WASP

WASP

Or, A Very Sweet Power

IAN GARBUTT

Polygon

First published in Great Britain in 2015 by
Polygon, an imprint of Birlinn Ltd.

West Newington House
10 Newington Road
Edinburgh
EH9 1QS

www.polygonbooks.co.uk

ISBN 978 1 84697 307 9
eBook ISBN 978 0 85790

British Library Cataloguing-in-Publication Data
A catalogue record for this book is available
on request from the British Library.

The publishers acknowledge investment from
Creative Scotland towards the publication of this volume.

Typeset by Hewer Text (UK) Ltd, Edinburgh
Printed by Bell and Bain Ltd, Glasgow

To Judy as always

A Visitor

Bethany Harris sits perfectly still on the soiled mattress, her legs drawn up, both hands loose on the dirty folds of her gown. She faces the room's only window, the frame lidded on either side with damask curtains hung with tassels. Beautiful curtains that catch the sun.

No draught ever disturbs them. The window is nailed shut and the glass panes are as thick as her finger. Outside, in the neat garden, rosebeds throw up a hundred pink faces.

A fly settles on her cheek. She tries not to blink and keeps her breath to a whisper. For hours she practises clearing her mind of thoughts. Every day is a struggle to diminish herself, to vanish. Then she might be forgotten, ignored, left alone. It's the only trick she has.

On her right is the door leading into the passage. She is attuned to it. The scrape of the key, the turn of the knob, a whisper as it swings inwards on greased hinges. She has learned footsteps as she had her letters. Friend's heavy tread, the scurryings of the younger girls, the ragged steps of the ill or crippled.

Parts of Bethany are missing. The satin bows from her stained dress. The heels from both slippers. Her ivory bracelet – stolen and likely sold. A hard slap loosened a tooth, and the nail is missing from her ring finger.

Her gaze shifts from the window. A chorus of dust motes are caught in a sunbeam and lifted on warm eddies of air. She focuses, bringing them into sharp relief. For a moment the room seems filled with twirling bits and pieces, forming patterns then breaking apart to shape others.

A noise in the passage. Bethany folds more tightly in on herself. A step, a break, then two steps in quick succession. The girl who brings water and eat-it-now things raided from larder scraps. She scuttles from room to room, performing all the dirty tasks Friend will not consider. Perhaps she lacks the wit to run away. Or maybe what awaits her outside the garden walls is worse than the things she has to deal with inside.

She always enters the room breathless and pink-cheeked, as if late for some tryst of critical importance. Today her hands are empty. She is on the bed in a breeze, stroking Bethany's hair, fingers like warm brook water trickling over her scalp. 'Don't know why Friend picks on you so. Before, he never paid much mind to one of us over another, 'less it came down to poking his pink stick. Even then it can't be said he was o'er fussy.'

Her eyes go egg-wide when she speaks, as if using some God-endowed talent to form the words. When Bethany chooses to consider the matter, she wonders what had prompted this young woman's mind to break, or whether she had indeed been mad when first brought here.

It won't happen to me.

Disconnected thoughts butterfly through Beth's head, collide, form images. She feels lice biting her scalp. Dust motes fade back into nothingness as a cloud covers the sun.

A frown splits the brow above the water girl's hazel, gone-away eyes. 'Friend's coming for you later,' she says. 'That's what he sent me to tell you.'

'What does he want?'

The water girl starts humming a melody that loops around and in on itself as her mind cycles through its seasons of lucidity and witlessness. Beth catches her wrist. 'I asked you what he wants.'

'Not likely to tell me, is he? Remember what I said last time. Don't be afraid to run away,' water girl taps her temple, 'in here. Friend can't get you when you've jumped that wall. I have my place. You'll find yours. Not bad places, though. I know you have some.' She leans forward on the mattress. A storm wouldn't knock a strand of her greasy, matted hair from its place. 'If there were no bad places you wouldn't be here.'

Dusk sees Bethany still folded on her mattress. She hears Friend's irregular tread. The door swings open. He slips inside, quiet despite his bulk, and pauses beside the bed. 'Not a sound,' he says. 'I'm taking you to my office. Mustn't wake anyone.'

Bethany obliges with silence. After a moment she unfolds her limbs, slowly, so cramp won't bite. Out in the hall, a smoky candle gutters in its holder on the wall. Upstairs, someone coughs in her sleep, mumbles and turns over. Bethany sucks in a breath and follows Friend along the low-ceilinged passage. The air is only a little fresher. Ahead is an open door with a fire flickering in a grate beyond. She can sense the warmth of it.

An oak-panelled room. A desk, a stool, a shelf bristling with quills. Bethany has been here before, on her first night, waiting while her name was entered in a leatherbound book. Now she stands with her back to the fire, eyes watchful. Whatever Friend has planned she will make sure to get some heat into her bones first. He regards her, lips thinning. 'That's right. Warm your arse.

While you're at it slap your cheeks to put a bit of colour back into 'em. Won't hurt to have you looking fresh.'

'Are you going to kill me?'

Friend leans forward. 'What's that?'

Beth knots her hands behind her back. 'It's what you've wanted from the start.'

A laugh splits his florid face. 'Killing you is the last thing I have in mind tonight.'

Her bottom lip starts to quiver. She can do nothing to stop it, but she won't cry for him. 'You're just a scrap of a man who takes pleasure in torturing women. Your mother should have smothered you while you were still in swaddling.'

His boot smacks into Beth's thigh and sends her sprawling across the floorboards. She smells dust and old cinders. Splinters prick both hands.

Friend stands over her. *This is it*, she thinks. *The next kick will catch me in the ribs. The third will fetch across the side of my head. He won't stop until I don't have a breath left in me.*

She braces herself. Friend remains standing, legs astride. She twists round to look at him.

'You're a bold lass,' he says, 'but don't give me cause to lash out again. You've caught someone's eye and that means a fat pile of coin for my purse. I have faith. I've had it since you tried to rip open my carriage door.'

Before she can reply he opens the yard entrance and calls into the darkness. A massive, midnight-skinned warlock steps into the room. He's dressed like a lord in a crimson satin jacket and a waistcoat that glitters with golden butterflies. Tasselled breeches top cream hose, which in turn are swallowed up by a pair of polished, buckled shoes. Above his dark brow is a silver-dusted wig pricked with a black satin bow as large as a man's hand. Ancient, pagan magic seems to crackle between his fingertips. Yet when he turns those big hands over, the palms are as pink as the girl's own.

Friend spits on his sleeve and scrubs grime from the corners of her face. 'A pretty one, just like I told you.'

'You cut it too fine,' the dark man's voice rumbles like grinding millstones. 'Another month in this hole and the worms would have her.'

'Nay, sir. Wouldn't pay to let this one die. She had to suffer for her sins, if you take my meaning. Honest gold bought her penance, just as you are buying her salvation.'

The visitor crouches in front of Beth. A mark colours his right cheek. A picture of a bird, small but perfectly drawn. A river dweller, but the name escapes her.

'We are going on a coach ride,' he says, pronouncing each word in an accent that knows no home in any vale or coast of this country. 'I need you to behave. If you can do that you will be treated fairly. Do you understand?'

'You're all dark,' she whispers.

He nods, his expression not changing. She reckons his face had been hewn out of coal. Then his mouth splits open and two rows of teeth, whiter than snowdrops, leap out at her. She blurts 'Oooh' like a child and scrabbles backwards onto her knees. The dark man reaches under her arms and hauls her upright as if she weighs no more than a bag of cobwebs. The girl shrugs free. Perhaps he's a slave. She's heard city folk take to dandying up their darkies, though she's never seen one.

He scours her with those big eyes. 'Can you walk a short distance, Miss?'

No one has called her 'Miss' for what seems a lifetime now. Liar, harlot – those things and more. But 'Miss'? Any other time Friend would laugh until his breeches split.

The dark man turns. 'Do you have a coat or cloak?'

5

Friend snorts. 'She goes out the same way she came in. I ain't a parish charity and I don't earn so much that I can afford to give clothes away.'

'I have lined your pocket well enough.'

'Aye, and who am I going to have to bribe in turn to make sure you get away with your trick?'

'Very well. The blanket in the carriage will have to do.'

The girl touches the dark man's arm. 'I'm going home?'

'Yes,' he says, no longer smiling. 'In a manner of speaking.'

A summer aberration whips bitter rain across the back yard. Beth kicks off the broken corpses of her shoes and presses both feet into the gravel. Pinprick sensations run across her soles as the stone chips crack her toes apart. She raises her head to the sky, mouth open, both hands stretched out. When was the last time she had felt rain on her skin? She licks her top lip, her chin, as far as the tip of her tongue will reach. She lets it soak her dirty gown and plaster her hair against her skull. A rain orb hangs pendulously from a strand of hair, reflecting the night world in tiny entirety.

The darkie closes the yard door. Now it's only the light of Friend's fire bleeding through the curtains and a wind-bobbed lantern dangling from a carriage waiting in the lane. Beth needs nothing more. From her square window she'd mapped the contours of this pretty, deceitful garden. Her visitor doesn't push or rebuke, but follows softly along the path as she flits between the flowerbeds. Water trickles from the corner of his tricorne and runs fingers down the front of his coat. His face is unseeable.

Beth plucks a sodden bloom from its stalk and crushes its petals against her cheeks. A peck of muddied earth pressed to her nostrils fetches memories of rutted village lanes, her mother's vegetable gardens, the meadow behind the church which always flooded in the winter rains. All the evergone things.

The darkie is waiting beside the gate, and here the night has coughed out a new curiosity. A lumpen figure standing by the carriage, in a too-big coat and grasping an oiled whip easily twice his height. Rain threads currents of hair across the brow of his misshapen head.

'You took thy time, Kingfisher,' the figure says, voice muffled by his upturned collar.

'That may be, but I've hooked our fish and want to land her before the night is done.'

The dark man, *Kingfisher*, lays a hand on Beth's arm. Beth's feet splash in one of the many puddles dotting the lane. She falters at the carriage door, caught in an instant of memory. The grip on her arm tightens.

'Don't cause trouble, little one.'

'Show me the door handles. And the windows. I want to see them working.'

The grip relaxes. 'You have a terror of coaches? Look,' he demonstrates, 'everything is as it should be.'

She snatches a lungful of air and climbs inside. The floor is smothered in rugs which are soothing against her toes. On the wall, a smaller lantern burns with a frail light. Beth slumps against the soft upholstery. Kingfisher offers a blanket but Beth pushes it away.

'You will catch a fever,' he warns.

'That pigsty didn't kill me so I doubt a slap of fresh water on my skin will do so.'

'As you wish.' He lays the blanket aside and holds out a pewter flask. After a moment's thought, Beth takes a sip. A smoky-flavoured brandy spreads fire through her belly. She opens her mouth to speak but he seals her lips with one finger. 'No, you must rest now. We have a long journey ahead.'

He leans back and raps on the roof with his knuckles. A crack of the reins and the carriage stumbles into motion.

'What do you want with me?'

A shake of the head. 'Do as I say for now.' He pulls the hat down over his eyes, deepening the shadows around his face. His voice is cultured, almost gentlemanly, but he wears it like a coat that doesn't quite fit.

The coach springs swallow the lumps and bumps of the rain-lashed road. Beth's eyes grow heavy. She wonders if the brandy is drugged, but makes no fuss as the motion of their passage lulls her into a half-sleep, the deepest she dare allow herself to fall. No dreams visit her. The Comfort Home has knocked even that pleasure out of her head. Instead she grasps the belief that, whatever the dark man's purpose, at least she is going home.

At the River Mouth

'This one's got a smile. Wide and toothy. Say I cut her another one.' The knife trembled above her throat. 'How'd you like that, darkie? A big red grin?'

'Do not touch my wife.'

'Look here. One that speaks the mother tongue. Thinks he's civilised.'

Their voices were guttural and flecked with spit. Unlike the singsong English he had learned from the missionaries.

'Might have a use for you. Ain't that so, Jack?'

'Might indeed. Listen, blackie, do what I say if you want your woman to keep breathing. Tom there is a very patient man and he's got himself comfortable. He can hold that knife at her neck for a long time. Ain't that so, Tom?'

''Tis so,' Tom said.

'I shall do what you say.'

Jack spat a yellow gobbet onto the forest floor. 'Good boy.'

He gathered his people, told them that the danger was coming from the north and they had to go. Now. They followed him down the riverbank to the mouth of the Big Water. Senses dulled with trust, they did not see the slavers' nets. Three tried to resist and were shot or clubbed. The rest had wrists and ankles chained.

'You said you would spare us.'

'And so I have,' Jack said. 'You're both alive, ain't you?' He nodded at Nanyanika. 'Take her to the Captain's cabin. She can warm his belly for the trip.'

Tom relaxed for a second. Nanyanika looked straight at her husband, caught Tom's wrist and drew the blade across her throat. Her body slid onto the planking.

Tom grinned. 'Seems she's got more balls than you, blackie.' He nudged her body with his boot. 'Throw her carcass into the river.'

He lost his woven cloak trimmed with feathers. His headdress and jewellery were gone. The carved boar's tooth pendant gifted by his father when his boy became a man was torn from his neck, snapping the hide cord. The only thing not taken was the armband made with twists of Nanyanika's hair. He had sold his people for the sake of his wife and she had been murdered anyway. He had not understood the slavers' greed. Standing on their dock had taught him the depth of his mistake. He made no complaint as his authority was stripped. He no longer deserved to lead anyone. Even then his people turned to him for help, believing there was something he could do. He would not look at their pleading faces. Some fell to the wooden decking and a great howl went up, a ululation. The slavers laughed and dragged them up by the manacles. Those who persisted were beaten into silence.

Rain poured through the cut in the forest canopy and hissed

on the water. The slavers cursed it. These creatures did not live with the land but cut it to their own shape and size. Dozens of trees had been slaughtered to build this landing, the riverbank beneath split to the rock.

'The world is crying for us,' one of the tribesmen said, tears sliding down his own face.

The ship sat at the dock in an ugly spider web of timber. At the hold's open mouth the women squealed and dragged back on their chains. Something bitter had been burned to hide the stink, but it had gone into the wood. Blood, sweat, all the body's foulness. A thousand sorrows.

Anyone who tried to struggle had his calves whipped. In the semi-dark men and women were bound on their sides to flat wooden boards. The hatch slammed. Sobs and muttered prayers in the gloom. A feeling of the world shifting as the boat cut free from the bank and caught the river's current.

Day and night fell through the lattice from the deck above. He felt the sores grow on him, the cramps bite his muscles. When he was taken up to exercise on the deck of the great boat he would not look at the water.

In the chained darkness, a woman's voice, breath soft on the back of his neck. 'What have you brought upon us? Where is my child? You have to do something.' He thinking but not saying, *No, I can do nothing.* Hour after hour as the shackles bit deeper into wrists and ankles. Here, there, people died and became still, finding release at last in the embrace of the Spirit. But still she spoke to him. Day after day until he wondered if she too had died, and this was some residual demon inhabiting her husk. Always asking 'What have you done? *What have you done?*'

Sometimes rain leaked from the deck, cool and sweet on the tongue. Rough weather brought floods of seawater which burned their wounds. A storm tipped and turned their cramped world.

Those who had fished from dugout boats had the bellies for it. Others were sick over their neighbours, who were sick in turn.

What they were given to eat tasted of nothing and failed to blunt their hunger. He remembered the fish his father had caught, smoking on a stick over the fire. The sweet things his mother had made from milk and fruit. He willed flavour into the slavers' lumpy mush, textured it with memories, swallowed it down. He would not die. The Spirit had turned its back on him. He knew he was cursed to live his life seeing his wife collapse again and again, lifeblood streaming from her throat. He should have known that would be Nanyanika's way. Girlhood saw her practise hunting with the boys, her father's admonition for tradition's sake falling on ears that wouldn't listen. She was fast with a knife, agile as a hunted deer and could fashion jewellery to break the soul. Hers was a life that would not, could not be captured. In the end, though he believed he had betrayed his people for her sake, she had refused to share his guilt.

I did not deserve you.

The rolling sea had no answer.

A Most Peculiar Establishment

Beth jerks upright, mind filled with momentary confusion. Her gaze settles on Kingfisher, who is watching her with that same easy indifference. She peers outside. Nothing to see but her own weak reflection in the glass.

'Why are you staring out of the window?' he asks. 'Have you never seen the night before? There is nothing out there.'

'You're taking me the wrong way. I remember my first trip to the Comfort Home. I couldn't see anything then either but I recall every bump and jounce, the creaking of the trees and the smell of the lilac bushes. Stop the coach and let me out. I don't know who you are or what your plan is but I want none of it. I'll run in my bare feet if need be.'

'And why would you do such a thing?'

'You said you were taking me home. I thought Lord Russell had relented, that he'd sent you. What new cruelty is this?'

Kingfisher favours her with a smile. 'For now we go this way.'

She glances at the door handle. The carriage is cracking along. Jumping might send her under a wheel or into the ditch with a broken neck. Her fingers twitch then settle.

Wherever he's taking me, Beth thinks, *it can't be worse, can it?*

They travel in shared silence until the splashing of the wheels outside turns into a low rumble. 'We are in the city now,' he says.

Outside, buildings hug the roadside in a jumble of roofs and gables. Torches throw off sparks, figures flit between the puddles of light. Carriages pass the other way, outlines softened in what has now become a persistent drizzle.

The road widens. Buildings grow taller and merge into terraces. Wheels clatter over cobbles. On either side, walls of glass-pricked stone slip past. Beth is captured by the clamour, smoke and stench of this terrible, astonishing place.

'Sit back from the window if it frightens you.'

'No town can be so big. I've seen pictures, but nothing like this.'

Kingfisher smiles. 'The world is larger than a few tumbledown hovels at the side of a country road.'

'The noise, the smells. How can anyone live this way?'

He taps a finger on the knee of his breeches. 'Not everyone favours the ceaseless chatter of the city. Some are brought here by circumstance, others by necessity.'

'Why have I been brought?'

'Be patient. We are almost there.'

The coach rattles to a halt. A few moments later the dwarf stands framed in the light, eyeing Beth. Perhaps he thinks she might run. Despite her earlier bravado, Beth doubts her legs would carry her a dozen yards.

Kingfisher stands, huge in this cramped space. 'Stow the carriage once we're inside,' he tells the dwarf. 'I doubt our foundling will put up a fight.'

He offers Beth his hand. 'Only a short walk now. You are perfectly safe.'

'Where are we?'

'A place where there is food and warmth, and a chance to be free of those filthy rags. You will be in a soft bed before the night is out.'

She shrinks back against the seat. 'It's a trick.'

'It is no such thing. This has been a hard journey. The worst is over. I shall help you if need be.'

She grasps the hand. Warm and soft. Without thinking she rubs it between her palms, feeling the creases, the hard nub of each knuckle.

'See,' he says, gently pulling free. 'I am a man like any other. This way.'

The rain has died altogether and the air is losing its bitter edge. He leads Beth along a lane squeezed between two houses, his legs taking big bites out of the path. Lights glimmer behind curtained windows. A stink of bitter smoke hangs over everything. Beth coughs and presses a sleeve over her nose and mouth. She struggles to keep up, forcing her escort to slow his pace.

Concentrate, she tells herself. *Don't get fooled again.*

A lamp burns in a holder beside a door reinforced with iron bands. Kingfisher slips a key out of his waistcoat pocket. A soft click and the door swings open. He takes the light and beckons. Beth follows, arms wrapped tight about her. Figures stare at them in the gloom.

'Who's there?'

'We are alone,' Kingfisher says.

'No. I can see others. I knew this was a trick.'

His feet are heavy on the wooden floor as he crosses the room, light falling in puddles around him. He puts a taper to the flame and ignites candles set in sconces on the wall. Shadows melt away. Tall mirrors, spaced at regular intervals, throw back a dozen reflections. Beth eyes herself from beneath a thatch of stringy hair. Both feet are caked with mud. She is thin enough to snap.

Is that me? Is that really me?

'Welcome to the House of Masques,' Kingfisher says.

She plucks at one of the holes in her ruined gown. 'I have no money.'

'You've no debt of that nature to settle under this roof.'

'Then what is this place?'

'This is your new home. Do you understand?'

'My . . . home.' Her lips work the words over. 'Does it belong to you? I didn't know darkies could own things.'

'It is the property of the Abbess. You will meet her in time. First I must fetch the Fixer. He will treat your discomforts. He may also ask you some questions. Answer as honestly as you can.'

'You are going to leave me here?'

'I shall only be gone a moment. You do not intend to harm yourself or break anything, I take it?'

'No . . .' Her head sags. A clump of still-damp hair falls over her face.

Is this merely a sweeter hell? she wonders.

Life Pieces

The horses are settled by the time Kingfisher crosses the yard, his business in the mirrored hall concluded. The room above the coach house is plagued with damp, but tonight the wind sent the rain in another direction and his walls have escaped the worst of it. He removes his clothes and hangs them in the wardrobe. The laundry girl has already laid out tomorrow's shirt and breeches.

Kingfisher walks naked within his chamber. He dislikes wearing the clothing these people have given him. Even the finer materials rub his skin like gorse. The bed dominates the corner and not once has he used it in the years he's lived at the House, preferring instead the bare floor in front of the hearth. Three times a week a maid comes in to change his bedding, the linen she takes away as clean as the blankets she puts on. Nothing is ever said. The daily business of the House goes on, and demons, quirks and eccentricities keep their affairs to themselves.

The girl. A risk. He recalls the way she stood in the downpour, revelling in it. Not like the rain he knew at home. The air surrounding these people's dwellings always smells of old food and ashes. Clouds of a different kind swirl behind the newcomer's eyes, yet a bigger menace is brewing under the House's own roof. The Fixer knows it too.

Kingfisher runs his hands over the bangles, necklaces and other pieces arranged on the table by the window. Jewellery he had bought and bartered for. Pieces of home. Shards of his people. Some are from tribes he recognises, others are new. Each one he touches speaks to him of a life stolen, a nation scattered across the markets and hawkers' stalls of this country. The only connection with his past life, he collects them as if doing so could draw his land back around himself.

He fingers the armband under his shirt. Her name meant *gift from god*, something his father told him long before the wedding. 'I see the way you look at her,' the old man said, grinning.

'Nanyanika, I am sorry,' Kingfisher whispers to the empty room.

A boat was coming in.

The potboy banged on the door. He was up with the rooster, or earlier if the Mango captain wasn't willing to anchor offshore 'til dawn. The Fixer was already awake. The plank hut he lived in caught all the muck the sea threw inland, and last night the rain hadn't let up.

'Fire up your pot,' the Fixer called. 'I'll be down within the hour.'

He turned on his back and stretched arms and legs, flexed fingers, turned feet this way then that. Shrugging off the blanket, he eased himself out of bed and laid out the leather jerkin and breeches thrown over the chair beside the bed. A piss-poor day. Waxy light filtered through the cracks in the plankwork. Dark stains on the floor marked where the roof had leaked again. Plug one and another sprouted. A hard storm would have the lot off and then the Mangoes would have to let him sleep in their precious warehouse and never mind the cargo.

He elbowed the nearest shutter open. The rain had eased into a gasping drizzle. Below, the harbour front seemed out of focus, the edges softened by the weather. The Mango boat had reached the harbour wall. He fancied he could catch its stink already. Beyond that was nothing but a leaden murk.

The Fixer checked his stove, blew some life into the embers, and threw on the last of yesterday's wood. Fragments of old barrels, broken crates, anything he thought might burn. A cough cut his lungs in two. The spasm lasted a few seconds. Afterwards he rubbed his chest and breathed in. Another cough. He spat into the bucket beside his bed. No blood in the spittle. Good. Mornings here could shrivel the lungs.

He threw handfuls of water over his face, picked up his razor, strapped it, then shaved off his body hair, starting with his head.

Harbour folk claimed the darkies carried lice but he got 'em from the Mangoes. Dirty bastards were worse than their cargoes.

When finished, he tipped the water out of the window and onto the warehouse roof. Shrugging on leather shirt and breeches, he crammed both feet into his work boots and picked up the Judicator. A three-foot length of thick knotted rope. He'd learned about the darkies fast.

'Even after months at sea some still carry a bit o' fight,' the slave agent had explained. 'If one eyes you hit 'im right away. Don't worry about killing 'im. A darkie with too much spit in 'is gut can't be sold.'

'I thought I was here to heal them?'

'You don't heal slaves,' the agent had said. 'You fix 'em. There's a difference. Don't forget.'

A sharp wind kicked up, filling the harbour with seaborne murk. The steps leading down from the Fixer's cabin were treacherous when wet. The warehouseman who used to live there had ended up at the bottom in a gin-sodden jumble of shattered bones.

The Fixer recognised the ship's figurehead. *The Bo'sun's Lass.* John Stark's tub. The harbour men were quick in tying her up. They were Sabbath breakers and wanted the Mango's bribe.

The potboy slept in the tar shed. The Fixer went in and found a good fire burning. The air was thick with the smell of hot tar. 'Almost done, sir,' the boy said, pulling his forelock. His bare forearms were streaked with old burns.

'Let's get this done,' the Fixer said.

The cargo was unloaded equally fast. Some of the buggers could barely walk. Their gaze flicked over everything. *Probably wondering what this godforsaken place is*, the Fixer thought. They were forced into a shivering line, chains jangling, men and women bound indiscriminately.

'Clean them up.'

The potboy fetched the hand pump and ran the pipe into the harbour. Cold water sprayed across exposed backs. The Fixer walked down the line while Stark stood by. Months at sea had given him a bleary face that knew no change between sun and rain.

'How many lost this time?'

'Only twelve thrown overboard.'

'Your cargo's always the worst, Stark. Pack 'em loose. More will live. Won't need so much fixing when they get here.'

'Tight pack weeds out the weak. Saves time later. Strong stock means good money.'

'It's like you to bring your barge in on the Sabbath.'

'Those who choose our trade can't be o'er concerned with their immortal souls. I'll wager there's not a church pew felt the weight of your rump in years. We both work outside the circle.'

'You'll do no selling today.'

'I don't aim to. The cargo can go in the pen tonight and the agent can take them up to Liverpool on the morrow. Cur takes too fat a slice but I've no notion to keep my ship idle.'

'I wouldn't keep sick dogs in that.'

'As well we ain't talking about dogs then. You'd best get fixing my cargo if you want paying.'

'The boy put a flame to the tar as soon as he spied you at the harbour wall.'

'As well he might. I need to get down the coast and resupplied.'

'You push your crew too hard.'

'Think so? The bastards are as greedy as me.'

The Fixer walked back up the line of darkies while one of the Mangoes kept a musket levelled. Usual sores in the usual places. All would survive. The dead weight had been culled. He felt bones, fingered a few faces. Checking mouths was a formality. The darkies always had good teeth. He thought of the society girls laughing at him with their rotten stumps.

The cargo had quietened. They were more bearable with the shit washed off, but Stark would have to burn sulphur in his hulk all night to quell the stench. Most stood, quivering, eyes down.

Apart from the big man at the end. The one with the look on his face.

The Fixer's fingers tightened around the knotted rope. He shifted, ready to swing. He'd seen that look before and often it meant trouble. The darkie's eyes didn't even twitch. Something bad, something beyond fear of chains or whip, was going on inside his head.

'That one's prime meat. Fix him good,' Stark said.

'I don't need telling. I'm a doctor.'

'You might be many things, my friend,' Stark laughed, 'but you ain't a doctor. Not any more.'

The boy lifted the cover off the tar pot. The Fixer dunked the brush and started applying it while the Mangoes kept the slave chains tight. The potboy laughed as the darkies squealed. The Fixer wondered how much he'd like his arse rubbed raw after weeks at sea bound to wooden slats. Let sores fester and they'd gnaw a body into the grave piece by piece.

The big man didn't flinch when he felt the tar. Not once did he glance at his fellows, nor they at him. Everyone, it seemed, had their politics.

'Can you understand me?' the Fixer said.

Still no reaction.

'Got a wife?'

The eyes swivelled, fixed.

Aha.

19

Wind blustered and cursed the wooden planks of the watchman's cabin. Rain, thick with spite, pummelled the roof. The night was black as the tar boy's pot.

The Bo'sun's Lass had made it out of harbour and a good lick beyond the coast before the foulness set in. Stark had offered the Fixer a belly warmer in return for keeping a watch on the cargo, but he was having none of that. He clipped the potboy's ear and told him to put food and pails into the pen. 'I put buckets in but they just shit on the floor,' he complained. The Fixer told him to do it anyway.

Two hours to midnight according to the clock nailed to the wall, and the Fixer knew it'd be no sleep for him that night. The cabin groaned like an old maid under the wind's hard hand. He sat at the table, the stove behind him spitting smoke. Medical papers lay scattered underneath the dripping candle. He'd tried to concentrate but the constant battering ragged his nerves. To distract himself he tried the columns of the society papers, looking for the familiar names.

A sound. Another. That wasn't the weather. Someone was on the stairs outside. The potboy had gone into town with a shilling tip from the Mangoes and the Sabbath breakers were all in the gin house.

The Fixer dropped the papers and stuck his head out the door. The lantern had blown out. Figures on the steps. Three, maybe four. He heard cursing as boots scrabbled on the wet boards.

'Who are you?' the Fixer called down, voice strong even in this wind. 'What do you want?'

'We have a woman. She needs help.'

The Fixer met them halfway. A cloaked figure supported by two rain-lashed men, a third behind. 'Very well, bring her inside. Easy now. These stairs could break your neck.'

Inside the cabin, the Fixer drew back the woman's hood. Her

eyes were glassy, the pupils wide. Slivers of blue circled the corneas. Her breathing whooped as tremors rippled through her body. He looked at her belly then back at her face. Barely more than a girl and possessed of a beauty even her condition couldn't blunt.

'Who are you men?'

'We are her brothers. She has taken ill.'

'Ill? She's in labour. Couldn't you have found a surgeon sooner?'

'We don't have time to go hunting round this pig's pit of a town. Are you not the harbour quack?'

The Fixer stared at them. 'A doctor, yes. She should have been confined hours ago.'

'The roads are mired. We brought her downriver by rowboat.'

The Fixer took in their clothes. All were of a fine cut that not even the rain had managed to disguise, yet they seemed ill suited. One of the men's hands were bleeding. 'You rowed her here yourself? Where are your servants? And what about the baby's father?'

'Unless you want to feel my sword tip you'll mind your questions.'

The Fixer regarded him for a moment then removed the girl's cloak and settled her on his bed. He pressed the back of his hand to her forehead. Strands of hair clung to his skin. He lifted her eyelids, one at a time, nudging the candle closer to the cot with his free hand.

'What have you done?' he said, turning to the men.

'Done?'

'She is near insensible.'

'A pinch of laudanum for the pain.'

'No. Something else.'

Glances were exchanged. 'Laudanum, as I said. How long until the birth?'

The Fixer ran careful hands over the girl's midriff. 'Any moment now. You cut it fine. Her waters have already broken.'

'We shall go and secure the boat then find lodgings.'

'Won't one of you stay with her?'

'What do we know of childbirth? You're the doctor. You fix her.'

He sucked in his teeth as the men left. *Fixer by name, fixer by trade*, he thought. He checked the girl again. No odd smells on her breath. Skin was clammy. Lungs continued to whoop down air with each contraction. Little apparent pain.

'What have you been taking?' he asked. 'More than laudanum, yes?'

She smiled. On that face it should have been lovely. It wasn't. 'The dream makers.'

'What are they?'

She sighed but didn't answer. He realised how he must sound to her. A voice once polished, now neglected and losing its shine. Cracks spread through his sentences, throwing up ugly words like rough stone through plaster. But the next few minutes were critical. 'You have to help me. Listen . . .'

He squeezed one hand and told her what to do, unsure if she understood half of what he said. Instinct seemed to drive her body. Her youth was in her favour, and a strength that might partly come from whatever other than blood ran in her veins.

I could use a little gypcraft right now, he thought, but skill took over, both hands moving deftly as he whispered encouragement into her ear. The baby slid into the world without complications. He slapped its arse. Lusty cries. He cut the cord and wrapped the newborn in linen. No time for delicacy – the afterbirth would go to the gulls. Not much blood loss. Good. A clean birth. He'd seen some horrors, oh yes.

'Listen. Can you hear me? You have a daughter.'

For the first time her eyes focused. 'They want my baby dead.'

'What?'

She whispered something else. 'They know who you are.'

The Fixer wondered if she was delirious. Her face was intent, the words quiet but carefully pronounced.

'Bringing you down the river in this condition might have killed you even if the night wasn't blowing a storm,' he said. 'Those men should've known better.'

'They don't care either way.'

'They are your brothers.'

The mouth twitched. 'Brothers?'

'Why here? Why me?'

She turned a slack face to him. 'Because of what you did before.'

The Fixer recoiled. He pressed fingers to his temples, tried to quieten his blood which seemed to sizzle inside his head. He glanced at the clock then at the baby. Small, peaceful. Her mother was gazing at the ceiling, making odd noises at the back of her throat.

'What will happen to you?' he heard himself say.

'I shall be taken back. Forced to be a good daughter. A pretty prisoner. The child will disappear. You will be blamed. A baby killer twice over, that's what they'll say. It's the gibbet for you.'

The Fixer scooped up the newborn and was out the door. Rain slapped his face. He clung to the railing and took the steps as fast as he dared. Splinters spiked his palm. The harbour yard was a swirling demon of wind and wet. He pressed the baby to his bare chest, leather jerkin slapping against his skin. He could hardly see. It seemed the gale had picked up every bit of shit from the quay and was throwing it in his face.

He opened the warehouse side entrance. A squall almost blew it from its hinges. The warehouse itself was a cantankerous, timber-creaking hole of a place. He dodged coils of rope, rusty clanks of old chains, broken crates. At the back was the slave pen. The Fixer laid the baby on top of a crate and grabbed a jemmy. Rust browned the cage, though the padlock was beefy enough. The Fixer worked the jemmy behind the hasp and tore out the screws. The big darkie squatted in a corner as far from the others as the cramped space allowed. The chains binding their wrists and ankles were gone – stowed back on the *Bo'sun's Lass* for the next cargo. When the Fixer swung open the iron door, they shrank back, winding arms and legs together. The big fellow didn't budge, didn't even look up. Leaning into the cage, the Fixer remembered that he'd left the Judicator in the cabin. If the darkie decided to turn on him he'd have to use the jemmy.

'I know you understand me,' he said. 'I saw it on your face by the quayside. I need your help.'

The head turned, eyes fixed. Four limbs stirred. The Fixer backed out of the cage door. Even if he could swing it closed in time there was nothing to lock it with. The darkie was moving towards him, impossibly silent.

I'm a dead man.

Outside the cage, the darkie unfolded and stretched, like a big old tree creaking in the wind. Tar patches stood out as blacker spots against his skin. 'How do you know I'll not snap your neck, white man?'

Good English.

'Because I trust what my instincts are telling me. If you run, there is nowhere you can go. With me, with a *white man*, there are many places we can both go. That's the way of this country.'

'Perhaps I do not want to run. Perhaps I do not deserve freedom.'

'There is a woman and newborn child. We have to leave, now.'

'Something has gone bad for you?'

'Very bad. I need your help. They need your help. This is the bargain I offer. We are in fear of our lives. If I read your face right

24

beside the dock today then such a thing means something to you. I don't know why. I don't care.'

He nodded back towards the cage. 'What of their lives?'

'They can't come with us. Otherwise they may stay or flee as they wish. What do you say?'

'I abandoned them long before reaching these shores. I shall go with you.'

'An old barouche – a cart – is stored back of the warehouse with a nag to pull it. Take the child and fetch them. I shall collect the girl.'

The Fixer ran back across the yard and scrambled up the cabin steps. *I'll get her down if I have to put her across my shoulders*, he thought. When he entered the cabin the three brothers were waiting for him. Two had drawn swords. The third was seated on an upturned box beside the newborn's empty swaddling.

The Fixer caught the first one square on the face. Bone crunched under his knuckles. An elbow to the midriff took care of the second before a blade sliced across the Fixer's temple, knocking him to his knees. He covered his face with both forearms and rolled across the floor. A boot cracked into his ribs. Hot pain across his chest as another blade cut into his skin. He saw the first brother, nose gouting blood, raise his sword. The Fixer slithered out of the way. The blade missed his throat and sliced a thick splinter out of the floor. Another sword caught him across the forearm, then another across his belly. He was done for, and he knew it.

The door crashed open.

A figure demoned out of the night. A sweeping hand caught one brother and hurled him through the closed shutters. Wood cracked. A breathless thud of a body hitting the warehouse roof. His sibling tried to bring his sword around but the angle was too tight. The darkie grabbed the hand holding the pommel and crushed it in a savage grip. His victim dropped the sword and stared at his broken palm. The darkie kicked him on the kneecaps and he went down like a sack of turnips. The third brother leapt up, fell over the Fixer's legs and clanged his head on the end of the bed where the girl still lay, wide eyes drinking in the mayhem. The darkie grabbed him by his shirt and hauled him to his feet.

'You cause any more trouble and I shall eat you whole.'

The man had wits enough left to nod before the darkie packed him out of the door. For good measure he picked the other one up and sent him sprawling down the steps after the first. Quiet settled on the cabin. The Fixer climbed to his feet and checked his wounds. Clean, but they would need stitching before the night was out.

'They will come back?' the darkie asked.

'Yes.' Blood trickled from one of the Fixer's nostrils. 'They will come back. We have to go.'

In the Mirror

Again the tread of those large feet. A click. A gentle draught on her skin. She looks up and he is gone. No door. Only those reflections.

She pads over to the nearest mirror. A scarecrow girl stares back. She tugs at the frame. It won't budge. She debates whether to try the others. One must hide the way out, but which? And even if she finds it, what can she do? It is likely locked. He would not have left her if he thought she could escape. Perhaps she can smash one of the mirrors and use a glass shard as a weapon. He's big, but he won't expect her to attack him. She can catch him the moment he steps back through the door. He's much stronger than she is but a quick stab in the neck might do it. Her skinny limbs are no use for anything else. She doubts she could break an eggshell.

Look at you, standing here plotting murder. Not so long ago you were reading Greek and Latin, or listening to pretty melodies played on Lord

Russell's harpsichord. The only weapon you ever held was a knife for cutting cake or spreading butter over the baker's scones.

Bethany returns to the middle of the room, sits beneath an unlit dome lantern and draws her legs up under her. After a few minutes a mirror swings open. The dark man steps back into the room, followed by a swarthy, white-skinned fellow. Cloth breeches hug the newcomer's legs. Apart from a sleeveless leather jerkin his upper body is bare. Not a single lick of hair. Pale, puckered streaks furrow his skin. He closes the door and approaches the girl. Square feet are crammed into a pair of thonged sandals, the toes as thick as carrot stubs.

'My saints, what a pretty piece of pastry we've bagged,' he says. 'Can't be more than eighteen. Maybe less.'

'A children's tutor,' the dark man says behind him. 'Locked up in a private madhouse.'

'Not so vicious a find, Kingfisher, compared to some of her soon-to-be-Sisters.'

'She would be dead enough if she remained there.'

'True.' He nods at the girl. 'What's your name?'

A pause while she hooks it from her memory. 'Bethany Harris.'

'You can read and write?'

'Yes, sir.'

'What else can you do?'

'I can count. Do needlework.'

'How about singing or dancing? I don't mean these cloddish country reels, but a proper gavotte, say. Have you ever been to the theatre or the opera?'

'I watched the mummers at Moorcott fair. A travelling company also put on Shakespeare.'

The bald man grimaced. 'What about languages? Have you any musical ability? Can you play cards?'

'I know a little Greek and Latin, and I play the harpsichord passably well. My employer taught me the rules of piquet.'

'Thank the gracious God for His mercy. Walk over to the door and back again. Go on.'

He watches as Beth gets up and shuffles across the polished boards. 'She must have put a right bee in someone's bonnet. Look at her.'

'She made an accusation against the local squire's son. Nearly caused a scandal the breadth of the county. When will she be ready to meet the Abbess?'

'At least a day. I wonder if her belly will hold a bite of decent food.'

The girl turns and peers at them through limp strands of hair. 'Am I in a nunnery then?'

Both men burst out laughing. 'In a manner of speaking,' the bald man says. 'Now open your mouth.'

She hesitates, then obeys. Baldy walks over, grasps her chin and checks her teeth. 'Much work to do. Good food and careful cleaning should take care of it.'

'Are you a surgeon?'

He grins. 'Fixing people is what I do. Broken people. Like you. Now, hold out your arms. Good. Pull up your skirts. No, don't go coy, I'm not some cully with stiff breeches and a shilling in his pocket.'

Beth lifts her hem. Bug bites pepper both wrists and ankles. Baldy unslings a canvas pouch from his shoulder. Taking out a vial he dabs foul-smelling paste on the sores. 'These can't be allowed to fester.'

'What difference does it make?' she says. 'I didn't ask to be brought here.'

'No, you didn't,' he concedes, 'and if you're so keen to go back to where you came from you can be returned with little trouble. So far, all you've cost us is a purse of coins and some inconvenience. You'll have the rest of this night to dwell on it.'

He stoppers the vial and returns it to the pouch. 'You are running with lice. I shall have to shave you. All of you. Do you understand?'

'Shave me?'

'Yes. It won't hurt, and the hair will grow back clean. Afterwards I shall give you something to make you sleep and a good clean bed. Kingfisher, you are finished here for the night.'

The dark man nods and leaves by the mirror door.

Baldy lays down a large square of canvas and fetches a table littered with ceramic bottles and strips of linen. 'Stand there,' he said, gesturing at the canvas. 'We won't tarry.'

Bethany waits on the square while Baldy loosens her gown's fastenings and lets it drop around her ankles. His touch is delicate, almost ticklish.

'Please don't.'

'I'm a doctor. You mustn't forget it.'

'Then why do this in here? Why must I stand and face a hundred reflections of myself when a plain room would serve as well?'

'This is a glasshouse, my little seed. You need to watch yourself grow and blossom. To believe it you must see it happen. This is where we start. Hold still.'

He takes up a pair of shears and begins to cut her hair. A blizzard of matted chestnut wafts onto the canvas as the blades work around her head. 'Lean this way,' he encourages. 'Now that. Turn around, yes, very good.'

In the Comfort Home she had been stripped and beaten. She'd had her hair pulled until she thought it would come out by the roots. Every nook of her body had been violated in one horrible way or another, yet this is somehow worse. The gentle smiles, the soft *snip-snip* of sharpened metal.

Finally he puts down the shears, picks up a bowl and brush, and soaps the top of her head. She squeals when she sees the open razor. 'Close your eyes if you wish,' he says. 'I promise you shall hardly feel it.'

She shivers at the first touch of metal against her scalp. But he's as light as a fly. She opens her eyes, aware of his closeness, his smell. She eyes the stitching on his leather vest, the stubble along his forearms as they move.

He wipes the razor on a strip of linen, snaps closed the blade and sets it down on the table. From one of the small porcelain bottles, he pours something onto a soft cloth and rubs it into Beth's head. A warm flush spreads across her skin and a curious herbal smell fills her nostrils.

'Did you get this from a Wise Woman?' she asks.

'Old Bobbo down at the apothecary, more like,' Baldy laughs. 'He's no woman and definitely isn't wise, but he gets his stock directly from his own herb garden. He mixes and bottles the preparations and he sells them on. Much better than the rat poison you get off some of these hawkers.'

'My skin is tingling.'

'Good. That means it's working. Now we'll get your underarms and crotch done. Lift up.'

Beth raises both arms. Baldy picks up the razor and works on her armpits. When he applies the soap brush between her legs her muscles clench.

'Don't worry, Kitten. It's not that kind of touch.'

She tries to relax. It's hopeless. She's trembling from her toes to her teeth. Baldy squeezes her hand. 'A minute more, I promise.'

Eyes close. She feels the wet warmth, the kiss of the bristles, the razor's gentle scratch. Then a soft towel and more ointment.

'What about your courses?'

'My what?'

'Your monthly time.'

'I don't have any.'

'How long since you did?'

'A while, I think.'

'You were with child?'

'I lost it. As best I can remember I've been dry since.'

'Did it happen at the Comfort Home?'

'No, before.'

Baldy soaks scraps of linen in another concoction and ties them over the raw patches of skin. 'Don't take them off,' he warns, 'no matter how much they sting.'

He turns back to the table, picks up a glass bottle and hands it to her. 'Splash this around the inside of your mouth twice a day. Make sure you spit it out. Don't swallow any or you'll give yourself a belly ache.'

A clean garment is pressed into her other hand along with a linen cap. She tugs it over her bare head and knots it under her chin. Her fingers are shaking. The garment is a plain smock but kind to her skin when she slips it on. When she's finished, Baldy turns her to face one of the mirrors.

'Look there. What do you see? No, don't be afraid.'

'I can't.'

'You've come this far, Kitten. Tell me what you observe.'

She cracks open an eye. 'Something ugly. A gargoyle.'

'That will change. The House of Masques works a special kind of magic.' He grins. 'Soon you will forget you ever laid eyes on the starved, beaten creature reflected in that looking-glass.'

Beth backs away. 'I don't believe your smiles. I've seen them before. In the other place. Heard the sweet words. Felt the slash across my face. A wet towel. Or a strip of my own soiled linen. Afterwards I'd sometimes hear the man who beat me talking in the passage outside. About sons or daughters, about his home and what he planned to do for the harvest festival. I was an interruption between the gin jug and the fireside hearth. A bit of filthy business that had to be dealt with before he took to his warm bed.'

She fingers the smock. 'Every Sunday after service he brought back a parson who pressed a handkerchief to his nose while he prayed for me, the lost sheep. You never saw a blessing spat out so quickly, or a man so pale about the gills. I thought he could help me. I slipped him a note scribbled on the corner of a page of Scripture with a sliver of burned candlewick. He took it to my captor and I had to sit in the dark for a week. So don't go grinning at me, doctor man. I doubt you're even a real surgeon.'

Baldy regards her for a moment. 'Bed for you now, I think,' he says. 'You've earned your rest. I shan't torment you any more tonight.'

The Dream World

Nightingale sits on the bed, pomander caught in her slack hands. Any interruption and the fingers will snatch tight on the draw-strings. No scent tickles out to delight the nostrils. It is full of the dream makers, and she takes it everywhere.

She had returned to the House earlier than expected. An awkward Assignment. Some city buck come of age and wanting to make a mark. He walked fast and talked faster, eager legs tangling in his walking stick. At dinner he spat food over the tablecloth. Twice he dropped his fork into his quail. Then he knocked over his wine, most ending up on his cream breeches. His wits unravelled and the evening threatened to do likewise. He stared at his feet when she delivered the Touch, his formerly proud face threatening to collapse in on itself. She was trained never to show disdain, always to keep her tone moderate and her expression interested.

'I saved my allowance for months for this,' he said. 'I fear I've become something of an oaf.'

'Don't be concerned, sir,' she said, delivering a smile. An oaf was exactly what he'd been but he brightened at her warmth, knowing nothing of the frost behind it.

Nightingale checks her face in the looking-glass. Powder and rouge have survived the night, though her eyes show too much red. Her client's choice of club was fog-thick with smouldering tobacco.

She examines both hands, flexes her fingers inside the velvet gloves. Stains darken the material. Clumsy. The marks smell of bitter fruit.

She opens the dresser drawer and finds a plain cotton pair that will serve the night. Keeping gloves in her room is a privilege Nightingale guards. The fresh pot of hand salve the Fixer has provided sits next to a vial of scent.

Everything is in its proper place. She can't suffer another mistake. Squeezing both eyes closed she peels off the soiled gloves and lets them drop onto the rug. Working by touch she applies salve into her hands and wrists. Her nails will need clipping soon.

She fumbles for the cotton gloves. Too quickly. Her fingers catch in a seam and one of the gloves tumbles into her lap. She scrabbles in the folds of her house gown. Nothing. Colours have begun to burst behind her eyes. What if it's slipped under the dresser? She will have to get down on hands and knees and grope for it.

Stupid, stupid.

There, by the leg of the chair. Fingers snatch it up, burrow inside. She is safe. Long, deep breaths. Let the panic pass. In the looking-glass, her now opened eyes are still red-tinged. She touches the polished silver key which hangs pendant-like around her neck. Clients often enquire about it. She tells them it belongs to a chest full of her mother's things. A sentimental trinket with no real value. The box it fits belongs on a waist-high shelf beside her bed.

Above her pillows a crucifix is nailed to the wall. She often muses over which is the darker vice.

Other clients don't notice the key. It's one more shiny bauble amidst a glittering spray of jewellery. Clothes shed, it lies naked against her throat. She's always conscious of that smooth, cool metal, feeling it move with each breath.

She has not always possessed the key. The Fixer would have given it to her sooner had she demanded, otherwise it remained tucked away in his bag of potions. Winning his trust had proved a bitter task.

Indeed, Nightingale has never used the key. It's symbolic, a talisman to convince herself she's in charge of her own fate. The box itself is unlocked. No maid would find anything of value inside.

Sometimes Nightingale imagines touching the box. In these daydreams her hands are perfect, and her bare fingers trace the grain of the wood, smooth and firm under her skin. A flick of the wrist and the box will open. No one is there to stop her. She can take what is inside and return to the go-away place. But if she does, the Fixer can never bring her back.

This is my purgatory, she thinks. *God willing it never turns into hell.*

What she needs to keep the horrors away is in the pomander. A pinch. A sprinkling. Barely enough to register a taste. When empty, the Fixer takes her pomander and an hour later, perhaps two, hands it back. A voiceless transaction.

There was a time when the dream makers drew the skin across her bones, tightened her mouth to a gash and put darkness under her eyes. Shapes and colours swirled in her mind. Distinct memories were rare. Everything else was a stew of brandy, music, bodies and, always, laughter. Fights had broken out over her, she recalled. Men had been badly injured. A single sentence from her father.

'No bastard will get its fingers in our pot.'

The Fixer demanded she break the dream makers' hold, no matter the cost. Nightingale had endured it for him and for the life she'd birthed. No child would call her mother while she was *dirty*. She suffered the sickness that stretched hours into eternities, the convulsions, the foulness. The thing that kept her head out of Bedlam was the Fixer's lips mouthing the promise that if she could do it he would return her daughter. Yet when she hauled herself partway out of that dark tunnel he had changed his mind.

'You don't deserve to be a mother,' he told her. 'At best you might open a crack in the clouds where your head abides. But you need more than a crack to raise a child. You've done well to get this far, but not well enough. Prove to me you're capable and then perhaps we'll talk.'

'Haven't I been through enough?'

'No. What if you're lying glassy-eyed and she's bawling through want of food or a clean behind? What if an ember tumbles from the hearth while she's lying squirming on the rug? You can't look after yourself, let alone a baby. This House is the only life you have. It's as potent a drug to you as anything you swallow, and no place for an innocent.'

The dream makers were waiting to soothe the blow. To Nightingale they were sweet medicine, yet she had not entirely fallen back into the tunnel. The Fixer's crumbs were enough to keep the hunger away. The poisoned light filled her up, made her walk and talk, but she would go no further.

I must prove I'm worthy, became her mantra.

Her injured heart warned against the guiles of men yet perversely this made her more sought after in her House Assignments. The ice girl from whom everyone hoped to chisel secrets.

She had convinced her Sisters that she wore gloves around the

House because of sensitive skin. A cheap and easy lie. Once, when the poisons in her mind swirled the wrong way, she saw the satin curl and turn black. Ripping off the gloves, Nightingale found her hands charred into crone-sticks. She screamed herself into insensibility. Eloise, arms pregnant with laundry, found her collapsed across the dresser. She ran to fetch the Fixer who came with the medicine and changed the colours of the world.

Another time she cut herself when a brandy glass broke in her grasp. A shard sliced through the material of her glove. The Fixer said it had to come off if he was to treat her. 'You can throw a tantrum if you like,' he told her, 'but if you do I shall leave you to bleed and they can bury you in those gloves.'

Nightingale had struggled to no effect. The Fixer removed her glove with a long blade. When he touched her bare fingers she thought she would faint. The cut was not as deep as he feared and once he'd stopped the bleeding he bathed her skin. 'Beautiful,' he declared, 'like a dove wing. So pale and pretty.' But she would not believe it.

She knew what she owed the doctor and the dark man. She had been scrutinised and somewhere within her fevered bones was revealed the shade of what she might become. In the Fixer lay something the dream makers could never have granted. He opened the door in her head and let the real world back in. She ought to have hated him for that, but through the hard weeks of near madness he was there, not with comforting words but challenging, daring, provoking. As he wiped clean her sodden face his eyes filled her world. 'Now you must decide whether to live or die. Show me if I have wasted my time.'

Nightingale returns to her bed. Kingfisher is bringing a new girl. He has sent word ahead and will arrive with the Kitten tonight. That is the second newcomer this month. Nightingale must ensure the proper order of things is maintained. She intones her prayers, leans over to kiss the crucifix then throws herself into the rich, silken swaddling of her bedclothes.

The Gilded Cage

Beth opens her eyes. A flat plaster ceiling. Cream walls topped by elaborate coving. Junk everywhere. Wooden crates, coils of rope, an old broom, other things she doesn't recognise. She tries to turn her head. Everything aches.

Footsteps. Heavy, measured. A face bends over her. That bald head again. Glittering blue eyes. The nose sliced by a puckered white scar. A hand cups her chin and turns her head one way, then the other. He fingers her cheek. She sinks her teeth into his wrist.

He steps back, hand clamped around the bite. Blood seeps between his fingers. She waits for him to strike her. He shakes his baldy head and walks over to a dresser. He pours water into a basin, bathes the wound and binds it with a strip of linen.

She casts about. A pair of shears lies on top of a canvas bag just a couple of feet away on her side of the bed. She flexes her hands. They aren't bound. Good. She glances at Baldy. His back is still turned. She gauges the distance and gets ready.

'If you're fixing to stick me with those things,' he says, 'the base of the neck's the best place.'

She wants to ask him if he's got eyes in the back of his head but the words won't come. She falls back on the mattress. Baldy turns and watches her. He's taken his jerkin off. He sponges down his chest and under his arms. The marks on his body resemble scars.

The room has one window and one door. The window is small and square. The glass is grimy and she can't see anything outside.

37

The door's made of barred wood and looks like a bull couldn't smash it down.

Baldy stops washing and comes over to sit beside the bed. He doesn't bother putting his jerkin back on. Droplets ripple over his chest. More slide down his forearms.

'That's the only way in and out of here, and I'm keeping it locked, at least for now. You can't open the window so don't try. Stay away from it. If I'm outside in the alley and see your face anywhere near that glass I'll put the shutters across and you can sit in the dark.'

He waits for that to sink in. She manages a nod.

'You'll still be wondering where you are. All that will come. You're safe as long as you don't cause trouble.' He leans forward. His breath smells of onions and hot mutton. 'When you're allowed outside you might think about running away. The man who brought you here knows the ins and outs of this town and can sniff your trail better than any hunting cur. Don't make him fetch you back or I'll have to tie you to this bed. I've got a few days only to get you fixed then you'll be taken to see the Abbess. She owns the house and will explain what's wanted from you.'

He dabs fresh paste on her bug bites then brings a pan from the hearth. 'Herb-infused broth,' he explains. 'My own recipe. Whatever shit you've been fed before, it's done your belly no good. We have to be careful or you'll bring this up as quick as you can swallow it.'

He goes away often. Sometimes for a little while. Other times longer. She hears him outside, talking, moving things around. Other voices reply. Sometimes it is the dark man. Usually it's women. When alone, she sits and learns every crack and cranny of the roof and walls. She doesn't go near the window or bother to try the door. Usually when he returns his face is grave and he doesn't say much. He feeds her before eating his own dinner.

At night she lies in the dark. It can be a long time before she gets to sleep, if at all. He says he can't trust her with a candle. It might fall off the table and set something alight. The fire is stoked up. It has a metal door with a grate on the front, which he's bolted. It traps most of the heat. 'I'll fetch an extra blanket if you're cold,' he says.

Mice scurry inside the walls. Sometimes when she closes her eyes it's like she's in the Comfort Home again. Baldy is snoring somewhere nearby. The noise seems to rattle through the rafters. She wonders what he's dreaming about.

In the morning, when he brings breakfast, she has a question for him.

'Am I supposed to thank you for all this?'

He puts down the trencher. She smells hot coffee. A treat. 'D'you reckon you should hate me instead?'

'Why not? I'm a prisoner just the same. You're not feeding me out of compassion.'

He points to the ugly marks on his back and chest. 'See these? I showed a young woman compassion. I fetched a beating and lost what little I had.'

He strokes her forehead. Nothing much, but she pulls away. How many other women have those hands touched?

'Where's my dress?'

'I burned it. The thing was stinking and riddled with bugs. I brought you something else.'

A linen gown. Brown with a cream apron. Something a milkmaid might put onto go to a harvest dance.

'The fit looks about right,' he says. 'Might have to tuck it in here and there. There's a pair of slippers too, and some woollen stockings.'

'Where'd you get them? From someone else you kidnapped?'

His cheeks pink. 'You can do without if you prefer.'

She wears the garment and he brings supper. Real food. A strip of beef, potatoes in butter. A smattering of carrots.

'You can feed yourself,' Baldy says. He places a chair in front of the table and a set of wooden cutlery beside the trencher. It's the most Beth's had in a while and she has to struggle not to bolt it.

'What's your name?' she asks between mouthfuls.

'My name isn't any of your concern.'

'I have to call you something.'

He laughs. 'I'm the Fixer, and right now I'm the only father you've got.'

Bethany finishes the meat and the last of the potatoes. 'Why are you so bald?'

'Sometimes I have to work with filthy people. Lice get in your scalp, your eyebrows, under your arms, in your breeches. Shaving's the only way to keep them off.'

'Filthy like me?'

He nodded. 'Like you.'

'Why am I here?'

'You've been bought and I'll deliver you on time.'

'Bought for what?'

'That's not for me to tell. Be glad you're alive.'

He goes out again. Bethany naps for a while. Afterwards she gets up and wanders about, picking things up and putting them down again. She feels itchy and foul. Pulling the brown linen gown over her head, Bethany tosses it on the bed, kicks off the slippers, bends over and peels off the stockings. Standing naked in the middle of the room, she picks up a sponge and starts bathing herself with water from the Fixer's ewer. She wipes her arms in long, lazy strokes, dabs her breasts and slips the sponge between her thighs. Water dribbles down her legs and pools at her feet. It's like being caressed by angels.

Beth's so lost in herself she fails to hear the Fixer come back. He's standing in the doorway, looking at her. Three long strides bring him across the room. His face is black with anger.

'Put your clothes back on.'

'You've seen me naked before, tended my wounds, cleaned up my blood. Why should it trouble you now?'

He scoops up her crumpled garments in his fist and holds the bundle under her face. 'That was different naked. Put on your clothes.'

She takes the gown and slips it back on. He waits, back turned, until she's dressed.

'I don't know why you're angry. I was bare enough when you slapped those ointments on me.'

'If I need to doctor you then that is an agreement between us. Otherwise you will treat me like a gentleman, whether you still believe yourself a lady or not.'

It's the end of her last day in this room and the sun set an hour ago. The Fixer sits in front of the hearth. Bethany is perched on the edge of the bed. They don't say anything. They don't look at one another. He has the iron doors on the fire open and flames paint his face orange. He stares right into them but Beth doesn't know what he's really seeing. She's wearing her smock. A trencher of bread and cold meat sits on the table beside the bed but there's no hunger to satisfy. Instead she's fidgeting as if a nest of ants lies under her rump. She opens her mouth to say something then closes it again.

Footsteps outside the door. A knock. The Fixer rises from his stool. 'Your Sisters are here to bathe you properly and provide fresh clothing. Do whatever they say and don't pay any heed to their japes. They like a little blood sport with the new girls.'

The Fixer is gone in a breath. Two young women dressed in plain smocks carry a sloshing tin tub into the room. They are maids, the girl supposes. Her 'Sisters'? Is that her future? Working as a servant in a big house? At Russell Hall she'd been little higher than a kitchen wench anyway, and ripe for teasing from the other staff. Pepper in her tea, nettles in her bed, even a toad from the ornamental pond stuffed into her shoe. That had sent her screaming down the hall and out the front door.

In one of her mother's magazines she'd read of a house for fallen women in London where harlots were scooped out of jail and reformed into seamstresses or washerwomen. A humble new life, her mother supposed, but better than dying of the pox.

The maids are watching her. One has a look that could slice butter and a prancing horse, painted all black, tattooed on her cheek. The other is softer about the face and sports a red flower design. They lower the tub to the floor and the woman with the horse motif beckons.

'Off with that sacking, Kitten.'

Beth is confused for a moment, then starts to tug at her smock. The maid snorts. 'Too slow, too slow, you are as idle as you are ugly.' She grasps the top of the gown and splits the fastenings from neck to hem. Cool air wafts over the girl's body. She crosses both arms over her breasts but the maid bats them away. 'No tomfoolery. Get in the bath.'

Warm, scented water envelops Beth's feet and she sighs despite herself.

'Another one from the madhouse,' the maid remarks to her companion. 'Where does Kingfisher get this refuse?'

'From the gutter, the same place he found us.'

The woman laughs. 'Looks like he cut it fine with this one. I don't know why I should be tasked with pampering her.'

'We all take our turn, Ebony Mare. 'Twas the same when you first arrived.'

'Oh very well, let's turn this weed into a blossom.'

For all their scorn, the maids' hands are as soft as butterflies. Face, hands and body are carefully cleaned. When satisfied, they dry Beth with a thick towel that smells faintly of jasmine. Her smock is exchanged for a linen gown that matches their own.

'Now,' the flower-cheeked woman says. 'I think you are ready for the Abbess.'

A Good Prospect

Bethany's parents waited until she'd turned sixteen before they sat her down at the kitchen table and laid out her future. Beth was forced to admit she hadn't given much thought to the matter. She considered her education a lure to attract a well-appointed banker or corn merchant. Certainly she hadn't foreseen pegging her future to the village and Russell Hall.

'Lord Russell's had an eye on you since you were a lass,' Mother said, while Father folded and unfolded his hands. 'You'll do right by him and his family.'

'You said we should mind our place.'

'Our place just got bigger. Your father paid good coin to have you lettered. Lord Russell wants you at the Hall and that's where you're going. He's too old to be running after children, his housekeeper's a prune and his lad can barely keep a leg out of a hunting saddle. It's time you chased the butterflies out of your head and put the things you've been taught to some use.'

Mother was a woman you did not argue with unless you were ready to let a month pass and still not hear the end of it. She lifted a hand to no one, but her ability to wear a body down with words was as persistent as the tide. Though professing to be a fervent disciple of God she also believed that to spare the rod was to spare the body unnecessary hurt. Unlike her fellow parishioners, who beat their servants and children with equal impunity, Mother believed the doorway to contrition lay in the will.

'You can blacken a rump with a leather strap but you can't knock pride out of a person,' she often asserted over the supper table. 'Pride is the chief cause of disobedience. Some of those village boys think it a mark of bravery to suffer a beating at their father's hands. They show off their bruises as if they were honours from the king. Only through humility can you find repentance and humility can be taught just like anything else.'

She did charity work for the Wesleyans, giving out dead children's clothes to the local urchins from a huge wicker basket tied to the back of her husband's wagon. Sometimes these garments were little better than the rags the youngsters already wore, but their mothers could work patchwork miracles with the material, and many rainbow-coloured breeches were seen scurrying around the lanes outside the village. Most Saturdays mother and daughter spent the morning loading up the basket before taking it around the farms. Local children – a whirl of bare feet, bad haircuts and missing teeth – tumbled into the yard as the wagon squeezed through the gate. Beth's ears were soon filled with whispered secrets, and forests of small fingers opened to reveal treasures gleaned from the fields surrounding their fathers' steadings. Ever-in-a-hurry Mother kept her peace over this because it made the job go more easily.

'You have a gift for working with children,' she acknowledged, perched crowlike above the now empty basket. 'More use could be found for that, I think.'

Later that afternoon Bethany slipped into the village for bread and found a lad fetching a hiding from a boy twice his size. She swung the breadbasket across the bully's ear. He was a good head taller and built like a barrel. Beth returned home with swollen eyes and her nose swimming with blood.

Father took her into the kitchen. 'I don't understand what's possessed you, Bethany. You have no friends to speak of, and at every turn you taunt the older village lads. I'm proud of my position, but not so high-handed that I forget who bakes the bread in this village, or puts shoes on the squire's horses.'

She gazed at him above the bloodied rag pressed against her nose and said nothing.

'When I speak you look at me as if I'm not there, when you choose to look at all. You're my flesh and blood yet sometimes it hardly seems I know you. Why can't you be like everyone else?'

'Why should I? I don't see so many things in someone's face as I do in a flower or an evening sky. Nor the sense in saying what isn't meant. The truth might hurt, but being lied to then finding out later is worse. You all talk and think in loops. It hurts my head to try and work out your meaning. I try to be truthful and I'm scolded. I make an effort to play your games and say what I think you want to hear but only court more trouble. You say I'm clever in one breath then stupid in the next. What am I supposed to do?'

Father struck his fist against his chest. 'You think me a man happy to be caught in the middle of everything, too low for some and too high for others? We all have our place, Beth. If everyone sat in gilded drawing rooms no crops would be harvested, no homes built, no ships captained across the sea. Without me or my kind, Lord Russell would see his estate turn to ruin. Without the village seamstress, your dress would fall as rags from your shoulders. If every farmer disappeared in the night your belly would cramp in its craving for a meal, and without smithing my horse would limp for want of shoes. I have my position, Lord Russell has his, and you have yours. You can't cross from one world into another any more than a milkmaid can turn into a silversmith. What I do is enough to put a sound roof over your head.'

'It's not your house, and neither is the land it sits on.'

'By rights no soul owns anything in this world except God, but the squire has charge of it and we're safe living here because of that. Don't go envying the lace-clad ladies who turn up at the Russells' tea parties. Such creatures don't own the satin slippers they stand up in. They live in their fathers' pockets and then their husbands', men who were likely chosen for them. How'd you like that, Beth?'

'I don't see the difference, since any time one of these older village lads you mentioned looks at me you seem intent on breaking his jaw.'

It was true Beth had enjoyed occasional attention when she was out bramble picking or pruning the roses in her mother's garden. Her only actual suitor was a buck-toothed farmer called Toby Wetheridge whose first wife went under a cart two weeks after their wedding. Toby wanted to fill the cot he'd made from two old barrels and a length of planking. He called on Beth's papa one Sabbath after church, wearing clothes that were only marginally less disgusting than his usual rags. He brought a spray of wild-flowers for Mother and a fill of pipe tobacco for Father. 'I aim to court your girl,' he declared.

Father chased him off with an old army pistol. Once nothing was left of Toby Wetheridge but a retreating cloud of dust, Father called Beth downstairs and stood her in the middle of the parlour rug, where he shoved a Bible into her hands. 'Did that man ever kiss you?' he demanded. 'Have you ever let him touch you anywhere?'

Beth, conscious of the scrutiny of both parents, shook her head. 'No. Never.'

'Swear it.'

Beth swore. Papa took the Bible and nodded. 'Good. No daughter of mine is going to end up as some farmer's brood mare.'

She wondered whose brood mare she would end up as.

'They have their world too,' Father said now, 'and you can't go there either. Find a respectable merchant, or perhaps a young barrister. Men like that will fall into your path soon enough.'

'So I've no more choice than those fancy ladies?'

'You can't do anything you want whenever you want. None of us are that free. Lord Russell knows it too. I've worked for that man longer than you've lived and I'll respect him till the breath is gone from me.'

'What if I reckon I do have a choice?'

'Then you'll likely bring calamity on yourself. Us too. Love is more than a tumble in the hedgerow with some comely village buck. It means doing what's right for everyone, no matter the sacrifice. I don't believe you ever understood that. I don't know if you ever will. I pray I'm wrong.'

In terms of Beth's immediate future, Mother was more practical. 'Your education will stand you in good stead at the Hall,' she said over supper. 'Working for the squire will knock some of the flighty notions out of your head.'

So there it was. She was to look after Lord Russell's niece and nephew whom she had never met. Not long after their birth, their mother had fallen down the village well. Her neck broke on the stone shaft before hitting the water. The incident oiled the gossips' tongues for weeks.

As for their father, he took a cannonball through the belly in the American War. Rumour said he sported a hole you could push your head through.

Dressed in her Sabbath gown, Beth was summoned to the big house and into Lord Russell's reception room. Oak panels gleamed in the light from tall windows puncturing the end wall. Lord

Russell stood gazing into the gardens, fingers curled around a silver-topped walking stick. Though small in stature, he boasted a broad flat back and hands as thick as stumps. His land was said to stretch for forty fields across all points of the Dunston crossroads. It took in the fish-swollen stretch of the river Dun, most of Mapleberry forest and all of the village. Nobody starved on his land or went without a roof, even when one vicious summer had the corn withering on its stalks. Village folk cooked his meals, tended his gardens and kept the poachers from his woods.

Beth dipped a curtsey.

'Ah, the estate manager's daughter,' Lord Russell said, turning.

'Yes, m'lord. We have met before.'

'Indeed, and you were barely higher than my jacket cuffs as I recall. Well, I am happy to engage you at your father's recommendation. I shall familiarise you with my household, then take you to meet the children.'

'I have to say I'm no teacher, m'lord.'

'I don't require a tutor as such. I need someone to play with them, indulge them, permit them their fantasies while ensuring they are not starved of responsible company.'

'A friend of sorts?'

'Of sorts, yes. This part of the county is quite remote and they see little of their peers. You will provide a suitable distraction for the time being.'

It was customary, he explained, for the squire himself to introduce new staff to their duties. 'I like to know who's under my roof' was how he put it.

As a ten year old she'd first met Lord Russell when her father took her round the grounds. Six years had not much weathered him. He was one of those men who, early in life, gains a comfortable face and exists happily with it into old age. He showed her all the in-and-out places of his grand house. Lord Russell was famed for collecting oddities. Rooms bristled with rare plants, primitive pagan masks, weapon collections and obscure texts. Rumour had it he once kept a lion in an upstairs bedchamber. Guests could hear the pad-pad of its paws across the floor. When Beth entered the greenhouse abutting the Hall's eastern face, the heat and moisture hit her like a fist, and she tumbled backwards in a half-faint. With wiry strength, Lord Russell scooped her back to her feet and into the fresh air.

Yet when shown the pretty bedchamber she was to make her own she blurted, 'I dislike blue. It is a cold colour.'

'Be thankful you are not packed into the attic with the servants,' Lord Russell said, but his eyes were smiling. He tapped his skull. 'You seem a quiet young woman, but your head, now that is a busy place.'

'In the village talking too much earns a scold's bridle.'

'Indeed? I am sure it will never come to that here. Now you will meet the children. Their needs are as persistent as they are varied. You will not visit home often, I suspect, even living on my doorstep as you do.'

Sebastian and Julia were presented to her in the schoolroom. Eight years old and so alike, as if someone had painted a boy, folded the paper while the colour was still wet to make a mirror image and, surprise, come up with the girl. Fair-haired, fair-eyed and with skin like milk, they carried little of their uncle's rugged sallowness apart from a thin-lipped twist to their mouths. Julia dipped a sweet curtsey while her brother bowed.

'What are you holding behind your back, Master Sebastian?' Lord Russell enquired.

He revealed his secret. A hunk of bread goldened with honey.

'Another illicit feast with Julia in the coach house, is it?' Lord Russell waited, face serene, while the boy shifted on his feet.

'It's for my pet,' he confessed.

'And what pet would this be?' Lord Russell said, faking a frown. 'A new hunting hound? A mare that I don't know about?'

'No,' he said. 'Smaller.'

'Do you want to show us where you keep it?'

He nodded towards the windowsill. Lord Russell smiled. 'Shall we have a look?'

He took the boy's hand and was led across the room. Beth followed, shoes whispering like dry paper on the rugs. At the window Sebastian stopped and pointed.

'There.'

Beth could see nothing at first except the corner of the frame. The afternoon sun threw fingers of light across the oak, and little patches of green mould seeped through cracks around the edge.

Should I pretend to see something? she thought. *Will he think I'm teasing him and get cross?*

Sebastian dropped the bread onto the sill. 'Supper for you,' he said, seemingly talking to the air.

Beth looked again, then spotted it. On the wood, wings spread to catch the sun, was a small brown moth. She almost laughed but Sebastian looked so earnest she didn't want to break the spell. He nudged the bread with his little finger. The moth remained indifferent. Beth thought about saying something when the door banged open and George Russell blustered into the schoolroom. George in cream riding breeches and glittering leather calf boots, always with that slightly startled look in his blue eyes. His smile was as wide as a river, a tumble of golden curls spilling out from the edges of his velvet tricorne. Beaming at them, his grin shone brighter than the sunlight.

'Well,' he said, 'if it isn't the new girl.'

The first night in Russell Hall found Beth in her quarters examining the bed her employer had provided. A real four-poster, not some put-together box. Big and sturdy, with an oak headboard carved into the shape of a dozing cat, and drapes on top. It could sleep four at a pinch.

A fire had been left burning in the hearth. The glow from it turned the room orange. Beth undressed and slipped into bed, relishing the soft kiss of the embroidered coverlet. The pillow was gentle on her head and she closed her eyes.

An hour later she was awake and sweating, her breathing laboured. The fire was a demon. She'd never been this hot, even in midsummer with her bedchamber windows sealed. She pushed the coverlet onto the floor and pulled off her shift. Lying naked on the mattress, Beth struggled to get comfortable. It was hopeless. Frustrated, she picked up the wash jug from the dresser, stumbled over to the grate and doused it in water. Orange embers hissed and turned grey. Smoke whirled up the chimney.

Retrieving the quilt, Bethany returned to bed. The room quickly cooled but she lay, wide-eyed in the dark, conscious of the high ceiling, the open space around the four-poster. Pulling the drapes only increased her isolation. In her cottage the walls were an arm's reach away. Sometimes she'd soothe herself by running fingers over the plaster, tracing cracks or small imperfections, enjoying the comfort of their solidity.

Finally Beth got up and dragged everything closer to the bed. The washstand, the chair, the footstool. She tried to move the dresser but a corner caught on the rug and it wouldn't budge. She built her own walls with whatever else she could find.

The estate, with its clumps of woodland and rolling lawns, was as quiet as the bottom of a well. Already she missed the sound of the wind stroking the tree outside her bedchamber. Mother twitching with dreams in the room below, her breath whispering in the dark. Father's guttural snoring.

Drowned embers settled in the hearth. Her slipping-away thoughts didn't linger on George Russell, or the things she believed she had read on his face. Instead she thought of the easygoing charm of Lord Russell, and those exceptional children. She knew even then she would love them.

Forever.

Morning. A maid stood laughing in the doorway. What was so funny? She gestured at the horseshoe of furniture gathered around the four-poster and said, 'You're supposed to sleep in here, not shove everything about. And look at that bed. Were you fighting with the coverlet?'

Short and pasty-faced, this servant bore an accent that put her nowhere within the county borders. But words weren't needed. Every gesture was a sentence. Each step across the rug, hand on the bedclothes, cough or sniff said something. *Who is this clod? Look at what she's done. Wait 'til I tell everyone.* The stuck-together mess of drowned ashes in the hearth didn't improve her demeanour.

'I was too hot,' Beth explained, cheeks pink.

The maid cleaned out the fire and set a new one. 'I shall not light it. You can do that yourself, or not at all.' She lifted the water jug out of its basin and shook it. Empty. 'I'll bring you more, and a clean gown just as I've been told. But don't think I'm going to run around after you if you make a sty of this room again.'

In the days that followed, Bethany learned the politics of her station. Servants took breakfast at six of the clock. Too high for the kitchen, too low for the dining room, Beth was an in-between person, not quite gentry or servant. Everyone seemed uncertain around her. Eventually she took her meals in her room.

What day was it? Tuesday or Wednesday? She'd lost count. Daffodils bordered the lawn and the air whispering through the crack of the open window carried the change of season. She paced the rugs, ate whatever she was given and stood in the corner when the maid grudgingly brought a fresh pot and changed the bed linen. Some nights sleep came easily, others were starved of it. Each morning Beth dressed herself in the clothes Lord Russell had ordered for her. Practical yet still finer than anything she'd worn at home. The fastenings proved slippery. That mopsqueezer of a maid did nothing to help.

Beth had hoped to see Julia and Sebastian immediately but both children were in Bath and wouldn't return before the week's end. 'This will give you time to settle,' Lord Russell explained.

What to do? A few books sat on a shelf above the hearth but most were either printed in what she thought was Italian or turned out to be heavy, scholarly tomes that tied her head in knots. The weather chose to be fickle. One day the wind blew the wrong way and smoked the room out. She nearly choked before the maid arrived, muttering, to damp down the fire.

'I'm going out of my wits,' she whispered to herself.

She'd hoped to spy her father working around the grounds, but he'd been sent off to arrange new plantings for the spring. Lord Russell was also noticeably absent, his interests taking him off to every corner of the estate. Beth thought about asking if she could go home until the children returned, but realised if she did so settling here would prove impossible. Besides, she needed to draw up a daily plan for her charges. It was so hard to think.

Finally the overcast sky split into blue and grey patches. Beth decided to risk a stroll in the grounds. Outside, cool air gusted over her. She lingered on the step, closed both eyes and breathed deeply. This was unlike Dunston air, which even in winter was thick with woodsmoke, horseshit and stewing vegetables. Instead it was akin to standing on top of Farley Hill with a fresh northerly in her face. Her lungs burned, her blood sang.

Invigorated, she took a few steps across a yard paved with broken stone. Ahead was a fountain. Bethany had only seen one other, in Dunston square. It never worked. The bottom was choked with dead leaves, bits of sacking and rubbish tipped in from the weekly market. Men watered their horses at the village trough.

She remembered the back-cracking work of hauling a pail up from the stream behind her cottage so the family nag could have a drink, yet water squirted unchecked from the outlets of this elaborate sculpture in a fine, clear spray. The centrepiece was a naked stone boy, a jug raised in both hands. Rainbows coloured a wet mist which coated Beth's face and hair.

Outbuildings clustered around the courtyard, hemmed in by a wall twice a man's height. Through an arch, she glimpsed a bridge over a reed-peppered moat. Hooked by curiosity she passed through, listening to the ticky-tack echo of her heels. Beyond, grass lawns sloped gently away. At the bottom sat a round pond like a big silver eye. More reeds poked through the water, and lily pads spotted the surface.

A tardy sun appeared and began warming the land. A duck floated in the middle of the pond. Another two lurked in the rushes, beaks tucked under their wings. Sunlight shimmered off the coloured feathers. Any travelling man would have their necks wrung and their carcasses plucked. Dunston went without ducks for winter upon winter when the tinkers were camped on the common.

On the far side of the pond stood a short, round tower of grey stone topped with crumbling battlements and studded with slit windows. It reminded Beth of a gnarled thumb poking out of the soil. Patches of moss greened the stonework. She glanced at the sun. Still early in the day, so she drifted down the slope towards the tower. Beyond lay a row of trees. Crows dotting the upper branches took flight, black wings flapping.

The tower was more strange than ugly. The door lacked latch or handle. It was plain wood, stained dark, with no bolts or keyhole. Beth stretched her neck, trying to peek into one of the windows. It didn't look the sort of place anyone would want to live in. She glimpsed snatches of things but couldn't tell what they were. For a second she thought something moved, but wasn't certain. Clouds rippled over the sun and odd shadows flew everywhere like swooping blackbirds.

A splash from the pond. One of the ducks stretched its wings. The land was still half asleep.

She ran a hand over the door. Wood felt warm where sunlight played across it. A splinter dug into her finger. Beth yelped and slipped it into her mouth. She glanced back at the walled-in house. For a moment she fancied she could see George Russell galloping across the grass on his hunter, a breathless fantasy in cream cravat and tasselled tricorne. All this supposed freedom and she didn't know what to do with it.

The door swung open. Beth screamed. The noise sent the ducks flapping off. Hot air wafted over her, and queer smells flooded her nose. She couldn't make another sound. A figure stood in the doorway, clad in a brown smock, with long grey hair tumbling about its face. Its mouth opened.

'Come in,' it said. 'I've been expecting you.'

Friends and Enemies

Bethany tingles all over; a warm, fresh feeling. She's been scrubbed to her roots and no longer feels greasy or smells of old sweat. The tattooed maids sprinkle her with rosewater, pull a clean linen dress over her drying body and slip her feet into a pair of cloth slippers. After retying the linen cap, the flower-cheeked woman leads Beth out of the room and along a lantern-lit passage hung with tapestries. They all depict fierce beasts and dense pagan forests.

'How long have you been a servant here?' Beth asks.

'I'm no maid, Kitten. As you heard me say to Ebony Mare, we all take our turn pampering the new girls. It reminds us what we once were.'

'What were you?'

'Cold, hungry. The same as you.'

'And what are you now?'

'Think of me as a business associate.'

The corridor ends in a scarlet curtain. Beth is ushered through. Beyond lies a dazzling hallway draped in more of the scarlet cloth. Marble pillars climb to a domed ceiling from which dangles a chandelier that glitters like ice. The floor is also marble, and cool even through her slippers. Black-and-white rings ripple outwards from the centre. Directly across from her lies a wide staircase, carpeted in red, that spirals upwards to a gallery. To her left is a closed door, painted a glossy black. Beside it stands a desk similar to a lectern in a church, only bigger.

Two tall windows either side of the door throw slabs of daylight across the marble. Beth cranes to see if she can spy anything of the street outside but the tops of some railings are all she can glean.

Ahead stands a set of double doors. Beth's escort pushes them open and enters the room beyond. 'The Kitten as requested, Abbess,' she announces. Bethany creeps in and finds a circular chamber with more scarlet drapes that loop and swoop around cream walls. Underfoot, a red carpet splashed with white goatskin rugs swallows up her steps. In the middle of everything a crescent of embroidered sofas, fat as pregnant cows, have been arranged around a polished table.

Seated is an old woman, slim and finely boned. Coloured patches cover her face and arms, leaving no scrap of bare flesh bigger than a farthing. And that hair. Long, almost to her waist, and lightning white. But her eyes are blue, like the sky during the height of summer when all the clouds have been baked out of it.

The Abbess pats the cushion beside her. 'Come, sit down. I like a busy face and yours is full of questions.'

Beth slips onto the sofa beside the older woman. It's impossible not to stare at that patched visage. Painted emblems colour her cheeks and brow, and plunge down the neck of her shimmering gown.

'You like them?' The Abbess smiles. 'These patches are copies of all the Emblems in the House. I wear my girls, proud as you like, on my skin for everyone to see. There's a space for you here,' she taps an inch of bare skin beside her left ear, 'just as soon as we decide who and what you are to be.'

'And what shall I be?' The girl knots both hands together in her lap. 'A whore? D'you think I haven't guessed where I am?'

The Abbess sucks air through her teeth and leans back. A gentle cloud of honeysuckle drifts into Beth's nostrils. 'I've read about places like this,' she continues. 'My employer was a regular subscriber to *Town and Country*. He didn't care where he left that scandal sheet lying. Even the local milkmaids know about these city vice-pits, and not one of them can read a word.'

'No immoral earnings are obtained under this roof. The House of Masques is not a market hall for bawds or courtesans. We do not need such creatures to advertise our services, nor are we a facility by which they can fill their own purses. Notoriety of that nature is not welcome. A client who has endured a difficult day may come to us desiring no more than a soothing voice or cheerful melody. We smile, hold hands, whisper reassurances into their ears.

Brows are cooled in summer and hearts warmed in winter. Men's vanity does not wane with the passing months, and our services are always discreet.'

'Whore, courtesan, it's all the same. Why was I chosen? The madhouses must closet a hundred girls with faces fairer than mine.'

The Abbess leans forward. Her eyes catch the light and seem to shimmer. 'For the first few weeks of your stay here, you will work as a maid. You will fetch and carry for your Sisters, clean out their hearths, turn down their beds, empty their pots. You will address them with courtesy at all times. You were nothing when you arrived at the House. Nothing you will remain until you have proved yourself. However, we are not slavers. First you heal. Then you work.'

'Nothing? But I am—'

A raised hand. 'You are nobody. The person you were will die on her bed in the Comfort Home. She will be buried under quick-lime in a pauper's grave with no tombstone or flowers. She will be forgotten.'

'Who are you?'

'As you heard, I am the Abbess, and we are going to be friends.'

Beth's escort is waiting in the hall. 'I shall take you upstairs. Hummingbird is waiting for you.'

'Who is Hummingbird?'

'She will be your tutor.'

Before they reach the bottom step, a tall, slender woman in a gold-trimmed linen gown blocks their path. Sun-coloured hair is gathered behind her head and tumbles down her back in a long tail. Blue eyes glitter under sweeping lashes. Her skin is pale, her lips plum dark. On her right cheek is a picture of a bird. Her left sports a second emblem, a pattern of four diamonds – two red and two white – forming another, larger diamond. When she tilts her head the light catches the emblem, turning it blood red. She smells of roses.

'So, a new Kitten fresh from some country ditch.' Her bladed voice cuts the length of Beth's spine. 'We get our share of farmers' daughters.'

'I worked for a squire and his family in a fine house.'

'Draw in your claws, Kitten. I'll not have you scratch me. Go on twisting your fingers like that and you'll have them out of their sockets.'

'My name isn't "Kitten".'

'I've no doubt your real name is very lyrical.'

'And what are you called that is so much better?'

'I am known in the House as Nightingale.'

Beth snorts. 'Not a proper name either.'

'Inside or outside these walls, it's the only one I have. You would do well to commit it to memory as soon as you are able. I am not in the habit of repeating it.'

She walks off across the marble floor, gown swishing around her legs.

Into the Night

The cart and Shire were waiting in the yard when the Fixer arrived. The beast was starved to its ribs yet the darkie, big as he was, looked dwarfed beside it. He scooped the girl into his arms and laid her in the back amidst a pile of straw. Next to it was a make-shift crib. 'I took bales from the stable,' he explained.

The Fixer climbed into the cart, checked the baby and covered her with loose straw. The darkie took the driver's perch and clicked off a series of sharp notes using his fingers. The cart lurched forward, back axle squealing. It should've been greased days ago but there'd been enough work to do around this stinking port.

Another job lost, the Fixer thought, *and here I am running away again. The same fear. The same pain in the gut.*

The Shire's steps were laboured. It smelled of leather and stale dung. The potboy was supposed to see to the animal's welfare but was getting more idle by the day. A taste of the rope across the backs of his legs would sort him. Not that it mattered now.

The quay remained quiet. No light appeared. No one came running. The watchman was gone, his brazier choking in the drizzle. He'd be in the gin house with his toothless doxy and fetch no grief because of it. Who, after all, would steal from a slaver port?

Into the lane. The squealing axle settled to a low whine. After a few minutes the cold started to bite deep, even under the straw. A distraction from the Fixer's wounds. He'd had no time to stitch the cuts but had cleaned the worst with alcohol and bound them tight. None of the sword strokes had hit anything critical. He might not bleed to death but the buggers were going to scar. He took a vial of laudanum from his salvaged doctor's bag and risked a few drops. Any more and he'd be no use to anyone.

They reached a crossroads, handpost stark against star-punctured clouds. The rain had fizzled out. 'Go that way,' the Fixer told the darkie, nudging his tar-spiked back. Another click of the fingers and the cart turned, wheels settling into soggy ruts.

Don't let us get bogged down. Not now.

He fiddled with a tinderbox and lit the lantern hanging beside the driver's perch. They were too far into the trees to be seen from the docks. In the yellow glow the young mother's face was pale and drawn above the mound of straw under which she'd buried herself. Her baby had settled in the makeshift swaddling. The darkie muttered words in some incomprehensible tongue but the Shire's tread on the road seemed sure enough. The Fixer settled in the straw next to the girl and slipped a warming arm around her. Already the pain was receding. As the laudanum deadened his body he couldn't tell where his troubled thoughts ended and the dreams began.

He sat up, wide awake. The cart had left the road and was standing behind a screen of trees. They were in a sloping clearing, thick with wild grass and the skeletons of old brambles. Using the lantern, the darkie had set light to a small pile of grass. As the Fixer watched, a bundle of twigs was added to the guttering flames.

He checked the girl. Her eyes were closed, her breathing low but irregular. Sheer exhaustion had knocked her into sleep. The Fixer fumbled under the straw. No fresh blood. He'd take a proper look as soon as chance allowed. He eased himself away from the girl and out of the cart, throwing both arms around himself like a shroud.

The darkie stared at the smoky blue flames. 'Bad wood,' he said when the Fixer joined him. 'Burns like wet hide, but we need to get some heat inside our bones. I have known cold before, but not like this.'

'Is that why you left the road?'

He nodded towards the Shire. 'The animal needs to rest or it will fall between the shafts.'

'How far have we come? Did you see whitewashed stones spaced along the road with markings on them? Can you remember how many?'

The darkie marked them off with his fingers.

'Sixteen miles. No sign of anyone coming after us?'

'We joined a better road a thousand paces back. I saw no one.'

'That'll change. Dawn's about two hours away. I slept harder than I meant to.'

'I saw you swallow something. It made you snore like a wild hog.'

'That may be, but it's wearing off and I'm starting to hurt. We can't linger here.'

'Tell that to your horse.'

'Hunger will soon wake the baby. She'll get nothing good from her mother's breast. We need to find milk or she might not survive the night.'

'The girl cannot feed the child?'

'I doubt she can feed herself.'

The darkie dropped another handful of sticks into the flames. 'Warriors, in my land, sometimes eat a root before fighting. It unchains their minds. They go wild, see things others cannot see, but they forget to eat. To clean themselves. This one is in such a place. Her blood is singing. You cannot go there too. Keep your potion in your pouch. Use your pain to keep alert.'

He threw the last of the wood on the fire. It spat like a sick dog and billowed smoke into the freezing air. The Fixer mused over the idea of being needed. The darkie could snap both their necks, abandon the baby and slip into the trees. The journey over the ocean had eaten at his muscles, but enough strength remained, as had been demonstrated in the Fixer's cabin.

No, my friend, you also have demons to answer to. I suspected as much on the quayside and I'm more sure of it now. I'm banking on those to get us through this.

They still had time. The port watchman would be well in his cups and the potboy seldom budged before cockcrow. The girl's supposed brothers posed the biggest threat but the Fixer knew their sort. They'd whip up some men, likely from their own estate, to do their chasing for them.

'How is the girl?' the darkie asked. 'She was speaking through much of the journey, saying things I did not understand.'

'Sleeping, or as close as she can come to it. The straw is keeping them warm enough. I daren't wake either. Noisy mouths will serve us ill.'

'If not for them I would still be in that cage?'

'Yes.'

'Then I must be grateful to them if not to you. I know what you were thinking, that I could kill you all and take my chances in the forest. You are right to do so, because I am a murderer. I have killed or enslaved my entire people, and what would be three more among these dark trees? But that is not how my heart works. I am a stranger in this country and will take your offer of life, if only to remember what I have done.'

'D'you have a name, darkie?'

'You could not say it. Your tongue is too stiff. Your race has forgotten how to speak. You do not name your children after living creatures. You are given nonsense titles that cannot be found in the skies, the land or the forest. I cannot speak to you of names.'

'Fine. No names. Not for now. But I'd like to know why my language is so familiar to you. You speak better than many English born.'

'My village once traded with your kind, until you found a better use for us. So, do you have a plan, healer, or shall we wander like this and let fate decide what becomes of us?'

'I've fooled myself for months that working those docks was the only choice open to me. But no, there's another.'

'Another?'

The Fixer said nothing more and the darkie didn't press it. Half an hour later they were back on the road, the fire kicked into ashes behind them. An orange smudge lined the horizon to the east. They had to pull onto the verge to let a post coach gallop past, but so far that remained the only traffic.

The darkie had a haggard look. The Fixer sent him into the back of the cart and took over the driving. When the baby woke and started crying she was soothed with gentle songs never heard in this patch of the world. The miles rumbled by. Every sound caused the Fixer to flinch. The nag snorting. A crow flapping out of a hedge. Soon the land opened out into pasture and the grey-green fuzz of trees lay well behind them. Not much of a forest. Any pursuers could likely comb it within an hour.

Another crossroads. The handpost marked eleven miles from the city. The right-hand road disappeared into the fields. Ahead, the lane rotted into a track. The brown husks of last summer's weeds still poked out of the middle. Dead brambles encroached from either side.

The Fixer snapped the reins across the Shire's rump. All around them fences were broken, walls had stones missing, the land looked bare and neglected. No good for grazing or farming. The only house they passed had lost its roof. The garden was thick with gorse.

The darkie was still awake. 'Are we looking for something?' he asked.

'An acquaintance of mine. His home is tucked well off this track. We may have to walk part of the way.'

The horse strained against its harness. Thorns scratched the wooden sides of the cart. Ahead, the lane ran beside a line of tall, untended hedges. The Fixer halted the cart next to the crumbled bones of a wall almost entirely swallowed by undergrowth. All that remained of an old drover's cottage. Beside it sat a ragged hole in the brush, not much bigger than a man.

It's even worse than I remember, the Fixer thought. *I've more chance of sprouting wings and flying than getting the horse down that.*

He slid off the driver's perch. The nag snorted its relief. The Fixer tethered him to the branch of a stunted tree and let him chew the verge. If he was found, nothing could be done about it. The Fixer lacked the time or patience to hide him.

'Get the girl. I'll take the baby.'

'We are going through here? What lies beyond?'

'A house with many paths to its doors, not all of which are safe. This way we won't be seen.'

The darkie placed the child into the Fixer's arms and scooped up the girl, again with no apparent effort. They had to duck through the undergrowth, but a few paces further on the bushes had been widened and the path cleared. Ahead lay a hunting lodge fashioned from stone and stout oak beams.

'It suits my friend to keep a back route,' the Fixer explained. He tucked the baby under his arm and banged his fist once, twice on the door. A crow clattered out of a nearby tree and flapped off, squawking.

The glade settled back into silence. The Fixer thumped the door again, harder. The girl stirred a couple of times but didn't wake. In a sense he envied her. His ears and his nose were turning numb. They had no money and no other place to go. Besides, the Shire needed proper feed and a long rest.

If I'm wrong about this I'm taking the girl to an inn even if I have to sell the nag to pay for it, he thought. *The darkie can take his chances.*

The door ghosted open. A man appeared on the step, his profile mottled orange and yellow by the fire behind him. An old army musket was clutched in both hands.

'You know that's as likely to blow up in your face as cause any hurt to us, Crabbe,' the Fixer said.

A lengthening silence. Even at this distance the Fixer could feel the heat spilling out of the parlour hearth. His bones sighed for want of it.

The gun lowered. Crabbe spat into the dark. 'On the run again, John? I thought you'd had your fill of trouble over women. Yet here you are, out of the night with a lass in tow and, cross my heart, a baby too. I hope that big fellow is your rightful slave and not something you stole.'

He studied the darkie in the light from the door. 'Cross my heart, the tar's barely dry on this one. He's fresh off the boat and not even sold, I'd wager. And what about you, John? Someone's cut you up pretty fine by the looks of it. What trouble are you bringing to my door?'

'We got a good start. Nobody knows we're here.'

'Not yet, they don't. But you know what these Mango buggers are like when they're sniffing out a blackie's trail.'

'Are you alone?'

'Bless your luck, I've no other visitors tonight. Now get inside. I near broke my back feeding logs to that fire and I don't want its heat leaking into the hedgerows.'

Crabbe stepped aside. A leather armchair hugged the hearth and, without being asked, the darkie sat the girl down. Her eyes opened, took in the orange-flooded walls, the stoic furniture, the animal trophies peering gawk-mouthed from their mountings.

'That baby's only hours old,' Crabbe said, gesturing at the bundle in the Fixer's arms. 'You delivered it?'

'I did.'

'I never thought you'd have the courage. You took a fine chance bringing the mite and its mother out on such a night. When it comes to certain things you've got dust floating between your ears, John.'

'D'you have milk for the child?'

'Yes, fresh from the cow this very morning.'

'And something for the mother?'

'A pot of stew. Might still be warm.'

'What's in it?'

'Don't ask. I did you a big favour last time, John. My charity don't stretch every which way.'

'You'll get a fat enough purse on the girl.'

'Ah, so that's your notion? You're right, I shall, but the baby won't get past their doorstep. House rules. Besides, I'm retiring.'

'You? I thought they'd have to shoot you first.'

'Age is creaking my bones, and I can't go chasing over the country like I used to.'

'Maybe I could help there.'

'What, do my job? You're too bad with women. No subtlety. No discretion. You'd leave a trail wide enough for a boatman to sail his barge up. Tell you what, though. The House might be looking for a quack. You're good enough at that, despite your other failings.'

'We can find someone to take the child.'

'That we could. But I'm no baby farmer. If you want it gone you'll have to sort it yourself. I doubt the mother will stop you. From the look of her she'd not notice if her head rolled off her shoulders. So what's the tale behind that?'

'Some kind of opium and she'll want more of it soon enough. There are places in the city.'

Crabbe nodded. 'Indeed there are.'

'Are you going to take us to the House?'

'I shall. That's the prettiest lass I've e'er laid eyes on and she'll line my pockets well, even if fairies are flitting around inside her head. Where'd you get her? From the cut of her cloth she's no milkmaid. I thought you'd learned not to go dipping your fingers in this particular pot, John, so don't tell me she's your sweetheart.'

'She fell out of the night and landed in my lap. I believe she's from one of the big estates upriver.'

'Baby's a bastard, I take it.'

'I believe so. Those that brought her to me would gladly be rid of it at my expense, but this isn't just about my misfortune. The child's life is in our hands.'

'Your hands, you mean. You don't so much get dogged by ill luck as throw yourself into its embrace. Did you see any sign of pursuit on the way here?'

'Not so far, but these are men who won't let the matter lie. You can cover our tracks, Crabbe. Making girls disappear, both high and low-born, is your trade.'

'True enough. I don't care for the darkie, though. He can get his rump back on the road.'

'He comes with us.'

'Done you a favour too, has he? Must have been a bloody big one to run this risk . . . So be it. The Abbess might have work for him.'

'We have a bargain then?'

'We do. But I take the whole purse, and if things go sour don't come troubling my peace again.'

Crabbe leaned over the girl, who sat, hands spread in front of the fire, humming a pretty melody. Such a contrast between them, he with a face boiled by the seasons and curly hair that defied any wig to keep it contained. But he possessed a vain streak as wide as the Bristol channel. His fingers, fat with rings, embraced the girl's head and drew her eyes towards him. 'What's your name, lass?'

'I can sing,' she said, 'pretty as a nightingale. Everyone says so.'

'That you can. And what might this songbird be called?'

'Anna.'

'Well, Anna, you're going to have to travel some more. But first we'll get you rested and some food in your belly. Then, when your wits have cleared a mite, we'll talk about what needs to be done.'

'Yes.' She smiled, and this time there was no slackness in it.

Crabbe looked up. 'Clean yourself up, John, and pick a coat. You know where they are. They never did much fit me anyways.'

'I've got a nag and cart in the lane.'

'Stolen?'

'They belong to the docks.'

'Right. I'll leave 'em somewhere that'll knock the pack off the trail.'

'Just like the old days.'

'Too much like the old days.'

Crabbe's bedchamber also boasted a hot fire and the Fixer stole a few minutes to warm himself. The laudanum was wearing off and his cuts were beginning to hurt again. He couldn't risk taking anything else. The darkie was right, the pain would keep him alert. He checked his brow, his neck, running surgeon's fingers into his armpits and down his groin. *No fever*, he thought, *exhausted is all*.

The wounds had stopped bleeding. His ointments had done their job, but he was coated in a dirty brown rime. He crossed to the wardrobe, shoes soft on Crabbe's thick rugs, and gave the ewer a shake. Water sloshed inside. He poured some into the basin and splashed his face and hands. Refreshing. He peeled off jerkin, breeches and shoes. Beside the wardrobe was an empty drawstring sack and he bundled the clothes inside. After retying his dressings, he opened the wardrobe, glanced at the contents and selected new breeches, hose, shoes, shirt, waistcoat and jacket. His fingers worked intuitively on all the fastenings. Once clothed, he topped everything off with a tasselled tricorne and a cream neckcloth secured with a silver pin. When he gazed into Crabbe's full-length mirror a phantom stared back.

I've lost weight, he mused.

The door swung wide. 'Your friend thought you might want supper,' the darkie said, a trencher in his hands.

'Where is he?'

'Gone outside. The girl has been fed. Her child too. They are both asleep. No one else is in the house.'

On the trencher was bread, stew, a lump of cheese. 'Take half the food for yourself. And here,' the Fixer reached into the wardrobe, 'put on this overcoat. I don't aim for either of us to starve or freeze. Crabbe might not care whether you survive but I owe you a debt, my friend, and I've just enough honour left for that to matter. Does he know you understand our language?'

'He did not even look at my face.'

'Good. Don't say anything. Knowing English would make you more valuable. Crabbe would sell you behind my back in a spit, no matter the risks. I should have warned you in the lane.'

'You do not trust this man?'

'So long as a profit is involved he's entirely trustworthy, but his notion of a fair price doesn't always match mine.'

'A bad thing to say when you are wearing his clothes. Better than anything I've seen on missionary or trader.'

'These were my clothes once. That favour he did before cost me plenty.'

'I heard you both talk about money. Have I helped you save this girl so that she might be sold? Is that how it is done in this land also? You trade one another?'

'It's not the same.'

'How so?'

'She will have a life.'

'Had I stayed in the slavers' pen I too would have a life, but it would not lessen the bite of those chains.'

'If I'm caught I'll spend my life on a prison treadmill. Perhaps even hang. I don't have any place else to run. Trust me.'

'You do not trust Crabbe.'

'I trusted you. I had faith that you would help us. That you wouldn't run when I opened the pen or kill us and steal the cart.'

'Perhaps it is I who has lost too much faith.'

'Keep just enough to finish this journey. That's all I ask.'

'You have too many secrets.'

'As do you. Now eat.'

Friends or Foes?

'Just a moment.'

Curious thumps and bumps. Beth knocks again. The door is flung open. A wild-haired young woman, petite and bright-eyed, gazes out. She sneezes and a feather flies out of her mouth. 'Well, patience isn't one of your virtues,' she declares.

'I think I'm supposed to sleep here.'

'And so you shall. Come in.'

Beth slips past her into the room. It looks like a storm has gusted through it. Clothes lie everywhere. Over the floor, across the dresser and draped on the backs of chairs. A huge embroidered quilt is scrunched up in one corner. Feathers float onto the carpet.

'Forgive me for keeping you waiting,' says the girl. 'I'm forever getting into a fight with that quilt and I always lose. It's like trying to shift an elephant. Not that I've ever seen an elephant, you understand, except in a storybook, but the size and the weight look about right. Still, now you're here you can help. Perhaps we'll get the cursed thing on the bed while there's still some stuffing left.'

'You've got a lot to say for yourself. In my village, women who gabble as much as you do get a scold's bridle in the mouth.'

The other girl looks startled, then laughs. 'Yes, I know I talk a lot. The queen of light conversation, that's what the Abbess calls me.' She crosses to the dresser. 'Hummingbird's my name. You know what a hummingbird is?' She taps the picture on her cheek. A tattoo like the others.

'No.'

'A tiny, many-coloured creature that can hover in the air like a bumblebee.'

'It must be a very peculiar bird.'

The girl tries to pull some sense back into her tousled hair, gives up and reaches for a brush. 'Yes, it's certainly different. Now, are you going to help me with that quilt or stand and watch me tie myself into knots? Might be good for a giggle but it won't get the bed made.'

Beth doesn't move from her place on the rug.

'Right,' Hummingbird puts the brush back down, 'so I'm small. Well, a lot of men like that. You'd be surprised how many want me to pretend to be their daughter or niece. Women too. I'm sure Nightingale is half hoping I'll end up servicing old men. Can you see me doing that? No? Well, neither can I.' She made a face. 'Are we going to sort this quilt, Kitten? It's cool out tonight.'

'Why does everyone call me Kitten?'

'It's a nickname for new girls. I don't mind you sharing my bedchamber as long as you don't snore. I'll stuff a pillowcase up your nose if you do. Apart from that, I'm sure we shall make fine companions.'

She plumps down on the mattress in a rustle of petticoats and kicks off her slippers. 'The Abbess warned me she was putting a Kitten in my room. I always seem to play mother. Well, a maid will soon be huffing up the stairs with two possets to warm our bellies. I'd sooner enjoy a snort of brandy, but this is the only nightcap we're allowed. Here, would you help me with my fastenings? The chambermaid is so clumsy; her nails are always ploughing my back.'

'Have you many servants?'

'Oh, we've all sorts in here. Titles tend to slip a little.'

'This is a brothel, isn't it? You're a harlot and soon I'll be one too. I rotted in a locked room for six weeks. This place is just another cage. Are you to be my jailer, Hummingbird? Or are you a prisoner just like me?'

'I'm nobody's jailer and this isn't a bawdy house. Bodies aren't sold here, Kitten, only company. Didn't the Abbess tell you that? All you have to do is look good, talk sweet and the rest will be easy. New girls are always full of questions. I was too, and I think I gave everyone a headache with my pestering. You belong to our mistress now. She can do whatever she likes with you. And will.'

'She said I was dead.'

A hint of a smile. 'We are all dead. You had better get used to it.'

'How long have you been here?'

'How long is forever?'

'Don't you ever see your family?'

'I'd rather hang.'

'You hate them that much?'

'Of course. Don't you hate yours?'

A knock on the door. A round-faced woman blusters in, dressed in mobcap and apron. She lays a silver tray with two glasses on the bedside table. The candle glow catches her face, highlighting the pink scar on her right cheek. She notices Beth staring and says in a singsong voice: 'You see something funny, *enfant*? Something to make you laugh perhaps?'

Before Beth can utter a word, Hummingbird scoops up a linen shift and tosses it to the maid. 'Thank you, Eloise. Fix my quilt then take that shift down to the washroom.'

'You knocked your bedding onto the floor. You can pick it up.'

'Please?'

The maid flaps her hands. 'Am I to do everything? You English girls are so prissy. You drink water and think you piddle fine wine.'

She leaves, muttering, the shift tucked under her arm. Hummingbird waits until the door closes then explodes into a fit of giggles. 'Well, I thought it worth a try.'

'She looked angry.'

'Don't worry about Eloise. If she didn't complain I'd think her ill. Here, drink this. You'll feel much better, I promise. And afterwards you really must help me with the quilt.'

'Where am I to sleep?'

'With me, of course.' Hummingbird pats the mattress. 'Sit down. I won't bite. We've more than enough room. A pot is under the bed if the need arises. You've had a bath, I take it?'

'Yes, I thought they were going to scrub me down to my bones.' She touches her cap. 'All my hair is gone. Even my eyebrows.'

'A precaution, Kitten. All sorts of vile things crawl around in jails.' She glances at the marks on Beth's skin. 'That's where you were, wasn't it? Jail, or somewhere similar? We've made ladies out of worse. What was your crime?'

'The local squire's son attacked me.'

'And you told on him, did you? Silly girl.'

Beth grimaced. 'I thought I'd see justice done. I should have known better.' She rubs her arms. 'That man, the Fixer, he put some sort of ointment on me. It smells horrible.'

'I'm used to his concoctions. The Fixer knows his business. Always do what he says and you'll be well.'

'He unsettled me. So did the dark man, and that Abbess woman. I thought I'd fallen into a madhouse, not been lifted out of one.'

'A madhouse, was it? Your wits seem solid enough.'

'It was a bid to silence me.'

'We've all been cast into the gutter in one sense or another.' Hummingbird picks up her glass and takes a sip. Beth does likewise. Honeyed milk, warm and sweet on her tongue.

'The Abbess is devoted to this place,' Hummingbird continues. 'Kingfisher too.'

'Doesn't anyone want to leave?'

'And go where? For all its pretty terraces, horrors fester in the streets of this town. Step off the path and they will cut you up. Be a good girl and you'll enjoy food in your belly, clothes on your back and a roof over your head.' Hummingbird put down her glass. 'Where do you hail from? Your milkmaid voice suggests Sussex, or maybe the bottom of Hampshire.'

'Dunston. A farming village mostly. I was no doubt quite the talk of the place for a while. I left by carriage. And what a carriage it was. People thereabouts must have had enough to keep their tongues wagging a whole season.' She gulps her drink. 'I'd forgotten a posset could taste this good, yet my mother used to make them every night.'

Hummingbird nods. 'I know it's easy to say, but don't let the past haunt you. Memories can stick in your thoughts and turn sour. If my mind starts to cloud, I think of horses. One of my regular clients owns a fine stable and I often go riding with him. We all find our own way to survive the snarling demons of our past. You will too. Very quickly. Don't be a screamer, Kitten. It will do you no good at all.'

'A screamer?'

'Some of us talk freely about the people we once were – strictly within the walls of the House of course, for a client must never know anything, not even the real name of his escort. Other girls don't talk so much, but you can read their past in their eyes or in the set of their face during an unguarded moment, perhaps as they sit by the fire or sup a hot drink before bed. Sometimes these ones will smash crockery or beat themselves. Broken items are discreetly repaired or replaced, and bruises heal. So long as we behave like angels with our clients the Abbess will overlook our tantrums.'

'She said I was to work as a maid.'

'And so you shall. You need time to get better, to put a little meat on your bones. Light duties first. You'll have an easy time of it. Now, if we're finished with the inquisition, I've had a long day and am feeling snoozy. Eloise won't make this bed, the lazy French sow. She says I rumple the covers too much. What does she expect me to do, sleep on the floor?'

Beneath the friendly chaos is a nice enough room. Pale pink walls, white plastered ceiling with elegant cornices, a thick rug and burgundy curtains.

'She seemed impertinent for a maid.'

Hummingbird stares at Beth for a moment. 'Well, hark at Miss High-and-Mighty. What were you before you came here? Daughter of a duchess?'

'No, I looked after well-born children and I'd have felt the end of a strap if I'd spoken to my betters like that.'

'So you're Eloise's better, are you?'

'No . . . I mean . . . What I meant . . .'

'Understand, Kitten. Even the girl who helps Leonardo sweep the manure out of our stableyard is higher in the scheme of things than you are right now. Eloise used to be a Masque, just like I am, and that scar on her cheek was where she used to wear her Emblem.' She taps the picture on her face with a forefinger. 'It's not a lifetime job. Afterwards we're grateful to still have a home and a bit of work.' Hummingbird stands and grabs a corner of the quilt. 'Now, please help me. Between the two of us we'll have it done in no time.'

'I don't even know if I shall sleep. I can't believe this is happening.'

'The first night is always the worst. Some newcomers settle quicker than others. I'm sure you won't prove difficult.'

Beth snatches up the other end and together they manage to force the bed into a semblance of tidiness. Satisfied, Hummingbird pulls her shift over her head and lets it fall in a linen puddle to the floor. Beth is startled at the girl's nakedness. She has an absolutely beautiful body, like a porcelain sculpture. Her skin is clear and fresh. She seems to know no shame at all. Sweeping back the coverlet she climbs into bed and pats the pillow beside her.

'Snuff out the candles before you get in.'

Beth moves like a ghost from flame to flame, extinguishing each with a puff of breath. The fire in the hearth has already smouldered to ashes. She is conscious of the rustling of her linen dress as she tiptoes across the rug in the dark.

'Not going to take it off?'

'No.'

'My, aren't you a shy one.'

'I'm cold. Sometimes it feels as if I've been cold all my life.' She slips between the covers. So smooth and clean against her limbs. Yet her mind is a buzzing nest of thoughts. The strange words Hummingbird had used. Masque? Emblem? What did it all mean? *Not a bawdy house*? Beth doesn't know what to believe, though it couldn't be any worse than the Comfort Home.

Could it?

An arm slides around her waist.

'You are beautiful,' Beth sighs.

'So are you.' Hummingbird's voice whispers into her hair. 'You would not be here otherwise. Now go to sleep. Everything will be better in the morning.'

I won't sleep, Beth thought. *I've gone from a stinking mattress to a soft bed and I can't believe it. How can I possibly sleep?*

But sleep she did.

A Sense of Injustice

'A fish is swimming in your pond. Come and see.'

'Nothing lives in the pond. The gardener cleared it out weeks ago.'

'No, a fish. A trout perhaps.'

'I don't believe you.'

'Then Alice and I shall catch it. Our shawls will serve as nets. It'll make a fine supper.'

'You can't take anything from my garden. It's theft.'

'You said there's no fish. How can we take what isn't there? Come, Alice.'

'Wait.'

Anna Torrance surveyed her two visitors. Both were smiling, but Anna's eleven-year-old mind knew that their eyes didn't match their tucked up mouths. On arriving with their parents, Alice and Emma's excitement had been real enough. While the adults took tea Anna had shown the girls her pony, her wardrobe of London clothes, her watercolours. She had played the spinet, then stood in front of her father and his guests to sing. Her efforts had brought the girls' mother out in tears. 'A nightingale,' she had gushed. Her own daughters were clumsy on the keyboard and sang like frogs.

'Take the girls for a walk around the garden,' Anna's papa instructed her. 'I have business to discuss with their father.'

Anna dutifully took her cue. Papa often invited people to the house. Always these visitors wanted something. Often they left happy, other times not.

In the grounds, Anna pointed out the expensive topiary, the rosebeds, the greenhouse with exotic, out-of-season flowers. Somewhere along one of the perfectly straight gravel paths the dregs of her visitors' enthusiasm slipped away and they began whispering behind Anna's back. She had taken them to the pond with its sculpted fountain and was on the way back to the house when she finally rounded on them.

'Stop whispering. Stop keeping secrets from me.'

'Why shouldn't we?' Alice said.

'You're at my house, in my garden.'

'It's not your house, it's your father's.'

Anna became aware she was digging her nails into her palms. 'Tell me what you were talking about. My father's bank could reduce your parents to paupery if he wished.'

So now she had returned to the pond, peering into the water for the fish which, like everything else on the estate, she considered hers. The dark water was drawn from the gizzards of the hills. At its deepest it would not have passed her knees, even at the height of the spring rains, but it was black as a stone-clad cistern.

A hand caught her between the shoulders, propelling her forward. An entire world of cold crashed into nose, mouth and ears. Shock bubbled the breath out of her lungs. Trying to regain her feet, her soles slipped on the stonework that lined the pond and she crashed into the water again, backwards this time. The other girls stood watching her. All pretence at dignity was gone. Anna's hair lost its moorings and, in a cascade of pins, slopped around her cheeks. Her bonnet floated off like an upturned basin, ribbons trailing. Half blind with pond water, she slithered to the other side of the pool, grasped the stonework with a flailing hand and managed to climb out. Shaking her skirts, she set off across the grass towards the house without a glance at her tormentors.

She was aware they were trailing her. That was good. Father wouldn't have to go looking for them. She could picture the looks on their faces.

Anna didn't cry, in fact she hadn't been much hurt at all. In a sense that was a shame because it would make it so much worse for them. Her mind was focused, her thoughts fixed. Impinging on her sense of purpose was the realisation that her bonnet was still floating in the pond. That didn't matter. Father would get her a new one.

Her feet carved up the distance to the house. Arms swinging, she strode across the flowerbeds, dragging thorns and petals in her wake. The other girls had to hurry to keep up.

The outside door to the drawing room hung open. Soft voices chattered into the afternoon air. She walked in from the terrace, dragging a filthy trail across the carpet. Father was seated in an armchair opposite the hearth. A glass of Madeira and some papers littered the table beside him. The girls' parents sat on the couch, laughing at some jest Father had made. At sight of the wet apparition in front of them the humour died in their throats.

'They pushed me,' Anna said. 'Into the pond.'

'She slipped,' Alice said behind her. 'We didn't touch her.'

Father regarded the girls, then his daughter. Something rippled across his features, then settled.

'Anna, go back around the house to the kitchen and have the maid wash you,' he said. 'Then change for supper. I don't want mud on my carpets.'

'But—'

'Go, Anna. Now.'

She ran back across the terrace. Instead of heading towards the kitchen she clambered through her father's open study window and landed on the rug in a slither of soaked petticoats. From the desk she grabbed a fistful of pens and tried to cut her dress, but the crow quills broke in her angry fingers. Discarding them, she pulled at the satin bows on the front of her bodice. Her hands, greasy from the pond, slipped on the material. Both hem and petticoats offered similar resistance.

She slapped herself across one cheek, then the other. Pain, sharp and honest. She hit herself again, harder. Beside her father's inkpot sat a decanter. She pulled off the top, put the neck to her lips and glugged down the dark liquid. Fire split her belly and ripped up her throat. Nose and mouth seemed to fill with hot embers. She forced herself to drink more.

Mr Torrance, always sceptical of his daughter's capacity for obedience, found her sprawled and puking on the floor. He carried her to the kitchen and held her at the basin while Cook tipped jugs of bitter-cold water over her head. Hours later, when she woke in her bed with a dry mouth and her head cracking open, he came to see her.

'I'll run away,' she told him.

'You're already gone.'

'What happened at the pond wasn't my fault.'

'Aye, it was.'

'They pushed me. You'll have them punished.'

John Torrance's voice was tired and age-cracked. 'No, daughter, I shall not.'

'Are you saying I'm to blame?'

'Not to blame. Lost. I thank God it's not the same.'

'I hate you.'

'Aye, that is true enough.' He rose from the bedside chair and brushed down his knee breeches. 'Perhaps you have good reason to. But you can't fight the entire world.'

The door thumps open. Curtains swish. Dull light leaks into the room. Beth opens bleary eyes and spies the outline of a mobcap and apron.

'Well, what a pretty sight you two make,' the maid declares. 'Perhaps I leave you to it, *oui*? Let you doze on your idle backs until noon while the rest of us have work to do. You would like that, no doubt.'

'Eloise,' Hummingbird mutters, half buried under the quilt, 'I swear they should have caught and killed you before you ever lifted a foot off French soil.'

'Then what would you do, *mes enfants*? Drown in your own clutter? Starve to death because you could not stir yourselves to climb outside your warm bedcovers? And now that you are finally awake I suppose you want me to bring you a nice hot dish of tea to heat your tender bellies?'

'If it'll break your heart, don't bother,' Hummingbird says, sitting up and stretching.

'Then you'll go and tell the Madame Abbess that I am neglecting you, that I am cruel to her darlings?'

'What can be crueller than this? It must be midnight, if that.'

'It is well past seven. The sky is thick with clouds just as your head is thick with nonsense. Now, I shall bring in a fresh ewer then go and fetch the tea. Be sure you are up and clean by the time I get back.'

She ducks out of the door, reappears with a jug and sets it on the dresser. After favouring them both with a look that could slaughter a cow she leaves, muttering.

'I don't believe she ever sleeps,' Hummingbird says, yawning. 'I think she spends the whole night pacing the corridors devising new ways to torture me. Now you're here she'll be doubly delighted. Two souls to curse instead of one. Come on, Kitten. No warm fire for us this morning.'

Hummingbird whips the quilt away. Cool air gusts up Beth's bare legs. 'Ow!'

'Eloise isn't averse to pouring water over people who can't drag their feet out of bed. Don't tarry. I want my breakfast, and the sooner you're taken care of, the sooner I can eat. Take off that dress and I'll sponge you down. Maybe a quick splash on the face to wash the sleep out of your eyes.'

Beth shivers on the rug while Hummingbird rubs the sponge over her. The ewer water is warm and rich with the scent of herbs. Her skin tingles. Despite herself she giggles. When had she last done that?

'Ticklish, are you?' Hummingbird dabs the end of Beth's nose with the sponge. 'There, finished. Dry yourself then put on your smock and slippers.'

Beth towels down and dresses while Hummingbird cleans herself. No sooner have both girls donned their day gowns than Eloise reappears with two steaming dishes of tea. She gives a grudging click of approval and puts the drinks on the table before leaving.

Hummingbird pats the rumpled quilt. Beth sits and swallows the drink handed to her, savouring the heat on her tongue. 'When I awoke this morning I expected to find myself back in the madhouse,' she confesses.

'Then you saw my ugly, sleepy face and knew you had,' Hummingbird laughs.

'No, this is different. I don't think I've felt so comfortable in such a long while.'

During her time at Russell Hall she'd taken breakfast at seven o'clock every morning in her room. In the madhouse the days had blurred into each other, the fights and squabbles seemingly possessed of their own regularity.

Hummingbird eyes her over the rim of her tea dish. 'Well, I'm afraid the comfort can't continue, at least for a while.'

'Why? What is going to happen?'

'You're going to earn your place, and quickly. The House can't afford to give freely of its favours. More training awaits.'

'What will you do?'

'Me? I'm going down for breakfast. If I receive a day Assignment I doubt you'll see me again before dusk. Be of stout heart, Kitten. Your new life is just beginning.'

An hour later Beth is with the Fixer.

'I'm going to teach you to eat properly,' he says.

'What's wrong with the way I eat?'

'You stuff meals down your throat as if they're about to leap off the trencher and run for the door.'

'When you haven't had a decent meal for weeks you want food in your belly just as fast as you can shove it there.'

The Fixer doesn't answer. Instead he wheels in a trolley laden with plates and glasses and sets up a table by one of the mirror doors. At his prompting, Beth seats herself. The table heaves under silver cutlery of all sizes. A fancy-looking bowl features birds etched around the rim. Beside that is a glass goblet that's so clear it could've been made of air.

The Fixer serves all kinds of food in tiny portions. Beth doesn't know what half of it is. At home Mother often flung vegetables and meat scraps into one big pot and boiled it up. Sometimes a rabbit would be roasted over the kitchen hearth and the bones used for soup. Everything here is offered in bowls or covered trays. Potatoes appear in a big metal dish with a knob of melting butter on top. Mutton and beef are carved into slices no thicker than parchment. There are lumps that look like small dead birds, and fish with eyes that stare up at Beth from the plate. Oily things slick her tongue and churn her belly. Spices send her into a coughing fit. She doesn't know the proper way to eat or drink this strange fare. Everything she does is wrong. She uses fingers when a fork is required. Or she uses a fork when she's supposed to use her fingers. There's even a little bowl of scented water to dip her fingertips in. And small bites. Always she is told to take small bites.

'Your stomach isn't ready for rich food,' he explains.

This goes on for hours. Rehearsals for breakfast, lunch and supper.

'Pick up that knife . . . No, not that one, the other . . . That's right, let's try again.'

And that's not the half of it. The Fixer sets Beth walking around the room, staring at her as if she was an old nag barely worth a bent coin. A few circles around the polished floor and Beth is told that she moves too fast, that she's all arms and hips. She thinks if her tormentor were ever chased by an angry dog across a farmer's field he'd feel no urge to tarry either. But no, Beth has to take measured steps, hands clasped in front, eyes demure. She keeps this up for the fat part of an hour until her feet ache.

When she finally brews enough courage to ask questions, the Fixer goes deaf. Beth gives up and plays the games. As the light outside begins to fade, the Fixer points to the big spread of cutlery and asks for the umpteenth time if Beth knows what fork is for sticking into what fish or meat. Again Beth goes through all the spoons and knives. She shows what she would do with the napkins and how she is going to pick up her wine glass.

'Don't curl your hand around it like a fist. You're not going to hit anyone. Use your fingertips. Clasp the stem.'

'What d'you want with me?' Beth demands. 'Haven't I done enough?'

A smile flickers at the corners of the Fixer's mouth. 'Perhaps.'

'I was furious.' Beth frowns at her companion seated on the bed beside her. 'Wouldn't you have been?'

'Nothing to be ashamed of,' Hummingbird says.

'I felt clumsy. And small. In the end I felt like throwing everything on the floor. And you were gone all night. I was sure I'd see you before turning in.'

Hummingbird shrugs. 'These things aren't done to torment you, Kitten. Not long from now you'll be dining in high company. This training will ensure you're a credit to yourself and your guests. Now, I'm afraid you have to see the Fixer again. A mite more discomfort, then you can have breakfast and meet the other girls.'

Beth wonders how many more mites of discomfort she can bear. After draining her tea dish she follows Hummingbird downstairs and across the hall.

'When I first saw the Fixer's razor I squealed like a snared rabbit,' Hummingbird confides. 'I had to be dosed to the gills on laudanum before I would let him shave me.'

At least the Fixer's potions have soothed her injuries. That, coupled with the bath, makes her feel reborn. Her shaved body gives an odd sensation of cleanliness, and the catch-up on sleep has lifted the tiredness from her eyes.

The Fixer's examination is brief. 'A new woman already,' he says, grinning. 'A little fresh ointment on your injuries and you'll be ready for breakfast. I take it your belly stood up to the rigours of yesterday's training?'

'It was the best food ever forced on me.'

He shakes his head. 'You've had the best of nothing yet.'

Back in the hallway, Hummingbird takes Beth through a burnished walnut door trimmed with gold leaf. Beyond is a long table with six high-backed chairs. Two other tables at right angles stretch the length of the room, all shrouded in milk-white table-cloths and set with glittering silver. It's easily as elegant as the briefly glimpsed dining room at Russell Hall.

Hummingbird nudges Beth's arm. 'Don't look so awestruck. It's not a palace.'

Their feet are silent on the rich carpet. Lace curtains turn the daytime into a moonglow that makes everything shine. Above, a host of round-faced cherubs and trumpet-blowing archangels beam from the curved, frescoed ceiling. An iron chandelier, studded with crystal and a hundred candles, hangs in splendour over everything. A fireplace opens a black mouth in the far wall, the metal grate ringed by soot-charred bricks.

Beth runs fingers along the back of one of the chairs. 'I am to breakfast in here?'

Hummingbird catches her arm. 'No touching, Kitten. You haven't earned this place setting. Instead you'll dine at the low table with the other new girl.'

'Low table?'

A square of oak set near the hearth and partly covered with a grey linen cloth. Hummingbird gestures at one of two squat stools. 'Wait there and don't touch anything. I'll be back shortly.'

'You're not staying?'

'I have to enter with the other Sisters. It's all part of the game.'

Beth can't quell the fluttering in her stomach. Unsure of what to do with herself, she sits down. The stool is an unforgiving lump beneath her. A lot of places are set at those tables. In the Comfort Home no one could afford to make friends.

Newcomers were pestered for anything of worth then left to fade into the grey walls. During her first week the ribbons had been plucked from her hair and lace snatched from the sleeves of her gown. Two weeks later she stole them back. That was the way of it.

But food, real food, was something her near worthless possessions couldn't buy. Now here she is, in a dining room fit for a squire, waiting for breakfast. What would Lord Russell say to that? What would her mama?

Trouble is what you are, Bethany Harris. You'll bring ruin on us all.

Beth has been so lost in her thoughts she hasn't noticed someone else slip into the room. Clad in a linen smock, the newcomer has a fuzz of hair darkening her scalp. Round cheeks are cut by a long, straight nose. Eyes are mahogany dark and settle instantly on Beth.

'So I'm to share this table with someone at last,' the girl says in a voice that seems to loop around itself. 'Sometimes I feel quite forgotten tucked away here.'

'Who are you?'

She sits opposite. 'I'm Moth. A Kitten like you.'

'Moth? Is that your real name?'

'No, I got it from my father. He said I was always flitting about the house like a moth around a candle. I don't mind. I always thought "Sarah" a bit dull.'

'I'm Bethany.'

'You'll get another name. Supposedly there's a test that helps decide it, but I don't know any more than that.'

'Who is looking after you?'

'Red Orchid. Do you know her?'

'A girl with a flower on her cheek?'

'That's right.'

'She helped bathe me the other night.'

'Oh, she's nice enough but I think I'm taken care of out of duty, not fondness. Perhaps she's meant to stop me stealing something or hurling myself out of an upstairs window. Her eyes are never off me.'

'You share her room?'

'Yes, but not her bed. She makes me sleep on the floor by the window. To learn my place, I think. But I'm not complaining. I have a pillow, a nice soft rug for a mattress and all the blankets I want. Compared to snatching a nap in a draughty barn it's paradise. You're with Hummingbird, yes?'

'How did you know?'

'I saw you in the hall together. She'd be a sweet girl if she could manage to stop gossiping for more than a minute at a time. I hope for your sake she doesn't talk in her sleep.'

Beth chokes back a giggle. 'Not that I noticed, but I was so tired you could've lit a gunpowder keg under me and I doubt I would've stirred.'

'Did she put you on the floor too?'

'No, I slept in the big bed, with her.'

The ghost of a frown flickers across the other girl's forehead. 'The Abbess doesn't like the Masques to have favourites. You might find yourself moved before long. Not everyone is so free with their bed space, I've heard.'

Beth leans forward. 'Moth, how long have you been here? I thought I'd been brought to some kind of bawdy house but the Abbess says that's not so.'

'I don't know much about it myself. I only arrived two weeks ago and I slept a lot of the time. Girls of all ages live in the House. They are given Assignments, sometimes during the day, mostly in the evening. They go out and they come back. I tried asking Red Orchid if there's anything more to it than being paid to keep people company but she says I'll find out soon enough. All I've done so far is change bed linen and let the Fixer feed me his witchy potions. He's happy because my hair is growing back but it seems to be taking a long time. I had dark hair, long and beautiful. I spent hours just brushing it. Look at me now. I resemble a farm boy. You too.'

A bell sounds in the hallway. Women dressed in identical white linen file into the room and take up places behind the chairs. Each face is fresh, each tumble of hair tied at the neck with a plain ribbon. Beth spies Hummingbird but fails to catch her attention.

'What now?' Beth whispers. 'Are we supposed to stand?'

'No, sit there and try not to fidget. They don't usually pay attention to us.'

Four more girls in linen gowns, this time trimmed with gold, sweep into the room. Each sports a coloured emblem on both cheeks. They stand at the top table, hands resting on the chair backs. Among them is Nightingale. Her face is so delicate it could have been cut from pearl-coloured glass. She sees Beth sitting at the low table and a tiny knot creases her forehead.

Finally the Abbess appears in a dress of glittering scarlet. At her side is the dark man, Kingfisher, in jacket and breeches of deep blue embroidered with silver. Both seat themselves. In a sigh of rustling linen, everyone follows suit. Beth wonders if the Abbess is a Lady of Quality. Certainly she carries herself like one, but Beth can't believe it of the dark man. The fact that he's allowed to sit with everyone else, let alone at the top table, makes her suspect some form of twisted charade.

Conversation ripples up and down the long tables. Maids with scarred cheeks wheel in trolleys buried under tureens and dishes of food. Meals are served with whispering swiftness. Top table first, then the others. Beth's stomach cramps at the smell of meat and freshly baked bread. She spies fish and bacon, bread streaming with butter and layered with strawberry jam. Dishes of tea are poured and passed. Laughter punctuates the chatter.

The Kittens are served last. 'If you're wondering what you've got,' Moth says, already tackling her food, 'it's liver, kidneys, fresh vegetables and some fruit juice. New girls who gorge themselves are often sick, apparently. One arrived last autumn, thin as a stick and on the run. She'd been found eating grass on the heath. She stuffed herself on leftovers from the kitchen and spent the rest of the day casting into a bucket.'

Beth prods the food with her fingers.

'Can't use a knife and fork? What were you? A tinker girl?'

'I was a companion to two beautiful children and my father was a respected member of the community.' She gestures at the table. 'Why have we been given wooden cutlery? This so-called knife wouldn't slice butter.'

'Kittens aren't allowed metal cutlery unless supervised.'

'Why?'

'Weren't you told? They get all kinds in here. A few weeks in prison can turn even the most wilting bloom into a spitting wild-cat. If you want to tame a beast you don't leave it with sharp claws, that's what the Abbess said. Despite the table training we're both on trial.'

'Is everyone from prison?'

'Or worse, so I've heard.'

Beth tries a forkful of food. It's tender on her tongue. The fruit juice has a cool, sweet taste. Orange and lemon mixed with sugar, possibly. A comfortable feeling spreads through her belly.

At the end of the meal a red box trimmed with brass is set before the Abbess. Chatter dies away.

'She's going to give out the Assignments,' Moth whispers.

Names are announced. Girls rise and approach the top table where the Abbess hands each a parchment bound in red. Every face is a study in beauty, every movement elegant and considered. Even the most breathless heartbreakers of Beth's village are milk-maids by comparison. Ten minutes later the box is closed and whisked away. Not everyone has received a parchment, Beth notes.

'Look at Ebony Mare,' Moth whispers. 'She didn't get one again.'

Beth remembers the dark-haired girl from the night of the bath. She is staring bleakly at her empty breakfast plate. 'Why?'

'Her looks are fading. She is becoming very bitter about it.'

'She seems comely enough to me.'

'But she's old inside her head, and that's made her ugly. She believes she deserves to be a Harlequin, but the Abbess only assigns her the older clients.'

'Harlequin?'

'Senior girls who get the best jobs. They have the diamond pattern on their left cheek.'

Before Beth can ask anything else the Abbess claps her hands. Everyone rises and files from the room. The maids begin clearing away plates.

Moth stands.

'What do I do now?' Beth asks.

'Find your Masque. She won't be far away.'

Hummingbird is waiting in the entrance hall, ribboned parchment twirling in her fingers. She hurries over, small feet pattering on the marble floor. 'Well, Kitten, were you impressed with our dining arrangements?'

'I've seen naught like it.'

'You'll get used to such luxuries once you begin moving in the right circles.'

'Do you eat there every meal?'

'Only in the mornings. Most evenings the room is set aside to entertain callers. We usually take supper in our bedchambers.'

'What's in the parchment?'

'Perhaps an opera, perhaps a Ball. And you? D'you feel better for something in your belly?'

'A little, yes. The other new girl, Moth, put me at my ease.'

'Hmm, she's learned a lot.'

'She seemed put out that you let me share your bed when Red Orchid makes her sleep on the floor.'

'On the floor, is it? She's lucky not to find herself thrown into the corridor. Moth cries in her sleep. You can hear her halfway along the landing.'

Beth thinks about those rounded cheeks, the fuzz of hair already growing back. Moth had seemed confident but, on reflection, every gesture, every word had a fluttering of nerves behind it.

'I've already met one of the girls at the top table. Nightingale. She spoke to me as if I were a beggar.'

'Nightingale's one of the House's most favoured Masques. She enjoys a grand room, has the services of her own maid and usually only escorts the most high-born clients. I daresay she's never known aught but the touch of silk against her skin and the favour of princes. Come, Kitten, we both have work to do today.'

Eloise stands outside their room, an empty canvas sack grasped in one hand and a small brush and shovel in the other. How plump she looks. Every woman in the house except the Abbess seems fleshed out.

'Now,' Eloise says, handing the sack to Beth, 'time for you to earn your bread, *enfant*. I served you, now you serve me, *oui*?'

'Go easy on her, you mad Frenchie,' Hummingbird says. 'I have an Assignment later this evening and won't be here to look after her.'

'So it is fine for me to sweat blood and crack my backbone to provide your little comforts, my precious, but I must not break your new toy, *non*? Well, do not trouble your sweet brow. She will get her hands dirty but come back to you in one piece. You can tuck her into your pretty bed and smother her in rose petals while I, who work my fingers till they bleed, fetch your supper. In my grave I shall find peace at last, *oui*? 'Tis as well you are bound for hell else I'd fear you would come haunt me in heaven.'

Hummingbird pats Beth on the shoulder then slips into the room, closing the door. Eloise flaps her free hand. 'She is laughing at me in there, you know that? All the time she laughs, like this is some game I play for her amusement. Pray God you have some sense in that bare head of yours. Now we must get started. We are already late.'

Beth examines the empty sack dangling in her hand. 'What are we going to do?'

'Do? Why, we are going to clean fireplaces, that is what we shall do. What did you hope for, *enfant*? Some flower arranging? A little crochet perhaps? Sew a sampler for a young beau? Not under this roof. Ashes and embers, those are our business, and you'd better get used to their smell before you can think about dabbing sweet scent behind those little-girl ears. We shall do your bedchamber last. I cannot go in there and suffer that idle creature braying at me. Here, we shall start in here.'

Hours of work leave Bethany's back and legs aching. Each bedchamber, though a near mirror of Hummingbird's, is infinitely tidier. Apart from some hairbrushes and the odd trinket box there's little in the way of personal effects. It's impossible to glean anything about the occupants.

Along the whispering corridors of this huge house she some-times hears voices and odd snatches of laughter. Ghost women clean and polish, remove chamber pots, deal with the laundry. They are everywhere and as barely glimpsed as mice.

'Where are all the tattooed girls?' Beth asks.

'Your Sisters-to-be are either out working or in the Mirror Room practising their skills. No one other than Hummingbird sits idle in this house for long.'

One more room, one more hearth. After clearing it out, Beth collapses into a sooty heap on the floor. 'Finished at last. I'm exhausted.'

'What are you doing, *enfant*, taking a nap? A little beauty sleep to put some rosebuds on your cheeks? Our work is only half done.'

'Half done? What do you mean? There can't be a grate I haven't cleaned.'

'Cleaned the grates, yes, but now we have to fetch fuel and kindling. Our brave princesses will want something to warm their pretty hands by. The walls of this house are thick and it has a cold heart, whatever the time of year. A room without a flame is a dread place. We must work some warmth into its bones.'

Beth tries to get up but tumbles back.

'I can't do it.'

'Can't do it? Of course you can do it.'

She tries again. Her legs won't move. Both arms feel as if they are floating six inches out of their sockets. Her hands are two ash gloves and soot smears her face. 'I can't.'

Eloise stands over her. 'Must I take a stick to you? Will you be beaten like a stubborn donkey?'

'I'll kill you if you touch me, I swear it.'

'Brave words, *enfant*. You claim you cannot fetch a scrap of kindling yet in the same breath threaten my life. Look at you, trembling like a rabbit in a snare. I fear for my safety, I truly do.'

'Don't mock. I've been beaten enough, you French cow.'

Eloise claps her hands. '*Mon dieu*, now you sound like Hummingbird. Come, *enfant*, let me help you up. No, don't flinch, I shall take you to a place you can rest awhile. You have a stout heart and have worked hard today. I doubt the House of Masques will be any poorer for sparing you half an hour.'

Eloise guides her down the passage and into an alcove. 'Here we are, our little day palace.'

A plain varnished door opens into a parlour dotted with armchairs. Thick curtains are bunched at the windows. A coffee table, scattered with newspapers, sprouts from the polished floorboards.

Eloise lowers her into a leather armchair. Opposite, a figure lies snoring on a sofa. A woman in breeches and long leather apron. Her face is grubby, and she smells of manure and old rope.

'Don't pay any heed to her,' Eloise says, filling two cups with steaming liquid from a pot over the fire. 'This is where we come for respite. Our own parlour, though few of us have time to make much use of it.'

The rich smell of coffee warms Beth's nostrils. She lifts one of the cups and takes a sip. 'I've not had coffee in weeks.'

'Then it will taste all the better. I take pity on you, new girl, because you are so weak and wrung out, but do not think I shall treat you like this every day.'

'I'm grateful just the same.'

'What did you do before your life turned bad?'

'Bad? How would you know what happened to me?'

'We are all people who have had something happen to them, *enfant*. Only the details differ.'

Beth stares into her coffee cup. 'I looked after children.'

'Ah, little ones,' Eloise's face softens, 'they are our future, *oui*?'

'Who is the girl on the couch?'

'Another hard-working member of our family.'

'Why is she asleep at this time of the day?'

'She has spent all morning helping the dwarf with the horses.'

'Couldn't the stable boys see to them?'

'Stable boys?' Eloise laughs. 'We don't keep stable boys. Not with a house full of pretty girls, *enfant*. Men are pigs, don't you know that? They get ideas above their place. They drink and wag their fat tongues into the wrong kind of ears. They fight among themselves because they all want to be king over any pile of straw they find. And they would not suffer a woman as their master. They are not bred for it, you see? The poorest farmer in the country can sire six daughters and hold them dear to his heart, but as soon as he spits a boy from his loins then that son inherits whatever patch of mud his papa possesses. This is what all men are brought up to believe. And it is the men who make the laws.'

Beth settles back in the chair. It feels like sinking into a soft glove. 'My mother never saw a future for me beyond the walls of the squire's house. Father didn't object. Sometimes I hated him for that, sitting like a straw puppet agreeing with all her opinions as though he never had a single thought of his own. As it turned out, I was wrong. But what about Kingfisher? And the dwarf is a man of sorts.'

'Ah, but those fellows are cut from a different cloth. I doubt you will hear Leonardo bemoaning his lot. Kingfisher enjoys a high place here and, darkie or not, he is not so witless as to send himself back to the slavers. He claims he was a leader in his own country who was tricked into captivity. The Abbess bought the collar off his neck and exchanged it for a cravat. He can knock the wits out of any so-called bruiser and still flourish a silver fork with the grace of a dandy. Yet he never touches the girls, not in that way. He jests that they are pale and horsy, with the fire drained out of their veins. The women of his own country are seemingly rich and exotic, like a strong spice, yet the humour leaves his face when he talks of them.' She takes a mouthful of coffee. 'Nevertheless he is a hunter. He sniffs out girls – good ones, not common trash. Everyone under this roof is well educated. He knows all the shut-away places families hide their black sheep. His net is huge and he caught you, my little minnow.'

'Why did you become a maid here, Eloise?'

'Maid?' She taps her cheek. 'You see this scar? I was once a Masque, a girl not much different to you, enjoying the company of landed gentlemen. However, rules are in place, and if rules are broken there should be consequences, no? My Emblem was taken from me and now I spend my days running after little *mesdames* like Hummingbird. I tell you, some days when she is difficult I wonder if working the streets would not be kinder.'

'Emblem? You mean one of those tattoos? How was it removed?'

'With a hot knife. A quick enough job if the Fixer puts his mind to it. That is one task only a man could do well. Don't ever upset the Abbess, *enfant*.'

'Why did you let her do that? Why were you not dismissed, or leave of your own accord?'

Eloise laughs but there's a hollow sound to it. 'You'll soon learn not to ask certain questions. Asking in itself can't get you into trouble. It's the answers you won't like. The House is a refuge in many ways but if we are not careful our pasts will fester inside us. We look for any means to lock our histories deep inside ourselves. Sometimes a hot knife is the only remedy.'

They sit quietly for a moment. Apart from the snoring the only sound is the hiss of steam from the pot on its hook above the fire. Eloise drains her coffee. 'Now we must go back to work, *enfant*. I shall take care of most of it. All you have to do is hand me the kindling. Can you manage that?'

'I'll try.' Beth holds out her arms. Soot blackens both sleeves. 'Why didn't you give me an apron?'

'Because you would have dirtied your gown just the same, then there would be two lots of washing to do. I doubt the washer-woman would thank you for that. She complains loudly enough as it is about the amount of laundry we give her. Fear not, *enfant*, you will get your scented bath at the end of the day, and a crisp fresh gown for the morning.

'You make me look a sluggard.'

'Once your strength returns you will surprise yourself with what you can do.'

They progress back through the rooms. Sometimes Eloise chats, sometimes she sings little French ditties. The day is beginning to soften into late afternoon when she declares their work finished.

'Now you can go back to your bedchamber. If that idle friend of yours comes home early I shall bring supper so she can gorge her flabby face even more. There will also be a fresh pitcher of water and some towels. You at least have earned them.'

Nightingale is standing outside the door. Beth nearly walks into her. The Harlequin's face is so pale it almost shines. Thin lips cut a pink gash in that icy skin. Beth drops the kindling bag. Behind her, Eloise draws in her breath.

'Did the Kitten work well?'

'Well enough,' Eloise replies.

'She did as she was told?'

'She did, *oui*.'

'No tantrums? No rebellion?'

'Not so much.'

Nightingale turns to Beth. 'So, you are a good girl? We shall see how far that obedience extends.' She brushes past and glides off down the passage, linen gown whispering.

'What did she mean by that?' Beth asks.

Eloise cocks an eyebrow. 'Ever trained a puppy?'

'No. We never had a dog. Mama got the gripe whenever one came near her.'

'Well, Nightingale is good at it. Very good. Now, let's get these things put away. Be back here tomorrow at a quarter past the hour. We shall need to clean the fires out again in the morning.'

'And this is done every single day?'

'Don't worry, *enfant*, it's not forever. In a few days you might be changing bed linen.'

Beth finds her own way back to Hummingbird's bedchamber. Every muscle in her body creaks. *I'm going to sleep smelling of soot and old chimneys*, she thinks. *If I never wake up I don't care.*

A stranger stands in the bedroom. A white-faced creature with rouge ringing her mouth. Dark eyes glitter above rosebud cheeks. A gown almost swallows her whole, massive loops topped with velvet bows sweeping across her skirts. Her head is smothered by a powdered wig topped with a tiny blue tricorne.

'Did you clean out those ashes or take a bath in them?' she says in Hummingbird's voice. 'I thought you a sweep's boy.'

Beth struggles for breath. 'And . . . and you look like an earl's doxy.'

Both girls burst into a fit of giggles. 'I don't know who fetched the bigger fright,' Hummingbird says. 'Me, I think.'

'You'll have to duck every time you go through the door,' Beth retorts. 'Where did you get those garments? I saw nothing like that in the wardrobe.'

'These are my working clothes. I'm only allowed to wear them when I'm on Assignment. No, don't touch, you'll get dirt on them. Strip and wash. A clean shift is on the back of the chair and some water left in the ewer. Did our darling Eloise mention anything about supper?'

'She promised to bring something up.' Beth pulls off her soiled smock and lets it fall onto the rug. She nudges off her house shoes and pads over to the dresser in her bare feet. Water splashes into the basin. 'That woman, Nightingale, was lurking in the corridor when Eloise and I finished working,' Beth says, washing the soot from her fingers. 'I don't know how long she'd been standing there. She was like a cat waiting to pounce on a starling. She *scared* me, even after all I'd suffered before coming here. She's harbouring some sort of gripe, I'm sure of it.'

'She's like that with all the Kittens. I think she's laying down the pecking order.'

'That's what Moth said, but there's more. It's not just the way she wafts around in that golden gown and elbow gloves. She's beautiful, the most beautiful woman I have seen, yet at the same time she's like some unholy sculpture by a mad artist.'

'Ah, those gloves. She has more than a hundred pairs. A little privilege the Abbess grants her. They infest every corner of her room. I've heard she even bathes wearing them.'

Beth cleans under her arms then across her breasts. The water is cool against her skin. 'Eloise took me to a parlour to rest for a while. Will Nightingale likely go on haunting me?'

'Harlequins have their own parlour. You'd have to scratch and scrabble to step through that door, Kitten. Beware, always beware. Your Sisters can quote Latin with the eloquence of a poet while pushing a hatpin through your throat.'

A knock on the door. Beth grabs the fresh shift and hugs it to herself, but it's only Eloise carrying a tray and teapot which she sets on the dresser.

'*Et voilà*. Scones with cream and sweet bramble jam, if that suits your highnesses.'

Hummingbird launches herself at the tray. 'Give me anything so long as it has cream on it. In fact, leave the cream and forget the scone.'

'I hope you are ashamed, Hummingbird, displaying such piggery in front of this girl, and her only recently arrived. Don't expect me to patch your stays when the stitching bursts. Can you please take the Kitten to the Fixer before you go out, provided you can still move after gorging yourself of course?'

Hummingbird dollops cream on top of a scone. 'Yes, yes, I'll do your job for you, as always. Please go now, Eloise, your twittering gives me a headache.'

The maid withdraws, mumbling something in French. Hummingbird breaks another scone in half and spreads a generous portion of jam over it.

'Come on, Kitten, put that shift on and eat something before I finish it all. I'm sure a morsel won't kill you, provided you don't tattle to the Fixer.'

Beth, whose belly feels like an empty pot, picks up the butter knife. Hummingbird snatches it out of her grasp. 'No.' She taps the blade against the side of the tray. 'Silver. You don't touch it outside of dinner training. Next time I'll remind Eloise to bring you a wooden knife. She should have known better.'

'Don't you trust me?'

'One of my papa's friends had a sheepdog. He reared it from a puppy. I used to pet it until one day it bit me. Just like that. So, no, Kitten, I don't trust you. Not entirely. And even if you didn't hurt me you could always slip it out of here, perhaps up your sleeve, and use it on someone else. We've had girls try all sorts of things with the most unlikely implements. We even had one Kitten run off with an entire case of spoons and try to sell them to the local silversmith. You're in my room because it is my job to watch you. The Abbess would have me strangled if she caught you with a silver knife. Now, take this scone and eat up. The Fixer wants you, and the city is expecting me. We can't afford to keep either waiting.'

Art Lesson

Beth felt as if she was standing at the bottom of a huge cannon with a floor of black powder primed to go off. One wrong step could cause her whole world to explode. Daylight spilled through the thin windows, creating beams of sunlight like the spokes of a huge carriage wheel. A flight of stairs circled up through the ceiling, hugging the wall. A fire crackled in an iron grate, adding a smoky tint to the air.

Lord Russell was dressed like a visiting town merchant with blue breeches gathered at the knee with ribbons. Coloured hose sank into glittering shoes with rosettes as big as the moon. A dark satin doublet was embroidered with silver butterflies and a neck-cloth circled his throat in milk-white folds.

Beth stole a breath. 'May I ask why you were expecting me, m'lord, and what you could want of me in a place such as this?'

Lord Russell seemed to consider for a moment. Fingers, shiny with rings, ran through his hair, a flowing brown mane that fell over the shoulders and down his back. A sharp widow's peak mixed with threads of grey stabbed his forehead. He resembled a tall, white-cheeked wolf. Beth half expected his teeth to be as sharp as needles. As it was they were polished to an unholy shine.

'Such impertinence,' he said through a smile. 'You did not think to curtsey or wait until you were required to speak. If you were in any other service a birch would be laid across your back.'

He spoke in little bites, picking each word from between his teeth. His fingers scurried up his shirt, twiddled the fastenings, played meaningless games. 'Fortunately I am not so disposed. I was expecting you because curiosity would inevitably lead you here. I have a penchant for painting and believe you can be of use to me.'

On top of a folding table lay a flat piece of board spattered with coloured blobs. Half a dozen thin-handled brushes were piled on one side. Beth had seen painters at Pendleton fair. Sixpence for your portrait.

'Is this where you work? Don't you have a canvas?'

He swept his hand around the room. 'Men's fascination for erect, cylindrical objects never ceases to amuse me. In a round house nothing can hide in the corners and canvas, for all its versatility, is not a living thing. It stands without protest and suffers the indignities thrust upon it by the great and incompetent alike.'

He positioned himself behind the table. 'But how could I paint you? You are cold, locked up – everything hidden away as if in a cupboard. Your body has nothing to say. It does not speak to me.'

'I don't know what you mean. You hurt my head with all these words.'

'Take off those gloves. Your fingers will resemble bloodless worms if you do not permit the sun to colour your flesh.'

'The sun is a painter?'

'Indeed. Every man with a brown face will testify to that. She is the world's greatest artist, colouring the land with greens and yellows, the gold of autumn, the crisp whites of winter. Flowers follow her movement across the sky like eager children, folding up their pretty faces in petulance when the day ends and she takes her brush to the other side of the world.'

He beckoned Beth over and grasped her shoulder. 'Be still. The brush will not bite.'

It circled then touched. Bristles kissed her knuckle. A hairy tongue slid down to her fingertip, leaving a trail of wet scarlet. The paint dried quickly on her warm skin.

He smiled. A whisper of air as the brush returned to the palette to feed. Returning, it gave Beth a blue thumb. Yellow, green and white coloured her other fingers. Ochre whirls spiralled up the back of her hand, chained her wrist and dipped back into her palm.

She giggled like a child. 'It tickles, like being licked by a friendly cat.'

'The brush is my friend. It takes what is in my heart and mind, and gives those visions substance. Now, move your hand. Waggle the fingers. See how the colours blend, become a single entity the way a painting is the sum of its many parts.'

'It's like watching a flower dancing in the air.'

'Now you must try.'

'I can't paint. I have the hands of a milkmaid.'

'If you can hate, if you can love, if you have ever felt angry or sad, or brimmed with joy so that you wanted to burst. If you have watched a beautiful sunset and cried, or felt melancholy because the sky was choked with rain clouds. If you have felt some or all of these things then of course you can paint. You do not work these miracles with this,' he touched her hand, 'but with this.' His fingers alighted between her breasts, lingered, then fluttered away. Beth fancied she could feel her skin tingling.

He passed her the brush, which felt awkward in her many-coloured hand. His fingers curled around Beth's and led them to the palette. The brush dived and wrapped itself in a bright shawl of purple then was guided to her other hand, where it made a shiny grape of each fingernail.

'See how easy it is.' His voice was a tickle in her right ear.

'I'm no painter. Your hands are guiding mine.'

'Parents help their infants to walk. Finally they take their own steps, unsteadily at first, but growing in confidence. Once you have a feel for things you won't need help.'

He reclaimed the brush, wiped the end with a rag and dropped it into a pot beside the others. Stooping, he dipped a finger into the palette, turning moist pink into vivid green. He knelt in front of Beth and hooked his thumb over the lip of her gown. A sharp tug and the stitching parted. Air breathed over her exposed breasts. Before she could react his painted fingertip circled the left nipple. Beth was betrothed with a ring of green. Shivers cut like glass along her spine. She was ice, freezing and melting and freezing all over again.

He leaned forward, mouth filling with her body, but his eyes spoke directly to her soul.

I'll paint the sky across your heart. A forest will sprout from your belly and, rooted in your feet, red roses shall stretch thorny necks up your calves. Gold for the centre, only gold. What other colour for so priceless a treasure?

An Odd Sort of Prank

The Fixer looks up when Beth enters the mirror chamber and nudges a chair with his boot. 'Sit down. First I'll attend to your upper limbs, and then we'll look at the rest of you.'

'It's warm,' Beth says. 'I don't see a fire.'

'A furnace sends hot air under the floor. The architect borrowed the idea from the Romans.'

A vague smell of cinnamon wafts into Beth's nostrils as he bends over her. His touch is gentle as arms, hands and fingertips are examined. 'The nails are filthy,' he says. 'What have you been doing?'

'I was given a dirty job. I tried to wash away the worst.'

He checks arms and legs, the soles of both feet. 'You are healing well enough, but try to keep the dirt off.'

He applies ointment to a few stubborn rough patches of skin then inspects her scalp. Seemingly satisfied, he bids her open her mouth and peers inside.

'Stay like that for a moment.'

He reaches into his bag. Beth strains to see what's inside. A rough object presses against her gums and she recoils.

'Watch out,' he says, 'you nearly had my fingers off.'

'What did you just do?'

'It's a strip of bark. Work it around your mouth and it will help clean your teeth and gums. Don't forget to spit.'

'My tongue will be scratched into a raw lump.'

'A few minutes each morning and night should do it. Now I'll bathe your eyes. Tilt your head back and fix your gaze on the lantern.'

He wipes each eyelid with lumps of wadding treated with a sweet-smelling oil, then everything blurs as something drips onto each eye. 'A soothing concoction of my own,' he explains. 'Bear it a mite longer. Such dusty work has served you poorly. There, you can sit up now.'

Light floods her vision. The Fixer wipes his hands and returns the items to his bag. 'I am finished for today. Can you find your way back to your room?'

'I'll manage.'

He snaps the bag closed. 'Don't wander where you shouldn't, Kitten. For your own good.'

Hummingbird is out on Assignment when Beth returns to their bedchamber. A sickly sweet odour taints the air. Not perfume but something more earthy. The supper tray has been cleared away and a candle burns on the bedside table. She checks the window fastenings. The night seems innocent.

Beth drops her day gown onto the rug, yawns and pulls back the coverlet.

A dark stain spreads across the mattress. A yellow-and-black blemish that undulates as she watches. Hundreds of tiny bodies swarm over one another, silvery wings glinting in the candlelight. And now a sound: a low, ominous buzz as the mass shivers in the sticky warmth of the bedchamber.

She backs away from the bed, biting her tongue in a panic-stab effort not to scream. Her hip catches the edge of the dresser. Basin and ewer clatter to the floor.

Her grasping hand finds the doorknob. Fingers slip on the brass. She scrabbles and it turns. The door whispers outwards. Cool air. Blessed silence. Beth concentrates on placing one foot behind the other. At any second her mouth, ears and nostrils could fill with that buzzing, furious horde. Each nerve seems to draw tight then break.

She stumbles into the corridor and slams the bedroom door behind her. The world turns upside down and sanctuary arrives in darkness.

Bethany awakes to find a blanket wrapped around her and a foul-smelling vial held under her nose. She pushes it away and tries to sit up.

'Are you all right?' a voice asks. 'Can you hear me?'

'Yes.' Beth waves towards the bedroom door. 'In there.'

'Eloise is clearing it up now. You must have spilled some jam on the bed. Wasps flew through the open window, attracted to the scent. You should be more careful in future.'

Beth's belly cramps and she leans over, retching. Nothing comes up, but the effort leaves her trembling. 'The window was closed,' she whispers. 'An entire nest was hidden under the coverlet. Someone put it there.'

'And who would want to play such a trick? Come, Kitten, you are in shock. Let me help you to your feet. You will recover in a moment.'

A sliver of anger cuts through Beth, but she accepts the offer of help. Her benefactor is tall and well-bosomed, with an oval face and auburn hair that hangs loose over her ears. A plant picture is etched onto her right cheek.

'I am Nightshade,' she says, answering the unspoken question. 'My room is further down the corridor.'

Eloise appears clutching a damp bundle. 'Got them all, I think. An easy task. I threw on a towel and poured water over the little devils.'

Nightshade squeezes Beth's arm. 'Can you face going back inside? If not I'm sure we can find you another place to sleep, though Hummingbird will return soon, I think.'

'I shan't be driven out of my own bed.'

'I'm sure it was all a misunderstanding.'

'Then you won't mind checking the room with me?'

'I don't know what further horrors you expect to find, but very well.'

Beth follows Nightshade inside. The coverlet has been drawn back and a dry, fresh sheet spread over the mattress. A hint of sweet scent still hangs above the bed.

'Look,' Nightshade says. 'All gone.'

'No,' Beth whispers. 'She missed one.'

On the floor a solitary wasp, wings broken, transcribes an agonised circle. Its striped, tapered tail arches again and again, plunging the sting into the rug. Nightshade stamps it into a viscous smear.

'There, Kitten,' she touches Beth's elbow. 'It's dead.'

Fingers of hot, salty perspiration trickle down Beth's forehead. 'I hate those things.' Her voice is a hiss. '*I hate them.*'

Nightshade sits Beth on the bed and wipes her brow with a strip of cloth. When Beth has calmed enough to hold a cup without dropping it, Nightshade pours a measure of cool water. 'Drink,' she instructs. 'You're acting as though a mad dog has attacked you. It was only a stupid insect.'

'I hate them.' It's all Beth can think of to say. She winces when her fingers encounter an egg-sized lump on her forehead.

'You struck the wall when you fell,' Nightshade explains. 'I shall fetch something for it.'

She finds fresh linen in a drawer and moistens it with the last few drops from the ewer. Beth presses the material against the lump until the coolness dissolves the pain. 'This is a madhouse,' she says. 'I shall be dead before the week is out.'

Nightshade gives a thin smile. 'You are not badly hurt, but I can have the Fixer look at you if you wish. He'll not be abed yet.'

Beth shook her head.

'Would you like me to sit with you awhile?'

'That's kind, but I've caused enough fuss. I need to sleep.'

'Do you know where the maids' parlour is?'

'Yes, Eloise showed me.'

'If you are uncomfortable go and knock on the door. Someone is always there, no matter the hour. Promise me you will do that and I shall leave you in peace.'

Beth promises. The girl squeezes her hand and leaves, closing the door. Beth checks under the bed. Nothing. She pads over to the window and opens the curtains. Nothing there either.

Climbing onto the bed, Beth props her back against the bedstead, draws up her legs and wraps both arms around her knees. She is sitting like that when, an inch of burned candle later, the door gusts in. Hummingbird wears fresh linen but her skin carries the scent of smoke and dark gin-sodden corners. Her hair is tied back, her face creased with grime.

'I know you're fond of me but you didn't have to stay up,' she says.

Beth doesn't answer or move from her place on the bed. Hummingbird kicks off her slippers. She picks up the ewer, tips it and frowns when nothing comes out. Returning it to the basin, she plucks a towel from the back of the chair and begins rubbing her face and neck.

'A nightmare,' she exclaims as the towel breezes over her skin. 'An absolute nightmare. There I was, looking like Queen Charlotte, all ready for a fine dinner and a concert afterwards and do you know where I ended up? Do you?'

She throws the towel across the room. It flops over the top of the looking-glass. 'A cockpit, that's where. No opera house for me. Instead, a foul, smoky room filled with fat men piddling their breeches over two scrawny birds scratching each other to death in a circle of sand. And that wasn't the worst part. Women weren't allowed inside, so my beau for the evening made me dress in jacket and breeches. Can you believe it? Three hours to get dressed and I had to pull the whole lot off. My hair went under a cap, my breasts into a tight shirt and soot went over my face to hide my Emblem. I looked like a gutter urchin. My client kept telling everyone that I was his manservant but I don't think they believed it for a minute. They all kept winking and sniggering at one another. I believe my client was more interested in my boy's clothes and watching my reaction to the fight than wagering anything on the birds. Next time I'll cast a sharper eye over my Assignment.'

'Someone tried to hurt me tonight.'

Hummingbird pulls off her house gown and drops it onto the chair. 'I daresay a cockpit is no worse than any other place. I've watched bear-baiting before and don't mind a bit of blood and fluster, but if a client's going to put me on show I wish he'd leave me dressed for the occasion. Not that there's anything I can do about it, mind. He didn't fumble me, didn't break any of the rules. As soon as I gave him the Touch he was off. The Abbess will get a fat fee and I'll be left to die of embarrassment, to Eloise's delight no doubt.'

'Someone smeared bramble jam on our bed and dropped a wasps' nest over it.'

Hummingbird frowns. 'Odd sort of prank, but I've seen the like. Some of the older girls feel Kittens should undergo an initiation. You'll get sharp to these games. Now, are you going to settle? I'm eager to go to sleep and forget this night existed.'

'This was more than a prank. I could've been hurt. As it was I fainted and nearly cracked my head open. One of the other girls, Nightshade, found me sprawled over the corridor floor. I hate wasps. You don't know how much I hate them. I thought I was going to die of fright. That girl's an angel.'

Hummingbird sits on the edge of the bed. 'Actually she's a poisoner. Killed her entire family. She was an ace away from getting hanged before Kingfisher stole her from the noose. As for this so-called prank, perhaps Eloise tipped the jam over when she fetched the tray and was too tired to notice. We tease each other ragged, her and I, but I'll be first to admit that she works herself too hard. The jam was spilled and wasps caught the scent, that's all. Every summer we have to smoke their nests out of the roof. This big old house is home to every bird and bug in God's creation.'

'The coverlet was pulled up.'

'Then I daresay a clumsy ghost has come to haunt our bedchamber. Perhaps his spectral tongue had the taste for a fine spread of bramble jam.'

'Don't make fun of me.'

'I'm not, leastwise not in a cruel way. It's easy to wallow in misery and start thinking the whole world is against you. Sisters have better things to do than scare one another.'

'Why am I here? What have I done to warrant it?'

'Those the House chooses have no other future. We are all dead people, Kitten.'

'Are you a criminal? A murderess? What manner of creatures are kept penned in this place?'

'It's not a gaol.'

'Isn't it? Then am I free to walk out the front door? Can I leave now, without a word to anyone?'

Hummingbird cocks her head, rises from the bed and hurries to the window. She parts the curtains and presses her face against the glass. After a moment she teases the window open.

'Don't—'

Hummingbird presses a finger against her lips. Beth hears noises in the alley below. The rustle of velvet. Soft voices. A man's grunt followed by a guttural, throaty sound. A woman's moans, hurriedly stifled.

'Someone is enjoying themselves,' Hummingbird whispers.

Beth feels her cheeks redden. From where she sits there's little to see beyond the open curtains. No moon. No shadows. A distant flickering from a linkboy's torch bobs and weaves before being snuffed out. 'I thought Masques didn't . . . You told me this wasn't a whorehouse.'

'Oh, don't stir yourself, Kitten. 'Tis only a street girl and her tup.' Hummingbird makes a face. 'If they don't rein in they'll likely find a chamber pot tipped over their heads. Once a week, sometimes more, I am serenaded from the alley. Being so close to the House seems to give these creatures a thrill.' She giggles. 'He'll knock her through the brickwork, methinks. Don't pretend not to know what I'm talking about. That blushing face doesn't fool me.'

'Does the Abbess know?'

'Perhaps. Perhaps not. She's had her own share of admirers. Rumour has conjured up a string of lovers, but relationships are a dangerous pastime. Not so long ago a client grew too fixed on one of our girls. He was bundled out of the back of his gambling club, thrashed and dumped in a trough. When a few days later he plucked up the courage to return he found his credit withdrawn and his debts called in. He works as a menial in the church now, I believe.'

'That's an appalling thing to do.'

'He was given fair warning.'

'What about the girl? Did something bad happen to her?'

'No. It was agreed she'd done nothing to encourage him. A lesson nonetheless.'

'Is love so frowned upon here? Have you never dreamed of marrying?'

'And spend the rest of my days in a draughty parlour with a dish of tea in my hand and a tiny dog panting at my feet? Marriage can bleed a woman of power the way a quack might open a vein in her arm.'

Hummingbird turns back to the window. 'Renowned painters, fashionable poets and leaders of men have all haunted the square. A peek from behind drawn curtains is enough to drive anyone into a frenzy. Some of the younger rakes, desperate for a stolen glimpse, have been known to scale the drainpipes. Every so often Kingfisher goes out and shoos them away.'

'You tease men to distraction yet live as nuns? How can you bear it? Surely you have desires?'

'Good training and a strong will can turn you from the most handsome of faces. Grow too hot between the legs, however, and the Fixer will give you something to cool your passion.'

'Surely some things are beyond even the Fixer's bag of tricks.'

Hummingbird laughs. 'He's a fine caster of spells. Should he wish, he'll have you believing you can fly, but don't be careless.'

'Why, what would happen?'

'You'll learn,' she says, 'in time.'

Beth slips under the coverlet and pulls it up to her chin. 'Will you close the window and come to bed? I don't want any more surprises creeping out of the night.'

'I might. I might not. It's my room, remember. I've noticed you've been tidying up after me, straightening this and that.'

'I'll never sleep if you don't.'

'Ask the Fixer for a draught.'

'I don't want to keep going to him. Anyway he says I'm getting better.'

'Very well.' She closes the window and draws back the curtains. The mattress shifts as she climbs into bed. 'Happy now?'

'Don't you ever say any prayers?' Beth whispers.

Hummingbird leans across and blows out the candle. 'To whom? God abandoned us a long time ago. Being damned is part of the game. Those pretty gowns don't come without a price.'

Beth listens to the tic-tic of cooling metal as the last embers die in the grate. 'Hummingbird?'

'What now, Kitten? I'm tired. I've had a hard day and may receive another Assignment tomorrow.'

'What if I can't do the things I was brought here for?'

'That won't happen. I shall not let it. Now go to sleep.'

'But—'

'Go to sleep, Kitten.'

Beth turns onto her back and stares into the darkness. Beside her, Hummingbird's breathing settles, and soon a tickly snore escapes her nostrils.

What if I don't do it? What if I decide not to be a good girl any more?

She rolls back on her side, wondering what Hummingbird dreams about, what nightmares, if any, she suffers. Then, before

115

Beth knows it, sleep rolls a blanket over her thoughts. The rest of the night passes in a confused fug of sounds and faces. Julia, Sebastian, Lord Russell and George, always George, asking the same thing. *Where are you going with the children, Miss Harris?* Much later, just before dawn has a proper hold on the skies above the city, she's awakened by a scream.

Blood on the Road

The Fixer pinched the bloodied shard between thumb and forefinger. It glittered red in the carriage lantern light.

'How did she get it, Crabbe?'

'I don't rightly know. I gave her a brandy and she seemed to settle a bit. I thought there was no harm in it. She must've tucked the glass into her cloak. You could hide a barrel in there.'

'See if she has any more. Strip her to her shift if need be.'

Crabbe shook his head. 'She's got a wish for death, that one. Can't force a soul to stay alive if it has no mind to.'

'Come on, you know her worth. Not losing your nose for the business, are you?'

'The deal's getting worse by the minute. The Abbess can turn shit into silk but even she has limits, John. Throw the girl out of the door and let me sell the brat to the gypsies.'

'No. I've given up too much to lose her now.' The Fixer caught the struggling girl by the shoulders. 'Anna, listen to me. D'you have any more glass?'

She twisted her head from side to side. The Fixer prised open her gloved hands. The shard had sliced through the fabric and into the flesh beneath.

'The blood's gone over her gown,' Crabbe said. 'Could've fetched a few coins, that.'

'Still got that pig sticker tucked into your boot?'

Crabbe reached into the calfskin boot and drew out a polished spike. 'What are you aiming to do with this?'

'I need to get both gloves off and see what I'm dealing with before the material sticks to the wounds.'

'No, don't show my hands,' the girl said. 'Not *my hands*.'

'Damn it, Crabbe, she's throwing a fit. Grab hold.'

'I ain't putting a finger on her. Get your blackie friend to help.'

'We can lay her on the seat. Come on, Crabbe, grab her legs.'

'She's got a kick like a Shire horse. Have your blackie do it, I tell you.'

'His eye's on the baby where it should be.'

'All right, then. But listen to her. Sounds like a cat howling at the moon.'

It took both men a deal of puffing and banging around to get her straight. 'Those gloves need to come off if I'm to treat you,' he told her. 'Throwing a tantrum won't help.'

'My hands are ugly,' she whimpered.

'You're hurt and I aim to fix you. Close your eyes if you don't want to look.'

He removed each glove with a quick flick of the spike. The cuts bisected the tops of both wrists and were not as deep as he feared. Once he'd stopped the bleeding and bathed her skin using his water flask he was able to examine her hands. They were beautiful. Beautiful like dove wings. So pale and pretty, without any blemishes. Yet fear was in her eyes all the while the Fixer ministered to her. The first time he touched her bare skin she swallowed down a scream.

'Stop biting your lip,' he said. 'Now, look how sweet your hands are.'

'No,' she said. 'They're *burned*.'

'Will she live?' Crabbe asked. 'If you won't ditch the wench then I still aim to collect on her.'

'She'll live. It's not so bad as it looks. If someone has a mind to slit their wrists this isn't the right way.'

'I don't want any more of her blood fouling the inside of my coach. And I'm not just talking about her wrists.'

'I thought you more compassionate than that, Crabbe.'

'You've gone and worn it out of me.'

'A clean birth, like I told you. I didn't have to cut her. But we'd better keep her head in this particular cloud or she's going to hurt. I might have to risk a pinch of laudanum after all. Tell that lump of a driver to spur himself.'

'Leonardo takes his own good time. Push him and we'll fetch a broken axle. If you ain't happy climb up there and tell him so. These lanes ain't the London turnpike.'

The darkie sat in silence on the seat. Though his eyes were placid he seemed ready to pounce on Crabbe in a blink. The baby lay on the seat opposite her mother, sleeping in a basket Crabbe had drawn from a footlocker and packed with rags. 'Better than Moses,' he'd said.

Crabbe had also filled the baby's belly with milk drawn from a jug in his back larder and warmed on the hearth. He'd brought more in an earthenware flagon which stank of some previous unholy concoction. 'Won't do the child harm,' he maintained. 'Might put a bit of spark in its blood.'

The Fixer thought the mother had more than enough spark in her blood without the baby following suit, but when Crabbe's mind was turned to a notion it took a mighty force to turn it back.

'I want the whole fee, John. Every penny. I'm peddling new lives for all three of you. Four if you count the little 'un, though I reckon you'd be showing it greater grace if you smothered it right here.'

'My baby.' The girl's eyes settled on the Fixer. Blue, impossibly blue in the dim lantern light. '*Please save my baby.*'

'Go back to bed, Kitten.'

'I heard screaming.'

'Go back to bed. I'll join you soon.'

Beth tries to shake off the fug of sleep. Figures haunt the passage, flickering candles dripping hot wax onto the carpet. Hummingbird puts a hand on her arm. 'Come away.'

Shadows dip across the walls as a maid ducks inside an open door. 'Someone's in trouble,' Beth says. 'We have to help.' She feels the tenseness in her body, the old aches and pains flaring up. The fear. Always the fear. Hummingbird's grasp seems to burn her skin.

'Just a nightmare,' the other girl whispers. 'A bad dream. Those women will take care of it. You can't do anything.'

Bethany allows herself to be led back to her bedchamber. Hummingbird closes the door and climbs back into bed beside her.

'How can you stand it?' Beth asks.

'Go to sleep.'

'You think I can? So easily?'

A pause. 'See. The noise has stopped. There'll be no further trouble tonight. Don't think about it any more.'

'That was Moth's room. Where is Red Orchid?'

'On late Assignment. She can't always be present to nursemaid her Kitten whenever she has a bad dream.'

'Dream? I thought she would scream the roof down.'

'Moth sees things. Things that slither. Things that go *hisssssssss*. When she was little her brother put a viper in her bed. Now she sees them everywhere: under the bed, sliding between the sheets, coiling around her throat. The Fixer is working to drive them back into the shadows. Perhaps he will succeed, perhaps not. Then who can say what will become of her? She can't be dosed with laudanum forever. Besides, you created a big enough fuss over those wasps, as I recall.'

'You mustn't speak like that. Snakes, spiders, horrors in the night. Everyone is tormented by demons at some time in their lives. You said so yourself.'

'Yes, but it won't do if she has us up out of our beds every other night. Don't gripe, she'll be given time. The Fixer usually lives up to his name.'

Moth appears at breakfast sporting haggard cheeks, dark sacks under the eyes and pale, drawn skin. She sits opposite Beth and curls her fingers around a wooden spoon. Looking up, she flinches as if noticing Beth for the first time.

'I didn't mean to startle you,' Beth says.

'I'm sorry,' Moth whispers. 'I'm tired.'

Beth pins her best smile onto her face. 'Bad dream?'

Moth makes an odd sound at the back of her throat. Not quite a gasp. Not quite a moan either. She drops the spoon and grips the edge of the table with both hands. 'I can't go to the Cellar. They can't send me to that place.'

'The Cellar?'

Blood rushes into the girl's pallid cheeks. 'Forgive me, you can't know what I mean. You haven't been here long enough. It's just stories. Don't pay me any heed.'

'Moth—' Beth has hardly opened her mouth when the doors swing wide and the Masques file into the room, followed by the Abbess and Kingfisher. The breakfast trolleys rattle in a moment later. Moth has picked up her spoon again and is staring darkly at her place setting. When the food is served she pushes it into her mouth, barely giving herself time to taste it.

120

'Moth, you'll make yourself ill.'

'There's no room for dead weight in the House,' she says without looking up. 'The Sisters told me that.'

So it goes for the next two weeks. Sometimes Moth joins Beth at the table, sometimes not. Everything seems to upset her. She eats her food quickly and with intense concentration as though afraid to leave a scrap on her plate. Yet if anything she is getting thinner.

The fuzz on Beth's scalp thickens. Her sores have healed, though the Fixer insists she keep rubbing in his foul-smelling potions to keep the skin supple. Her eyes are brighter and her body is filling out. Climbing the stairs no longer leaves her breathless, and she's better able to keep up with Eloise in the course of her daily chores. *I look like a boy*, she thinks, regarding the slim, short-haired creature reflected in Hummingbird's looking-glass.

Other jobs swallow up her time. She fears the Masques will run her ragged with errands. Sewing, laying out their night shifts, fetching books or evening possets. But they are kind. Generous even. 'Let me help you with that,' a girl called Dragonfly says, watching her struggle with a pail of scented water for someone's bath.

When Beth spills red wine over an embroidered kerchief belonging to Raven, she is favoured with a dry smile and told it will probably wash out, though they both know it won't. At certain tasks she is good, at others hopelessly clumsy. 'We can't be perfect at everything, *enfant*,' Eloise says when Beth drops a basket load of scrubbed linen the washerwoman had just delivered. 'A quick rinse and those garments will be good again.'

'I'm not very skilled at washing,' Beth mumbles.

'That is so, but you have to try, *oui*? We need to prise all your hidden things from you, find out what talents lie in that head and those hands. Perhaps you will surprise yourself.'

'Perhaps I shall turn out a dunce.'

'But you can smile beautifully. I have seen it. Sometimes such a smile is all that is needed. It can buy hearts. Don't forget.'

There are lessons of another sort. When Hummingbird is not out on one of her Assignments she and Beth share supper in their room at a table in front of the hearth.

Beth pokes a lump of stewed vegetables with the tip of her wooden knife. 'When shall I have some proper meat? My belly stopped aching days ago. Everyone says I'm looking better. It's torture sitting here watching you eat roast chicken, and that beef pie you had yesterday looked like it had come straight off the king's table. All I get are fish, vegetables and fruit. This lime juice makes my cheeks pucker.'

'You'll get more hearty food when your teeth are better,' Hummingbird replies. 'They still look ready to drop out of their sockets and your breath is a fright. I got a faceful of it last night when you rolled over in your sleep.'

'Blame those draughts the Fixer makes me swill. I don't know why he doesn't just poison me outright and be done with it. And he keeps prodding me like I'm a shank of pork hanging from a flesher's hook.'

'The Fixer needs to check his handiwork. Don't be hard on him.'

Beth stirs her food and swallows it. 'It seems I'm always being examined, observed or corrected.'

Hummingbird puts down her cutlery. The window behind her throws most of her face into shadow. 'We both know where you were before you came here. You can't survive a place like that without growing claws and scratching. All the pretty things your mama taught you are soon forgotten when you find yourself fighting to live through another day. That'll always be a part of your life, Kitten. You can't cut it from your mind like a surgeon hacks off a rotten leg. While you share my room I'm responsible for you. I have to make you fit for our society, and there are harder ways to learn than the methods I use.'

'You make me sound like a trained animal.'

'Trained is exactly what you're going to be.'

'Or?'

'There isn't any "or" about it. If you don't perform it reflects on me and I don't want the Abbess on my tail. Now eat that supper and I'll share a word with the Fixer. It may be we can slip something a little tastier onto your plate for a night or two.'

'Is Moth sleeping better? Is she taking a draught?'

'Too many for my liking. The only way you'll quieten that one is to knock her with a brick. Laudanum can make you dull-witted. Herbs may help. He knows a good apothecary who can supply him. The other quacks aren't much use. Most of the concoctions they peddle will likely poison you. That would certainly cure the sleeplessness. Moth's remedy will need more than a few roots crushed in a pestle, I suspect.'

Bethany's visits to the Fixer continue. He bids her walk in front of the mirrors, sometimes naked, then stand, then turn, then sit. He runs his hands down her legs and along her forearms. 'Your limbs are strengthening,' he says. 'I can feel the muscles taking shape, growing beneath the skin.'

He makes her talk and hum, then open her mouth and go 'Ahhh' in a great drawn-out sigh. He bathes her eyes again, turning the world into a bright blur. He shaves under her arms and checks between her legs. She draws away, covering herself with her hands. 'I don't think it right for you to do that any more.'

He grins. 'Rediscovering our modesty, are we? That's good. The lady within is beginning to assert herself. But you're right. There's no need to do it now. You're as clean as a freshly scrubbed pot and, coming from where you did, you can count that as something of a miracle.'

That evening, Beth sits with Eloise in the empty parlour, sipping coffee and chewing a selection of soft fruit. 'Why do we always have this room to ourselves? I think I've counted three other people in the time I've been here.'

The maid is swaddled in a tall armchair, slippers off, her feet propped on a stool. She draws on a long-stemmed clay pipe and blows a lazy cloud of smoke towards the ceiling. 'This is a place of come-and-go people, *enfant*. We are busy all the time. Running errands, keeping our little family happy. Friendships are difficult. The House makes so many demands, as you will discover when you sport an Emblem on your own pretty cheek.'

'When is that likely to be?'

Eloise shrugged. 'Depends on you, *enfant*. Some are born with a gift for the work. Others learn slowly. I would say you are doing well enough. But the real tests are yet to come. Then we shall see what you are made of, *oui*?'

Beth clears her throat. 'What tests are these?'

Eloise sucks on her pipe and says nothing. Beth feels a stab of irritation. 'In my place of employment servants never mixed with the rest of the household. Most were beaten if found to be lazy or impudent. They expected to be treated that way.'

'Is that so?' Eloise replies. 'And how would you know such a thing? Did you ever ask what they thought of all that hard work they dealt with so obediently? The scrubbing, washing, fetching, cooking?'

Eloise leans over and taps her pipe out into a bowl. 'Tell me also,' she says in a gentle voice, 'what makes you think you are now any less of a servant?'

Beth stares at the smouldering ash.

'I thought not. Think before you speak, *enfant*. You cannot bring such high-handed baggage into this dangerous new world. There are those who are less forgiving than I. *Alors*, more coffee?'

Beth wakes from a shallow sleep. She slips the cover off and rolls out of bed. Hummingbird's place is empty, her pillow a bunched-up shape in the dark. Already Beth is getting used to her companion's toing and froing.

She kneels and fumbles under the bed, her fingers catching the rim of the pot. Liquid slops onto her hand. Full. She stands, groping for a hand towel. A privy lies at the end of the corridor. Beth steals out of the door and along the corridor, fingertips brushing the wall. No lights under any of the doors. No other sounds in the dark. She reaches the end of the passage and ducks into the cupboard that serves as the privy. Sprigs of fresh lavender cluster in brackets on the wall. Beth hoists her shift and settles on the wooden board. Outside, a muted chime announces the second hour of the new morning.

I shouldn't have drunk such a large posset before turning in, she thought. *Not on top of all that coffee.*

Beth stands, dabs herself with a square of linen and steps back into the corridor. The House never truly sleeps. Girls often return from Assignments at three or four of the clock. Beth wonders if the front door is ever locked, if anyone has risen in the night and left, gone away, taken their chances in the darkened streets dressed only in a shift. Every evening, Eloise takes their house gowns away and brings fresh ones the following day. Where are the beautiful dresses worn on Assignments?

Perhaps I could hide in an alley 'til the morning and pluck garments from a wash line, Beth thinks. *Or I could filch an item from the House, a clock or small tapestry, and trade with a beggar for their coat.*

A noise jolts her out of her thoughts. She pauses, straining to hear in the gloom. The House settles around her. Walls and floorboards creak as they relinquish the previous day's heat. But there it is again. A low hiss followed by a muffled whimper.

Beth inches along the passage. The hissing sound repeats itself. Has a cat got into the House? Dare she run the risk of treading on it in the dark? She leans forward, trying to gauge the distance. A soft laugh echoes in the dark followed by another hiss. No cat, then.

She takes a few cautious steps. A figure looms out of the shadows, bent against one of the bedroom doors. A finger of light spills from underneath, revealing stockinged feet and the hem of an elaborate gown. Hands, pale even in this light, are cupped against the keyhole.

Hissssssssss.

A yelp from inside the room follows muffled sobs. Beth coughs. The figure jerks upright, then scampers off down the long passage. Beth fumbles to the door and presses an ear to the wood. Inside, a voice, hoarse with crying. 'Go away.'

'Moth?'

'Please go away.'

Beth creeps back down the passage to her bedchamber. Moth is not at breakfast the following morning. Nor the day after.

A Trip to the Woods

Beth tugged at her riding habit. The garment was green and velvety, and as heavy as a sack of potatoes. A tall hat was tied onto her head with ribbons.

Under her feet was a cobbled yard. She'd never walked on cobbles before and twice nearly fell flat on her face in the boots she'd been obliged to wear. Stable doors lined the yard on two sides, the wood painted a shiny black.

'Let's go riding,' George had said, striding into the schoolroom where she'd been trying to bend her mind around one of those thick books. 'I know you can handle a mount passably well. It's too fine a day to tuck yourself away here.'

She put down the book. 'The children—'

'Are deep in slumber. We won't see them until tomorrow, I'll wager. The games you had them play this morning left them quite exhausted.'

'Is there no one else who can go with you?'

'My kipper-faced groom has put his back out, the fool, and I'm in the mood for some fair company. Come now, don't make me ask again.'

Of course she'd had no choice and had to suffer the help of a pouting maid to put the riding habit on. *What am I really doing here?* she thought, watching bugs skit lazily across the surface of the water trough. She wasn't that good a rider. Father got a horse from the squire, a stout old thing that was no use to either plough or hunt, but it plodded the miles around the estate without fuss. He kept it in a woodshed turned stable and taught Beth the basics of riding. Though she had no grace for the saddle, the beast bore her clumsiness with good humour.

George strode across the yard. Calf-high boots kicked up puffs of dust. Tight breeches were topped by a sharply cut brown jacket and he slapped a riding crop against his thigh as he walked. 'I thought we might ride up to the ridge. Give you a chance to spread your wings a little.'

A boy walked out of the stables with a face so riddled with spots he looked poxed. He gave Beth a look of such cheek she wanted to bury the end of her boot in his rump and see how he felt about that. A horse trotted out behind him, already bridled and saddled. A hunter, sleek and grey, the flanks like satin. Better than anything Beth ever saw at Pendleton horse fair.

'This is Odysseus.' George slapped the beast's flank. 'I had him brought from Spain. He's the fastest horse in the southern counties.'

'Have you ever raced him?'

'His reputation is solid enough.'

'But you haven't actually raced him?'

'Let's see what we can find for you.'

Beth is given a wheezy old nag with its ribs sticking out of its flanks. 'I shan't get far on that.'

'You're not meant to go far,' George said with a dry smile.

'Oh, I see. It'll drop down dead if I decide to stray.'

George put his boot in a stirrup and swung his leg over the saddle. Beth eyed her nag doubtfully then climbed up onto the side-saddle. The beast snorted when she settled on its back, and all four legs shuddered.

''Tis a nice enough day. We'll settle for walking pace.'

'As if this sack of bones could manage more.'

'Be patient, Bethany. He's very experienced.'

'So was my grandfather, but he could hardly walk.'

A bridleway skirted the edge of the lawns. George led his hunter up the muddy path. Beth's lump of bones plodded along behind. She hated riding side-saddle. You couldn't feel the horse properly. The riding clothes weighed her down and the hat made her head itch. As a girl she never had her hair fettered, even with ribbons. Father cropped it every half year and it went its own way after that.

'Shouldn't you be riding with someone of your own station?' she called ahead.

George shook his head. 'I daresay I should, but local ladies are too fond of their carriages. They refuse to tolerate saddle or bridle, and prefer a stroll on the lawns to a hearty gallop. Every so often I like to go to the ridge and scare the birds off their perches. Today, however, we shall enjoy a gentle pace. I don't always risk a broken neck.'

He closed his eyes and breathed deeply through his nostrils. 'Smell that air. It's sharp enough to cut your lungs.'

All Beth could smell was the flyblown hide of the stinky old nag she was perched on. She sniffed a couple of times to keep George happy, but her backside proved ill company for the saddle and began to hurt. She'd just as soon return to the children.

The bridleway widened. George hung back until Beth was alongside. 'Julia and Sebastian would like it here,' she said. 'They would love to smell the air, the way you just did.'

'You are fond of them?'

'Very much so.'

'And would prefer their company to mine?'

'That's a foolish thing to say.'

'You have a remarkably frank tongue for a young woman in your position.'

'If you want me to behave like a servant then treat me like one. Don't favour me with fancy clothes and take me riding across land that isn't mine.'

The bridleway opened into a rutted lane. Neat hedges gave way to clumps of gorse and scratchy bramble. Patchwork meadows rolled away in all directions. Sheep, fat with unborn lambs, grazed the rough grass.

Ahead, a fist of trees crowned a gentle rise. George nudged his hunter off the road and between the scraggy trunks. Beth squeezed the nag through the gap, ducking as twigs scraped the top of her hat. Inside lay a dark circle of musty forest loam. A cramped spot, but her nag could probably do with the rest.

George was out of the saddle in one easy movement. Beth wasn't sure whether to remain seated or dismount. He walked over to the nag, boots quiet on the soft mulch. He breathed in snipped gasps. Surely that plod of a ride couldn't have worn him out?

He reached up a hand. Beth grasped his fingers and slid out of the saddle. Her boot caught in the stirrup and she landed on George in a flurry of petticoats. Both rolled over in the dirt. Damp seeped through the back of her dress and a pebble dug into her skull. George's breath was all over Beth's face like a rash. The air was squeezed out of her lungs. She tried to wriggle free but couldn't budge for the weight of him. He kept saying things but she couldn't hear a word. His thighs pushed against her, his breeches making a faint rasping against her gown. She didn't know whether to laugh or retch. Finally she managed to get a hand free and shove him half off her. It was enough to let her roll out from under his pawing hands and scramble to her feet.

Shadows seemed to flit across George's face, then lifted. 'An unfortunate accident,' he said, picking himself up.

'But—'

'An accident, as I said. You understand, Miss Harris?'

A fox broke out of the undergrowth, stared at them impudently for a moment then disappeared back into the dark greenery. Nothing else stirred among the ferns.

'Yes. I understand.'

'Good. Then nothing more need be said.'

Beth brushed dark loam from the creases of her riding habit then tucked a wayward string of hair behind her ear. 'Perhaps we should go back to the house.'

George swallowed air, then fetched his horse and mounted. Beth eyed her nag. The stupid thing seemed to be grinning at her. On the way back she poked it in the ribs with her heel. It barely stirred.

George rode in silence. The knees of his breeches were grubby and his boots scuffed. He'd probably say he fell off his own horse or some such thing. He kept breaking into a canter and Beth had to shout for him to wait. Her useless beast hadn't a hope of keeping up. This couldn't go on. They had to talk about something. Finally George drew his horse to walking pace. The usual expression of lazy confidence had settled back on his face.

'We are almost home,' he said. 'I look forward to riding with you again, Bethany. I hope you feel likewise.'

'As long as there are no more unfortunate accidents.'

A snap of his reins sent him galloping forward and this time he didn't turn back when she called him.

Beth perched on the edge of the bed. She still wore the riding habit, feeling too wretched to take it off. The material was soiled where she'd rolled in the dirt.

I can't just sit here like this.

She tied her hat back on and stepped onto the landing. She met no one on the stairs. Outside it had grown colder. A thin layer of cloud watered down the dipping sun. There were too many shadows in this warren of a garden. What was the point of it anyway? Why keep all this land if not to grow crops or graze cattle? Smallholders in Dunston worked themselves ragged trying to make a living on less ground than this.

She passed the gardener's hut. Something rattled inside. A pigeon flew out the door, trailing feathers. Beth kept out of sight of the house as much as possible before deciding to head back. The grass was already damp and had soaked her soft leather boots. She thought about supper. Perhaps she'd get a strip of beef pie and some hot potatoes. Better than broth. But what would she say if she ran into George? He'd been around so much lately, always enquiring after the children, always trying to help her when she didn't need it, always standing too close or becoming too familiar with his hands brushing her shoulder or resting in the small of her back.

Beth closed her eyes, took a sharp breath then turned and set off down the meadow towards Lord Russell's tower.

Into Town

'We're going out today.'

Beth peeks from underneath the coverlet. Hummingbird is framed in the window wearing a gown of deep green velvet. Powder whitens her face and her dark hair is hidden beneath a wig.

'Out where?'

'To breakfast. A new tea room has opened in George Lane. Very fashionable by all accounts. It's time you stepped out and coped with a little society.'

'Why a tea room?'

'Good business can be found in all kinds of places. Tea rooms are often the knots that tie many threads together.'

'What business?'

Hummingbird smiles. 'The business of being seen. So stir yourself, girl, unless you want to spend another morning in that stuffy dining room?'

Beth slides both legs from under the covers and makes a grab for her shift. 'I'm allowed outside? Just like that?'

'Why not? The Abbess has to trust you sometime. You can't stay indoors forever.'

'Suppose I run away?'

'Then Kingfisher will catch you and I'll beat your silly arse blue.'

'You'd do that?'

'I'm the one who'll get into trouble if you don't behave, Kitten, and I've no mind to sour the Abbess's mood. Make a nuisance of yourself and it might be a long time before either of us will be permitted outdoors again. Besides, Moth will be joining us.'

'Moth? She is well?'

'A little calmer. The Fixer has tinkered with her wits. He's confident she'll behave. Now, we need to find you a suitable gown. Come with me.'

Moth is waiting in the hall. The shadows have lifted from under her eyes and she tucks a smile on her mouth on spying Beth. Hummingbird leads both girls round the back of the staircase and through a set of curtained double doors. Beth wonders how many tuck-me-away places exist in this house. Every tapestry, every alcove seems to conceal a secret. Here is a passage carpeted in green with full-length mirrors set into each wall at regular intervals. Above, a vaulted skylight sheds bright daylight while sconces, fat with unlit candles, fill the spaces between the mirrors. Beth wonders what it would be like to walk down here at night with nothing but stars overhead and a dozen flickering flames throwing their reflections across the floor.

Through another set of doors lies a rectangular room. Tall wardrobes hug the left side. Opposite sit half a dozen teak dressers. Windows set into the end wall throw bright planks of light across the carpet. Beth is lost in this place. The walls of the House are thick and hard. They don't creak in the wind like the eaves of her father's cottage. No birds skitter across the roof and no overhanging branches tap-tap the slates with their twig fingers. She's locked in a big stone box.

Bending over, Beth can see a pale blob, her face, staring back from the shiny floorboards. Rugs are white fur puddles. The glass in the window is cold. Tiny ripples cross each pane. It's like looking at the world from the bottom of a brook.

'Let's see,' Hummingbird says. 'Something light for you, I think.' She tugs open a door, rummages about and passes a gown to Beth. 'It should fit. I've a good eye for that sort of thing.' She glances at Moth. 'Blue for you, definitely, trimmed with white, and satin bows across the loops. Not too big, mind. A narrow border lies between looking like a princess and a harlot.'

She crosses to one of the dressers and slides open a drawer. 'Thin stockings only, it's hot out today, and you're both too skinny for corsets. One petticoat each and don't step on any horseshit, these slippers are satin and the Abbess will flay me if they come back ruined. Stay away from the gutters too. They're always full of swill, and they stink, especially in the middle of summer.'

'Why don't Masques have their own clothes?' Beth asks.

'Good merry lord, we'd all need bedchambers the size of the dining room. Every task requires a different set of garments. We put them on when we go out, we take them off when we come back. Some of the girls prefer maids to help them but I'm sure we'll manage.'

It takes the better part of an hour to dress. Beth's inexperienced hands shake on the fastenings. There isn't a part of her that doesn't itch. For the first time in her life she's wearing a proper society gown and it's the most beautiful thing she's seen. Pale cream with crimson sleeves and dozens of bows that swoop up and down the material like butterflies. Layers of petticoats swish-swish whenever she moves. There's a garter too. Crimson, like the bows. 'Don't harlots wear these?' she says.

'They might, I've never taken a peek myself.' Hummingbird fingers Bethany's growing hair. It's clean with a hint of copper. Beth's never realised that. She didn't know her eyes were such a rich shade of brown, like fresh horse chestnuts, or that her lips could look so full and red. Her skin is pale and clear. No scabs, no festering sores.

Full-length mirrors are fixed to the inside of the wardrobe doors. Moth, gown half fastened, dances in front of them, turning this way, then that.

'Look at you,' Hummingbird declares. 'You've never worn fine clothes before?'

'My da wouldn't let me have a good dress. He said I'd look like a trollop. I'd fetch a strap across my back if he caught me like this.'

Hummingbird stands behind Beth who's checking her now bewigged reflection in another mirror. 'What about you, Kitten? Do you like what you see?'

'I don't resemble a boy any more.'

'You'll need one of these.' Hummingbird reaches towards Beth's cheek, something tucked in her hand.

'What are you doing?'

'Don't be a turnip. You can't go out without an Emblem. This is only until you earn a proper mark. Look, it's made of paper. You can take it off when we return home.'

Beth examines the object in Hummingbird's open palm. A scrap of black paper in the shape of a mummer's mask. 'Ladies wear those to cover pox scars,' she blurts.

Hummingbird bursts out laughing. Grains of white powder fly off her cheeks. 'Not this sort, they don't. People need to know you belong to the House.'

'Why?'

'It earns certain privileges. Stop fussing and let me put it on.'

Beth feels a cool spot on her cheek as Hummingbird applies the patch. 'There,' she declares, straightening up. 'Almost like a real Masque. Now, bonnets for the pair of you, though not ones with feathers as they make me sneeze. And something for your faces. We have everything: rouge, milk of roses, pearl powder. Jewellery too, most of it gifted by generous clients.'

'They make presents of such things?' Beth says.

'Certainly, though we have to be careful a Masque is never seen in public wearing the wrong item. A few of our more smitten patrons have even donated horses. Our stables are full of such beasts.' She steps back. 'Now, let's see if you pass muster in the street.'

'I still can't believe I'm going out.'

'All part of your grooming, Kitten. You need to learn how to conduct yourself in the wicked city. No creeping down the back alley either. I'll sign the wardrobe book then it's the front door for us, as befits the princesses we are.'

The hot scent of the city smacks Beth across the face the moment she puts a foot outside. A foul mix of horseshit, smoke and human refuse. She has forgotten what the world can smell like beyond the gently scented corridors of the House. A dozen or so marble steps spread away from the front door onto a flagged pavement. Beth is reminded of thick cream spilling from the lip of a jug. Metal railings, glossy black with fresh paint, frame either side.

An ornate square faces the house. A few trees, a patch of green, a yellow peppering of flowers. Carriages rumble past, dogs bark, hawkers call from street pitches. Beth's senses struggle to cope. She has the impression of being buried in the heart of some huge beast. She can feel it all around her, smell it with every whiff of air. Beyond the roofs and chimneys, how many other streets?

Hummingbird squeezes Beth's arm. 'Stay close to me. It's often difficult the first time.'

'I'll be trampled.'

'Keep off the road and you'll be safe enough. You only have the length of this street to walk. From there we can hire sedan chairs.'

'No.'

A click of the tongue. 'I daresay you can go back indoors for now, Kitten, but I thought you had more courage. The Abbess might not be so generous with her favours in future. I'm sure you don't want to spend another month cleaning hearths. The longer you put this off the harder it will become.'

'Very well. You have such a sweet way of persuading people.'

Hummingbird's grin sweeps back. 'All the best teachers have. Come on now, don't look so glum. Three hours outside and I'll probably have to drag you back into the House.'

Moth harbours no such reluctance. She's down the steps in a breath. Hummingbird has to call her back. She comes to heel wearing a scolded look. People make way as they cross the square. None looks them in the eye.

'Have we the plague?' Beth asks.

'Keep walking. You'll get used to it.'

Beth steals a quick look back at the House. Not so grand as Russell Hall, though neat in its own way. She could easily lose it amidst the jumble of buildings.

Nobody accosts them. Nobody points or gawps, yet it takes the longest five minutes in Beth's memory to stroll to the edge of the square and turn the corner. She is conscious of everything. Her gait. The cropped hair beneath the wig. Her sense of awkwardness in these heavy clothes. She tugs down the brim of her bonnet and fingers the paper patch on her cheek, resisting the urge to peel it off. *We're like the bad women outside the market taverns*, she thinks. *The ones in the gaudy slammerkins and painted cheeks. Any moment now a man is going to stop one of us and offer a shilling for a tup.*

The clamour smothers her. She tries breathing through her mouth, praying she won't faint. Every chimney belches fingers of black smoke into the sky.

A figure appears on the path. A hag of a woman in a tattered green dress with a fright of ginger hair sprouting above her poxed face. She grins and gestures at the two rows of chipped, yellow-stained tombstones poking out of her gums. 'See 'em? Forty years old and I got all my own teeth. Forty, and they're mine, every one.'

'Good for you, Sally,' Hummingbird says, not breaking stride.

The creature darts after them with an agility that would shame a cutpurse.'You're ugly,' she tells Beth, plucking at her sleeve. 'Ugly. Not like me. I'm an earl's daughter, d'you know that? Used to have all the young men lined up and begging for my hand.'

Beth jerks her arm away and tries to move on. The hag scurries at her heels like a terrier on the scent of a rabbit. 'Shamed, are you? As well you might be. Bad times have hit old Sally. There but for the grace of God go you. But I've still got my looks. And my teeth. Count 'em. Go on. Every one still there. Every one still good.'

Beth groans. 'For pity's sake, give her a penny.'

'A mirror would suit her better,' Hummingbird says, 'though 'twould cost a shilling to have the glass replaced.'

The hag's squawking fades. Already she has tripped back into the throng. A glimpse of carrot hair then nothing.

'Who was she?'

'Never mind. We're going the rest of the way by sedan.'

Chairs are lined up by the kerb, the bearers standing nearby, some talking, others smoking clay pipes. Beth has never used a chair before, though she's spied them in her local market towns. 'An extravagance for those too bone idle to use the good legs God gave them,' Mother had said, happier to walk in a downpour than part with a few coppers for a bit of dry comfort.

Moth doesn't seem impressed either. 'Shouldn't we just walk?'

''Tis more than a mile, Kitten,' says Hummingbird. 'My feet are very important to me and I don't want to wear them out trudging through the city in a pair of satin slippers, so hush thy tongue, as Leonardo would say, and climb inside.'

The bearer tugs the brim of his hat as Beth seats herself. She grips the window frames either side as the sedan is hoisted into the air. The men set off at a cracking pace, the cabin swaying as passers-by scuttle out of the way. Street after street slips past. Gulls swoop in from the river, fight pigeons for scraps, soar off in a flurry of screeching feathers. A dog scampers after the chair, barking, heedless of the bearers' curses. Beth clings on, her rump jounced about on the hard seat, her gaze fixed on the bobbing chairs ahead. Soon they are climbing a cobbled hill. The chairs slow as the bearers take the strain. At a signal from Hummingbird, they halt on the crest.

Bethany takes a deep breath then steps out. Buildings rise in a zigzag on either side of the road and fall down the other side of the hill. Hummingbird dips into her reticule, pays the bearers and waves Beth over. 'Nearly there, Kitten. Did you enjoy the ride?'

Beth eyes the crowds lining both sides of the street. Beggars and beer hawkers share road space with finely powdered dandies. A legless man, face toothless and broken apart with some festering pox, holds out an emaciated hand. 'Charity, sweet ladies, a little charity?'

Beth edges away. 'Are we safe here? Should you give him something?'

Hummingbird grimaces. 'Hand over so much as a farthing and you'll have a mob on you before you can sneeze. There's nothing like a soft face and the glint of coin to bring the rats scurrying out of the gutter. Keep a tight purse and your good intentions to yourself and nobody will trouble you. Not in daylight anyway.'

She leads them down a breezy side street. Beth peeks through an open door. A well-dressed gentleman is seated on a chair, a beard of white soapsuds covering the bottom half of his face. Beside him, a barrel-bellied fellow in an apron sharpens a razor on a leather belt. Next door is a hat shop, then a stall selling sugared fairings.

'Ah, here we are.'

They've turned the corner into a terraced lane. Hummingbird climbs the steps of a lemon-coloured building. Inside is a good-sized room with a dozen busy tables and a fire flickering in a wrought-iron hearth. The windows are trimmed with lace, crisp linen smothers the tables and paintings of various city views hang on the wall. Above, wreathed in smoke, cherubs smile from a frescoed ceiling while a brass chandelier drips with fat, waxy candles.

Conversation abruptly stops. It's only for a moment, like a hiccup or someone catching her breath, then it resumes again. If Hummingbird notices she doesn't comment. She takes the only remaining empty table and gestures at the others to sit.

'It's like being inside a cake,' Moth exclaims.

A maid flusters up, fresh in white apron and mob cab. Hummingbird orders tea and raspberry tart.

'That red-haired woman yelling at us in the street,' Beth says, once the maid has hurried off. 'You knew her by name.'

'Screeching Sally? She's a tough old harlot. Been twice carted and none the worse for it.'

'Carted?'

'An old tradition in this city. Petty criminals are hoisted into a cart and driven through the streets for a pelting. Sally flaunts her scars like trophies and wanders the streets showing her teeth to every pretty young woman who passes by. She's especially fond of Masques. She thinks we're angels.'

'Angels?'

'She often claims to see them.'

'She must be soft in the head. Can't we help her?'

'Many harlots die a filthy death. Others are lucky enough to dodge that particular grave. Sally has enough wits left to survive. I'd say that—'

She's interrupted by shouting from a back room. A man's voice, words knotted in anger. They hear the maid twittering a reply then a sharp slap followed by more yelling.

'Oh dear,' Hummingbird says, 'I don't believe we are going to get our tea after all.'

From a door behind the counter, a big fellow dressed in knee breeches and waistcoat lumbers into view. A horsehair wig spikes his head above a pair of florid cheeks and piglet eyes. His forearms resemble shanks of beef and his feet are the size of barges. He approaches the women and leans both fists on the white tablecloth. 'We don't serve you.'

Moth spluttered. 'But—'

'You're just whores by another name. Get out.'

'Come on.' Hummingbird grabs hold of Moth. 'You too, Kitten. Let's not reinforce this gentleman's prejudices.'

'Did you see the way everyone stared?' Beth says. 'I thought that oaf was going to push us out the door.'

Hummingbird, tight-lipped, leads the way past the tradesmen's stalls. Her face is white, her eyes black buttons. Both hands are clenched around her reticule. 'We can hail chairs at the end of the main street.'

'Can't we try another tea room?' Moth says.

Hummingbird gives her an odd look. 'We could, but that won't solve this particular issue.'

'I just thought—'

'Don't dally, and keep away from those stalls.'

A haberdasher's pitch has caught Moth's eye. She lingers a moment before hurrying to catch up. In her haste she nearly sends a sewing basket tumbling into the gutter. 'I'll belt your arse,' the red-faced owner howls, but Moth only laughs. She skips after the other girls, snickering to herself every few yards.

'What have you got to be so jolly-go-lightly about?' Hummingbird demands.

Moth seems to curl into herself. An odd, sly look falls across her face.

'What are you hiding?' Hummingbird stops so abruptly Beth nearly stumbles into the back of her. 'Show me.'

Moth plucks something from a fold in her gown and unwinds it. A length of blue ribbon.

'Did you steal that?'

'Might have done.'

'What do you think we are? A gaggle of common footpads? Either give it back or I'll give you tuppence and you can pay for it.'

'No. He'll slap me if he finds out I filched from his cart.'

'You'll fetch more than that if you don't go back. He'll be happy enough with the money.'

'If he was too stupid to see me pinch it then he deserves to lose it, and he doesn't merit payment either. This is mine. I sweat for the Abbess all day and don't get a penny to show for it. I'm entitled to take what I can and if you don't like it then look the other way.'

'Do I have to take it off you?'

'You couldn't even stop us getting thrown out of that tea room.'

'Fine. So you want to end up like Screeching Sally, poxed and living on the street? Or maybe you prefer transportation? The gallows, too, will prove happy to welcome you. That ribbon won't look so sweet when they bury you under shovel-loads of quicklime.'

''Twill be the only way you or anyone else will take it off me.'

'The Fixer warned you about this sort of thing, Moth. Petty pilfering is against House rules. You can't go lifting other people's property just to make yourself feel good. Don't say I didn't tell you.'

Moth rolls up the ribbon and returns it to her gown. 'I shan't.'

Bits and Pieces

'That's not right.'

The Abbess surveys the combs and brushes spread out on her dresser. After a moment's thought she moves one of the larger hairbrushes two palms' width to the right. Then, shaking her head, she moves it back.

'Perhaps if I try *this*.'

She plucks up two bone-handled combs and lays them side by side next to the mirror. 'Better, but still not perfect.'

They had been given by one of her first clients, a long ago cleric whose church the Abbess and her Harlequins still attend to the horror of the latest incumbent and his outraged parishioners.

'Going to church is the law and we shall not be seen to break the law,' the Abbess told her girls. 'Any legal chink will allow those opposing us to prise fingers into our affairs.'

She rubs her right hand, trying to soothe the sharpening ache in her joints. These bouts are becoming more frequent and the Fixer's balms are losing their potency. Her previous loss of control hadn't helped and the litter of that particular tantrum still bespoiled her bedchamber floor. A jumble of stays, stockings and garters lies strewn like gutted fish across the rug. All due to a

143

bottle of lavender scent. Her favourite. It was not where she'd put it. A search through the dresser turned into a scrabble. Soon everything, drawers and all, was pulled onto the floor.

The Abbess started sobbing towards the end, throwing around curses that would make the saints blush. And she didn't know what upset her more, the missing pot or her loss of dignity.

The bottle was gone, lost to the clutter of the room or somehow ghosted away. Like the many pieces of her life her ailing mind had eaten up. A beloved cushion, embroidered by one of her best girls, which the Abbess swore she'd left on her coverlet. A garter embroidered with her maiden name. A lace-trimmed kerchief brought by a client from Paris. Those too had been swallowed.

I'm too afraid to move anything, she thinks, *lest it melt away. And if I turn my back for a second will things change again? Shall I even notice?*

She fetches an inkpot and quill from her writing desk. Like everything else in the House the quill is of the finest quality. Metal-tipped and hard as a dagger blade. She draws around each item, scoring the varnish of the dresser. Once these inky images are created she writes labels onto the wood in a bold, sweeping hand. Clear, solid letters taught to her as a girl by someone willing to bargain for the lessons.

Her fingers are steady on the quill. Good. She is not losing everything then. Not yet. She picks up the last item. A frown cuts her tattooed forehead. She turns the object in her hands, this way, then that, examining its different angles. Her stuttering mind reaches for identification, then fails. She remembers using it in the recent past, can picture it in her hand, but the name has gone, fled, leaked out of her brain. She casts out mental hooks, hoping the name is hiding in the back of her thoughts and can be coaxed out, summoned, drawn back into the light.

Nothing.

Up to now she has been hiding it. For the most part her girls have not noticed, though Nightingale may have an inkling. Kingfisher too. Before long too much will have gone wrong and the last pieces of her mind will spill out of their disguise.

Will anything remain of the House?

She looks up. An image in the mirror. A distorted reflection skewing nose and eyes. An outline of a face that haunts itself.

Will anything remain of me?

Betrayal and Retribution

'Send the Kitten into the Scarlet Parlour,' the Abbess instructs. 'She can surrender her garments later.'

'Well, haven't we been highly favoured,' Hummingbird says on the way to the dressing room. Her mood has not improved since the incident at the tea room. She glares thunderstorms at Moth, who's tied a strip of the stolen ribbon to a tuft of her hair. Since the sedans dropped them off at the corner of Crown Square she's flaunted it at every opportunity, especially in front of the Masque who would, Beth suspects, gleefully throttle her with it. And yet there is something in Hummingbird's expression that suggests a part of her is glad Moth overstepped some boundary or other. Beth has never been good at reading faces. She supposes she'd have suffered a lot less in recent months if she was. But the contradiction is there.

The Abbess is already seated when Beth enters the blood-coloured room. Again she is invited to sit on the fat sofa beside the old woman. Her gown billows around her waist as she settles.

'Now you have spent some time here,' the Abbess begins, 'what do you think of the House?'

'I've never known its like,' Beth says truthfully.

'I daresay. Perhaps it is the only one of its kind in the world. Perhaps not. What does it mean to you?'

'I'm not sure. A prison. A slave pen. A brothel in all but name. Or maybe a refuge. A haven.'

'You are still confused?'

'Yes.'

'I prefer to think of it as a place where the lost and broken can, shall we say, rediscover themselves.'

'But you earn money from them.'

'The pampering does not pay for itself, Kitten. Things weren't always as you see them.'

'What makes you different from any other bawdy-house madam?'

A smile cracks her patch-studded face. 'Once, I was just another runaway country girl come fresh-cheeked to the city with an ugly past behind me and a head full of hopes. Some flee home due to their pregnant bellies. Others because of their deeds. My village had me as a witch, a white-haired foundling whose very touch could wither flowers or sour milk. A crop failed and they wanted to pillory me for it. A stolen sovereign bought a coach ride into the city. No one came after me, and I've never been back since. I earned this house, Kitten, and everything in it. I don't know if you like stories, but here's an enchanting tale for you. I started in a ruin that stank of the river it stood beside. A leaking, rat-infested shell possessed of four walls, a hole for a roof and precious little else. I took the skin off both knees scrubbing it clean. I found my first girl bleeding in a gutter by the docks, beaten half to death by some sailors who'd taken their pleasure then vented their spite when she'd asked for a shilling in exchange. I took her in, nursed her, fed her and turned her into a queen. The black butterfly tattooed on her cheek gave me the idea for the Emblems. She told me some witch-man straight off a ship from Africa had painted it on her cheek with a touch of his black finger. She always was a whore, and a lying whore at that, but her looks put paintings on my walls and rugs on the floor. Each room took a year of our lives, and there were so many rooms in that house, Kitten, so very many. New girls sold their company to have the windows fixed, new doors, a ton of fresh slate and a warm fire in the hearth. Women spat at me in the street, yet at night their husbands crept up my path. No matter how fat their purses I vowed no man would ever ill-use the bodies of my charges again. Think on that tonight when you lie on your comfortable feather mattress.'

Beth lets her gaze wander. 'It seems you have done well for yourself.'

'This building was given to me in payment for a debt by a lord who was too fond of the cards. He got the better side of the bargain, for in giving it to me he no longer had to maintain it, or pay window tax. The deeds are as solid as the foundations and none shall have them from me unless I so wish. Some years ago a troop of soldiers came to close me down. We barricaded ourselves in and emptied pisspots over their heads. Our clients brandished both their swords and their purses. A few hefty bribes and the matter was resolved. Now we are careful not to break the law.'

'I still don't know why I was chosen. The madhouses must closet a hundred girls with faces fairer than mine.'

'That may be so, but wits are another matter. Listen to the way I speak. Impressive, is it not? What you say when you open your mouth will leave a mark more powerful than any expensive dress. Many a comely face has been ruined by a milkmaid's squeak. You are a fighter, Kitten. That place had the power to snatch the last breath out of your lungs. Had you died you would have done so with defiance in your eyes. As it is, you will become so enchanting that men will gladly empty their pockets for the privilege of conversing or playing a hand of cards. Within a month you'll know the name of every noted theatrical performer. You'll sing like an angel and play whist or hazard with enough skill to bankrupt a gambler. At the table your manners must be without fault.'

'You've the Fixer to thank for that.'

'Indeed. Any clod is capable of cramming food into their mouth, but most can't tell the difference between quail and mutton. Pass something the wrong way or pick up the wrong knife at an inopportune time and your charming social veneer will be irreparably cracked. This sort of thing is important to these people and word gets about. "Did you hear about the milkmaid Geoffrey had for dinner? What, tried to eat pheasant pie with a soup spoon?" You'd become a laughing stock.'

A door opens at the back of the room. A girl appears carrying a gilt tray piled with tea things. An ebony-eyed, round-faced lass of solid build, younger than Beth perhaps, with a tumble of chestnut curls sprouting from her crown. Freckles buzz around her neck and forehead. She wears a white shirt and embroidered waistcoat above a pair of buff riding breeches. A black bird swoops across her right cheek.

The tray is placed on the table. 'Thank you, Raven,' the Abbess says. 'I shall take care of everything.'

The girl withdraws. The Abbess pours two dishes of tea and passes one to Beth. 'We have stables at the back of the House. Can you ride?'

Beth nods. 'My father was given a horse to travel the squire's estate. He taught me.'

'Leonardo will take you around the yard and appraise your style. Side-saddle only of course.' The Abbess smiles. 'Schooling a girl is akin to training a good mount. First you have to break it in. Then comes the finesse.'

'Is that what this house is? A place full of broken people?'

'The maids, the kitchen girls, even the wench who brickbats the front step – all have their place here. Nobody ever leaves.

Nobody ever retires. Play your part and no man shall ever ill-use you again. Life here can be very comfortable if you follow the rules. You will continue to learn these as you progress.'

'Not much of a choice, is it?'

The Abbess sips her tea and nudges a plate of cream fancies towards Beth. 'You have earned a treat, I think. I'm sure your belly will cope in any case.'

Beth picks one. Her tongue nearly bursts with the exquisite taste of it.

'Your first clients will be carefully selected,' the Abbess continues. 'You will also be accompanied. At the close of the evening touch the client on the cheek with your gloved fingertips and that will conclude the contract. Hummingbird will show you how to do it properly. Avoid skin contact. If he wishes to hold your hand then keep your glove on. Clients are not escorted by the same girl more than three times in any one year unless by special arrangement. This is to discourage them becoming over fond of any one Masque. Never ask a client's name. If he wishes you to know, he will volunteer it. Otherwise it's "sir" or "madam", never "m'lord" or "m'lady". Everyone is equal in the presence of a Masque. Sometimes they'll want to address you by a name of their own choosing. Indulge them. Memorise the name, use it as your signature and answer to it for the duration of your hire period. Once your contract is fulfilled, push it out of your mind unless the same client hires you again.'

Beth cradles her tea dish. 'Who's going to want me with my tired face? You might as well give me to a travelling fair.'

'Don't belittle yourself. The Fixer is a master at his trade. Ours is a very select circle catering to unique tastes. One of our girls has a hook. Cuckoo. She's in Florence on a long-term Assignment. A client once gifted her a ring. She was foolish enough to accept it. He became besotted, so Kingfisher warned

149

him off. He managed to send her a private message, to meet him in his carriage by the wharf. And she, her head full of sparrows, went unaccompanied and stepped inside his coach, where he cut off her hand to get his ring back and dumped her in the harbour. Two dredgers found her in the mud, barely breathing. They were going to rob her of her silks, I believe, but then noticed the Emblem and brought her back to the House for a better reward. Stories like this are rare, however. Most of the time my girls enjoy a fulfilling life.'

'This girl, Cuckoo, is still a Masque?'

'As you heard, we cater for clients of all persuasions. Your first will likely be a local lady.' She laughs. 'Don't look like that. It's not what you think. We have a small female clientele. Some of these women are lonely, others have lost family members. They need a "daughter" or a "sister" to take to the theatre, sup tea or sit in the park. If more is involved then the same look-don't-touch rules apply. A few tip very nicely too. You can keep whatever they give you, within reason.'

'If I'm not to become a whore, then what am I?'

'A companion.'

'And what happens when I grow too old?' Beth presses. 'You said nobody leaves. Shall I spend the rest of my days cleaning out hearths?'

'Ah, Kitten, such a black view you have of the world. Surely you are not finding it so difficult to settle in? I am told that you are performing your duties well enough, and you are comfortable with Hummingbird. A few weeks ago you had no future to speak of. Why trouble yourself now?'

Beth regards this strange, patch-covered creature. How very much at home she looks in her sumptuous, blood-red nest.

'Men . . . people . . . are different. I wouldn't rightly know how to please them all.'

'No need to, Kitten. Most please themselves. You just have to be there.'

'But—'

The Abbess raises a hand. 'Don't be too clever. More than one eloquent Kitten has talked herself out of a home. Trust what I tell you. Now sip your tea then tell me about your visit to the tea room in George Lane.'

Beth gives a brief account of the afternoon's events. The Abbess listens without comment. 'You were not hurt?' she asks after Beth has finished describing the tea-room fracas.

'No. It was shameful though. Moth's antics didn't improve things.'

'Really?' The Abbess leans forward. 'What antics were those?'

'What's happened?'

Two of the elegantly framed windows of the George Lane tea room are boarded up. The brass knocker has been ripped off leaving a bare oak scar.

'These streets can be lively,' Hummingbird says. 'Things can happen if people aren't careful. Shall we go in?'

'Hummingbird, this is a mistake. You saw the look on the proprietor's face. I've suffered enough troubles in my life without walking into more, especially over something as stupid as a dish of tea.'

'No one is going to cause trouble.'

Beth glances back down the lane. Leonardo is waiting with the carriage around the corner, whip clutched in his hand. On the way here a group of jeering urchins had been sent scattering by a few expert flicks of that leather coil.

Hummingbird is halfway up the steps. Beth follows. Inside, the blocked windows cast a gloom over the tea room and motes of dust swirl in the light creeping through the one remaining window. Candles have been lit and placed along the mantelpiece. The air is stuffy and smells of hot wax. Patrons, fewer than before, sit at tables, sipping tea or squinting at newspapers. Someone coughs.

'Sit down, Kitten,' Hummingbird says.

'Are we being punished?' Beth asks. 'Why isn't Moth with us?'

'I believe the Abbess wants her for something, and no, this isn't punishment.'

Bethany notices, as she pulls back a chair, a group of young men playing dice at the table in the bay window. Overdressed, faces blanched with powder, rouge painting little kiss-me mouths. Teetering on their heads are wigs as big as pillows. If it wasn't for their striped and tasselled breeches they'd pass for girls. As the maid goes by, a pot of tea in her hands, one of the dandies squeezes her rump. She squeals and tips forward, spilling hot liquid on the carpet. The group dissolves into giggles. The maid, blushing, retreats with the pot, rubbing her backside with her free hand.

'Who are those oafs?' Beth whispers. 'That poor girl could have been burned.'

'Another gang of puffed young dandies,' Hummingbird replies. 'There seem to be more plaguing the streets every day. I'm surprised their heads don't collapse into the witless gaps between their ears.'

More laughter. Beth snatches glances around the room. An old fellow dozes in one corner, newspaper open on his lap. Near the door sits a lady in a wide-brimmed bonnet hung with ribbons. A child is beside her, a tiny mirror image of the older lady in a looped dress freckled with satin bows.

The maid, composure regained, approaches their table. Beth's fingers are knotted in her lap. *Now there'll be trouble*, she thinks. *What's Hummingbird doing, bringing me here again? We'll be back on the street in an ace.*

The maid opens her mouth then gets a good look at Hummingbird's smiling face. Blood rushes out of cheeks that were bright red only a moment before. 'Pray how . . . how may I serve you?'

'You can get me the landlord,' Hummingbird says. 'I would have him attend to us.'

Beth tries to nip her under the table but Hummingbird seems resolute. The serving girl hesitates a moment then skitters off. A few seconds later the landlord appears. Beth, who has resigned herself to an almighty row and possibly a thump across the ear, feels her breath catch. A mass of black and yellow bruises colours his face. One eye has closed completely. The other is watery and bloodshot. His arm hangs in a dirty sling, the fingers bandaged together. He stands at their table and stares at his feet.

'Tea and a selection of your best sweetmeats,' Hummingbird says.

'Yes, Miss.' His voice is barely more than a whisper. He fetches their order, bows and leaves without uttering another word.

The young men's laughter fragments into whispers. They stare and nudge one another. Hummingbird pores over a magazine as if nothing untoward is happening. The dandies finish their whispered debate. One shoves another who rises and approaches the girls. Beth wants to bury her head in the tablecloth. If he speaks how will she respond? She peeks at him from beneath the rim of her bonnet. Impossible to tell his age under the powder and rouge. Her mother could guess a person's years just by glancing at their hands. This fellow wears satin gloves ringed with lace. Bright blue eyes, sharp with mischief, glitter beneath the soft wig.

But he doesn't say anything. He reaches inside a jacket pocket and produces a calling card. His friends watch as he drops it on the table. Hummingbird lifts her dish of tea and takes a sip, gaze not shifting from her magazine.

Bethany stares at the card. Should she pick it up? Is the fellow an admirer of Hummingbird's and this some complicated social ritual? The youth has returned to his seat and is talking to his companions.

Hummingbird, as if sensing her friend's discomfort, slides her periodical aside, plucks the card off the tablecloth and drops it into her reticule. Beth opens her mouth but the other girl silences her with a waved finger. 'Try one of these.' Hummingbird offers the plate of sweetmeats. 'You'll burst your stays but it's worth it.'

Sugar and cream explode across Beth's tongue. Hummingbird calls the serving girl over and orders more tea.

'D'you want the master to bring it, Miss, like last time?'

Hummingbird shakes her head. 'No, I think we've frightened him enough.'

The girl scuttles off, apron ties flapping at her back. The tea room fills. Merchants, bankers, ladies in frilled summer gowns. Beth begins to relax. Up till now she's wondered if this has all been some perverse game. The hubbub of voices soothes her frayed nerves. The three lads have stopped staring and returned to their dice game. She settles back in her chair and glances at the discarded magazine, which lies open at the society pages. Tea parties, seasonal Balls, names of people Beth doesn't recognise. All look pompous and important. There are lists of births and marriages; families securing dowries and heirs being born. Then, on the facing page as if of secondary importance, is parliamentary business. The 'den of donkeys' as Father once denounced it. Beth has no knowledge of politics. It's a part of the strange world of men and she can't make any sense of the words printed there. Why is Hummingbird reading this?

Cries of delight and outrage explode from the dice table. Purses are opened and coins exchanged. Beth regards the young man with the blue eyes and feels her stomach pinch. His name is printed on the calling card but that's at the bottom of Hummingbird's reticule. And the card itself? Clearly an invitation of some sort but to whom, and for what? It had not been handed over, merely left on the table.

She steals a glance at the lad's powdered face. Is he disappointed? Should Beth have said something? Would that have been proper? Even the way these young men move is exaggerated, every gesture overplayed. Beth shifts on her chair. The heat is back in her cheeks. She's conscious of Hummingbird watching her, the trickle of a smile on those dark red lips. But Beth can't afford to let her mind off the leash, to go down the path to the brink of the pit, the pit which held George, the children, and her life at Russell Hall. Friend should have killed her, or refused Kingfisher's bribe and let her rot.

Then it happens twice more.

The first is a uniformed army officer. He slaps his card onto their table, scattering crumbs. The second is a fat fellow in black garb who resembles the fire-and-brimstone vicar from the church on the east side of Beth's home village. He slips the card from his sleeve as if palming a guinea to a tavern whore. Such is his haste to return to his seat that his hip catches a table edge and sends a teapot clattering onto the floor. Scarlet-faced and puffing, he mutters apologies and buries himself in a newspaper.

Both calling cards follow the first into Hummingbird's reticule. No words have been exchanged. She drains her tea, scrapes back her chair and stands. 'Time to go.'

Who Are You, Bethany Harris?

August. A wasp became tangled in her hair. She ran screaming from the garden, shoes kicking up gravel from the path. George found her slumped on the terrace, red-faced and shaking, hair a broken haystack around her face.

'Where is it?' she said. 'Has it gone?'

George bent and picked up a broken yellow-and-black shape by the tip of one stilled wing. 'Look.'

'Get it away from me.'

'Are you stung? Let me see?'

'Don't touch me. And throw that thing away. I don't want to see it.'

She'd spent the morning beside the flowerbeds with Julia and Sebastian where they'd been identifying the different blooms. The children were sunbursts of life bound by neither tact nor guile and she had taught them through a three-season glory of glittering frost, spring shoots and hot summer meadows.

'The flowers are like jewels,' Bethany told them. 'Close your eyes, breathe deeply, smell their pretty scent.'

'I am told when I come of age I shall have my mother's jewels,' Julia said.

'Really? My first jewel was a polished chestnut my father brought home. It was perfectly round, the only one of its kind I'd seen. He placed it in my cupped hands and I spent minutes running my fingers across its smooth skin.'

'It wasn't worth anything.'

'Not true, Julia. It was a treasure. My father found it and made the effort to keep it for me. He knew I loved such things.'

In the reds and golds of autumn, Father brought back more horse chestnuts. Beth laid them out in rows across her dresser, the fat clunky ones on top, the tiny brown pebbles at the bottom. 'Aren't you going to make something more out of those?' Father asked, but Beth thought them perfect arranged as they were.

When clopping around the grounds Father hung dun-coloured sacks from his pommel. In these he collected the small detritus any estate of significance attracts: a broken flower, a wing-shattered crow, a poacher's illicit snare. Other items he thought might interest Bethany found their way into his pockets. She pressed oddly shaped leaves, like green and brown faces, into a scrapbook received one birthday. She filled the corners of her room with everything. Father had whitewashed the house from kitchen to attic. 'White is the best background for furniture and other things,' he claimed. Then Mother discovered 'tapestries' and smothered the walls of her bedchamber. Given leave she'd have spread them across the parlour and hall, but Father wouldn't consider such a notion. She spent hours running her hands across the material. Beth thought they resembled old rugs with bad stitching. Her own treasures came straight from nature's mouth. Finally Father built shelves for her using odd cuts of wood begged from the Russells' stables. Beth laid out her larger pieces, arranging then rearranging until each was in its proper place.

'Move just one and they all end up looking wrong,' she explained.

'You're a peculiar sort, Bethany, make no mistake,' Father said, shaking his head. 'How much of me is in you? How much of your mother? And where did the rest come from?'

Peculiar or not, she taught Julia and Sebastian to take delight in simple things, and to find wonder in almost everything that grew or lived on their uncle's estate.

Then the wasp appeared, and the day was ruined.

Beth shut herself in her bedchamber. An hour passed before she brushed civility back into her hair and returned to the schoolroom. Despite the children's protests she did not go outside for the rest of the day. Eventually they gave up and dabbled with watercolours. Beth's brittle face warned she would not be swayed. As the paints swirled over paper, however, she softened, remembering her time in the round tower and the soft kiss of the brush against her skin. Julia looked up from her work, a dab of blue smeared on the end of her nose. Beth felt a flood of affection for her and Sebastian, whose face was folded in concentration.

I wish I could do this forever.

George caught her while she was hanging the paintings on the schoolroom wall. Julia and Sebastian were off for their afternoon nap. Russell Hall had, for a short time, settled into a warm silence.

'On the terrace today. You were impertinent,' George said. 'The children were crying. They thought you'd taken a fit.'

'I ask your pardon. I was upset.'

'Do you wish to discuss the matter?'

She put down the watercolours and faced him. 'I dread this time of year. Those things are everywhere. Week upon week of perdition. They haunt you like devils.'

'Did something bad happen? With wasps? Before you came here?'

'Yes,' she said. 'Something did.'

Through most of the previous August Beth's home had been tight as a stewpot, thanks mostly to a rain-sodden summer which had warped most of the windows in their frames. When the weather finally broke, it brought a heatwave which baked the lane into a river of dust. Mother prised open every window from larder to attic. Some hadn't been touched for weeks and put up a squealing protest. Mother's wiry forearms brooked no opposition. She put a jagged crack across one pane but Father knew better than to gripe. Not content with that, she marched into Beth's room and dragged the covers to the foot of the bed. 'No sneaking up for a nap today,' Mother told her. 'This place needs airing. You can spend your time outside.'

Beth worked her chores in a simmering broth of heat and bugs. A listless, drooping air settled over everything. After a cold supper she splashed water on her face and climbed the stairs.

The dusk had spawned a faint breeze which tickled her bedchamber curtains. She tugged off her clothes, rolled onto the bed and drew the thin coverlet up to her chin. A moment later she collapsed into sleep.

A sliver of late summer light still coloured the sky when a sharp pain pulled her from her dreams. She lay in confusion, taking in the ceiling, the walls, the now stilled curtains, wondering if she'd imagined it or if night-time cramps were beginning to bite. Another pain needled into her leg and this time she yelped. Something was crawling across her thigh. More pain on her calf, her rump, her belly.

Screaming, Beth hurled herself from the covers, caught her foot on the bedpost and crashed onto the rug. Tiny legs scratched across her flesh. She slapped herself, eyes thick with tears. 'Get off me. Get *off*.'

Feet thumped across the landing. The door was thrown open. Mother stood, frowning, candle in hand. 'Bethany?'

Flickering light caught the tiny yellow-and-black bodies squirming on the carpet. Three. No, four. Mother crushed them under her slipper.

'They were in there with me,' Beth whimpered. 'They were in my *bed*.' Angry, flushed circles, punctured in the middle, spread across her leg. She could *feel* the holes, as if the wasps had burrowed into her flesh.

Mother became a tight-lipped picture of capability. She delved into her kitchen concoctions and produced a poultice which brought cool relief to her sopping daughter.

'A bit of a nightmare that,' Father remarked.

'She'll get over it,' Mother said, not knowing how deep the roots of that particular horror had wormed into Bethany's mind.

George looked grave. 'I was sore for days,' Beth finished explaining. 'Mother could never make me go near that room for weeks.'

He reached a hand towards her face. She stepped away.

'No.'

'Bethany—'

'No, George.'

He let his hand drop. 'Why don't you seem to care? What do I have to do to reach you? Is such a thing even possible?'

'I shall not be your doxy. I'm not a horse you can mount whenever you please.'

'How can you talk of our relationship in those terms?'

'We don't have a relationship. We never will. These things always end the same. Broken promises. Broken hearts. I've no feelings for you.'

'Because of who you are? A paid companion for the children?'

'No, because of who *you* are. Rich, handsome George who should be loved by everyone. That's the real tic in your skin, I think. Don't try to pretend that I'm different from any milkmaid or tavern wench you've tupped during your adventures. All those treats you insist on – the riding trips, the walks in the garden, the flirty looks you give me whenever the chance arises – are games and nothing more. You're forever strutting about or posturing like some pampered dandy. Why d'you assume I'd be impressed with such things?'

'They are not games.'

'Really? It seems the rules are simple enough. Every girl wants you, so that means I must want you also.'

'I could hand that back to you, *Miss Harris*, and say because I am the squire's son you assume I must play the rake, that my role of heartbreaker is assured. You cannot believe me capable of harbouring genuine feelings for someone outside the circle of society butterflies Father parades in front of me. So I ask, do you think so little of me that you imagine I could love one of those featherheaded girls? Everything about them is artifice. But then we are taught both to know our place and to keep it, are we not? Some things, some people, make courting disaster a worthwhile enterprise.'

'How full of words you are. I'm surprised you don't choke on them.'

'And what of you, whose mouth says one thing while the rest of your face says something else? What is it you truly want, Bethany Harris? What do you have your sights set on that you should lure my father into your bed?'

The picture fell from Beth's hands, shattering the makeshift frame the children had made for it.

'Yes, I've heard about it,' George continued. 'I've no doubt the whole household knows. I even confronted Father in his study, and God help me I had murder on my mind. His desk was awash with documents. All estate jiffery. He looked at me as if I were an ignorant boy who would never learn anything of worth. He was not angry, merely disappointed. Not one word passed between us. He went back to fussing with his papers and I walked out without looking back. For days afterwards I'd catch the servants whispering and drawing me looks. Everyone knew, right down to the stable boy, and all thought me a fool. What are you if not another breed of servant, yet you take it upon yourself to tup the master of the house? Even when you went about with the marks of his mouth fresh around your neck I did not thrash you into the floor as I ought to have done. Suppose you had a child?'

Beth's fingers squeezed together, then loosened. 'You did not kill him, obviously?'

'Men such as I have resources to fall back on should we find ourselves financially unseated, so I tried to pretend that you were merely in his thrall and would grow weary of it once the shine had dulled. Am I a coward as well as an imbecile?'

'Neither coward nor fool, though in your heart you don't believe that.'

'How could you use an old man in such a fashion?'

'Because there was no usury.'

George's face tightened. 'Are you telling me he seduced you?'

'Yes, and it was lovely. And it meant a lot. Seduction isn't the same as force. A girl isn't obliged to lift her petticoats at a gesture from you.'

'But he's my *father*.'

'And? He was gentle when I wanted him to be, and passionate when my feelings called for it. He made me feel that I was *someone*, that I was worth *something*. Not a notch on your scabbard.'

'I could have given you passion.'

'You demanded it from me. It never occurred to you that I could refuse. Poor George, future darling of Parliament, cuck-olded in his desires by his own father. What a blow to your pride.'

His hand split the air, carving through sunshine and dust motes. Clumsy. Only his fingertips connected with her jaw, but it was enough to melt her mouth into a wide 'O' of surprise. She touched the point of impact and stared at her own fingers.

'You hit me.'

'Nothing,' he sucked in his breath. 'It was nothing. Don't say otherwise.'

'*You hit me.*'

'Damn it, girl. You have twisted this household enough. I doubt I can persuade Father to have you dismissed but I'll ensure you never see the children again.'

'You can't mean that? Julia and Sebastian are everything to me.'

'Really? You should have thought of them before tickling my father's breeches.'

'George—'

He strode towards the door. 'This is one thing you can't influence. Don't even try.'

Beth stared after him. *You'll see what I can do, George Russell.* And it was only on feeling a warm trickle between her fingers that she realised how far her nails had dug into her palms.

A Sisterly Lesson

'I know what you're going to ask.' Hummingbird clutches her bonnet against a stiff breeze. 'You were squirming in that tea room as though a hot poker had punctured your chair. So you might as well say it.'

'Those calling cards—'

'Yes, the cards. A morsel of business to accompany a fine lunch. You don't think the Abbess sent us out to take the air, do you?'

'From what I saw, the idea was to humiliate the proprietor.'

'He needed a lesson, true, but in the end the tea room will benefit from the notoriety. Those young men are potential clients.'

'Then why act with such indifference?'

'I need to stay aloof until the Abbess gives her approval. It's part of the allure.'

'Approval? Which is based on the size of their purse, I suppose?'

'Their purses can contain cobwebs or half the Treasury for all the difference it makes. It's *who* they are that matters. There's more than one way to choose a plump goose.'

'So are there fixed rates or are we priced according to our skills? I suppose the Harlequins attract a fatter purse.'

'That's certainly true. I don't know the exact sum, it varies from person to person, but I'll wager these prices would make your mouth flap open.' Hummingbird winks. 'Wealthy men are in danger of being crushed by the weight of their own fortunes. The Abbess is keen to relieve them of their burdens.'

'A burden that is obviously not shared with us.'

'Mind what you say, Kitten. One not-so-clever Sister thought to demand payment from the Abbess – made quite a show of it. The Abbess handed over the money then promptly charged for bed and board, rental of gowns and jewellery, and a dozen other things the girl had taken for granted. She ended up with the choice of keeping her gripes to herself or retiring to a debtors' prison. If it came down to it, the Abbess could sell us for a cart load of sovereigns and we'd not have a say.'

'Are we always given cards in public?'

'Usually. On a good night out we can snare twenty or more, though you never do it whilst in the company of a client,' she lowers her voice, 'unless his back is turned.'

Beth laughs. Both girls skip out of the way when a sedan lurches towards them. Once it has passed, Hummingbird takes Beth's arm.

'Listen, Kitten, if you get carded when I'm not with you, whether I'm off in search of a pot or whatever, do as I did. Don't speak, don't look. Take the card, slip it into your reticule and go about your business. Do you understand?'

'Yes.'

'Good girl. You'll be a Masque before you know it. Now here's Leonardo with the carriage, patient pup that he is.'

They climb inside and the coach sets off, wheels rumbling on the dung-spattered road. Dogs chase and bark around the wheels. A hawker runs beside their window holding up strips of lace. 'Fine for a bonnet, ladies, or a gift for a beloved aunt.'

A warning grumble from Leonardo and he falls away into the crowd. Beth squeezes her hands together. *Can I really complain?* she asks herself. *I have the chance to live better now than I've ever done, even at Russell Hall. Yet why am I uneasy?*

First she'll concentrate on getting her strength back, that'll give her time to think. The House is not the Comfort Home. If she decides to leave there's bound to be a dark night, an unlocked window or door. She'll head west. Perhaps to Bristol, which by all accounts is fat with slave trade money. She can forge a letter of recommendation, maybe gain a post working with children again.

But first. *Oh yes, but first.*

The coach hits a bump. The cake Beth had eaten in the tea room turns in her belly. It had tasted delicious and she'd felt hungry enough, but the proprietor's face, bruised and discoloured as rotten fruit, loomed large in her thoughts. He had brought them their tea the way a child might after a scolding. Though resentment lingered in his battered eyes, the defiance was gone, purged like a bad fever. Beth last witnessed such an expression on the face of a local scold who, hair foul with eggs and bits of old cabbages, had spent a day in the village stocks.

The carriage lurches again. They pass a church, spire pricking the grey underbelly of the clouds. 'Time we showed a little devotion,' Hummingbird announces, rapping her knuckles on the roof. Leonardo brings the team to a snorting halt.

'We have an errand to take care of,' she tells him. 'Don't bother waiting. We'll hire chairs.'

Leonardo's voice rumbles from the driver's perch. ''Tis my duty to return thee to thy House.'

'Well, don't worry thy head. Thou canst return thyself to thy stables with a clear conscience.'

Her slippered feet are light on the church steps. Beth follows, almost tripping in her haste to keep up. Hummingbird pauses by an arched door, the oak black with age and studded with iron. 'This is St Serf's,' she declares. 'It boasts a very fine cut of parishioner.'

Beth takes in the tall stained-glass windows, the statue above the door, the gargoyles grinning on their rooftop perches. From inside, the mournful sound of singing leaks into the vestibule. 'You can't mean to go in?'

Hummingbird shoves open the inner door. Beth tries to grab her but misses. Two days left until the Sabbath yet the church is packed to the rafters. A hymn drones to an end. With coughs and creaking bones, the pious seat themselves. Beth hopes to tuck herself away at the back but the devil has come to St Serf's and is squatting right inside Hummingbird's head. She's off down the centre aisle, skirts swishing, bonnet cocked on her head. People stare or glance at one another.

Where is she going? Beth thinks. *Not to the head of the church surely?*

But that's exactly where Hummingbird is bound. She sweeps down to the rented pews where the gentry sit, plumps herself next to some powdered dowager and pats the bench. Mortified but helpless to do anything else, Beth sits beside her. 'What are you doing?' she whispers. 'This place is thick with popery.'

The cleric has begun his sermon. He's a young man with unfashionably cropped fair hair and sharp cheekbones. An affliction of the voice melts all his 't's and 's's together. Hummingbird keeps snickering. Beth hunches in her seat and wishes herself on the other side of the world. While talking, the cleric's eyes flit around, his gaze alighting on the floor, ceiling, windows. Murmurs ripple through his congregation. He then launches into a series of prayers.

Hummingbird leans across and whispers, 'Are you going to take bread?'

Beth feels nailed to the pew. 'I don't think I can.'

'It's easy. Watch.'

People are leaving their seats and filing to the front of the church. Beth grasps Hummingbird's arm. 'Go up there, and I'll run out and leave you, I swear it.'

Hummingbird shrugs her off and joins the other supplicants at the altar rail, leaving a strong scent of jasmine in her wake. The young cleric is working his way along the line, dispensing bread and wine. A choir sings some dirge from an upstairs gallery. Occasional sneezes punctuate the music.

He reaches Hummingbird. She raises her face to him, expression unreadable. The priest's hand wavers, bread paused in the air between his hand and her mouth.

'Child?'

'Amen,' says Hummingbird. Her tongue snakes out, pink and wet in the light from the stained-glass windows.

'I can't believe you did that,' Beth declares as the two girls push through the city throng.

'Why not?' Hummingbird bats a fly away from her bonnet. 'Putting some wind in the preacher's sails teaches him a little of the humility his holy peers preach from their pulpits. These clerics love to sermonise. Sometimes their mouths need reining in.'

'You behaved like someone from a travelling show.'

'Our attendance always throws the pure at heart into a dither. No vicar will condemn us, no bolt of lightning strike from the sky. We are the devil's daughters seated among the lambs. Yet we give generously to charities. Nothing confounds the fire-and-brimstone preachers more than fallen women filling the pockets of the poor and destitute. Last year a visiting clergyman hired a Sister with the sole intention of taking her to church and praying for her salvation. The Sister put on a suitable show of repentance then everyone returned home.'

'That cleric's cheeks turned so scarlet I thought they'd burst. We were lucky not to get kicked out on our tails.'

'I doubt it, Kitten. He's one of our best clients.'

'No!'

'It's true. His visits to our particular den of delights are discreet but regular. However, his debt has grown heavy and he needed a reminder to settle. Besides, most of those fine-suited men stinking out the front rows with their expensive cologne spend much of their time whoring and gambling. They find absolution in muttering a couple of prayers then go and sin all over again. God is merciful, God is forgiving. The more money and status you've got the more merciful God tends to be.'

'It's not what I was taught.'

'Where did those lessons get you? Listen, Kitten, everyone knows us. Some call these Emblems on our cheeks the mark of Cain, yet gallants often send their footmen to dog our path home in a bid to arrange an unofficial assignation. These unwelcome shadows can usually be perplexed by a fast carriage or sedan bearers who know a back alley or two.'

Hummingbird squeezes Beth's fingers. 'We don't pretend to be anything other than exactly what we are, and that gives us power. A very sweet power. You will learn more about this once you wear an Emblem.'

Next morning finds Moth at the breakfast table, her eyes big and raw. Her left hand is bandaged. She won't look at or say a word to Beth. Halfway through the meal she gets up and runs from the room, knocking her stool over in the process.

'What's the matter with her?' Beth asks the serving woman.

The maid's mouth thins. 'Moth got a hot hand.'

Eloise catches Beth in the corridor and asks her to hang out the linen from the washhouse. Apparently the washerwoman has the gripe. 'We've had a poor morning and it will rain again later,' Eloise explains, both hands black with coal dust. 'If you peg it up now we might get most of it dry before the heavens decide to open again. Either that or we suffer a kitchen full of wet bed sheets. Cook is very jealous of her space. I don't want her sour face ruining the rest of my day.'

Beth hurries downstairs, scoops a basket from the alcove beside the courtyard door and steps outside. A flagstoned area, square as an executioner's yard, is hedged by the House on three sides with the stables flanking the fourth. Wooden poles support washing lines that spider-web above ground made slick by the morning's rain. Beth squints past the tall chimneys. Clouds grey the sky, thinning in places like the strands of some ageing dandy's hair. The air feels clammy.

Two dozen steps take her across the yard, basket swinging at her hip. The washhouse door hangs open. Tubs, like huge wooden barrels lopped off at the base and banded with black iron, hug the space beneath the window. Scrubbing boards lean over the rims like gravestones.

Against the far wall, an untidy pile of linen lies heaped on the draining board. Already it's beginning to smell of washing left too long. *If the rain catches it there'll be no comfortable sleep for some of us tonight*, Beth thinks.

She piles the washing inside the basket. The damp cloth feels horrible against her bare forearms. A grey sludge of water covers the bottom of the nearest tub. Soap suds hiss as they dissolve.

A noise outside. Beth peeks round the door. Nobody there. A few pigeons coo from the slate roof. The linen basket is a dead weight in her arms. She dumps it under the nearest peg-spiked drying line, half throwing, half draping sheets over the twine. Taking a mouthful of pegs she creates white, billowing rooms for herself, the walls made of linen ghosts.

Another sound. Then another. A breeze funnels into the yard, catches the sheets and sends them flapping. A speck of something strikes Beth's forearm and she looks up, panicking, thinking the rain has tricked them all. But the sky remains stuck in its grey doldrums. A pinch of soot, then? In a city of a thousand belching chimneys it must prove impossible to keep anything clean for long.

She rubs her arm and picks up the last of the washing. A sharp gust sends the corners snapping at her ankles. After this, Beth thinks, she'll go to the parlour and steal a few minutes with some coffee. Perhaps Eloise will be waiting by the fire, her face fat with smiles and gossip.

A shadow falls across the sheet in front of her. For a moment Beth thinks a bird has caught itself in the folds. The shape turns into a fist and strikes her square in the face through the material. Beth staggers back. Gloved hands appear, plucking the pegs from the line. The sheet slithers onto the wet flagstones. Beth squeals. An apparition. A white-faced spectre with dark, slitted eyes and bloody lips open in a demonic pout. Wild patterns of blue and black swirl over its death-white cheeks. It wears a green satin gown with creamy sweeps of lace looping across the skirts. A peg is scissored between fingers and waved in front of Beth's face.

She hears a wet slap as another sheet hits the ground. Then another. More figures, more white faces. Some are emblazoned with flames, others with birds or flowers, or strange winged creatures out of some poet's dream. Beth is caught in a rustling cage of skirts and petticoats. One of the figures speaks with lips frozen in a scarlet kiss. The voice is hollow and filled with winter. 'Quite the tattle tale, aren't you?'

Masks, they're wearing porcelain masks, that's why their faces don't move.

The circle closes around her. 'Tattle tale.' A blow between her shoulderblades. 'Tattle tale.' Another in the ribs. Beth tries to back away. She trips over someone's leg and jars her spine on the hard stone. Thoughts tumble into one another. Her eyes water and she blinks to clear them.

An initiation. She clings to the idea. *That's all it is. I'll wager all new girls undergo something like this. I'm nearly a Masque, Hummingbird said so. They'll tease me a little, try to scare me and then there'll be hugs and kisses. I'll be one of the girls. Hummingbird and I shall laugh about it later.*

They lean over her, masks dark against the gunmetal sky. One of the faces ducks out of sight. Footsteps crack across the flagstones. A pause. A muffled scraping sound. Then the face returns. 'Hold her up.'

Hands hook under Beth's arms and wrench her into a sitting position. The figure crouches in front of her, the mask inches from her face. Hot breath from those brittle lips tickles her nose. 'Got a dirty tongue, haven't you?' the voice says. Beth doesn't know how to reply. Who is hiding behind the porcelain? Is it someone she knows? Her back and ribs throb. The jest is wearing thin.

The figure holds out cupped hands. Manure, turned to ochre sludge by the rain, drips between the gloved fingers. 'Open her mouth.'

An arm slides around Beth's neck and tightens. Thumbs prise her jaws apart. Filth pours over her teeth and gums. She tries to scream and only makes choking sounds. The mask fills her vision. Beneath the thin slits, eyes glitter with anger.

'Sisters don't snitch on one another. Nor do Kittens. Remember that the next time you want to win a smile from the Abbess.'

The hand lets go. Beth rolls over, belly heaving. Manure pours out of her mouth and splatters onto the cobbles. Her eyes and nose sting.

Footsteps drift away. Muttering voices. Some faraway door opens and closes. Alone in the yard. Sheets flap as another gust blows between the chimneys. Others are crumpled phantoms lying prone on the ground.

I'll have to wash them. The only sane thought Bethany can squeeze out of her mind. She blinks, brings things into focus. A flagstone, tiny crack splitting its surface. Grains of dirt. A clothes peg, splintered into pieces.

Beth spits out the last of the muck and pushes herself into a kneeling position. Her breath is coming in loud whoops. Black threads wriggle across her vision.

'I'm going to die,' she whispers.

A pair of hands heave her into the air and carry her across the yard like a sack of oats. She tries to struggle but the arms holding her are firm. Ahead lies the horse trough. 'No—'

Cold water smacks against her skin. It fills her ears, swills out her mouth. She swallows. Cool fingers slide down her throat into her belly. A hand pushes her deeper, sluicing the last of the manure from her nose.

Out. Fresh air. The world smelling as it should. Floods of water course down the front of her day gown. Hair flaps about her ears like wet reeds. The hands lift her out of the trough and smooth threads of sopping hair off her forehead. Leonardo's face swims into focus. 'Better now?'

'Hurts . . .' Beth splutters.

'But thou art clean, and will live. Pride injured more than anything, I wager, as was their intention.'

'Why?'

'Thy Sisters have punished thee for a reason only thou canst know. Give thyself a moment, then I shall take thee to Kingfisher where thou canst dry in front of his stove. I shall fetch a fresh garment from the House.'

'I can't go back.'

'Thou canst not stay here. Best make thy mind up.'

Beth eases herself upright, clinging to the edge of the trough for support. Her knees quiver but keep her on her feet. 'The mess—'

'Stable girl will clean up. 'Twas her fault horseshit was there in the first place. Do as I say. Thy pride will mend.' He nods towards the House. 'After thou hast dried out, things must be mended in there.'

Settling Accounts

Rain starts falling in long, wet lances, smacking forcefully on the cobbles. Kingfisher pulls his coat tighter and peers into the muddied skies. Many times he had stood outside his hut in the forest of his homeland, revelling in the fresh, cleansing downpours that sometimes blew in from the coast. Here, the rainwater is harsh and choked with soot.

'No darkie is ever going to extort coin out of me.'

Kingfisher draws his attention back to the squawking buffoon in front of him. 'Your debt grows heavy and is long overdue. I am afraid I must insist, sir, especially as you have enjoyed yet another long session at the gaming tables.'

'I barely step out of the coach and you accost me in my own stableyard. How long have you been lurking here?'

'Not long, sir. Your whereabouts was common knowledge. The account must be settled. The House has granted you good grace for long enough.'

The client glances at Leonardo, standing like a misshapen boulder by the yard gate, then turns back to Kingfisher. 'Very well, I shall fetch your cursed payment out of my strongbox. You can wait out here and get a soaking, and if it costs you a fever then so be it.'

The back door slams. Kingfisher tugs his hat lower across his forehead. A foul night to go chasing bad debt. The client is as obnoxious as they always are but everyone pays in the end. In one manner or another.

Movement by the stable door interrupts his musings. A shape

is hunched over the ground, hands scrabbling over the cobbles. Kingfisher steps forward for a better look. A young woman, her skin as dark as his own. She is trying to winkle manure from between the stones, but the rain is turning it into a foul sludge that slips between her fingers and splatters her knees. She hears the scrape of boots coming towards her and looks up, water smearing oily drops down the course of both cheeks. His eyes know the cut of her face, as she knows his.

Kingfisher does not believe this encounter to be fated, though there are those whose lives are channelled by such things. Rather, this is another example of the great, endless roll of numbers that determines the way of the universe coming up with an event, a moment, a point where a decision one way or the other can change lives. It doesn't matter whether this woman had remained cowering at the back of the slaver cage until sold, or whether she fled with some of the others, only to be recaptured somewhere down the dark road. She is here. Now.

The words come to his mouth before his mind has time to consider them. 'I am sorry,' he says in their mother tongue. 'I shall try to make this right.'

She looks at him, mouth shivering in the cold, eyes full of disbelief. 'Can you make it right for those who died on the boat? Can you make it right for those who have died since? You could not save your own wife, Osei, so how can you help me? I am a slave now.'

'I know your voice. It was you who whispered into my ear during that long voyage. Even above the groans of the ill and dying I heard you. I know what I have done.'

'Truthfully, Osei? You walked away with that white man, leaving us in our cage, not looking back. Here you are now, driven in a carriage and wearing those foolish clothes. The man who holds me here is in fear of you, despite his noisy words. How did you come to have such power, Osei? Who else have you abandoned or betrayed?'

174

The back door opens. Kingfisher slips a hand under the girl's arm. He half expects her to jerk away, but she allows herself to be helped up without protest. The client is halfway across the yard with a purse dangling from his fingers. When he sees them an oily grin slides across his mouth. 'Like the look of that one, do you? She's not much of a belly warmer, I can testify.'

'Give her to me and your debt is settled.'

The client laughs. 'Want one of your own do you, blackie? Then take her by all means. Like the rest of your breed she's of scant use to me.'

Leonardo drives them back to the House. If he has any thoughts on the matter he keeps them to himself. Kingfisher smuggles the girl up to his chambers, wraps her in the coverlet from his bed and feeds her the cold supper that is waiting for him. She gives the thanks her father taught her to and says nothing more, watching him with those moon-pool eyes while she eats.

'You will stay in here for now,' he tells her. 'I shall talk to my mistress. A place may be found here for you.'

'So I am still a slave then, Osei? As are you?'

'Every village has its chief, even in this cold-lashed land. It is a blessing that some are kinder than others.'

'My family calls to me. I want to go home.'

'So do I, little one. So do I.'

She sleeps with him in his bed and, whatever she expects, he doesn't touch her. Next morning he collects the breakfast tray and smuggles a little extra. Later, in the kitchen, a commotion outside draws everyone to the window.

'Looks like the Sisters are punishing one of their own,' Cook says. 'It's that new girl.'

Along with the maids, Kingfisher watches the events in silence. When the yard has emptied he goes out to the stables. He studies the shivering girl perched on a stool before the stove, horse blanket wrapped around her shoulders.

'You are making a pretty mess of the tack-room floor,' he observes.

'Pardon me, but it was your friend Leonardo who dunked me in the trough.'

Kingfisher nods. 'Better water than horseshit.'

'Don't pretend to care, darkie. I didn't cry. Not a tear. Nor would I if my hand had been cut off.'

'You are not very civil in your tongue, English girl, no matter what table manners they might have taught you.'

She doesn't appear to know what to say to that. They look at each other for a moment. He doubts he can stare her down. She seems ready to wait until next winter before moving that hard gaze. Fingers run across her shorn head.

'I always had pretty hair,' she mutters. 'I doubt it will ever grow back the same.'

'That may be, but do not complain to me. I am forced to wear these rancid wigs. My scalp feels as if angry insects have bitten it. The cologne makes me sneeze and the food turns my stomach.'

'Look, Kingfisher, I—'

'Kingfisher is not my name. It is something I was made to take, trained to answer to as if I were a dog. If I spoke it in the forest the trees would not hear. It has no meaning.'

'You don't like it here?'

He glances out the window. 'It is nearly always raining, and cold. Clouds never seem to lift from the rooftops, and there is no friendliness in the wind. Even the birds have nothing to say, and your horses are stupid. They do not think for themselves because you bind them in saddles and harnesses, and make them pull huge wooden tombs crammed with noisy people. Their spirits are chained, like your women are chained. In my tribe old men died with a full set of teeth. Here, even children's mouths are rotten.'

'Well, it's better than being a savage.'

'What exactly do you believe?' Kingfisher faces her. 'That we eat babies fresh from the womb? That we garnish our food with their brains and slaughter their mothers to appease some form of animal god? Yet you murdered us by the hundred, perhaps the thousand. You are the interloper in our country: the savage, the barbarian. Your god is foreign and pagan in our eyes. Our land, the ground on which we lived and died and worshipped for generations, has become your killing ground. Now your blood has mingled with the blood of our ancestors and poisoned it.'

He rolls up his sleeve. 'See this bracelet? It is beautiful, is it not? Yet the slavers did not deem it worth stealing. No cold gems or dead metals went into its making. It is fashioned from a piece of my wife's hair and decorated with bones. You look disgusted, but she spent hours crafting it to perfection. She was clean. She washed herself every day. She did not smell of stale sweat or foul breath. Lice did not plague her hair the way they infest people here. Even the wigs on your heads are plastered with animal fat. You hunt deer for sport instead of for food. Everyone is a savage.'

He remembers coming into the city with Crabbe and the Fixer, the baby a bundle in his arms. The place thronged with traffic. Little black carriage boys in sparkling feathery turbans clung to the backs of their masters' coaches as if their palms had been nailed to the panelling. Buildings, larger than any he'd seen before, crowded around one another. He stared until his eyes hurt with the sight of it.

'What is that smell? It is like a rotting food,' he'd asked.

'That there's the city, you heathen monkey,' Crabbe said.

'It stinks of burned wood and dead things.'

'More life there than among your tree trunks, I'll wager.'

'People should not live like this.'

'Preacher now, are you?'

From boyhood, Kingfisher could run silent and unseen through the trees. The city is just another forest, teeming with life and death. He learned that during his first month at the House and had used it to his advantage since.

'You and I are the same,' he tells Beth. 'We were both captives. We are both captives still. I came from a slave pen, you from a madhouse. As I've been obliged to tell someone already, some prisons are worse than others. Make the best of this one.'

An Unusual Assignment

'You were all a part of it. Every one of you. Eloise sent me down to the washhouse on purpose.'

Hummingbird sits on the bed, wads of linen spreading her toes. She attacks the nails with a pair of scissors. 'You'd better come in, Kitten,' she says, blades going *snip-snip*. 'It won't do to yell in the corridor.'

Beth throws her ruined day gown onto the chair and slams the door behind her. 'Don't even pretend you don't know what I'm talking about. For all I know you might have been there, hiding your face behind one of those masks. I could've choked to death.'

Snip. 'Perhaps next time you'll think twice about snitching on one of the girls.'

'Don't talk of it so lightly. I have bruises.'

'Moth got a hot hand.'

'And what's that exactly? A rap across the knuckles? A smack on the fingers with a leather belt? If so, she deserves it for thieving.'

'She was branded.'

Beth's mouth closed. Opened. Formed a word. 'Branded? You mean *burned*?'

'Do you know what it's like to have a hot iron pressed against your skin? You can hear it sizzle like bacon on a skillet.'

'She suffered that for a tuppeny length of ribbon?'

'Theft cannot be tolerated. Who would dare admit a Masque into their home if she might lift the silver? Besides, the Abbess didn't burn her so much for filching that ribbon as for disobeying me. In the House, discipline is everything. I was willing to forgive her because Moth is impulsive and was maltreated as a child. Usually we fetch a cane across the rump for breaking minor rules but the Abbess wanted to make an example. She's mother to all of us, Kitten, but she doesn't spare the rod. Or the brand. Your bruises will disappear, and that's more than can be said for Moth's little memento.'

Beth stares at the rug. 'I never thought—'

'No, you didn't.' Hummingbird tosses the scissors onto her bedside table, plucks the wads from between her toes and swings her legs off the bed. 'You'd best get that soiled gown back to the washhouse.'

'How can I face anyone? How can I sit in that dining room with everybody watching me? Or go to the parlour, or even look Eloise in the eye again?'

'The Sisters have already punished you. No one will stare. No one will mention it. What's done is forgotten. Just remember to keep your tongue still in future.'

Bethany faces another surprise when the Fixer sends for her. She meets him in the Mirror Room where he's clad in satin jacket, breeches and hose. A white wig is perched on his usually bald head, fastened at the back with a black ribbon the size of two spread hands. He seems at ease in this dandy's garb.

'Dance,' he says. 'A gavotte first, then we'll try you with a few couplets. I need to examine your style. You can dance, can't you?'

'Yes.' Beth smooths her fresh day gown. 'No music?'

'I can't conjure an orchestra out of the floorboards. Don't worry, I'll mark the time. Give me your hand. Now, one . . . two . . . three . . .' Up and down they go, feet whispering on the oak floor. 'A little less stiffness in your legs. That's right, work with me, don't fight.'

They move. Turn. Move again. 'You are too stiff. You're not fumbling with a wheelwright at some country harvest festival. At least try to feign interest. Grip my hand properly, don't let your fingers go flabby. And look at me, find a smile even if you have to imagine you're gazing at someone else – a sweetheart or old beau. This can't be the first time you've danced with a man.'

Every touch, every brush of the Fixer's body digs a shiver out of her belly. In the great ballroom at Russell Hall, Lord Russell had held her so close their breath mingled. His face was slick with smiles, her nostrils full of his thick, spicy cologne. His eyes on hers. She looking *at* them but not daring to look *into* them. He'd had one of his footmen, a musician by a previous trade, tinkle a melody out of the spinet. His face was impassive enough but Beth knew she'd catch hell from the servants later. Getting above her station. Getting improper notions into her head. Getting this. Getting that. And the housekeeper asking, 'Why should the squire give you favours, a while-away-the-hours village girl?'

Lord Russell moved with her, and did not complain about her sluggish limbs. 'You dance like a princess,' he said, and they'd both laughed at the lie.

'But what if your son should catch us?' Beth said, not really caring whether he did or not.

'Oh, I think he should wish to dance with you himself.'

The Fixer keeps walking and turning her. Nothing Beth does meets with his approval. She trips, stumbles, treads on his toes, turns left when she ought to turn right. He works her until both feet hurt.

'How do you know how to do this?' she asks. 'Aren't you just a tradesman?'

His lips thin. 'A tradesman, yes. Once I thought I was more than that.'

Finally he instructs her to sit beside the potion table. He fetches a stool and sits opposite. Any notion Beth might have that the hard work is over is soon dispelled.

'At dinner your client will generally have a great deal to say,' the Fixer explains. 'Such people can't resist talking about themselves. Let him order the food. If it's something you can't stomach then push it around your plate. He'll be too interested in your face and the sound of his own voice to notice.'

'How do I meet these fellows? Will Leonardo drive me?'

'With established, reputable clients a coach will arrive to collect you. At other times you'll be driven to an Assignment in one of our own carriages. When a client has no specific Masque in mind, he'll come directly to the House and choose. On those nights we have a Parade. The Abbess will instruct you in that later.'

Afterwards he takes a piebald mare out of the stables and perches Beth on the saddle. Walking around the horse he checks her poise, her grip on the reins. 'Not too bad. Your skills are unlikely to be stretched beyond a canter round the park.'

When Beth finally drags her feet up the stairs to her bedchamber, Hummingbird is already snoring. Beth crawls in beside her, blows out the candle and is asleep within moments.

A quiet dining room confronts Beth the next morning. Moth is already seated, eyes studiously examining the table top. Throughout breakfast the two women avoid looking at one another, although it seems Moth makes no attempt to hide her bandaged hand.

Despite Beth's fears, there are no whispers, nudging or sidelong glances from the Masques' tables. Hummingbird receives an Assignment then, surprisingly, is called to the head of the table a second time, where she collects a scroll bound with a pink ribbon instead of the customary red. After breakfast, Hummingbird waits until the other girls have filed out of the dining room then drops the scroll into Beth's palm.

'Congratulations, Kitten, your first Assignment.'

Beth regards the roll of white paper with its sliver of ribbon.

'Don't look as if I've handed you a snake,' Hummingbird laughs.

'But . . . I'm not a Masque.'

'We're all Sisters of the House. Do this and you'll be on your way to earning an Emblem.'

'Shall I open it here?'

'Best take it upstairs.'

'Do you know what's in it?'

Hummingbird grins. 'I might.'

They scamper up to their room. Hummingbird pulls the curtains wider then pokes life back into the small fire. Beth's hands are shaking as she tugs the ribbon loose and unfurls the paper. 'One of the clock, Charlotte Street. House driver,' she reads.

'Well done, Kitten. You've drawn Mother Joan, and I'm to go with you. An easy job. Two hours at most. Perhaps half that.'

'Mother Joan? Is that a nun?'

Hummingbird's face nearly folds in on itself. 'No, not a nun. By a cully's breeches that would certainly be something. It's only a nickname, though don't ever say it in front of her. You'll discover soon enough why she's earned that title.'

'How shall we get there?'

'Kingfisher is taking us.'

'I didn't know he worked as a common coachman.'

'This is your first Assignment. The Abbess wants it to go well. And don't let Leonardo ever catch you calling him "common".'

'When does Moth get her first Assignment?'

'Moth will probably be sent out with Red Orchid within the next week. She hasn't progressed as quickly as you. She needs . . . more work.'

'What is it I have to do with this Mother Joan person?'

'I'll tell you,' Hummingbird says. 'On the way.'

The Fixer steals Beth for the rest of the morning. He reviews her etiquette, then bids her read passages from a book of verse. 'Only a formality,' he explains. 'I'm in no doubt you know your letters.'

It's a little past noon when Hummingbird joins her in their bedchamber. 'Time to go, Kitten. Excited?'

'Nervous.'

'Nothing amiss with that. Come on, Kingfisher is bringing the coach around.'

'Don't we have to go to the dressing room?'

'Keep your day gown. You'll find out why when we arrive.'

'Mother Joan's husband is a politician,' Hummingbird says as the carriage rattles out of Crown Square. 'He holds an important position in government.'

'I'm not well versed in politics.'

'I suppose not. What could you know about the workings of Parliament, living out in the meadows as you did?'

'My papa read newspapers.'

'You can read all your life and still not know what the roosters in that particular coop are up to. Mother Joan's husband already has them squawking, so I'm told. I love it when things get stirred up. 'Tis good business for us.'

'How?'

'As the Abbess may have explained, men need the calm of a soft voice, the comfort of a pretty face. Every political storm brings them yowling to our door. Most of these fellows should never have left their mothers.'

Beth gazes at the passing buildings. She meshes her fingers together. 'Where are we going? What will happen when we arrive?'

'Our destination is a family house on the outskirts of town. Constance, the maid, will likely answer the door. If so, follow her into the parlour on the left side of the hall. Put on whatever clothes she hands you. If the fit isn't right you'll have to make the best of it.'

'What exactly is this Assignment? The scroll didn't say much.'

'No need to. It's always the same. You sit, smile, drink tea and eat whatever Mother Joan puts in front of you. Cakes usually. She bakes them herself and they lie in your stomach like charred bricks, but no one's died yet. When she talks to you keep smiling and agree with everything she says. Whatever you do don't react if she calls me Polly. You'll get a name too, but we won't know what that is until she greets us. Just be sure not to forget it.'

'I don't understand. Why does she call you Polly?'

'It's her daughter's name.'

'Where is she?'

'Fell under the wheels of a carriage. Must be about, oh, eight years ago now.'

'You're going to pretend to be her dead daughter? That's foul.'

'Not exactly. Mother Joan has accepted her daughter's loss. However, she likes to imagine how it would be if Polly had grown up, what sort of society she would keep. The grief hasn't ever let go, but doing this helps keep it locked away for a while. The House offers all kinds of services for all manner of people, Kitten.'

'And who am I supposed to be?'

'One of Polly's friends. It changes with every visit. We've all taken turns. You don't have to be an actress of any talent. Just look on it as a sort of tea party.'

Their arrival is exactly as Hummingbird described. The maid takes them into the parlour and provides garments from a trunk almost big enough to live in. Most of these are over-laced fancies. The hem of Beth's gown barely reaches her ankle. 'The waist is too tight,' she complains. 'I can't breathe.'

'No gowns, no tea, and likely no fee,' Hummingbird warns.

The door opens. A tall, elegantly garbed woman stands framed against the hall. She has skin the colour of fine paper left in the sun and turned by its warm fingers into the deepening tints of autumn.

'Polly, darling.' Her bright eyes turn to Bethany. 'And this, why, this must be Alice.'

'Um . . . yes,' says Beth.

'Well, you both must come through to the withdrawing room. Constance has laid out a tray of cakes.'

She leads the way across the hall to a spacious, well-lit room draped in lemon-coloured fabrics. A settee as big as a double bed sits in front of a gilded hearth. The fireplace is full of dried flowers.

'Sit down, dears.'

Hummingbird settles on the end of the settee; Beth takes the place beside her. The dress immediately rides up to her knees but Mother Joan seems not to notice. She seats herself in an armchair on the opposite side of a laden coffee table and offers both girls a sweetmeat. Dominating the wall above the mantel is a portrait of a staid-faced gentleman in a flowing periwig of the sort a magistrate might wear. Beth supposes this is the important husband.

Treats given out, Mother Joan starts to talk. She talks about her day in the park, about the blooms she bought from a flower seller, about the ducks on the lake and how they seem in danger of being poached by beggars. 'Fewer and fewer eggs each year,' she declares. 'A scandal, but the constable does nothing.'

Hummingbird sighs and shakes her head at appropriate intervals while Beth forces a smile whenever Mother Joan's eyes settle on her. The maid brings fresh tea. Mother Joan shoos her away and pours. Beth has never felt so foolish in her life, but she eats the cake, drinks the tea and keeps her mouth shut because, despite herself, her heart aches for this silly, twittering woman.

'So,' their host rubs her hands together, 'tell me how you have spent the morning.'

Hummingbird spouts some fanciful story about how she and 'Alice' sat on the riverbank to sketch the skiffs on the water. Mother Joan nods as if her neck is on iron hinges. 'Oh, but, dear, you know it's dangerous to go down by the river. The current can be strong, and there are lots of unsavoury types who skulk about the towpath, hoping to cut the purse from some unsuspecting victim.'

Hummingbird nods in return and says, 'Yes, but Alice was with me the whole time and we never strayed far from the watchman's hut. Besides it was such a *lovely* day.'

'I daresay. A young lady has to go out and take the air, even in the city. What are you looking at, Alice, dear?'

'Oh,' Beth spills tea onto her napkin. 'I was just . . . thinking you have lovely curtains.'

The older woman smiles. 'Very gracious of you to say so.'

And so it goes on. As the mantel clock ticks off the hour, Constance returns to clear the tea things away. A distant, distracted look settles in Mother Joan's eyes.

'Go into the parlour and enjoy a game of chequers,' she says. 'Polly, you know where the board is. I can never find it. I enjoyed meeting you, Alice. I hope Polly brings you to visit again soon.'

Back in the parlour, Hummingbird starts undressing.

'Aren't we going to play chequers?' Beth asks.

'We're not playing anything. This is her way of saying goodbye. It allows us to slip out without any awkward farewells. Mother Joan plays a clever game but she's not stupid. She knows she can only fool herself for so long. We have to depart before the cracks begin to show. Change quickly, then we'll leave.'

'Good job, Kitten,' Hummingbird says on the way home. 'You did well, though I had to fight to keep my composure when you told Mother Joan how nice her curtains were. The Abbess will be delighted.'

Beth grimaced. 'Mostly I sat and smiled. I barely understood what she was talking about half the time.'

'But she's gone sweet on you. I saw it on her face. Don't be surprised if she asks for you again.'

'I hope not. It was terrible. I felt like some sort of ghost and that dress kept hitching up my legs. It smelled too. Of dust and dead moths. Almost as if Polly had been buried in it.'

'Perhaps Mother Joan dug it back up.'

'Don't laugh. How horrible for that sad old woman to have to play games like that. If her husband's as important as you say he is then he should know better than to encourage her in such a farce.'

'It was her husband's idea to begin with, and it saved her life, Kitten. Mother Joan was wasting away. Wouldn't eat, was up all night, refused to let the maid light the fire in the parlour. Old Slocombe tried everything. Spent a fortune on London quacks who bled her and charged two guineas for the privilege. Every queer potion an apothecary could concoct went down his wife's throat. In the end he tried seers and Wise Women. As his purse got lighter so did Joan Slocombe. Shrank to a stick.'

'So what happened?'

'He persuaded her to go out for a walk in the hope fresh air would put colour back in her cheeks. She hadn't left the house since Polly died, wouldn't even allow the curtains to be drawn. Mr Slocombe was overjoyed at this little victory. And out there, on a blustery autumn day tripping out of the door of a hat shop, was a girl who looked like Polly.'

Hummingbird adjusts one of her sleeves. 'Not exactly like her, of course. Grief was killing Mother Joan but it hadn't dulled her wits. The similarity was enough. According to her husband, the light returned to her eyes. Her steps picked up and she started talking in more than a whisper for the first time in weeks. At home she ate a pot of soup and half a round of bread. That's when Mr Slocombe had his notion.'

'You know a lot about it, Hummingbird.'

She shrugs. 'He called at the House, and we brought their daughter back to life. It's no secret among the Sisters. Ah, here we are. If Eloise doesn't gripe too much I'll get her to bring a tub up to the room and we can both bathe. Then the Abbess will likely want to see you. This has proved a big day for you, Kitten, and bigger ones lie ahead.'

A Matter of Some Importance

Bethany Harris never forgot George's threat. And she would not be silent. After an entire day locked in her bedchamber she was summoned to Lord Russell's reception room. She stared at the floor and dipped a curtsey. How different it had been when she had last met her employer, her *lover*, in here.

'You have brought an accusation against my son,' he said without turning from the window.

Beth swallowed. 'M'lord.'

'You are aware of the consequences this could have for my family? For the village?'

'I can imagine some of them, m'lord.'

He stepped away from the glass. 'No, you cannot imagine the half of it. George has a future in Parliament, Miss Harris. He could do a great deal for this country. Would you see that brought to ruin?'

Beth studied his face. It was entirely without tenderness. Nothing of the man who had danced with her, coloured her flesh with his paints and whispered beautiful things in her ear was there. She bowed her head. 'His character has a twist – something dark and deeply rooted. He believes he can take his pleasure from people the way he might pluck a sweetmeat out of a bowl. I was engaged to look after the children, not service his desires.'

'My son is a man of passion. In that respect we are alike, though it is true he is possessed of an exuberance that can sometimes prove difficult to contain. Nothing has been denied him in life, consequently he is accustomed to getting his way. In politics such attributes are to be admired.'

'He attacked me.'

'Come now. That is a severe word to use. You must have encouraged him.'

'I did no such thing.'

'Local maids would throw themselves at my son just to win a smile.'

'His attentions weren't welcome.'

'You still insist I involve the magistrate?'

'Yes.'

'Were this to go no further than these walls, the situation could be dealt with compassionately.'

'I have to think of the children.'

'Ah yes, the children.' He returned to staring out of the window. 'Go home, Miss Harris. I shall send a message ahead to your father. Stay there until I have dealt with the matter.'

When Beth walked into the family parlour her mother cracked her across the cheek with the back of her hand. 'Where did you learn to spit such poison? What is it you can possibly want, Bethany? Haven't the Russells – haven't we – given you enough? How can I go to church? How can I face anyone? Who else have you lied to?'

And so it went on. Mother castigating her for trying to get attention by telling vile fibs, for most likely whoring with a tinker or gypsy, and if she got roughed about it was her own fault for everyone knew what she was like. When Beth tried yet again to explain, Mother pushed her across the kitchen yelling 'Liar, liar, liar' until the words fell into one another, becoming a continuous howl.

Speechless, Beth fled the house, nursing her stinging cheek. A stroll down the lane to the village would clear her head. Outside the churchyard something hard hit her on the temple. A flash of pain turned the world red. Through a haze she saw village children running through the trees that bordered the lane. Dazed, Beth stared at the chip of flint that had struck her. She dabbed her head with her fingers and was relieved to find no blood. Giving up all hope of visiting the village, Beth did the only thing she could and returned home. Her parents were in the kitchen, seated at the dinner table. Mother's face was pale and puffy.

'You used to walk to and from the Hall with your head up,' Mother said. 'Now you skulk around like a thief. You'll bring disaster upon us.'

'I can't change what's happened,' Beth said.

'None of us are blind, daughter. We'll all suffer if you're cast out of the Hall.'

Next day Jane Harris, who believed that shame alone could purge sins, peeled off one of her woollen stockings, tied a knot in the centre and looped it around her thin, white throat. Pulling a stool over to the centre of the kitchen, she climbed up and fastened the other end to the chain supporting the brass candleholder. Satisfied that everything would support her weight, she clasped her narrow hands behind her waist and stepped towards eternity.

Jane's sense of penitence was ruined, however, when an errand brought Father home. He leapt at his wife's dangling legs and hoisted her up while she flapped about like a fish on a riverbank. 'Beth,' he yelled. 'Beth, come here now.'

Finally, desperation gave him the wings and strength of an angel. He hurled himself into the air and ripped the makeshift noose from the candleholder. Husband and wife collapsed in a heap on the rug. Father held her head between his hands and whispered things that had remained unuttered since their courting days. That's what he told Beth later.

Bethany knew her mother wouldn't die. The look in Father's eyes said he wouldn't let her die. He smiled and cooed like a youth, coaxing the will to live back into his wife. Beth slipped out of the house with the silence of a ghost and spent the rest of the afternoon yanking weeds and flowers alike out of the garden, ignorant of the dirt blackening her hands.

That evening she crept into Mother's bedchamber, struggling to find a tender phrase. She reached out to the figure in the bed, but Mother turned her face to the wall. 'How dare you do such a thing,' she said, voice coarse from the noose. '*I taught you*. Now you've shamed us and made a fool of yourself. You didn't listen to me. You learned *nothing*.'

Next morning Beth stepped into an empty kitchen and sat in front of a fire half choked on ashes. The night had yielded neither sleep nor comfort, though no sounds seeped through the lath and plaster wall separating her from her parents' room. She supposed Mother was still in bed, that Father thought she was no longer a risk to herself. The remains of a poultice littered the kitchen table. Perhaps, worried for her throat, he had thought it inadequate and gone to fetch a surgeon, though the local quack couldn't thread a needle let alone tend to injuries with any certainty.

So Beth sat there, feeling useless, as the last of the embers collapsed. Eventually the lack of movement from upstairs proved too much for her nerves and she dared a peek into Mother's room. The bed was rumpled but empty.

Back in the kitchen she tried a taste of milk, but either time or the weather had soured it, and she spat it into the slop pail. *You'd never catch one of George's society ladies doing that*, she thought.

The sky was turning into a cloudy patchwork when a coach and four pulled up at the gate. Beth ran out to meet it, wondering if it was news from Russell Hall. However, this wasn't the polished walnut panels of Lord Russell's private chaise, but a stout construction of weathered oak.

Her father stepped out and held the door open. He explained that she was being sent away. A lodging house in Pendleton would take her in. What chattels she owned would be sent on later.

'Are you putting me into hiding?' Beth asked.

'Look on it as an adventure,' Father said. 'For your own benefit until all this blows over.'

'Where's Mama?'

'At the apothecary.' Father's smile was brittle as dry mortar. 'My healing skills aren't so polished it seems.'

'I shan't see her?'

'It's not as if you're gone for good.'

'Will the children be told? Julia and Sebastian?'

'Best you forget them for now, lass.' A hand on Beth's waist guided her up the step and into the gloom. The door slammed. No kiss. No goodbye. Fumbling in the dark, Beth discovered locked wooden shutters instead of blinds. She ran her hand over the inside of the door. No handle. She pushed hard. It wouldn't budge.

The carriage lurched forward.

She scrabbled at the wood panelling. Nothing. She smacked her fists against the shutters and screamed. The coach's pace didn't slacken. After a few hopeless miles she pressed her hands to her face, voice spent, nails broken. In the near silence, she realised she was not alone. In the opposite corner a big man sat watching her, a cropped white wig perched on top of his turnip head. He didn't move or speak. Cracks in the shutters threw thin bars of light across his small blurry eyes.

'Who are you?' Beth demanded.

'You can call me Friend,' he said.

Anxiety boiled in the well of Beth's stomach as the extent of her father's deceit struck her. She fell back, exhausted, against the seat. *It's only until everything calms down*, she thought. *Papa wouldn't do anything really bad. Not to me. Lord Russell wouldn't allow it.*

Some hours later the carriage halted. The driver climbed down and unbolted the door. An oblong house squatted amidst gardens in the middle of woodland. Beth took in the cream walls, scissor-cut lawns and prim beds of red and yellow roses.

'Have I come here to die?' she asked.

Friend was at her shoulder. 'Maybe. Maybe not.'

'What is this place?'

'A Comfort Home. A dainty hideaway for families too squeamish to have their loved ones committed to the madhouse. Too many ears in Bedlam, too many people who might be interested in even a madwoman's outpourings. So I take care of them instead.'

'I haven't taken leave of my wits.'

He leaned forward until his breath tickled her ear. 'Almost ruined it for your family, you did. Your papa could have lost his job and his house. Why couldn't you take a tupping and keep your mouth shut?'

He pushed her inside. Through a door off the main passage lay a square, bare-walled room. A wooden bed frame hugged one corner. No dresser, no pitcher or washbowl. Friend caught her expression.

'You aren't here for comfort, my girl. You're here to learn penitence.'

Courage

'Obedience,' the Abbess says, lacing her fingers together on top of the desk, 'is the most important quality I demand from my Masques. Without it the House would lose cohesion. This is a very narrow ledge we walk along and the fall, should we slip, would be both long and hard. Many of our girls are headstrong; most have experienced difficult circumstances. Loyalty to each other as well as to me is a prime concern.'

She leans back, candlelight flickering across her coloured patches. Kingfisher stands immobile beside her, a silver wig forming a halo in the subdued lighting of the Scarlet Parlour. His attention never leaves Beth as the Abbess talks. A scattering of candles send shadowy half-ghosts flitting across the drapes. Outside, a dense, muggy night presses against the walls.

'The Fixer tells me you can now accept simple Assignments within city society. Hummingbird, too, has been loud in her praise concerning your behaviour during your trial. Becoming a Masque, however, demands more than an ability to dance or eat a certain dish with the proper utensil. A final step is required, an act of boldness tempered with dignity. Are you ready for that?'

Beth dips a curtsey. 'I hope so, Abbess.'

'You hope so, do you? Well, so do I.' The Abbess removes an object from under the desk and places it in front of her. A large ornamental jar, the glass shaped into flower patterns and secured at the top with a cork lid. At first Beth thinks it's empty but, no, something is moving inside. She scrunches her eyes to get a better look.

'Come closer,' the Abbess instructs.

Beth's nose is a whisker away from the glass. The thing inside hovers then alights on the wall of the jar.

Beth recoils. A wasp.

It's a wasp.

With summer drawing to a blustery close she thought they'd died out. The thing in the container, magnified by the curved glass, is a yellow-and-black monster. She imagines its sting, sharp as a pin and dripping with venom.

'Put your hand inside,' the Abbess says.

'No. *No.*'

'Do it. Face your terror. Touch it, feel it sting.'

Beth backs up a pace. She bumps into Kingfisher, who's moved from the desk to stand behind her.

'Must you remain a mewling Kitten?' the Abbess continues, holding out the jar. 'Perhaps you would like to return to the Comfort Home, be locked up like a beast? Women are either slaves or predators. Which are you? There is no half way. Kingfisher secured your release; a word can put you back. By suppertime you will be forgotten.'

Her voice drops to a whisper. 'You're sweating, Kitten. Your first instinct is to recoil. All you can see in your mind is that sting piercing your flesh, filling your veins with poison. Look again, harder this time. An insect. Hardly bigger than a fly. You could squeeze it between your thumb and forefinger – crush the life out of it with a single twitch of your hand. So tell me, who is the stronger? Everything you fear is inside that jar.'

The Abbess removes the lid. Beth feels as if the entire House will collapse in on her. She remembers George Russell, face cut with fury, threatening to deny her the children. And just days later, Friend plucking at her soiled bodice. She thrusts her hand into the jar, whimpering as the wasp crawls over her fingers, its legs blunt needles against her flesh.

'Don't kill it,' the Abbess warns. 'Only a child lashes out without control.'

Beth can't prevent tremors rippling through her hand. The insect stings once, twice. Fiery agony. Her eyes blur with tears. She becomes aware that she's shaking her head like a simpleton throwing a fit.

Please . . .

She falls backwards. Kingfisher's big arms catch her. She's carried to a divan tucked into the stairwell where he sits her down and pushes her head onto her knees. A minute, and the nausea passes. He releases her and Beth leans back, gasping. A fingertip rubs ointment into the stings.

The Abbess stands above her, the jar in her hands, the lid replaced. 'Your name is no longer Bethany,' she explains. 'It is Wasp. Do you understand? Everything you were has gone.'

'My name is Wasp.'

'You have done well, daughter, but you are only halfway through the door. You may have a moment before the next step, then you must go to the room of mirrors where the Fixer awaits you.'

'What new hell is this?'

'Not hell, daughter. A rebirth.'

Kingfisher escorts her through the curtain and along the passage, his hand resting on her arm. She knows the route so well now, could close her eyes and pace out the distance, the hem of her day gown *swish-swishing* on the thick carpet. The Fixer is ready for her, as always, with his chair and his small folding table, a hundred reflections of a hundred bald men like an approaching army. In his hand is a glittering needle. Pots of coloured ink cluster in a semi-circle on the tabletop.

'Sit down,' he says. 'I'll give you a drop of laudanum to help soothe you.'

'What are you going to do?'

'You are to receive your Emblem. No paper patch now. It's time to grow up.'

Wasp drinks from the cup he gives her. He's mixed the drug with fruit juice and it slips down her throat. Kingfisher nods at the Fixer and leaves the room.

'Now,' the Fixer says, leaning over her, 'this will hurt, but you're a brave girl. Keep as still as you can. I've done this many times before.'

Wasp thinks herself hardened to discomfort but whimpers when he presses the needle into her cheek. It's like the insect sting pricking her flesh again and again. Her instincts scream at her to push him off. Instead she locks her hands behind the chair's back rest. Pain flares then melts to a heavy numbness which spreads across her face.

The Fixer pauses to dab her eyes. A brief respite before he dips the needle back into the inkpots. Yellow and black. A contrast to Hummingbird and her rainbow-winged Emblem.

'Nearly done,' the Fixer whispers. 'A moment or two more. There.' He wipes the needle on a cloth and slips it into a pouch. 'No, don't touch. I'll apply a light dressing. Your cheek might ache for a while but keep your fingers off.'

'Can I see it?'

He gestures. 'Mirrors all around.'

'I don't think I can stand.'

The Fixer chuckles. 'Laudanum knocked the bones out of your legs? Here.' He passes her a hand mirror. She holds it up to her face. There, in tiny perfection, is a picture of a wasp, its wings spread, back arched down, sting a dagger thrusting out of the tail.

A whisper of oiled hinges. Feet take measured steps across the floorboards. The Abbess's voice: 'That Emblem is for life, Wasp, never to come off unless I decide otherwise. It binds you to me and to your Sisters. Once you feel recovered come to the Scarlet Parlour. The other Masques are waiting to embrace you.'

With the Abbess at her side Wasp stumbles back up the long passage and into the hallway. The door to the Scarlet Parlour lies open and candles set on tall iron stands flicker beyond. Stepping through, a rush of warmth envelops her. She resists the urge to touch the dressing over the still raw tattoo. Her Emblem. A wasp.

A twitch of a curtain. Figures drift like white, wingless angels around the furniture. The Abbess's voice punctures the silence. 'Masques, this is Wasp. Welcome your new Sister.'

Each girl steps up, embraces Wasp and places a soft kiss below her Emblem. Each press of those lips is devoid of either warmth or malevolence. Simply a gesture, an elementary initiation into the fold.

The Masque at the end of the line, a tall woman in a gold-trimmed gown, locks her in cold arms and places a kiss as bitter as winter on her face. Through those chilled lips, teeth nip Wasp's skin. She pulls away in surprise. Eyes, brittle as icicles, stab her from beneath corn-gold hair. Two Emblems puncture her cheeks. One a pattern of red and white diamonds, the other a bird.

A nightingale.

In the general hustle of House life Wasp has mostly forgotten about the Harlequin. She seldom attends breakfast and it has been some time since she last haunted the corridors. Wasp watches as she rejoins the line.

You don't frighten me, she thinks. *I shan't let you.*

And then she is once more alone with the Abbess. The older woman curls her arm around Wasp's waist and draws her into her bony arms. 'Welcome, daughter,' she whispers.

A hot bath awaits Wasp in her bedchamber. She flings her clothes onto the bed and slips into the water, appreciating the soothing warmth. Afterwards, she rubs herself briskly with a towel, lights the bedside candle with a taper from the hearth and climbs between the sheets. She's still awake when Hummingbird arrives.

'Hello, Sister.'

'Sister?'

'Kitten is gone. You have a new life. You've grown up.'

The world buzzes around Wasp's head in shades of yellow and black. 'Why weren't you at my initiation?'

'I couldn't get back from my Assignment in time.'

'Someone snitched on me.'

'What do you mean?'

'The Abbess had a wasp. A wasp in a jar. I had to put my hand inside. Someone must have told her how much I hate them. My fingers are all swollen.'

'I doubt it was much of a secret, Sister. We've all noticed how you flinch at the mention of one. Sometimes our fears are written all over our faces.'

'Nightingale bit me.' Wasp prods the tender flesh.

Hummingbird bends to take a closer look. 'I thought she might pull a trick like that. Nightingale is still the Abbess's best Masque, but this doesn't stop her intimidating the other girls. I've heard she even bleeds herself to keep a pale complexion like the ladies of the Royal Court a century ago. Her tactics are well known. Don't let her bully you.'

'She seems to hold a particular grudge against me.'

'Nightingale will hook her nails into anyone who neglects to pay her the attention she believes she deserves. Take it as a compliment. A newcomer rarely finds herself so favoured.'

A sombre morning sky breaks up into patches of blue. Facing the mirror, Wasp peels off the dressing the Fixer applied the night before and feels the scab with the tip of her finger. Thanks to the laudanum she slept reasonably well and now there's no pain to speak of.

'Doesn't look very fetching,' she remarks.

Hummingbird splashes water from the basin onto her face and pats both cheeks with a towel. 'The dead skin will be gone within a week. You'll get a paper one to cover it in the meantime. Not one of those monstrosities you've had to wear up 'til now but a proper one, nicely cut and drawn. We've a Sister who's good at that sort of thing. She painted in watercolours before poisoning her local magistrate.'

Wasp turns away from the mirror. 'Why would she do such a thing?'

'Do what? Paint, or poison the magistrate?'

'Don't play games, *Sister*.'

'Oh Wasp, if only you could see your face. 'Tis absolutely priceless. I'm sorry, but you are so easy to tease. Now if you're finished preening I want to go and breakfast. A busy morning lies ahead.'

'Cleaning hearths, I suppose?'

'Your days of sticking your head into sooty fireplaces are over. Eloise will get someone else to help bag up her ashes. For you the real work is about to start. Not today though. Today you'll join me in the dressing room sampling as many gowns and bonnets as you like, and afterwards we'll take a coach ride around the park. We need to see what suits. Each of us is different. A girl can look a sow in a gown that turns another into a princess. The joy is in finding out.'

'What about the dress I wore to the coffee shop?'

She grins. 'That was merely skimming the top of the water. I'm sure we can do better. Have you seen yourself lately, Wasp? I mean really *looked*, not just peeked into a mirror? You've become quite the rosy apple and I unashamedly hate you for it. Now will you come to breakfast and allow that lovely waist to gain even more curves?'

Wasp nods. 'I have appetite enough to eat my shoes.'

'Good. No Kittens' table for you. No more oak trenchers and wooden knives. Now it's silver cutlery and a proper chair. Only the best. The Abbess always insists on it. Those wasp stings bought more than you bargained for.'

Dining at the top tables proves a whole new experience. Conversation ripples around the room. Wasp watches the busy hands of her new Sisters. A few wear gloves: white, pink, kid leather or satin. What secrets did they hide? Nightingale's hands are encased in embroidered velvet that stretches to her elbows. She concentrates on her food, her forehead pinched.

If she glances up and catches me staring at her I shan't look away, Wasp promises herself.

Despite her training, the metal cutlery feels oddly heavy in her hands, and the crockery is so delicate she fears it might crack if she breathes on it. Everything is perfect. The napkin rings, the condiment holders, even the tiny cherubs decorating the rim of her tea dish. The steamed fish is manna on her tongue, the bread soft as a pillow. Wasp eats everything.

Seated at the Kittens' table Moth looks small, like a child. Her hair has grown to her ears and gives her a sweet, girlish look that belies her increasingly miserable countenance. Her wooden knife works up and down, slicing her slab of fish into rough strips then cutting the strips into squares. She's so thin. Like a wisp of smoke in a linen gown. Every so often she catches Wasp's eye and turns her head quickly away. Pink tinges her gaunt cheeks.

Wasp notices the bandage is gone from Moth's hand. Just below the knuckle of the middle finger is a livid red circle.

Conversation fades as the plates are cleared away. Kingfisher lifts the casket onto the table. The Abbess unlocks the lid and removes the scrolls containing the day's Assignments. Masques rise to accept their commissions. Nightingale receives one, Hummingbird too. Wasp holds her breath, lets it out again.

Nothing.

'Aren't you going to open that?' Wasp nods at the parchment.

'Later. We have a carriage waiting. Remember, I promised you a ride around the park.'

Wasp thinks for a moment. 'Hummingbird, why is Moth here? I mean, why did Kingfisher bring someone like her to the House? I can't guess at her age but in her head she's a child. If the Abbess sent her into the city she'd scarce last a night.'

Hummingbird settles back on the bed and laces her fingers behind her head. 'I've heard all manner of stories concerning Moth and I can't begin to tell which are true and which are just gossip. Kingfisher, for all his skill, sometimes makes mistakes. Perhaps Moth is one of those, perhaps she's here for a reason I can't fathom. The clock is ticking though. Moth is expected to get her Emblem by the end of the month. If not, I'd hate to think what might happen. Remember what I told you – the House doesn't carry dead weight. Ever.'

The Rise and Fall of Anna Torrance

'Keep your money, Torrance. I shall not marry any son of mine to that petalhead. No decent-minded family will have her. She's cursed, and any child of hers will prove likewise.'

'Any child can stray. It's easy to be a sinner casting stones.'

'Stray, aye, not fall into an abyss. Neither man nor gospel will bring that one back.'

'I could call you out over this, Hammond.'

'If you believe I'm wrong, do so.'

'Dear Lord, it's a fat enough dowry I'm willing to settle on her. I know you need the money. This could be a way out for both of us.'

'Pay a farmer to take her. You'll get your way out and the rest of us will be spared a catastrophe.'

'This is my daughter you're talking about.'

'Aye, a daughter you're so desperate to be rid of you've gone through the entire society list in a bid to find some halfwit of a husband. And now you've come to me, after poking your business into mine and finding the bank howling at my door. Well, damn you and your kind, I shan't do it. Even if she wasn't sporting a swollen belly I'd suffer penury before letting her under my roof. Get a quack to rid her of the baby then send the girl to a convent and have done with it. Good day to you.'

Hammond crammed his tricorne on his pinched skull and left, muddied boots scuffing the tiles. Papa watched him go, kept looking even after view of his visitor had been cut off by the stable wall. A minute later, Hammond's gelding took the drive at a gallop, sending gravel showering across the lawn.

Sometimes, when the dream makers worked a certain way, they added clarity to Anna's senses and silence to her feet. The world shrank around her so that she could pick out tiny details. Everything could be heard, smelled, touched. She was aware of her own heart beating too quickly, even though she felt as calm as a breeze-blown meadow.

She stood in the alcove beside the stairs, as still as the porcelain pot perched on the stand next to her. At that moment she had little concept of time, or that her days in this household had now become mere hours. Her father's raised voice had drawn her down to his study as it had once before, and again before that. Always there had been threats, warnings, denouncements, and a man storming from the house with his hat crammed askew.

What had changed were the words her father used when speaking to her afterwards. 'Disappointment' became 'shame' then 'anger' then 'outrage'. Anna was aware of the contradiction she seemingly posed, and that her father still could not get his wits around it. He appeared to think a greasy purse was the solving of any problem and that expensive tutors might achieve what his private counsel could not.

In the social graces Anna proved an apt pupil. She had a natural elegance that swept her around the ballroom floor with ease. She memorised the steps of each dance as naturally as some take to numbers or letters. At first the expected invitations had come and suitable young gentlemen would attempt to engage her. She found them boring to a man, and took refuge in claret or the brandy punch. All she had to do was cross a room and, in mid dance or mid conversation, men's eyes would drift from their partners. Even with a wine-spun head her legs never betrayed her. She ate with the manners of a queen and drank like a tavern sot. A swan among ducklings, she left society's finest wilting on the periphery of the dance floor, smiling, wafting their fans and hating her with passion. She was *that Torrance girl* and fuelled the fires of gossips' parlours.

Soon the gallants bled away to be replaced by a different cut of suitor. She seemed to drag every charlatan or ne'er-do-well into her sphere, though it could be argued some bounded in willingly.

'I want to find you a respectable husband,' her father complained. 'Is that so unreasonable?'

'One respectable man seems much like any other.'

'And you think you can find happiness in villainy? These rakes you find so appealing, so glamorous, can give you a future?'

'I don't know, but they can give me a day, an hour, even a moment, that isn't exactly the same as every other. These respectable men you so favour seem to mouth scripts straight from some city theatre. I am inveigled into giving all the right responses in all the right places. You want me tidied away and everything well in your world.'

Because her father couldn't control her, Anna believed the same was true of other men. Her youth and beauty began to bestow delusions of immortality. But such beauty was a weapon she had no means of mastering. Like putting a musket into the hands of some halfwit savage, who might realise what he held was deadly but had no inkling of what to do with it.

Anna never mastered the art of polite conversation. When a man was in her company he had no interest in what she said. Later she was to discover that they also had no interest in what she thought. Men did not fight over her. What was the point in spilling blood when she would move as easily from one to another, and all a fellow had to do was wait his turn?

When the wine lost its lustre another threshold presented itself, another line to cross. It arrived via a sallow-skinned libertine who wore his hair tied like a woman's and sported shoe buckles the size of blackbirds.

'We don't need to sour our bellies in order to liberate the mind. Do you want to soar, Anna? Do you want to go places you've never been before? Open doors that wine or brandy can't unlock?'

'Yes, I want to soar.'

He unfolded his palm. An ivory trinket box lay snug between thumb and fingers. He squeezed it so the lid flicked open. Inside were lumps of a curious sugarlike substance, brown in colour and glinting like crude jewels.

'Is it snuff?'

'In a manner of speaking, though I doubt you'd want to snort this up your nose.' He stroked her cheek with his free hand, as if drawing her into him. 'Just a little on the tip of your tongue will suffice to change your perspective on a great many things.'

She took a pinch and slipped it into her mouth, her eyes never leaving his.

He smiled. 'At first—'

Anna did not remember the ride to his lodgings, only that he laid her on his bed with a mother's gentleness. Already the world was beginning to sprout odd angles. His taste in furnishings was exotic, his wall hangings embroidered with scenes that would make a parson blush. Yet her eyes fixed on a sliver of loose thread clinging to the bed curtain, which seemed to change colour as she watched, at once growing and shrinking. She tilted her head to try to bring some sense to what she saw, but her view was cut as her skirts were lifted and thrown across her face.

Afterwards, when each morning found her retching into her washbowl, she still could not equate the events of that night with the strange sensations occurring inside her body. This was something the loss of her mother had left her ill equipped to understand. Society ladies, with their rapier eyes, understood only too well. When Anna fell, that fall was spectacular. Invitations dried up like a brook in a drought. Her papa burned the scandal sheets that gutterised both their names, but always more turned up. He took them into his study and read them to their last word, leaving his door open so she could hear his displeasure.

Now he turned and caught her standing in the alcove, incapable of doing anything except smile at his disasters, both knowing that at least a dozen men had walked into his study and all had hurried out. Nearly a hundred years the family business had grown by the efforts of Father and fathers before him, and now one wayward daughter was causing it to wither at the roots.

'A trollop,' he said. 'I've given everything I could and what have I raised? A drunken, addle-witted trollop. Well, by God, I shall not go down with you, and no rake's bastard will get its feet in my house. It's time you came to heel.'

Wasp brushes out the folds of her gown as Hummingbird joins her in the front hall. Both girls drip with jewellery and fat satin bows.

'A mite fancy for a clop around the park,' Wasp observes.

Hummingbird slips on a pair of gloves that match the sapphire blue of her dress. 'An opera is not the only place to be seen. Our charms need putting on public display. How else will the good ladies of this dismal town know what is fashionable?'

'So what's involved in this "public display"?'

'We sit in the carriage and preen whilst Leonardo drives us around the flowerbeds. You don't have to do anything else except wear the face of a disaffected angel.'

They step into a bold, blustery day. Gusts send autumn seeds twirling past their pinned bonnets. Across the square, children throw leaves into the air and cry with delight as they fall in a swirling curtain of ochre and gold.

A carriage waits at the foot of the steps. Leonardo sports an impressive livery that turns him into a dandified dwarf. 'Don't tease him about it,' Hummingbird warns, 'or he'll sulk for hours.'

Both girls keep a tight expression as the coachman lowers the step. Wasp checks the door handle and window then climbs inside. The interior smells of polish, and a fresh rug has been spread on the floor. Wasp sinks into the generous upholstery while her companion seats herself opposite.

'Why do you always fiddle with the door? I've noticed that on a couple of occasions.'

Wasp serves up a waxy smile. 'An uncomfortable memory. Nothing worth talking about.'

Outside, the House shines in a fugitive spar of sunlight.

'Neighbours must be aware of the House's business,' she continues. 'Don't they ever cause trouble?'

'How can gentlefolk, mindful of their position in society, complain when such high-ranking men frequent Crown Square? You never know who you might meet stepping down from a carriage. We have also performed the odd neighbourly favour in return for discretion. Residents keep their curtains drawn, their gardens empty and their minds on their own business.'

The coach sets off at a brisk pace. Daytime scents gust through the open windows as Leonardo cracks the horses through one city street then another. Wasp feels her mouth curl into a smile. After a mile or so, they turn through a set of iron gates. Swards of lawn bristle with late season blooms. Bridleways crisscross the gardens with arterial precision while oak trees puncture the grass at regular intervals. For a moment Wasp, still flummoxed by the jostling city streets, feels the pull of the countryside she hails from, a fleeting sensation spoiled by the swarm of carriages and riders which soon joins the gravel track. Coaches of all shapes and dispositions, many with canopies lowered despite the breeze. Inside, elaborately dressed women regard everything with smiling indulgence. Others ride elegant horses, some in the company of a groom.

Standing at the side of the path or seated on benches lining the route, gentlemen and ladies alike watch the parade as it circles the park. Some wave. A few take notes.

'Who are those women?' Wasp asks. 'They ride like queens. Is there another House in this city?'

'None like ours,' Hummingbird replies. 'Those creatures are courtesans, mostly enjoying lavish lifestyles at the expense of rich admirers.'

'Are we much different? Is it not a life you would enjoy?'

'What, becoming a demi-rep? I've no fancy to sell myself to a purse and a pair of breeches, only to go and tickle some handsome winkle on the side. You wouldn't want to be one of those pampered fluffheads, mobbed wherever you go. All gilt and no gold. They can't sneeze without half a dozen society scandal sheets reporting the matter. These women seldom work for anyone save themselves. They have no loyalties, no sense of sisterhood. They guzzle money with a view to a rich wedding and a comfortable retirement. Many end up bankrupt, poxed, and scorned by the very society which now adores them. Such power as they wield only lasts for as long as they remain fashionable. Time can't be bought or bribed, Sister. When their chins sag and their bosoms start to founder watch how these multitudinous admirers scuttle back into the woodwork. Yet one glimpse of a fine carriage or expensive gown has every city gutter girl clamouring to join the Cyprian Corps. Neither the church nor the morally outraged can do aught to stop it. These women are fleeting. We don't wish our candles snuffed before they are halfway burned.'

'Cyprian Corps? You make them sound like an army.'

Hummingbird leans forward and clasps Wasp's knee. 'We all inhabit a half-world, a *demi-monde*. It draws admiration yet allows people to socially exclude you in the same turn. Ladies will curse you for a harlot yet slavishly copy your fashion. Society has built a complex house. We can ascend to the top, but only if we are shut in a separate room.' She gestures at the onlookers' rapt faces. 'They all come here to see us. To try and touch the stars. Never underestimate your power. You need only to be spotted in public wearing a new style of choker and within a week a score of society ladies will parrot the fashion. Charm is also a powerful weapon. With it you can turn a papist to a Baptist in the breath of a sentence.'

Wasp peers out of the window. 'Those men watching, they remind me of hungry dogs.'

'Things can get out of hand. Last month the landau belonging to one famous courtesan struck a pothole as big as a pit and snapped the axle. Her carriage was mobbed. Grown men scrambled like urchins around a dropped farthing. Items were snatched: a strip of lace from her sleeve, a bead from her reticule. She was plundered like a shipwreck.' Hummingbird laughed. 'Don't go so wide-eyed, Sister. Leonardo will look after us. Sit back and enjoy the ride.'

Eloise dumps a pile of newspapers and society magazines on Wasp's bed. 'Madame Abbess says you must educate yourself,' the maid explains. 'Anything you need to know about your clients can often be discovered here. A lot of reading, *enfant*, but better than cleaning out a sooty fireplace, *oui*?'

Wasp concedes that she has little else to do. After the carriage ride around the park, Hummingbird took herself off to the dressing room. She'll be leaving for her Assignment soon and will likely be out most of the night.

Wasp draws her chair over to the window and settles down to read. A few of the publications she's familiar with. Father brought old copies home from Russell Hall and he spent time at the kitchen table with Mother, turning the pages and marvelling at the lives of city folk. In truth these society bibles are much the same. Births, marriages, petty scandals and endless politics.

On a trip in search of coffee she steals a glance through Moth's open door. Hummingbird, dressed in her evening finery, is sitting on the bed. She's holding Moth's hand and speaking into her ear.

Wasp watches, unsure whether to interrupt. This may be a House matter and she's caused enough trouble for Moth as it is. But the girl looks frightened – there's no denying that – and

Hummingbird's expression is fixed in a carved grin. Wasp frets over it all the way to the maids' parlour. When she returns, the door is closed.

Dusk greys the sky. After hours of reading, Wasp's eyes feel fit to drop out yet the pile of papers remains daunting. Acknowledging defeat, she draws the curtains, disrobes and slips into bed. Both neck and back ache, doubtless a result of cramming herself into that narrow chair, and sleep won't come. She stares at the ceiling. Hummingbird returns, candle in hand, just after midnight. 'You're awake,' she says.

'Yes. Good Assignment?'

'A minor tea party. Some dancing. I suspect hiring me might have bankrupted the host but it bought the attention he wanted.'

She places the candle on the bedside table and climbs in beside Wasp. 'A quiet evening for you, I daresay.'

Wasp doesn't answer. She is thinking of Moth and those wide, wide eyes.

Next morning Wasp receives an Assignment. She regards the scroll lying on the coverlet. The ribbon is red, not pink. Imperfections mark the paper, dark traceries like veins. A simple knot crowns the ribbon.

Wrapped like a gift, she thinks.

'I'll wager you're with me again,' Hummingbird remarks.

'How so?'

'Too soon to be let loose on your own.'

'Shall I open it now?'

'Why not? I'll open mine too.'

Wasp tugs the knot free and smooths out her parchment. The instructions are clear enough. She and Hummingbird will make up part of a foursome. Their clients are a gentleman of some note in Parliament and his son. A private carriage will collect the Masques. Kingfisher will fetch them in a House coach after the festivities.

'Supper at six,' Hummingbird says, waving her scroll in the air. 'Take my advice and eat sparingly. I once swallowed a huge meal only to have my client change his plans and take me dancing at the Assembly Rooms. As well as avoiding being tramped on by his leaden feet I was obliged to force down cinnamon sweetmeats and a glass of viciously rich wine. I was up half the night with grumbling innards.'

'Couldn't you have refused?'

'You never decline, Wasp. Never. If you're offered a drink try not to take more than one glass of anything, and a small glass at that. Make it last. An occasional sip should satisfy your host. Have you ever been to an opera?'

'No.'

Hummingbird grins. 'I think you'll like it. Wait and see.'

The Abbess looks up from her desk. An open ledger lies in front of her. 'Your face wears a troubled look, Wasp. Misgivings about tonight?'

Wasp runs her fingers along the edge of the desk. The wood is cool to the touch. Behind her, maids rustle across the hallway, caught up in the everyday business of the House. 'I feel as taut as a starched sheet.'

'Such feelings can be put to good use.' The Abbess closes the ledger. Wasp notices that an outline of the book has been scratched in ink onto the desk's surface. Above it is the word 'Ledger'. Other objects have lines drawn around them too, and are similarly labelled: 'Inkpot', 'Pen', 'Letters'.

'I know, Abbess, but there's another matter I need to discuss.'

'You are concerned about Moth? I know you've been enquiring about her.'

'It's my fault she was punished.'

'How so? Did you filch that penny ribbon? Did you slip it into your cuff and defy Hummingbird's demands to return it?'

'No, but—'

The Abbess raises a hand. 'Scarcely a week has passed since you received your Emblem. There's still a great deal to undertake without burdening yourself with a problem like Moth. Bear in mind you are still sharing a room with Hummingbird and remain under her tutelage. Moth must accept life under the terms we have given her.'

'She can't go on like this. She's as fragile as a cracked pot.'

'If not for us she would have no life at all.'

'Not ball gowns,' Hummingbird says, closing the wardrobe. 'We won't be dancing tonight. You need something you can comfortably sit in. Here,' she opens another door, 'try one of these.'

'I thought I was supposed to choose. I'm not a Kitten any more.'

Hummingbird has already selected a green velvet gown for herself. 'We can't keep clients waiting just because you decide to be fussy. You'll become quicker with experience. In the meantime try this.'

A cornflower blue dress trimmed in white. Wasp has to admit the garment is beautiful. She makes no complaint as Hummingbird fastens it up.

'Now a wig each and a spray of jewellery. Pearls for you, something dark for me.'

The girls help each other to finish dressing. They arrive at the front door with minutes to spare, Wasp smelling strongly of the honeysuckle perfume Hummingbird has also chosen for her. A carriage of polished oak waits in the street, a liveried driver on the perch and a brace of candied footmen clinging to the back. Four piebalds snort between the shafts.

As the coach sets off with the women inside, Hummingbird reaches over and grasps Wasp's gloved hand.

'Anxious?'

Wasp stares out at the passing buildings, their windows yellow with candlelight. 'Yes.'

'Don't be. Like the park, we're mostly there to be seen. Our clients will make small talk but it's unlikely to go further than that. If anything awkward happens or you get into difficulties I'll deal with it. How's your Emblem?'

Wasp fingers the tattoo on her cheek. Most of the dead skin has already flaked off. Hummingbird rubbed some ointment into the Emblem before they left.

'Itches, but hasn't hurt for a while.'

'Good. Try not to draw too much attention to it.'

'Is my client the politician or the son?'

'It's their decision. Don't take it personally.'

'I hope I like him.'

Hummingbird squeezes her arm. 'Liking him has naught to do with it. This is a job, remember.'

The carriage rumbles to a halt. Wasp peers out of the window. A sensation of heat wafts across her cheeks. She can see very little. A hint of bodies moving in the dark, solitary flames bobbing along leaving wakes of orange sparks. And noises, like undercurrents slipping between the dark shapes of buildings.

Wasp steps out, followed by Hummingbird. Another carriage clatters past, lanterns swaying. Across the road someone mouths an oath. Someone else laughs. Ahead, a short flight of stone steps leads up to a pair of open doors. Light spills onto the street.

'This is the Royal,' Hummingbird whispers. 'A place for dandies to stuff themselves on over-rich food. I've met clients here before. The footmen are often more lofty than their customers.'

The footmen escort the girls up the steps. Their clients are waiting inside, recognisable by their pink cravats studded with cameos. One is a cheesy fellow of middling years with a bulbous face and tufts of white hair poking out from either side of a wig. His son is soft-faced with dark eyes and brows that curve over the lids in wide arcs. Both men are dressed in dark blue with cream hose, the cravats providing the only splash of vivid colour.

'So these are our fancies, are they?' the older fellow declares in response to the coachman's cough. 'By God they resemble a pair of Italian poppets. Any one take your fancy, Richard?'

Before the younger man can utter a word his father stabs the air with his cane. 'You. You'll do. What's your name?'

Wasp drops into a smooth curtsey. 'I am Wasp. At your service, sir.'

'Wasp, is it? Hiding a sting somewhere beneath those velvet skirts perhaps?'

She glances at Hummingbird, who swoops into a curtsey of her own. 'And I am Hummingbird, also at your service.'

Richard bows. 'It seems my choice has been made. Permit me to accompany you inside.'

Hummingbird nods. 'I would be delighted, sir.'

His father taps his cane on the polished floor. 'Don't look so po-faced, girl. I haven't emptied my purse to suffer a sour kipper at my side.'

Wasp bolts on her most charming smile. Her client guffaws. 'That's the spirit. You may call me James. Sir James. My boy there is Richard, as you heard. Let's get seated. This draughty hallway is killing my legs.'

A long rectangular room topped by a gallery from which a string quintet saws out a melody. Tiers of fat candles hang from the ceiling; the air is yellow with tobacco smoke. Talk, laughter, a coughing fit from the far corner. Tables under white linen cloths dot the floor like cream buns, with waiters flitting expertly between them. One greases up to Sir James. 'This way, sir.'

The hubbub of conversation dips noticeably as the party follows the serving man to their table. Sir James seems to puff up in front of Wasp. His rolling gait turns into a swagger and he gestures expansively with his cane. When he speaks his voice is much too loud. Every ear and eye is the place is captured.

'Not the best of tables for such company. Still, it will suffice.'

Once seated, Wasp feels less exposed. *You'll be stared at*, Hummingbird warned before they left the House. *By women as well as men. Even servants will peek when they think you don't see. Try not to be too self-conscious. It's what you're there for, and you'll get used to it in time.*

People certainly steal glances, but the talk soon resumes its previous level. This is a riotous place for anyone to try to have a decent supper, she thinks. No tea-room serenity. No civilised dandies exchanging pleasantries over coffee and raspberry tart. The men around her, while smart enough, have a keen, almost criminal look about their faces, and from the snatches of conversation she overhears their talk involves more than casual business.

'Welcome to our den of thieves,' Richard remarks, smiling at Wasp.

Hummingbird clasps her fingers under her chin. 'You are all villains, then?'

Richard laughs. He sounds nervous. 'Without a doubt. Politicians, peers, bankers — what greater villainy could you find under one roof? They should hang the lot of us in chains.'

'Then I would be robbed of enchanting company for the evening.'

'And does your friend feel that way also?'

'Um . . .' Wasp splutters. 'I know little of politics or commerce, sir.'

'Call me Richard, please.'

Wasp glances at her client. Sir James's eyes flick over a menu. He hands it back to the waiter and mutters something in the fellow's ear. The waiter slides off. He's replaced by a rumpled-faced man in a grey periwig who's seemingly popped out of the smoke. He and Sir James launch into some convoluted exchange full of incomprehensible words and parliamentary jargon. Wasp tries to say something to Richard but he's already distracted. That's more or less the last stab either girl has at conversation for the remainder of their supper. Patrons are constantly out of their seats, flitting from table to table, catching people in the aisles, shaking hands and talking, talking, talking. Richard attracts an equal measure of attention. Men slap his back or shake his hand.

'Ever felt like a trinket in a box?' Hummingbird whispered.

'They're ignoring us.'

'Men's business. Leave them to it. We serve our purpose by being here.'

Sir James excuses himself. Five minutes later he's back, only to disappear somewhere else. Richard concentrates on his wine glass. Hummingbird does not interrupt his musing or try to cajole him into speaking. A tall, wigless gentleman, black hair scraped behind his head and tied with a velvet bow, cards the girls. Hummingbird shakes her head and returns it. Crestfallen, the man slinks back into the throng.

Don't accept cards while you're with a client, she'd warned.

More cards arrive at their table, only to be politely returned. Sir James, conducting business with other diners, doesn't seem to notice. Hummingbird slips out a bone-handled fan from her sleeve and wafts it in front of her face.

Should I do likewise? Wasp has chosen a tasteful, oriental-patterned fan from the selection in the dressing room, but when she attempts to flip it open, the handle catches on her lace cuff and it tumbles to the floor. Richard is watching her and she's irritated to feel her cheeks go hot.

Supper arrives, carried above the patrons' heads by a brace of nimble-fingered serving men. Sir James, back from his excursions, downs half a chicken and three glasses of Madeira. His cheeks, already puffed and florid, grow redder as the minutes tick by. Bits of half chewed fowl catch in his teeth.

The girls attend to their own food. They cut it, slice it, push it around their plates and pass the odd forkful across their lips. Hummingbird is an expert at not drinking. Whenever she puts down her glass it contains just as much red wine as when she picked it up. When the meal is concluded it's as if a great feast has taken place. Sir James sits back, surrounded by the debris of his supper, and belches.

'Can't linger,' he announces. 'Richard wants a bit of culture.'

Culture is an opera. They travel to the venue in Sir James's carriage and are installed in a box so high above the other seats it makes Wasp dizzy. Having only ever been entertained by a travelling troupe, she thinks the woman on stage is an angel singing to God. Such a perfect voice, it shivers the nerves.

Richard presses a silk handkerchief into her gloved hand. 'Opera can do that to your soul,' he explains. 'There is no shame in tears. Enough divas have broken my heart in the past.'

'I didn't know men allowed themselves such feelings. Father told me it was a sign of weakness . . . of *unmanliness*. He once berated a neighbour's boy for crying when a cat scratched him. He was only six years old.'

'Very candid of you. I don't myself care for bullish men. They are too fond of themselves and their ideas. For a woman to marry such a creature is to sit forever in silence.'

The curtain drops. The orchestra slips into an easy melody. People murmur, stand, stretch limbs. Wasp steals a glance at Sir James. He's slumped in his chair, his head tilted forward. An uncorked flask lies on his lap. A gentle snore stirs at the back of his nostrils.

Richard wakes his father and helps him down the stairs. He staggers a little but once out in the night air seems to rally. His carriage is parked at the kerb, driver and footmen waiting patiently. There is, as yet, no sign of Kingfisher.

Sir James disappears behind one of the sandstone pillars supporting the entrance pediment.

'Help me will you, m'dear? I'm having a spot of trouble.'

She glances back at Hummingbird, who's talking intently to Richard. Without thinking Wasp steps behind the pillar. Sir James is slumped against the opera house wall.

'Are you ill, sir? Shall I fetch your coachman?'

'No, no, just a bit of bother with the old todger.'

A fumbling noise then Sir James urinates noisily against the stonework.

Wasp thinks the entire city must hear it. The splashing finished, he turns, stumbles and grabs her arm. She tries to pull away. His grip tightens.

'You are breaking the rules, sir, and hurting my arm.'

'My money makes the rules.' His breath, sweet with Madeira, invades her nostrils. Eyes glint as if the sockets are filled with cold diamonds. All the buffoonery has gone. Wasp's prior feelings of contentment sputter and die like a candle drowning in its own wax.

'What a timid lily we have,' he purrs. 'See how she trembles, or perhaps the air is a little too cool on that lovely pale neck?'

His hand slips along Wasp's arm and across her shoulder. She fights the impulse to lash out. Despite the cold evening, fingers of sweat slither down her face.

'Just a touch,' he whispers, voice bristling with traps. 'I've paid your Abbess handsomely enough, filled your belly with fine food and taken you to the opera. An out-and-out tup with a decent class of whore would cost a fraction of that.'

His palm flattens out. With flinty confidence it moves to accommodate the contours of her body and lingers at her breast.

Wasp meets his unblinking gaze. Her voice is full of sawdust. 'You are not allowed to handle me, sir.'

'Ah, but who is handling whom? Do you seek to fleece a man's pockets then tease him to distraction without consequence? That is neither business nor bargain. So I shall not move my hand. If you are able to hold that quivering body still for long enough then this business will be done and your precious rules will be none the wiser.'

'I think, sir, that we should join the others.'

She tries to step out from behind the pillar. Sir James snatches her by the rear of her gown and pulls her back into the shadows. 'I'll squeeze the juices out of that ripe little arse.'

The night opens its belly and disgorges Kingfisher. He strides up, velvet coat flapping. 'You don't touch the ladies, sir.' His voice is like surf rumbling over a rocky shoreline. 'Against the rules, as well you know.'

'Back away. I've paid for this tart and I'll have her any way I please.'

'That you won't, sir, and I'd be pleased if you'd turn her over to me now.'

Sir James raises his cane. It quivers in the air between them. Kingfisher spreads his hands. Rings glint on every finger. 'No need for that, sir. I shall be happy to leave you to your business once these ladies have taken their leave.'

'Curse your black hide, you silk-tongued lackey. I've a hot spike in my breeches and it's in want of a dipping.'

Richard appears, Hummingbird in his wake. 'Father, we have better places to go and other things to do.' He squeezes Sir James's arm. The cane wavers a moment then lowers.

'Yes, my boy, that we do. I daresay my business here is done, but I shan't forget this, not by a league.' He allows himself to be led away. Wasp expects some final insult, an over-the-cuff *whore* or *harlot*. But he walks off laughing, and somehow that's worse.

Desperate or Damned?

Nightingale has no idea where she's going or how long it'll take to get there. She tried asking the coachman but all she got for her trouble were tight lips and a stony face. The carriage lurches along the lane like a sow in a mud bath and it makes her sick to her belly. It's a fine enough box on wheels, though not so fancy it would get overly noticed. At a guess they've gone ten miles. Maybe a little more. Most of the milestones are covered in thick patches of bramble.

Voices outside. Sheep bleating. A bell clanging the hour. Nightingale presses her face to the window. A higgledy-piggledy market town. The carriage pulls to a stop. The driver's boots are heavy on the ladder. Blessed fresh air rushes through the open door. She doesn't have time to enjoy it. Stepping outside, pins and needles shoot up both legs and she nearly falls flat on her face. The coachman gestures with his whip.

'The Stoke Inn is over there,' he says. 'I'll be waiting when you come out.'

The whip is black and glistening in his gloved hand. Nightingale smells oiled leather. She nods. 'I doubt this will take long.'

Ferguson is half an hour late. Nightingale's so nervous her stomach wants to throw out her breakfast. The innkeeper has already set two cups of tea in front of her and twice she's asked him the time. A clock stands beside the hearth but one hand is missing and the other bent. 'Half past two,' the innkeeper says, putting down the teapot. He's frowning. Nightingale wonders what's in his head. Maybe he thinks she's a whore or a trickster. Enough of those plague the highways, she's heard. Will he want coin? She doesn't have any. She can't even pay for the tea. If Ferguson won't take care of it she might be branded a thief and see all her plans unravel.

The thought almost amuses her. *Brought to ruin over a dish of tea and some pastry. What would the Abbess say to that?*

She's doing her best. An insolent amount of powder and rouge was needed to hide the Emblems on her cheeks. The loan of a respectable dress and bonnet cost her a gilded necklace. Getting a message to Ferguson required a pair of earrings. At least he had been accommodating enough to send his coach for her.

Nightingale watched the ladies come off the stagecoaches at the posting house. She copied their voices, their walk, the way they spoke to servants. She never realised how difficult it would be to pass as anything other than a Masque. Though her pale grey dress and cloak were up to the part, there was more to this deception than being able to flick and flutter her fan the way a common woman would. Her father's solicitor is no buffoon and she doesn't know how long she'll be able to fool him. Her fingers are aching, she's twiddled and twisted them so much.

The clock has a long brass pendulum swinging in a chipped case. It's too big for the room. The ticking sounds are like mice gnawing the wainscoting. The first time it chimed its secretive hour Nightingale jumped, spilling her drink over the tea table. She had nothing to mop it clean and ended up using one of the cushions from the armchair, which would likely leave an ugly stain. The rug under Nightingale's slippers is worn. She contemplates getting up and slipping back out of the door but remembers, again, she has no money for the tea. If caught, the innkeeper with his big hands and blue-veined nose might not think twice about beating her.

Think, Nightingale. Think.

She has a bracelet. It's a pretty silver thing engraved with jade flowers and must be worth a tidy sum. Surely Ferguson will accept it as payment. Oh, why won't that clock shut up?

At last the door ghosts open and Ferguson breezes into the lounge. A smile splits his face. He glances at the tea and tosses the innkeeper a guinea. The man's frown disappears and he backs out of the room. Nightingale doesn't move. Usually so sharp, she's fumbling for things to say. Ferguson warms his hands at the hearth. He moves easily, as if this is his own parlour.

Nightingale puts down her tea dish. It rattles on the tabletop. Ferguson chuckles. That's good. She can feel irritated with him. Feeling irritated will help her cope with her unease.

He beckons and she gets up to follow him. Not a word has passed between them. They leave through a back door which opens onto a lane choked with rubbish. Rats scatter out of their path. From a gaping upstairs window a man's voice, hurling abuse, floats on the thick air. Somewhere within, a baby is crying. Its wailing jangles Nightingale's already fractured nerves. The man curses again. A woman's voice rises in protest. A slap. Silence.

A scuffed green door is set into the wall. Ferguson unlocks it and waves Nightingale inside. A flight of stairs, the wood bare and splintered, leads up into the gloom. She hitches skirts and starts to climb. The taffeta rustles like dried leaves in the confined space. She hears Ferguson's tread on the boards behind her.

Three doors lead off a cramped landing. Nightingale waits. Ferguson is wheezing a little by the time he joins her. He plucks a key out of his waistcoat pocket, jiggles it into the lock and pushes the door. It sticks in the frame. He shoulders it open. A smell of damp linen and dust smacks Nightingale's nostrils.

'Come in,' Ferguson says, gesturing. 'Come in.'

A bed hugs one wall. Underneath, a rug barely covers the stained floorboards. A wardrobe shares a corner with a dresser on which sits a pitcher, bowl and two glasses. The only window is closed, the ledge below littered with fly husks.

Perspiration stings her forehead. The air's stifling. The door closes behind her. The latch clicks.

Ferguson pours two drinks from a hip flask and hands one to Nightingale. Brandy from the smell of it. He smiles and takes a generous swig, half draining the glass.

Nightingale sips the brandy and smiles back.

'You must excuse the accommodation,' he gestures around him, 'but it was the best I could achieve at such, shall we say, short notice? Besides, I assumed you wished discretion.'

'Yes.'

'Indeed. Your message, arriving as it did, left me both surprised and perplexed. Your father, along with myself and most of society, assumed you lost to the ether. In honesty, many would claim it would be better if you stayed lost.'

'I can settle your mind on that account. I've no wish to trouble Father or his brand of society. Let me be as dead to them as they are to me.'

'If only one could be sure that this is the case.'

'Be assured. I've no desire to be dealt with in such a shabby manner again.'

'Then this meeting is not for social purposes?'

Nightingale squeezes her fingers together. 'No, it is not. I want my child, nothing more. Find her, and I'll never trouble you or anyone connected with my family again.'

'You genuinely do not know where it is?'

'No.'

'And you think it can be located, despite the coin your father spent trying to track it down? He can't afford such a loose end. The consequences for his estate could prove significant.'

'This is a baby you're talking about. My daughter. She is not an *it*.'

He spreads his hands. 'Of course not. You must pardon me. This is all a shock, as I explained. But tell me, how do you propose that I find your *daughter* if you don't know her whereabouts yourself?'

'A man took her from me. He said he was going to give the child to someone who could care for her. I want to know where she is, nothing more.'

'And you let him do this?'

'I was in no position to stop him. I was . . . compromised.'

'Compromised?' Ferguson empties his glass. 'That could mean a great many things. I assume this fellow is the quack who dealt so roughly with your father's men and spirited you off into the night.'

'Yes.'

'And you know where he is?'

'I can tell you where to find him.'

'Hmm, not quite the same thing. So you're still keeping secrets, Anna Torrance. Well, that's to be expected. However, my professional services don't come without charge.'

Nightingale slips the bracelet from under her sleeve and places it on the table beside the brandy decanter. Ferguson glances at it.

'You offer me this bauble?'

'You don't have to be a silversmith to recognise its worth.'

'So tell me where I might find this baby snatcher of yours.'

Nightingale lists the apothecaries, herbalists, Wise Women.

'And you consider yourself a fit mother now?'

'I'm in a better position to try and be one.'

'Would this fellow agree?'

'No.'

'I may have to use less than convivial means to obtain the information you desire.'

Nightingale swallows. Her tongue is dry as bark. She tries a sip of brandy but it's an unusual concoction and nips her throat. 'Don't let him know I'm involved. Get what I've asked for and nothing more.'

'And what is to stop me turning both the child and you over to your father?'

'Why would you? I'm not asking you to fetch her, only to ascertain her whereabouts. I've already explained that I shall not trouble Father again. He may consider us both dead if he wishes. You have my word.'

Ferguson taps the empty glass against his chin. 'And what might that word be truly worth, I wonder? You look like you've fallen a long way, Anna Torrance, standing there in that cheap dress with powder caking your face.'

'I didn't wish to draw attention to myself.'

'So why the face paint? Pox got you? How do I know you're any more a fit mother than you were before? You might be taking the child into a bawdy house. It would be remiss of me to permit such a thing.'

'Since when did your breed ever trouble yourself with matters of conscience? You've been paid. Do what I ask otherwise I'll take my jewellery and go.'

'I need to know what I'm dealing with, Anna.'

Before she can stop him, he takes his kerchief and swipes it across her cheek. Air brushes over exposed skin. She slaps a hand to her face. Too late, he's seen it. The powder-stained square of lace falls from his fingers.

'Dear Lord,' he says, voice drawn taut. 'It seems you have fallen in a way none of us quite expected.'

Nightingale forgets about the bracelet. She forgets about the brandy glass still clutched in her hand, and her exposed Emblem. She tears at the latch, runs out the door and skitters down the steps outside. In the hot air of the alleyway she trips over her own feet and slaps into the opposite wall. Pain judders up both arms. The alley seems to fall in on her.

Ferguson doesn't follow. Nightingale waits as long as she dares, hauling air into her lungs. When she thinks she can walk again she makes for the end of the alley, holding the wall for support. With her free hand she pats powder back across her exposed Emblem then pulls her cloak around her shoulders. Everything is quiet. Even the dogs have stopped barking.

She fights the impulse to run. Ahead is the twist in the lane beyond which the carriage is waiting. Nightingale can't see anything through the unkempt hedge. Has the driver become impatient and left? Perhaps it was Ferguson's intention that she never return to the city. If so she'll not get five miles on foot, even if she could find the proper road. Hiring transport is out of the question. Ferguson has her only item of value. Even if she did manage to drag herself back to the House what would she tell the Abbess? That she was jiggled by a footpad? If so, how would she explain the clothes? For all she knew, Kingfisher might already have been sent after her.

The coach is waiting. Nightingale scrambles up the step and collapses onto the seat. The driver sets off immediately. At this time of day the landscape is sleepy. No one pays her nondescript carriage any heed. The horses kick up a good pace despite the road. Nightingale leaves the window down, grateful for the breeze. It strengthens as they clatter into open country and she draws her cloak tighter around herself. The brim of her straw bonnet flutters like starling's wings.

What have I done? What am I going to do?

Undercurrents

'I can't believe I let him talk to me that way,' Wasp says. 'This wasn't supposed to happen, was it? I felt so demeaned. I thought he would hit me if I didn't do what he wished.'

'No need to get upset,' Hummingbird says. 'All sorts like to try their luck. Most are just a gaggle of blustering fools. First clients are usually the worst. They feel intimidated by us and try to lay down their own rules. Others, like Sir James, get drunk and think they can fumble us as they please. He'll get a black mark next to his name and a warning from the Abbess. Any real trouble and he'd have felt a hatpin in his pintle.'

'You make it sound like nothing happened.'

'Well, not much did.'

'Was it something I said? Did I provoke him?'

'From what you've told me I think you dealt with it well enough. At least you didn't laugh. That really would have pricked his pride. Five minutes in the company of a Masque and all these high-handed politicians turn into children. You need to know how to play them.'

Hummingbird casts a glance into the gloomy streets. 'I heard you put up with much worse in that Comfort Home. The brutality, the inmates who would steal the hair off your head. I'd thought you'd be able to cope with any trick from our ennobled friends.'

'Such a place would make a brute of anyone. I survived because I believed that, no matter what happened to me on the outside, inside I was still better than those who were abusing me. Has anything changed? Sir James was like a bully or a cruel big brother. Even when he was warned off by Kingfisher it all seemed a twisted game to him.'

'He hardly touched you. You said so yourself.'

'He opened the top of my head and stuck a barb inside my mind. I was assaulted as readily as if he'd lifted my skirts and bundled me into the gutter. He got the better of me and I let him do it. That's why he walked away laughing. That's why I hate myself. The Abbess said I was reborn, that when I became a Masque my past would die. I believed her. I thought my past could be cast aside. I had started to convince myself that my time in the Comfort Home never really happened, that it was a fictional episode from a novel or one of those dreadful stories in the magazines from the circulating library. My God-fearing father would've shot me if he knew the things I did in the Comfort Home, if he'd heard what came out of my mouth. And just when I thought I could be a sweet little girl again out jumps the past and screams in my face.'

Hummingbird doesn't say anything else, for which Wasp is grateful. By the time their carriage draws up in front of the House she's composed herself with the help of some borrowed rouge.

Rain starts falling when they step onto the kerb, a clinging drizzle that spangles their wigs and chases them up the steps to the front door. Like butterflies turning into caterpillars, the girls shed their glittering wings on stepping back into the velvet throat of the House. Greedily it swallows their charms. Gowns, hats and jewellery all vanish into the dressing-room coffers.

The Abbess is waiting for them in the hall. 'Did the night go well?'

'There was an incident,' Hummingbird says. 'Kingfisher was obliged to assist us.'

'Is Kingfisher nearby?'

'He's retired to the yard.'

The older woman laces her fingers together. 'I see. Neither of you is hurt?'

'No.'

'You will recount tonight's events, Hummingbird. I dislike the thought of trouble so early in your protégée's career. Wasp, go to bed. I may speak with you tomorrow.'

Next morning Wasp expects a summons from the Abbess despite Hummingbird's reassurances. However, the matriarch has another game in mind. At breakfast, Moth receives a pink-ribboned scroll, her first, and behaves as if she's been handed a live snake. The content of Wasp's own Assignment is clear enough.

'I'm to take Moth to Mother Joan's,' she tells Hummingbird in their bedchamber. 'Is this another test?'

'More of a distraction, I think.' Hummingbird pours water into the washbowl. 'After last night's adventure look on it as a token of the Abbess's faith in you.'

'Shouldn't Red Orchid be doing this?'

'The Abbess has her reasons.'

Wasp feels anything but honoured as she bundles a nervous Moth into a hired chaise. The House coach is engaged and the stranger on the chaise's driving perch does nothing to quell Wasp's feelings of unease. Throughout the blessedly short journey Moth bombards her reluctant keeper with questions, all the while pressing her gloved fingers together until the knuckles click.

'Stop doing that before I lose my wits,' Wasp warns, but the other girl can't settle. She seems to have forgotten the branding episode, or pushed it temporarily out of her mind. At their destination, Moth's gown catches on the step and she nearly sprawls into the gutter. Inside is no better. Nothing Constance brings seems to fit. Gowns are either too short, too long, too this, too that. Slippers pinch her feet or flap like landed fish. She turns queasy when Constance tries to pin a straw bonnet to her hair. In the end she's presented wearing more or less the same clothes she'd arrived in. One look at Moth's plain travelling gown and Mother Joan's face crumples. Nevertheless she makes a fair game of it, forcing a smile and passing round the cakes. Moth stammers through all her sentences and spills an entire dish of tea down the front of her dress. While Constance escorts her to the kitchen to clean herself, Mother Joan drops the pretence. 'Where did you find that pudding of a girl? I have never been plagued with anyone so clumsy.'

'I am sorry. This is her first Assignment.'

'She has a nice enough heart, but is very much in the wrong trade, I think. Take her home. The day is spoiled beyond repair.'

Wasp is stretched out on the bed in her nightshift, her belly full of hot tea, her skin tingling from the evening bath.

'The water might still be warm enough if you want to jump in,' she says, as Hummingbird breezes through the door.

'I don't fancy swilling about in your leftovers, thank you,' Hummingbird replies. 'I'll have one in the morning, or use a pomander to keep me sweet. Right now I could sleep in a mud puddle and not give tuppence for it. Besides, I have news.'

Wasp props herself on an elbow. 'What's happened?'

Hummingbird sits on the edge of the bed, nudges off her slippers and reaches across the mattress for her shift, which is folded neatly over the footboard. Her face is still ghost white, her lips bloody with rouge. 'It seems our little Moth has taken flight.'

'She's run away?'

Hummingbird nods. 'Flew the coop some time this evening, no doubt after stewing on her bad performance at Mother Joan's. Kingfisher's already on the scent. It's a big city, but there are only so many places a girl like her can hide.'

'Perhaps she'll give him the slip.'

'He'll have her back before she's gone two miles. Where d'you think she can go? In that day gown? Without any money and not a soul outside these walls who knows her? An inn won't take her. There are no straw-stuffed barns to snuggle into for the night. Even if she clambers into someone's stable yard chances are a dog will have her. Kingfisher is familiar with every doorway and alley between here and the river. Even if she does slip past him a constable will catch her. The Abbess knows most of them by name.'

'Will she suffer another branding?'

'Running away is more serious than pinching a strip of penny ribbon from a hawker's cart. Punishments are decided by the Abbess and, truthfully, I think she's been patient with that girl long enough.'

Hummingbird finishes undressing and slips between the covers. After a while, Wasp joins her and blows out the candle. The room surrenders to the night. Soon Hummingbird is snoring. Wasp lies on her back with her eyes open, the pillow soft beneath her scrubbed hair. She thinks of Kingfisher moving through the city like a shadow.

Next morning, the Kittens' table is empty. No one mentions the missing girl. Assignments are distributed as usual. Wasp and Hummingbird are to double up again.

'I swear you'll get your own clients soon,' Hummingbird re-assures her. 'I expect you're weary of me playing Mama.'

The Assignment is at a party held on a river vessel. The girls are collected by the client's private carriage and driven a few miles upriver, beyond the city boundaries. Both riverbanks are thick with greenery and remind Wasp of the hedgerows surrounding her village. The water is clear and fresh-smelling, not the foul sludge that creeps through the city's innards. Every few yards fishermen cast lines into the lazy flow. A cry of triumph as a fat trout is landed, wriggling, onto the grass.

'The party's in honour of an alderman's daughter who's just come of age,' Hummingbird says. 'She has a glorious day for it.'

The sky is a blue skillet without a puff of cloud. Guests chatter good-naturedly as they board the boat, which is a restored barge bedecked with blue ribbons. A string quintet plays succession of melodies from a raised platform at the rear, while the front has been scattered with trestle tables laden with food. A few gallants bow to the Masques while their sweethearts stand by and giggle at the boldness of it.

Hummingbird nudges her. 'Here comes the golden girl and her dear papa. Dip a cute curtsey and we might squeeze a decent tip out of them. At least the old man's wife isn't here. Wives always kick up a fuss.'

Petticoats rustle as Hummingbird bends her knees. Wasp follows suit. Their client spreads his hands and grins. 'Ladies, please, I'm not the king.'

Both Masques laugh politely. Their host introduces his daughter, Phoebe, who grasps her fan fit to crack the blades. Her smile, though timid, is sincere.

'Make yourselves useful,' her father tells Wasp. 'Meet my guests. Be friendly. Let them admire you.' He turns to Hummingbird. A look passes between them. 'I have further business to discuss regarding your House,' he says. 'Come and see me once my daughter has given you a tour. I know she is aching to do so.'

Phoebe takes them in hand and guides them around the barge. She gestures at the coloured bunting, expresses awe at the cost of the quintet – 'From *Italy* no less' – and shows them a table laden with silks, perfumes and all sorts of silvery nonsense. 'Birthday gifts,' she enthuses, 'but both of you are the best by far. My friends are quite cut with envy.'

She makes a pretty sight, moving light-footedly across the deck as she introduces them to guests of great importance or none at all. Finally, Phoebe is claimed by the makeshift dance floor with a string of young bucks eager to partner the birthday girl.

'Shall we be asked to dance?' Wasp enquires.

'They wouldn't dare. That would be akin to stealing a fellow's pocket watch. Our presence has been bought by her father, remember? I'd better go and see what he wants to talk to me about.'

Hummingbird goes off in search of their host. Some minutes later she and the old man disappear into the bowels of the barge. At something of a loss, Wasp decides to stand by the gangplank and smile at anyone who passes. She's aware of a mild sense of outrage at her presence – the House has already honed that instinct. Yet, like the coach ride around the park, the party would be diminished without her. Every curl and cut of her appearance has been noted, every act seemingly designed to win her approval.

An hour slips by. A footman arrives carrying a tall glass brimming with lemonade. Wasp, whose face is beginning to ache from all the smiling, sips the cool drink. What business could be detaining Hummingbird?

The afternoon grows sleepy. Another servant appears with a plate of bread and cold meats. Wasp takes enough to be considered polite. Further down the barge, tables and chairs have been moved aside to make room for mock sword fights. Young men weave and feint, clutching walking sticks instead of blades. Every so often a cry of triumph sends the ducks scattering from the water, followed by a smattering of applause.

The sky goldens, then grows red edges. Farewells are made, men and their ladies spill onto the riverbank. Where is Hummingbird? While these guests were feasting, had she managed to eat or drink anything? Wasp approaches the hatch leading into the barge. The footmen are gathered near the stern, smoking pipes and enjoying a quick respite before clearing up. No one tries to stop her. Skirts hitched, she patters down the stairs. Partitions have been erected and rugs thrown on the planking, but the barge still smells vaguely of damp and old fish.

An aisle. A half-open door. Sounds.

A peek through the crack reveals Hummingbird splayed out on a makeshift mattress thrown together out of bunting and tablecloths. Her skirts are bunched around her waist and her stockinged legs lie wide. Their host is on top of her, face flushed, bare rump quivering. Hummingbird's cheeks are pink, her hair a dark fantail on the pillow. She grunts with each thrust, fingernails ploughing bloody furrows down the alderman's back. He bites her ear, nibbles her neck. Then his mouth fixes around her nipple like a suckling babe.

Wasp falls back against the wall. *Did I just see that?*

A stifled gasp. A groan.

Yes, Wasp concedes. She did.

'A complete success, wouldn't you say? And a job well done. I'm grateful to you both. Give my regards to the Abbess.'

Their host slips something into Hummingbird's hand. She touches his cheek without looking at the gift and the contract is concluded. As he returns to the barge and his daughter, the Masques stroll across the grass to the lane and the waiting carriage.

'They don't come much easier than that,' Hummingbird remarks once both girls are inside. 'I told you it's not all pinched rumps and wandering fingers. Most clients are genuine, and that can make up for the disasters.'

'Hummingbird, how familiar are you with that man?'

'That's a peculiar thing to ask.'

'You were gone a long time.'

'We're well known in certain circles. Some pampering is good for business.'

'What do you mean by pampering?'

'A little talk, a little time, a little attention. He paid for this Assignment, remember?'

'He handed you something. Show me.'

'Why the fuss? Here, take a look.'

Wasp stares at the object nestling in the palm of Hummingbird's gloved hand. An opal shaped like a tiny egg. 'Why would he give you such a thing?'

Hummingbird grins. 'Most presents are fair game. The Abbess lets us keep them because it encourages us to do a good job. Don't be envious. You'll get your share in time.'

'Are they always so expensive?'

'Within reason. Some besotted Frenchman once presented Swift with a racehorse. He had it brought to the front door with a red ribbon tied around its neck. When the Abbess saw it I'm surprised she didn't birth a litter of puppies. In the end Swift had to be satisfied with a bracelet while her gift filled a stall in our stables.'

'You didn't see much of the party girl. I hope she wasn't disappointed.'

'I doubt it. According to rumour sweet little Phoebe has tumbled all her family's footmen, worked her way through the coachmen and now has her eye on the stable boy. Her Papa can't wait to marry her off. The party today had nothing to do with her birthday. Papa was trying to hook her a fish, and from his countenance he might have succeeded.'

'Is that all he hooked?'

'What a strange mood you're in today. Perhaps if you'd—'

The carriage lurches to a halt, nearly sending the opal flying from Hummingbird's grasp. The door is flung open and a young man in a feather-trimmed tricorne leaps into the carriage. He sits opposite the two girls, throws off his hat and wipes his brow with a lace kerchief plucked from a sleeve.

Wasp and Hummingbird stare at one another. It's Richard, Sir James's son.

'Forgive this abrupt intrusion, ladies,' he splutters, 'but I fear any other introduction might prove difficult given the circumstances. Our last meeting did not go as well as I'd hoped. My father is so accustomed to blustering his way through Parliament that he sometimes finds it difficult to detach himself.'

'Do you usually accost people in the middle of a journey?' enquires Hummingbird.

'Gracious, no.'

'Our driver is handy with a whip. He could've had both your ears off even if you are a gentleman. I'm right aren't I, Richard, in thinking you a gentleman?'

'Why, yes, yes indeed.' He drops his hat, picks it up, drops it again. 'Though I confess the sight of a guinea brought your fellow up sharp.'

'Ah well, offer a large enough bribe and I daresay even the most dedicated coach driver will turn from his duty.'

Wasp frowns. 'Your father was not a gentleman towards me.'

'Don't judge too harshly,' Richard says, giving up on his wayward tricorne. 'You need a stout heart to survive a den of snakes. Parliament demands everything of a man. As I've explained, it is sometimes difficult to step away.'

'Is that where your future lies? Parliament?'

'Good lord, no, not for any length of time. It'll be a foreign appointment for me, preferably somewhere warm and far away. The wretched English winter has me constantly snivelling.'

'Won't you miss your home?'

'Probably, but a good political career can be forged just as well under a hot sun as grey London skies.'

'Sounds like you have everything sewn.'

'Perhaps, perhaps.' His long fingers dance around one another. 'There are people, important people with whom we must first court favour. Out of one pocket and into another, as it were. In any case it's no talk for ladies.'

'I was a tart the other night,' Wasp reminds him.

'Regrettable, as I said.'

'Why are you here? How did you know we were in this carriage?'

A blush darkens both cheeks. 'A few shillings dropped in the right purse and you can discover anything.'

'You can't have gone to such trouble to chat about politics.'

'Indeed not. I'd like an opportunity to make up for the less than genial ministrations of my father.' He produces a calling card from his jacket pocket and drops it into Wasp's lap. 'I wish to hire your services.'

'After what happened before, the Abbess will need to approve this.' A fat leather purse joins the calling card. 'Consider it approved.'

That evening Wasp visits Moth's bedchamber. The door hangs wide. Inside, the four-poster has been stripped to the mattress. Drawers poke wooden tongues, the insides bare. No hairbrushes, scent bottles or powder caskets litter the top of the dresser. Both windows have been thrown open. Warm breezes gust the curtains into pink butterfly wings. Even Moth's smell has been purged.

'I don't understand,' Wasp says later while Hummingbird combs her hair in front of their own dresser. 'If you're all so certain Moth will be found, why strip her bedchamber?'

'Kittens aren't supposed to have rooms to themselves in the first place. She was only put there until her night troubles were cured. I expect the Abbess plans to give it to you.'

'I don't want Moth's bed no matter how many years I spend here.'

'You can't cling to my skirts forever. As much fun as we've had I'd like some independence.'

Wasp sits on the edge of the bed. 'Taking Moth's room feels like stealing. She's only been gone a day and you'd think she'd died the way it's been cleaned out. What will happen to her possessions?'

Hummingbird shrugs. 'We'll find out after she's brought back.'

Wasp thinks for a moment. 'Did you ever tease her? Or play any sort of prank.'

'Whatever makes you say that? Moth and I became the best of friends.'

Cracks in the Plaster

Moth is apprehended at the Meldrum coaching inn, ten miles out of the city. Wearing stolen clothes, she bluffed her way onto a southbound stage, ordered supper from the innkeeper and tried to skip paying. He locked her in his ale cellar and sent for a constable. According to Hummingbird, she's in the town jail. No one is allowed to see her until the tavern's debt is paid.

Later that day Red Orchid, Moth's one-time tutor, is ordered to accompany the Abbess on a visit to their prodigal Sister. Red

Orchid pleads a bellyache. 'A very convenient malady,' the Abbess observes, but Red Orchid remains unrepentant. 'I'll not stand by and watch one of our own in chains. I've felt manacles and heard the mob baying in my ears. I can't bear those ugly, dirty places.'

Instead of punishment she's given leave to fetch a draught from the Fixer then sent to bed. The Abbess tells Wasp to change out of her day gown. 'You will come instead, unless you too are gripped by a sudden discomfiture?'

Wasp leaves the House feeling that her own gut is full of cannonballs. The Abbess's private chaise, driven with whip-cracking enthusiasm by Leonardo, makes short work of city traffic. No dramatic arrival at an imposing courthouse or prison, but a jiggling journey through back allyes to a former tollhouse standing at the junction of three streets. The turnkey's office is a gin-smelling box, the man himself a grim-faced ape with cracked spectacles perched on his bent nose. He nods at another fellow who's busy warming his rump at the fire. He's the landlord of the Meldrum inn, and he wants a reward.

'I reckoned she was more than a common thief,' he says, winking. 'I get all kinds tumbling through my door. They can order pigeon pie and a glass of claret as haughtily as the rest of 'em, but no matter how fancy they look, I know a runaway when I see one.'

The Abbess turns to the jailer. 'How is the girl?'

'Been howling since we brought her in. We had to keep the chains on.'

'Wasp, go with this man. Try and get Moth to settle if you can.'

The turnkey takes Wasp downstairs and along a fetid passage. Three cells are built into the mould-spattered walls. Two lie empty. 'Been taken and hanged,' the turnkey says as if guessing her thoughts.

A low sobbing issues from the furthest cell. The jailer unlocks the door and pushes it wide. Immediately a rotten stench hits

Wasp in the face. A figure, indistinct in the shadows, springs back on the metal bed frame to which it has been chained.

'I ain't here to do ye harm,' the jailer growls. 'Ye've got a visitor.'

Wasp squints in the gloom. 'Do you have a lantern?'

'Lantern, my arse. The cost o' candles comes out o' my wages. There's a window high up on the wall. Give it a minute and yer eyes'll get used to the light. If ye want I can fetch a stool. Just don't get too close and don't try to sneak her anything.'

'No, no stool.'

'Suit yerself. I'll be back after I've done business with yer mistress. If ye want anything just yell. I'll hear ye.' He ducks back out and locks the door. Wasp listens to his heavy feet tramp back down the passage. The window he mentioned is no more than a slit in the masonry that allows a finger of light to filter through. The figure on the bed has stopped whimpering and is bundled up at one end, watching her. No blanket, just a layer of coarse sacking. Apart from a pisspot the cell is otherwise bare.

A whisper. 'Bethany, is that you?'

Ignoring the turnkey's orders, Wasp sits on the edge of the bed. She grasps Moth's hands only to let go on hearing a gasp of pain.

'Sorry, I didn't mean to hurt you.'

'I knew someone would come, from the House I mean. I didn't think it would be you. You're going to take me back, aren't you?' She leans her head against the wall. In the gloom her face is the colour of fat clouds about to sick rain onto the streets. Creases spider-web the corners of both eyes. Her lips are thin and white in a mouth that's never going to smile again.

'I've come because you need a friend.'

Moth lets out a sigh. 'When were you ever my friend, Bethany?'

'I'd like to think things have changed.'

Metal clinks as she shifts her feet. Her gown is torn. It smells of earth and rusty shackles. 'She's here, isn't she? The Abbess?'

'Yes. She's going to pay for your release.'

'Release? I want to die, that's all. Let them hang me. Or measure me for chains and have the crows peck my eyes out. I don't care. Anything would be better than that House.'

'You don't know what you're saying.'

'Is that so? You spend your whole life dodging death while people around you drown, go under a cart, or catch some foul pox and wither before your eyes, and for what? I know exactly what I'm saying. I've grown up fast. I'm an old woman. A crone. You can't stay a child after what I've heard.'

'I don't understand.'

Metal clinks again. A hand, ghostly in the gloom, snatches Wasp's wrist. She feels Moth's breath whisper against her cheek.

'The things she told me. The words she whispered into my ear. There is a place other than the House, a place we're not meant to see. Hummingbird said it's easy to find when you know where to go, which knobs to turn, the doors that will open and the ones that won't. The House can offer more than a pretty girl to put on your arm or take to the opera. Those who want it, get it. Dear Lord, they get everything. Watch where you walk, Bethany. You don't want to tread in the wrong place.'

She stares at her manacles, at the swollen wrists beneath the cuffs. 'I'll never leave here. My bones will be buried in the back yard and no one shall ever know I lived.'

'Hummingbird loves to tease,' Wasp says. 'That girl could convince you the world is made of suet pudding if she chose. We all know how exhausted you've been. Your imagination can play whatever games it likes and Hummingbird will always be around to stoke it. She can be a nuisance but means no real harm.'

'You believe that?'

'Of course. She's the closest I've had to a real friend since arriving at the House.'

Moth leans back against the wall. 'I couldn't become a Masque. Not for a lifetime of pretty gowns and dancing lessons. The Fixer can parade me in front of those mirrors as much as he likes and it won't make any difference. In my heart I'd still run away. Or perhaps go mad. What a sweet escape that would be.'

'Is life with us so terrible?'

'Do you see my brand? When I first arrived the Abbess asked whether I would be a slave or a predator. I'm nothing but a common thief. I can't help it. Whenever I see something pretty I have to have it. I'm a magpie. Many times I've sat with my plunder and had no notion what to do with it. Usually it's too late to give it back, and even if I did I'd likely steal something else. It's a feeling that rises suddenly inside me, as if I become a different girl.'

'Is it worth such a risk?'

'I don't just steal their goods, I steal a part of them. I think if I do that they can't hurt me, and if I do it enough times nobody can. People believed me too mousy to misbehave, and so I got away with it. Once, twice, then many times after. Even when I was caught with someone's fob watch in my hand it was thought I'd made a silly mistake, until my victim turned out to be a lawyer. Don't you understand, Bethany? I can't scrub floors or wash dishes in the House for the rest of my days. It's the thought of *not* stealing that brings the snakes slithering out from under my bed.'

Moth makes a hollow sound at the back of her throat. 'I was too quiet in my nature to say anything. Always too quiet, but the House has given me time to think.'

'Moth, I'm sorry.'

'Far worse tales are told. You'll hear things that'll make your ears bleed. Never forget that you're among killers, thieves and whores. Hummingbird will tell you. She knew all about me. And she knows about you too.'

Wasp finds herself shrinking away from this pale girl with the dark, dead eyes. 'How can she know so much?'

Moth sighs. 'Hummingbird flies higher than anyone except perhaps Nightingale. I don't know what she wants but it can't bode good for any of us.'

'I thought Nightingale was the one with the black heart. She's sour enough towards me.'

'Have you ever seen her bedchamber? No, I suppose not. You've no call to go to that part of the House. One of my chores was stripping the linen on her bed. What a strange place to be, piled with a hundred pairs of gloves and a box on a shelf no one's allowed to touch.'

'That means nothing. I've shared with Hummingbird since my first night in the House and she has her peccadilloes.'

'Don't notice much, do you? Nightingale turned absolutely poisonous when I fetched this brand on the back of my hand. She and the Abbess near had a catfight over it and Nightingale is the only girl who can get away with that. She makes more money than the rest of you put together, but she's not as spoiled as you think.'

'But she—'

'I saw her at the posting house when I was on the run. Her face was caked with paint and she wore a plain gown, not much better than a servant's. Even so I couldn't mistake her. You've seen the way she moves – a sort of half-glide. She was trying to hide it, but that's like a horse trying to walk on its hind legs. At first I thought she'd been sent after me, but she boarded a private coach, one I've never seen before. And she looked desperate. Whatever is going on, you might need to think about who your friends truly are.'

The door swings inwards. The turnkey stands framed in the lantern light from the passage. He steps aside and the Abbess walks into the cell. Moth scrabbles to the end of the bed, her bare feet slithering on the sacking.

'I think you two have talked enough,' the Abbess says.

Wasp grinds through the rest of the day with a dozen different thoughts shouting for space in her head. The Abbess had sent her back from the jail in a hired chair. Running upstairs, she'd found the bedchamber door locked. Rattling the doorknob achieved nothing. Eventually she went in search of Eloise, finding her in the maids' parlour with her feet propped up in front of the hearth and a coffee cup on the table beside her.

'No mistake, *chérie*,' Eloise explained. 'The time has come for you to fly the nest. Here, let me show you to your new palace. You will enjoy having a place to yourself, *oui?*'

Wasp followed the maid along the passage until she stopped outside Moth's bedchamber.

'I don't want this,' Wasp protested.

'Well, you've got it,' Eloise said, leaving Wasp standing at the door.

Fresh linen covered the bed, a fire was already crackling in the hearth and a clutch of fresh flowers had been placed next to a ewer brimming with water. Towels were piled beside the basin and a clean day gown hung in the wardrobe. Wasp tugged open the top of the dresser. Brushes, scent bottles, a pot of rouge and some powder. She slammed the drawer closed and sat on the edge of the bed. Could dark horrors really live behind these cream-plastered walls? Or were they rattling about, like the chains that bound her, inside Moth's own head?

Afternoon fades into dusk. Wasp tries to catch up on a few society magazines but finds it impossible to settle. Finally a weary-looking Eloise waddles into Wasp's new bedchamber and sets a tray of tea and buttered scones on the fireside table.

'Any news?' Wasp asks.

The maid tucks a few loose strands of hair back under her mob cap. 'Moth is home and with the Fixer. She keeps trying to send a message to the Abbess but no one will listen to her.'

'Will she be branded again?'

'Truly, *enfant*, I do not know.'

After Eloise leaves, Wasp sits on the fireside chair and stares at the pots of butter and blood-red jam. Her belly squirms at the thought of eating anything. The tea tastes sour and she spits it into the fire. Finally she slips out of her day gown, pulls on a fresh shift and blows out the candle. This room and its furnishings are nearly identical to the bedchamber she'd shared with Hummingbird, yet everything feels different. The sheets are stiff, the mattress hollowed in all the wrong places. She tries tossing her pillows every which way but still can't get comfortable. In the grate, the fire crackles and dies. Shadows soften and are swallowed by the dark.

I miss Hummingbird, she thinks. *I miss her soft hair brushing my cheek. I miss her cold feet shivering the backs of my knees, and her tickly little snore.*

Finally, alone in that barren room with the moon cycling in the sky outside like a pitted shilling, Wasp finds a door into sleep.

She wakes with a splitting headache and grit-encrusted eyes. She turns over to speak to Hummingbird then remembers with a clarity every bit as painful as the hammers thumping away at the front of her skull. Pulling herself to a sitting position, she rubs both eyes and tries to adjust to the sunlight streaming through the open curtains. A new fire crackles in the grate and last night's uneaten supper has been taken away.

'Eloise, with such quiet feet you would make a good cutpurse,' Wasp mutters. A splash of cold water and a fresh day gown puts her in the right mood to face the day. The day brings an Assignment.

Wasp stares at the name. Initially thinking it must be Richard, that he'd kept good on his word in the carriage that day, she'd slipped away from breakfast at the earliest opportunity and taken the scroll upstairs. But it isn't her bold admirer. It's Mother Joan. And the Assignment is for that afternoon.

Instead of Leonardo or Kingfisher a hire carriage arrives with a starched driver on the bench. His glance bites as she climbs inside.

Fine, she thinks. *I'll wager I eat at a better table than you.*

Mother Joan waits in her usual chair, a yappy white dog perched on her lap. The same old nonsense spills out of her mouth. 'Dear Polly' this and 'Darling Polly' that. Wasp's headache bangs inside her skull. She forces herself to drink the insipid tea and eat the cakes Constance brings in. Carriage wheels clatter outside and set the dog barking. It tries to leap out of Mother Joan's lap while she burbles soothing words. Wasp regards those sagging, powdered cheeks and thinks of Moth sitting white-faced and chained in a stinking jail cell. Mother Joan's mouth more and more resembles a ragged hole. Cake crumbs have lodged between her teeth. Her voice seems to gain in pitch until it becomes a ceaseless whine. Wasp feels as if needles are being shoved into her ears. She chokes on a lump of lemon cake and bends over, coughing.

'There, there, dear.' Mother Joan plucks a blue kerchief from the fireside table. 'Take a sip of water then dab your eyes with this. Look, it's your favourite colour.'

Wasp tears open her bodice in a shower of fastenings. 'These aren't my clothes and I am not your daughter. Neither am I your sister, cousin or grandchild. I have no place here and I don't belong with you. Blue is not my favourite colour, I hate this tea and your cakes turn my stomach.'

Off goes the dog again. *Yap-yap-yap.* Mother Joan shrinks into her chair. 'You are upsetting Belle.'

'As for that beast, I'd like to wring its flea-bitten neck for the way it makes me scratch. It stinks like a privy, and eyes everything I eat as if it didn't already have enough to stuff its fat belly with. Why d'you make me come here? Why do this to yourself? For pity's sake let the past die.'

There. That's it. Wasp falls back against the sofa, torn material flapping around her exposed breasts. To add to her indignity, the borrowed dress rips at the thigh.

Now I've done it. I'll get thrown out. No carriage to take me back. I'll have to walk. The Abbess will hear of it and I'll fetch a brand. Maybe on the back of the hand like Moth. Maybe somewhere worse. I might lose my Emblem. I'll have a scar on my cheek like Eloise and spend the rest of my life cleaning out fireplaces.

'Does my game really upset you so?'

Mother Joan's voice is evenly toned, as if she's simply asking the time of day or the state of the weather. Wasp buries her face in her hands. 'It's wrong. Polly should be allowed to rest in peace. You can't cling to someone by dressing a stranger up in a badly fitting gown.' She strokes her brow. 'I feel my head will burst.'

Mother Joan regards her with a hint of a smile on her lips. 'I'll wager your pride hurts more.'

Wasp takes the offered kerchief and blows hard, thinking of how the Fixer wouldn't approve of such an unladylike gesture. Mother Joan indicates the chair on the other side of the hearth. 'Come and sit over here. It's time we had a real talk. No games. No masks.'

What else have I to lose? Wasp does as she is bidden. Cushions sink beneath her weight.

'I take it you've had your fill of tea,' Mother Joan continues. 'Is there anything else you would prefer? Water? Lemonade? Perhaps a nip of Madeira? It's wonderful for settling the nerves. I speak from experience, believe me.'

Wasp shakes her head.

'Give me a moment to put Belle somewhere quieter. I'll also need to settle Constance. She'll be concerned.'

'I'm sorry.'

'Don't be. As a little girl I was never very good at playing Charades.' She rises from her chair in a rustle of petticoats and carries the dog, whimpering now, out of the room. Wasp closes both eyes and massages her temples. The headache softens from a roar to a dull *thump-thump* like an extra heartbeat inside her skull. A moment later her hostess is back, a cup in her hands.

'This is a herbal draught,' she explains. 'Cook makes them. She's no apothecary but her family is gifted when it comes to natural remedies. I always keep some nearby. It will help settle you.'

Wasp takes the cup and sips the contents. Warm spices swill around her tongue. She mumbles her thanks.

'Now,' Mother Joan continues, 'Constance has laid out your own garments in the withdrawing room. Once you have changed, come back here and we shall talk. This is one conversation, I think, that is long overdue.'

Something Right, Something Wrong

'Get that thing out of my House.'

'She cannot go back. She will be beaten. Perhaps worse.'

'Then throw it in the river.'

'Abbess, this is Mawusi, daughter of our village healer.'

'Not my concern. Or yours. Everyone in this House has left their past behind. I put the roof over your head, food in your belly and those clothes on your back. You are mine. *Mine*.'

Kingfisher cannot pretend to know the Abbess beyond the patchwork shell she presents. This woman is a hunter who's fought most of her life. Beyond the glamour of the House her trophies and disasters are things she keeps to herself. But milk turned sour can still look white, and something has spoiled inside her head. That much he *can* tell, because he's been taught by a man in whose hands dwelt miracles.

Tribes along the river called him the bone sniffer. Many came to see him, all bringing gifts. Not worthless trinkets, but fruit, live-stock or salt. Items important to the village's prosperity. Outsiders considered his skills godlike, though he made no claim to divinity. 'My magic lies here, in my eyes, nose, fingertips. If someone is ill his body will tell you. A man smiles. His mouth says "I am happy". But what claim do his eyes make, the set of his jaw, the stiffness of his shoulders? Are his hands relaxed and open, or curled into fists? Does he stand easy, or ready to pounce? Warriors ask these things all the time, yet no one thinks them mystics.'

Kingfisher looks down at the girl standing beside him. Her presence is neither fate nor coincidence, but due to one of those moments that can send a life down a completely different course, for good or ill.

The Abbess waves her arms. She's not wearing her porcelain teeth and their absence pulls her mouth into a puckered 'O'. 'I sent you out for money, good money that's mine by right, and you return with this baggage. The House of Masques is not a refuge for any heathen you have a notion to liberate. Throw it out, or you can join it in the gutter. Make your choice.'

Kingfisher returns the girl to the Mirror Room and the back door.

'What will you do?' she says in the song of their homeland. 'Am I to be betrayed again? That woman is full of bad spirit. She wants you to kill me. It was on her face. Will you shame yourself a second time?'

'I won't put your blood on my hands.'

'It is there already. It was there when those slavers put their chains on me. Take the chains away and perhaps then the blood will go.'

'It seems I am still in chains myself.'

The Other Side of the Page

'When Polly died,' Mother Joan says, 'when I saw her stretched out on her bed, her head caved in like a crushed egg, I came downstairs and spent an hour walking around looking at everything. There was the half-dish of tea, now gone cold, lying where she'd left it that morning. Her sampler was on its place beside the fire. Crumbs littered the dining-room table where she'd sat and had breakfast; ham and soft bread dripping with butter – she always loved it. My tears were a long way off. You could have pricked me with an embroidery needle and I wouldn't have noticed. I sat where she'd sat, on the chair, imagining it still warm. I refused to let Constance touch anything. One by one I picked the crumbs off the table, winkled them out until there was a pile in front of me. I couldn't brush them away. They were proof that Polly had lived, had smiled at me that morning, her hands stroking my hair.'

Mother Joan rubs the corner of her eye. 'I took her clothes out of the dresser and spent the afternoon running my fingers over the material. A couple of her bodices had hair around the shoulders – thick auburn strands, not thin and fair like her father's. But then Polly never wore a powdered wig, never hid her hair from the sun. She was always so healthy.

'I even found myself in the washhouse with my head in the laundry basket, her clothes pressed against my face, desperate for a scent of her. What a sight I must have presented. In the end I smuggled the garments upstairs and hid them at the bottom of my wardrobe. Every day I held them, often for an hour at a time. After a while the scent faded until I couldn't even imagine it was there any more.'

Mother Joan's hand curls around Wasp's wrist. The fingers are warm, pink kindling. 'I was quite the beauty in this city once. I certainly had my share of beaux, but Polly taught me what a daughter's love could mean. I'd played silly-girl games for most of my life. I love my husband, love him deeply. But you never forget your child's smile, the first words she utters or the first steps across the nursery rug. In many ways I was still a girl until she died. And I'll never be a girl again.'

She releases her grip. 'What must you think of me, going on like this? I'm old and foolish. "A mind like a butterfly" was how my husband once put it. Polly's death hit him hard too, of course, but he was better able to cope. Politicians need hard hearts in order to survive, and he wanted to be strong for me.'

Wasp doesn't say anything. She can see Mother Joan as a young woman, in love, with the summer blowing lazy dandelions across a face as smooth as a pillow, and soft laughter burbling out of her throat.

'The week I lost Polly there were flowers, condolences, a beautiful church service. Then, overnight, her friends stopped visiting. I never saw any of them again. No, that isn't true. One did turn up, shortly after what would have been Polly's birthday. The girl had been on the Grand Tour with her parents and sailed back from Italy the day before. She stood on my doorstep with a beautiful embroidered reticule made from Italian leather. A birthday gift for Polly. I suppose you could say I pounced on the poor child. I wanted someone to talk to. Needed someone – anyone. Constance was no use. I couldn't mention Polly without her bursting into tears, which set me off too.

'I sat the girl, Arabella, in my parlour and told her Polly was bathing and would come down presently. Over a tray of lemonade and sweet fancies I listened while she told me about her travels on the continent. But before long she started to fidget and kept checking at the clock on the mantel. I tried everything. Chocolate, storybooks, I even tried to show her my collection of pressed flowers. Arabella grew more and more agitated. "Please, Mrs Slocombe, where is Polly?" she entreated, and each time I answered with "She'll be down presently, you know how fussy about her appearance she is". I all but kidnapped the child. She was close to tears. In the end I mumbled something about Polly being tired or unwell. I watched Arabella hurry down the street, petticoats flapping about her legs. She looked back at me, once, as if I was some mad old witch. I never saw any of my daughter's friends again. As for my husband, Polly's death pushed him deeper into his political career. He practically lived in Parliament. Even on the rare occasions I saw him his mind never strayed far from the business of government. I know you say this pretend life I lead is unhealthy. But if it wasn't for this occasional mote of comfort I think I would have been packed off to a madhouse long ago.'

She frowns. 'And that would prove something of an embarrassment for a government minister. My husband has many reasons to be grateful to your Abbess.'

'I hope I haven't spoiled everything.'

Mother Joan shakes her head. 'Since we are finished with pretence do you mind telling me your name?'

'In the House I'm known as Wasp.'

'Hence that colourful picture on your cheek?'

'Yes.'

'Did it hurt?'

'Yes. I'm stuck with it, unless cause is given for its removal.'

'Do you have any brothers or sisters, Wasp?'

'The House is my family now.'

Mother Joan nods as if this is what she expected. 'Would you mind calling on me again? As yourself, I mean. No more masks. No more games. We could chat, or perhaps stroll round the park together. You can wear whatever you choose, talk about whatever you wish.'

Wasp smiles. 'I'd like that, though I'll need the Abbess's approval.'

'She has not disapproved of my money yet.' Mother Joan stands and walks to a cabinet beside the window. Sliding open a drawer, she takes out a slim case and brings it over to Wasp. 'I want you to have this. It was bought for a birthday Polly will now never celebrate. Please don't offend me by trying to refuse. My husband was always pressing me to sell it. I feel it has languished in that drawer long enough.'

Wasp prises open the lid. Snuggled in white velvet is a necklace, glittering with red and green jewels.

'If you ever decide you want a real family,' Mother Joan says quietly, 'you will always be welcome here.'

The following morning Wasp is dealt another Assignment. Her client will call at the House that evening. No name is given, but Wasp can sense Richard's hand in it. Intuition, she supposes.

She drops the scroll into the top drawer of her dresser. Has Moth been given breakfast? Is she still with the Fixer? Wasp could invent a pretext to go to the Mirror Room – brush up on her dancing, perhaps? She could beg a scrap of information, a word, anything that might tell her Moth hasn't been harmed.

You were such a quiet girl. Why couldn't you have stayed that way?

Wasp settles by the window to read a book but the light comes and goes at the whim of the clouds. Giving up, she stretches on the coverlet in a bid to catch up on the sleep she's lost in this foreign bed. Sometime in the early afternoon a knock on the door arouses her. She opens it to find Hummingbird framed against the passage.

'Settled in?' she asks.

'No.'

'Well, I can't help you with that. The Abbess sent me up. It's about your Assignment tonight. Because your client is calling in person extra rules have to be observed. This is my last piece of advice. I'm taking on a new girl in the next few days and she's a difficult little sow by all accounts, so my time is going to be full.'

'You'd better come in.'

Hummingbird declines a chair and waves away the glass of lemonade Wasp offers.

'When clients call at the House they're not allowed to see our faces. I don't know if there's a particular reason for this or whether it's tradition. You'll meet in the Scarlet Parlour.' Hummingbird presses something into Wasp's hand. A porcelain mask, angular and insect-like. The edges are trimmed with white fur, and sapphires splinter the gold with radiant shards of blue. 'This is yours. You would've had it sooner but the craftsman found an impurity in the material and had to start again. Put it on before you go inside and don't take it off again until you leave. Even if your cheeks are itching enough to make you scream you mustn't ever remove it in the guest's company. He'll be masked too. Sometimes we have several gentlemen callers waiting in the parlour at once and we can't risk them recognising one another. Remember: the same look-don't-touch rules apply. You might be asked to join him in a drink before you leave. Port or sherry is allowed. Don't speak unless prompted.

Stand at your place and avoid staring. Tonight of all nights you must close your ears and mouth. The Abbess will be watching, trying to decide whether her trust in you, and my ability to train you properly, is misplaced. We're both on trial tonight, Wasp. It has proved a fraught week. Don't disappoint me.'

Evening falls in a grey haze. The streets outside seem preternaturally quiet, as if the city is holding its breath. Wasp bathes, and allows Eloise to pin up her hair. Three other girls have Assignments and are already in the dressing room when Wasp arrives. She draws a cream gown looped in swathes of blue and tops it with a tall wig with curls tumbling down one side. Matching cream gloves and satin slippers complete the fantasy.

She checks herself in one of the mirrors. What would her father say now? No matter how hard Wasp tries she can't quite bring his face into focus. He's gone into hiding somewhere between her memories, and any image of him is smothered under a layer of mental gauze.

Her Emblem is perfect. A sharp yellow body, thin shimmering wings, the needle tip of a sting. The mask is painted to match. Wasp slips it on. Her face moulds easily to its inner contours. Whoever made this is a master of his craft.

Richard is waiting on a sofa in the Scarlet Parlour, immaculate in turquoise jacket and white hose. A black feather-trimmed mask conceals the top half of his face. He stands and bows when Wasp arrives. 'There you are, and don't you look magnificent. Yes, quite magnificent.'

Wasp dips her knees in a curtsey. 'I am at your service, sir.'

'Service, eh? No need for such formality. I thought we dispensed with that . . . eh, the other day. Come, sit with me.'

The parlour girl, Raven, has been standing quietly beside one of the looped red drapes. She flits over to a side table and returns with two glasses and a decanter of port. Richard tries to pour, but his hand trembles and some of the drink splashes onto the carpet. Raven remains professionally straight-faced but it's easy to guess what she's thinking.

Wasp sips the port through her mask. After a few minutes, Richard escorts her outside to a brace of hired chairs. They travel to a small inn, a spit from the cathedral, where they're able to liberate themselves from their masks. The low-ceilinged taproom is full of well-dressed men noisily discussing business. In one corner a book club debates the latest titles.

Richard plays with his waistcoat buttons. He makes small talk over supper. Food spits from both corners of his mouth and he drops a lump of fish into his lap. Every third sentence is an apology.

Afterwards they take a stroll in the park. The cooing seats are full of young beaux and their doxies, while the night watchman prowls the verges, lantern throwing bobbing yellow pools across the grass. Richard returns to fiddling with his buttons. He remarks on the moon, which is a pale splodge behind some clouds, and the stars, few of which are out. Wasp walks by his side, saying nothing, waiting for him to work himself up to whatever it is he really wants to tell her. Finally he says: 'You must have admirers. A retinue of them I'd have thought.'

Wasp shakes her head. 'I am merely an escort.'

'Surely you want more than that?'

'My personal wants are not important. Everything is provided by the House.'

'But—' One of the buttons comes loose in his hand. He fumbles it into a waistcoat pocket.

'Yes?'

'A home. Children. A husband. These are the things every woman desires.'

'Really? As a man you would know this?'

'It is common knowledge.'

'For men or women?'

'You say you do not want these things?'

'Some women are grateful to have any life at all.'

'It must be possible to come to some arrangement with your mistress. If the price—'

Wasp stops and faces him. 'Richard, I've enjoyed my time with you, but if you're looking for some sort of wife or concubine then I'd hardly suit. I'm a glorified courtesan – that's what they call them in Europe, isn't it? – and I doubt any member of your undeniably important family would approve. There must be dozens if not hundreds of eligible ladies in this city who'd fight for a chance to wed a young man with your connections. I'm flattered at your suggestion, really I am, but I think the Abbess's price might be too high, even for you. Now why not cherish this evening as a pleasant interlude?'

'The issue runs a mite deeper than that.'

'Whatever you want I'm not the answer. I'm a fantasy. You've hired a pretty gown, a mask, an educated voice. I'm here to provide a distraction, or something you might want to show off to your friends like a new hunting horse or a shiny pair of boots. You don't know anything about me or my past.'

'Really? Why not tell me? I want to know all about you.'

'It's well past the hour. I have a chair waiting at the gate.'

Wasp reaches for his cheek, goodnight fingers already extended. He catches her wrist.

'You must let go of me, Richard. Please understand I am permitted no interest in you beyond that of a valued client.'

His hand drops to his side. Surprisingly he laughs. 'And you must understand, dear Wasp, that it's not necessarily *me* who has the most interest.'

During the bumpy journey back, Wasp huddles in her seat, hands wrapped around her knees, staring at the flickering lights beyond the window.

I haven't heard the last of this. The thought wasn't welcome, but even in the shadows of the park she'd seen enough on Richard's face to recognise the truth of it.

A coach is drawn up at the steps when Wasp's chair delivers her to the House. Stepping into the halo of light thrown out by the carriage lantern is a breathtakingly beautiful creature in white gown and wide, silvery cape. Her face is hidden but that gliding walk, that *attitude*, is unmistakable.

Wasp chases her into the hall. 'Nightingale.'

She turns in one fluid movement. Astonishing how she does that, as though running on silent wheels. Her eyebrows raise and her head inclines. *Already putting me in my place*, Wasp thinks.

'What do you want, Sister?' Nightingale's voice seems to freeze the air between them. 'It has been a long evening and the hour is late.'

'What has become of Moth? Don't pretend you don't know.'

Nightingale's mouth purses. 'Our former Kitten is safe in one of the House's tucked-away places. The Fixer stalks her bed, not resting until she is soundly asleep. And she does sleep, Wasp. The draught she drinks each evening makes sure of that.'

'Has she been given food? She was half starved in that jail.'

'Moth is persuaded to eat.'

'Why such treatment? Does fleeing the House warrant torture?'

'She's reluctant to take meals, Sister. She's trying to run away again. Trying to be free in the only way she knows how. But the House won't let her go. You should see how slender she has become. Before long you will be able to cup her waist in both hands. I've heard that's how they like them in the Cellar.'

'Cellar? What do you mean?'

'Oh, don't you know? You seem proficient at thrusting your nose into everything else. After tonight our runaway is going to embark on a new career. It appears she won't be getting her Emblem after all.'

Wasp throws the mask across the room. It strikes the edge of the dresser and clatters onto the floor. She kicks over a chair, tears off her wig in a flurry of powder and throws her gloves onto the floor.

'If you are going to throw a tantrum, *chérie*,' Eloise observes, 'then you'd do better to take it out on the pillows or upholstery. Bruises will only spoil your pretty skin.'

'Take that food out. I don't want any supper. It turns my stomach.'

'As you wish, *chérie*, but you had better return your garments to the dressing room. Such fine things to be so poorly treated.'

'I don't care about them.'

Eloise puts the supper tray back down on the fireside table. 'I think we need to have a chat, *oui*?'

'A chat? Yes, we need to have a chat, but no more *chérie* this or *enfant* that. I want to know what's to become of Moth. She was terrified, and kept talking about another side to the House. Don't feign ignorance. I can stand here all night. No secrets, remember? So what will it be? Prison? A parish poorhouse? Will she spend the rest of her days at a bench seaming dresses, or touting for business round the back of a coaching inn?'

'I think,' Eloise says, 'you had better go to bed.'

'And I think you had better get that tongue of yours working. It's busy enough most other times.'

'Such impudence is not becoming. Don't think I shall not take my hand to you, high and mighty Masque or not.'

'And don't think I shan't pull your hair out by the roots. If there's one thing my time in the Comfort Home taught me it's how to fight like a bitch defending her pups. Moth was branded because of me.' .

Eloise clicks her tongue. 'You should not have become so involved with her. Remember if one girl spoils something it is spoiled for all of us. If you won't take supper then may I pour myself some tea? This *contretemps* has given me a dry mouth.'

Hot liquid sloshes into a cup. Eloise takes a sip and turns back to face Wasp. 'Look at this scar on my cheek. I am allowed to remain in the House because I persuaded the Abbess I make a good maid. My labours help pay for this pretty bedchamber, that gown, the sumptuous breakfast you will no doubt eat tomorrow. Moth will not be cast into the streets. A use will be found for her.'

'She can't take any more punishment. It will kill her.'

Eloise shrugged. 'That may be, *chérie*, but there are always other girls to take her place.'

Pleasures and Punishments

Morning dissolves into a sluggardly afternoon. A French lesson with a singsong tutor brought in especially from London. An evening of rich food and a fire that spits flaming hate into the iron guard. Night. Fidgeting in Moth's haunted bed. Mind filling the dark with faces.

Daybreak. Gritty eyes and cold water. Breakfast conjures smoked trout and an Assignment. Some lonely painter boy with indulgent parents. He mutters to himself throughout the course of their riverside walk, stopping only to declare that he'd love to paint her, but it will take a thousand Assignments and more money than his purse can stretch to in order to capture her perfection on canvas. Wasp, who has given him no more than half her attention the entire time, nods sympathetically. Then, at the end of it all, he surprises her.

'May I have a souvenir?'

'A what?'

'A memento of an enchanting evening,' he elaborates. 'Something modest. Perhaps a glove? The one with which you have so delicately touched my cheek?'

She thinks about it for a moment. No rule she's aware of forbids such a thing. 'This one,' she says, tugging off her left glove. 'The other has touched many faces. It would not be unique to you.'

He thanks her and cradles it like a treasure as he escorts her back to the hire carriage.

In the House, the Abbess calls Wasp over to her desk, gesturing at the bare hand.

'A glove? You handed him your glove?' she remarks once Wasp has explained.

'Was that wrong?'

The Abbess grins, a horribly out-of-place expression on her usually dignified face. 'They are welcome to their petty trophies. Kingfisher will add ten guineas to his account.'

'Ten guineas for a strip of cloth?'

'Chances are he'd come up with double if pressed. What he obtained was more than a glove. It was part of a Masque. Part of you. And if he wants it, he has to pay.'

She reaches beneath the lip of the desk and produces a letter. 'Joan Slocombe has written to express her satisfaction with your services and has offered to pay extra for the continued pleasure of your company. This is not the first good word I've heard concerning you. The Fixer said you were a natural the first night you stumbled through our door. You could become a Harlequin in two years, perhaps less.'

Standing in that candle-flicker hall with the deep drapes and hidden doors, Wasp grasps an opportunity.

'I would ask something.'

'And what would that be?'

Wasp opens her hand. Mother Joan's necklace spills across the top of the desk. 'This belongs to me. A client's gift.'

The Abbess glances at the string of sparkling jewels. She makes no move to touch it. 'Why do you show me this trinket?'

'I wish to engage a Masque for one night.'

The older woman's gaze remains even. 'It is not unknown. Masques occasionally find comfort in one another's private company. Do you have someone in mind?'

'Nightingale.'

A heartbeat. Two. The pupils of the Abbess's eyes widen into pitch pools. 'Nightingale is a Harlequin. She has dented the pockets of dukes and princes.'

'You don't need to look closely at the necklace to know it's worth ten of her.'

'Whatever game you are playing, my dear, ruffling the feathers of Nightingale is not lightly done. I won't tolerate a storm in the House.'

'There will be no trouble, I promise.'

A smile spreads across the Abbess's withered lips. 'She is beautiful, is she not? You wish to learn from her, perhaps?'

Wasp swallows. 'Yes, she's beautiful, but my reasons are my own.'

Tuesday morning. The Abbess hands out the day's Assignments. Scrolls for Dragonfly, Swallow and Hummingbird. Deportment practice for most of the others. Wasp stares at the remains of her meal. On the edge of her vision, the Abbess hands Nightingale a scroll tied with red ribbon. 'A special client for you.'

Nightingale catches Wasp outside her bedchamber. 'What is the meaning of this, Sister?' She waves the opened scroll under Wasp's nose. 'A jest? You seek to play games with me?'

She's not angry. She is too confident in her own power for that. But Wasp has gone too far to become intimidated. 'Tonight your life is mine, bought and paid for. You will give me your best, Nightingale, your very best, or you are not a Harlequin.'

'My best for what exactly?'

Wasp shakes her head. 'Later.'

Wasp finds Hummingbird in the maids' parlour, buried in an armchair in the corner nearest the window.

'Unusual place for you to spend your time,' Wasp observes.

'I'm ducking my new Kitten. She's an absolute shrew and keeps beating my ears about everything. Practically expects her meals brought up on a silver trencher.'

'I didn't see her at breakfast.'

'This one needs work before she can be allowed near the Kittens' table.' Hummingbird shifts in the chair. 'I hear you've hired Nightingale for an evening. Where do you propose to take someone like her? She flies higher than any of us.'

'Then it's time her wings were tied. Buying her was easy enough.'

'The Abbess herself would go on Assignment with you for the right price. How did you pay for it? Put on a highwayman's mask and hold up a coach?'

'I had something valuable I could barter.'

'The Crown Jewels?'

Wasp laughs. 'Not even Nightingale is worth that. It's no use giving me that puppy-dog look, Hummingbird, I shan't tell you a thing. Not until later anyway. I've a feeling this evening is going to prove dramatic enough.'

'Your Masque is preparing herself,' the Abbess says. 'Go and wait for her. You can forgo any disguises. Raven will serve as your hostess tonight.'

The parlour girl appears and places a gloved hand on Wasp's arm. Raven's eyes are swimming with a mixture of bemusement and curiosity. Word has indeed spread quickly through the House.

Wasp fixes her gaze on Raven's back as she leads the way into the Scarlet Parlour. Her bodice is a rainbow of glittering, gem-encrusted embroidery, the colours shifting in the candlelight as she moves. Heels click on the polished floor.

The divans in the Scarlet Parlour are freshly brushed, the cushions plumped and undisturbed. Raven makes a sweeping gesture. Wasp chooses a seat at random and perches on the edge, knees pressed together, hands clasped in her lap.

'What will be m'lady's pleasure?' the parlour girl enquires.

Wasp stares blankly for a moment. Of course. House custom with newly arrived clients. Wasp has experienced it before, but to be a recipient, to sit on the other side of the curtain, now that is a foreign land.

'Brandy.'

Raven lifts the crystal decanter and pours a generous measure. Wasp's hand shakes as she accepts it. She presses the rim to her mouth to steady the trembling. She's seldom tasted brandy. Wine, yes, and a little gin if in the mood for something sharp. However the colour appeals, and a tentative sip spreads warmth across her tongue. She swallows, eyes closed. The clock chimes the half hour.

No use, even the drink can't help her relax. Wasp stands and traces the pattern of the rug with her feet as it spirals out from the centre. Despite spending an hour with powder and rouge she feels terribly exposed, and her stomach is performing butterfly loops.

She fingers her Emblem. In the mirror it had seemed very stark sailing the pink, round ocean of her cheek. Her growing hair, now satin smooth and glossy with health, is tucked under a pink-tinted wig. A soft gown of sapphire taffeta hugs the now generous curves of her body. The garment looks spectacular, provided she doesn't stretch too far or bend over unexpectedly. The rich scent she'd dabbed behind her ears and on the underside of both wrists flowers the air.

'Don't let her scare you,' Hummingbird had advised, 'whatever you have planned. Be sure to dress like the Queen and use all the weapons a young woman can muster. Beauty is the best armour. You may not defeat her in those stakes but, by heaven, you can give her something to think about.'

The door opens. Nightingale glides into the room, lethally dressed in a scarlet gown trimmed with white bows. Her eyes are as sharp as flint. She plucks the glass Raven offers her, swallows the contents with effective grace then dips a professional if insolent curtsey.

'I am at your service.'

Wasp puts down her glass. 'Let's go.'

'So, my Sister, tell me what delights you have in mind. I take it this is no whim, that the evening's festivities have been carefully plotted? No destination was mentioned on my scroll and the Abbess refused to enlighten me.'

Wasp settles back in the seat of the hire carriage. The Abbess offered her Leonardo's services but he's the last person Wasp wants on this excursion. The Abbess didn't press the matter nor ask any questions. She seemed distracted.

'Actually, Nightingale, I want *you* to escort *me* somewhere.'

'Oh? An opera? A gavotte? Perhaps coffee in one of the finer houses? Or would you prefer a stroll by the river so we can chat. I promise not to laugh as you spill your secrets into my ear.'

Wasp shakes her head. 'Has Moth been taken from the House?'

'I beg your pardon?'

'Moth. Has she gone? Answer me.'

'Yes.'

'Then you will take me to her.'

The carriage lantern bleeds yellow over Nightingale's face. 'A mighty peculiar way to satisfy your curiosity, Sister. If you want to see her that badly then I'm sure a visit, or even an extensive stay in her new accommodation, can be arranged.'

'Save your poison for the House. I'm your client. Do as I ask.'

'Poison?' Nightingale leans over and, to Wasp's astonishment, grasps her hand. 'Whatever point you wish to prove, the Cellar is no place to do it. If your desire is to humble me then I'll clean out your bedchamber, serve you breakfast, help Leonardo sweep the stables, anything you like. But believe me, Sister, the Cellar is not an establishment where anyone in the House chooses to go.'

Wasp shakes her hand free. 'Lean out of the window and give the driver directions. I want to see this "Cellar".'

Nightingale, face pinched, does as instructed. The carriage jolts forward.

'Will it be a long journey?' Wasp asks.

'No.'

'Whatever happens when we get there I want your support, do you understand?'

'I am your paid escort, though I suspect this adventure will end up costing you a lot more than the Abbess's fee. May I ask what you propose to do when we arrive?'

'That depends on what I find.'

'What part of the city is this?'

Terraced dwellings, low-slung warehouses, higgledy-piggledy buildings dotted around as though they'd fallen out of the sky. Close by, the stink of the river. No carriages, drunks or hawkers. Somewhere a cat is yowling at the moon. Upstairs windows show few lights. Yet the feeling of a hundred hidden eyes shivers the spine.

'This is a borderland,' Nightingale says. 'An in-between place. A threshold between pretty parks and gin-soaked gutters. Two worlds living off one another need a place of parley, a market, a trading place. There are no such people as "withs" and "withouts". Both have things the other wants and here is where the bartering is done. No constables, no footpads. No face that will willingly recognise yours or be recognised in turn. In the pretty crescents they will cut your purse. In the gin shops they'll cut your throat. But here you can buy what you want or sell what you have to offer.' Nightingale flicks out her tongue as if tasting the night. 'We're not supposed to be here. If Kingfisher catches us—'

'Kingfisher doesn't know where we are and our hire driver is two streets away tending to his horses. Now where is the Cellar?'

The Harlequin gestures towards a house bracketing one end of a terrace. 'I tell you, Wasp, I don't like this. Masques or not, we don't fit here. Inside that house are people who wouldn't twitch at turning your gown inside out and you along with it. These are not common men I speak of but high-class sparks who, for sport, would slice a person to pieces with their sword tips. If anything goes wrong the Abbess will have us both branded.'

'Why? What is this place?'

'It's a brothel.'

'What?'

'A brothel. A whorehouse. Call it what you will. You cannot say you didn't suspect. There is more to the workings of the House than sending pretty girls out to sup with gentlemen. Tell me what man wouldn't wish to take his interests further after having been whipped up to a frenzy of delight by his charming companion? Carriages are always ready to whisk clients off to the Cellar. They are taken from abstinence to the feast table and it blows their senses to the stars. In such a mood they'd sell their own shirts for a tup. Whatever a man's taste he'll find an agreeable flavour within those walls.'

'You are lying to me.'

Nightingale looks exasperated. 'No, Sister, I am not lying. The Cellar is a place for men with bulging pockets and bulging breeches, both begging to be emptied. It is a place where dreams come true. Dark dreams. The House of Masques is only the gilding on a black lily.'

'I'm going in, and you're coming with me.'

'You won't be permitted. You enter by invitation or not at all.'

Wasp skitters across the street, satin slippers clacking on the paving. Windows beam at her with candle-bright eyes. In the moonlight the stonework resembles a dead face punctured by a dark, vertical mouth. The front door is painted some awful blood colour. 'I can't find a doorknob,' Wasp says, running her fingers across the wood.

'You have to knock to get in. One glimpse of you and the door will slam in your face.'

'Then I'll find another entrance.'

'You'll be caught.'

Stairs descend to the mouth of the basement, blocked at the top by a barred gate. Wasp hitches up her gown and mounts the iron railing skirting the front of the house. One wrong foot and she'll tumble head first into that dark hole.

I won't back out, not with Nightingale watching.

She jumps. Her petticoats catch on a spike and rip. Any other time it would prove funny, but at least she lands on both feet. The gate is secured by a single bolt. Wasp hurries up the steps, slides it back and admits a paler than usual Harlequin. *Why are you so afraid?* Wasp thinks. *What is it about this place that scares you?*

Bawdy music seeps through the windows. Laughter. Raised voices. Curtains block sight of the interior. Wasp grasps the brass latch. It won't budge. She rattles the metal in its fixings then pushes against the door with both hands. Nothing.

'Damn you all, where is she?'

A small wicket opens. Curious eyes peer out. A lock clicks. Yellow light spills across the step. An apparition emerges, a demonic figure in a red slammerkin and a wig that brushes the top of the doorframe. Her face is a hollow pit of powder and rouge as if someone has gathered up the soft folds of her flesh and pinned it to her cheekbones. And there is the scar, the blurring of skin where an Emblem has been.

The figure drops a lopsided grin. 'Oh, here's a pair of high-and-mighty Masques come to put us to bed,' she declares. 'Too haughty to arrange entry by the usual means? If you want us, you pay like the rest.'

'We're looking for someone.' Wasp's voice catches. 'You . . . You must let us in.'

'Is that so? Well, I wear an Emblem too, only it's on my arse. You're welcome to kiss it, my pretties.'

'I don't have time for this.'

'And I have no time for you. Go back to your gilded palace before I slam this door in your faces.'

Nightingale steps up. 'Indulge her, just for tonight. She has a lesson to learn.'

Wasp doesn't wait for a response. She barges into the hall and past a litter of squawking girls. Laughter and rowdy singing assaults her ears. Carpets, sticky with spilled wine, are littered with empty glasses, playing cards, a scattering of coins and the odd slipper. Men, many in their undershirts, chase girls from room to room. A hand grasps her thigh. She slaps it away. A leering face, breath foul with brandy, wavers in front of her. A man sports a woman's wig – an outrageous confection of fruit and paper ships – askance on his skull. Jewellery, enough to ransom a country, glitters on his fingers.

'Come to play, have we?' He makes squeezing motions with his fingertips. Wasp shoves him away, resisting the urge to sink her foot in his groin. Ribald laughter flutters down a passage to her left. Two men, dressed in breeches and nothing else, openly eye her.

'Best leave that one alone, Johnny. Look at her face. She's a Masque and beyond the reach of even your purse.'

'A Masque, eh? What's a stuffed petticoat like that doing down here? 'Tis a place for games. I want to pump a woman's well, not take her to the opera.'

More laughter. Wasp's belly squirms. She glances behind her but can't see Nightingale anywhere in the mêlée. Perhaps she's returned to the carriage. If so, Wasp will skin her to her bones and never mind the consequences..

'Moth.' She struggles to make her voice carry above the racket. 'Moth, are you in here?'

'Bethany.'

She presses harder through the throng. The voice issued from a white-panelled door set into an alcove. Before Wasp can open it someone steps in front of her. The woman who'd accosted her at the entrance.

'Move aside,' Wasp demands.

'This is no place for you. Go back to the House, to your silks and your silver. Read one of your hidebound books or sip tea out of a fine china cup. This is where the real work is done, pretty one. And where the debts are paid. Paid in sweat and tears. Leave now. Pretend you never came through that door. Hope you never come through it again.'

'I can do what I wish. I'm a Masque.'

'I'd say you just forfeited that privilege, m'dear.'

Wasp fumbles in her wig and draws out a fake rose attached to a long, vicious-looking pin. 'My name is Wasp,' she says, 'and this is my sting. Move out of my way or you'll fetch it in the throat.'

The woman shrugs and slips away. Wasp bursts into the room. Moth lies naked and spread-eagled on a bed. She's face down, her limbs tied to the four posts with velvet strips. Her bare rump glistens with some sort of grease. Pink lesions crisscross her back.

In the corner furthest from the door cowers a bony stick of a man, naked himself except for a black mask covering his eyes and a leather codpiece sporting a protuberance like an overgrown nose. It, too, is slick with grease. 'What is the meaning of this?' he blusters. 'I was assured privacy. You have no right—'

Wasp slams the door, scoops a chair out of the other corner and sets it against the doorknob. On a table beside the bed lies a riding crop. The handle is still warm.

'God, no—'

She slashes the crop across his face, putting everything into the blow. He screams and stumbles back against the wall. Her arm rises and strikes, rises and strikes, moving in rhythm like the water pump in a stable yard. She doesn't know how many times she does this or for how long. Voices yell in the corridor outside. The doorknob turns, fists pound against the door. The chair creaks but holds. Wasp is conscious of Moth crying. Her tears only spur Wasp on. The cully is folded in on himself. He lifts his arms in a pitiful attempt at defence. She slices the crop across both wrists, opening them to the bone. Blood speckles her lips. His blood. The front of her gown is covered with it.

The chair splinters and breaks. The door falls open and Kingfisher is in the room, Nightingale on his tail. Behind him a dozen faces ring the doorframe.

Wasp is panting. The wig has fallen off. Her hair is a tangled nest across her face. Kingfisher's dark face is as inscrutable as always. In the corner her victim sobs into the bloodied carpet.

Kingfisher holds out his hand. After a moment Wasp gives him the riding crop. The leather tip is frayed to ribbons.

'Come,' he says, 'I shall take you home.'

'I shall not leave without Moth.'

He doesn't look at the bed, or the creature whimpering on the floor. 'The girl will be taken care of. You have my word on that. Now you must return to where you belong.'

'I don't believe you.'

He lays a hand on Wasp's shoulder, softly enough, though she feels tension in his muscles. His voice lowers to a whisper. 'I have given you my word. You are a Masque. A Masque does not disgrace herself before others. You will walk out of here with dignity and you will do it *now*.'

Everyone's attention is on Wasp as she steps through the debris. Behind her, Nightingale unties Moth from the bed. Kingfisher wraps her in a coverlet and hoists her into his arms. Murmurs ripple through guests and girls alike. Someone giggles. Faces are illuminated with the scandal of it all.

The scarred woman is waiting at the front door, which is open to the street. She curtseys as Wasp passes.

'Perhaps you shall return after all,' she says, tapping her ruined cheek.

'You're going to be punished, Wasp. You have mistreated a Cellar client. He has complained to the Abbess.'

'What was I to do? He was torturing Moth.'

Hummingbird shrugs. 'Cellar games can get a little rough. I doubt she was in danger of her life.'

'How can such a place exist? How many girls are fed to that nightmare?'

'Buying your freedom is expensive. Costs need to be recovered.'

'Moth isn't strong enough for that sort of life.'

'I'm beginning to wonder if she's strong enough for anything. You're in no position to make decisions.'

'What will happen to me?'

Hummingbird fingers the key to Wasp's bedchamber. Wasp has been locked in all night. 'Corrective training followed by a week of serfing for the Harlequins. You'll go through House etiquette until you drop in your shoes.'

'Serfing?'

'Running errands, laying out our dresses, emptying pots, fetching our night possets. Demeaning work designed to teach you humility. If you're a good girl you get the brand. If not, it's the Cellar and this time you won't be going as an uninvited visitor.'

Wasp tents her face with her fingers. 'I shall be branded?'

The other girl nods. 'It's called being kissed by the flaming star. You'll likely get it here, on the soft part of your arm just below the shoulder. Believe me, it doesn't hurt as much as you think.'

'Apart from Moth has anyone else been branded?'

'Of course. No angels under this roof.'

'When will it happen?'

'Work hard and try not to think about it.'

'Where is Moth? Can I see her?'

Hummingbird leaves the room and locks the door behind her.

'Here, slip this between your teeth and bite down hard.' The Fixer hands her a wad of velvet. 'I'll need to keep the iron pressed on for at least a second else the brand might fester. If you're lucky you'll faint. That's nothing to be ashamed of. Everyone's equal when faced with the hot metal's bite.'

'Where are you going to do it? Here in the Mirror Room? Haven't I enough scars?'

'No, the Scarlet Parlour. And as for your scars, be thankful I don't have to remove your Emblem.'

'Why such barbarism?'

'Barbarism? You horsewhipped a client. He's cut to the bone and will carry scars for the rest of his life. I hardly think you can talk of barbarism.'

'Shall we be alone?'

'Your Sisters will witness, but they'll be as quiet as a whisper. I'll enter the room behind you and stand, hooded, to one side of the door. Beside me will be a brazier filled with hot coals and the branding iron. It's all theatricals, designed to teach our girls to be obedient. Sometimes I oil my body to make it glisten like a demon's. But you've already faced your fear, in a glass jar, and you can come through this. It won't hurt any more than it has to and the wound will heal quickly. Now, the sooner you get there the sooner this will be over. No more locked door. No more eating alone in your bedchamber. You'll be back in the fold before suppertime.'

'You're not taking me there? I have to go alone?'

'This is your crime. Your punishment. I don't expect you to be dragged or carried. You're a brave lass, and you'll demonstrate that bravery to us all.'

Wasp takes tiny steps along the passage and across the hall to the doors of the Scarlet Parlour. Not a soul anywhere. The desk and stairs, the candle-spiked alcoves are all empty. She strains her ears. Not a sound, as if the House is holding its breath in anticipation of a storm.

She wedges the velvet strip between her teeth as the Fixer had instructed. The laudanum is beginning to soothe the edges of the world, but her belly is swimming with nerves. She nudges open the door and steps trembling into the parlour. The rugs have been lifted, and laid out on the bare boards is the circle of glittering candles she'd been told to expect. All other lights have been doused. A dozen Sisters line the walls, vague ghosts in their white house gowns. All wear porcelain masks.

And there is the brazier, as if someone has torn the heart out of the fireplace and dumped it into a black iron witch pot. Wasp tries not to look at the coals, at the rod plunged into the brazier's glowing innards. Already she fancies she can feel the iron's heat, metal turned white from hours in the flames.

He is really going to do this, she thinks. *He is going to burn me.*

The laudanum seems to have fled her body. She's startlingly awake, her mind sharp, nerve endings raw. Nostrils pick up the bitter scent of smoke and hot candle wax. She can discern the individual perfumes of the sisters. Their breathing. Shallow. Nervous.

Excited.

Please don't let me scream.

The Fixer appears on the rim of the light circle, hooded as he'd said, and stripped to the waist. Shadows catch his scars and throw vicious lines across his upper body. Wasp bites down hard on the velvet. Her jaw flares with pain. The Fixer gestures at her to kneel then pinches her skin, hard, between thumb and forefinger. Then the iron's bite. An angry hiss, like sizzling bacon. A wisp of greasy smoke. And the smell. *Oh, the smell* . . .

Candles tumble as she slumps forward onto the floor. A collective gasp sweeps the room. The Fixer's arms curl around her shoulders and draw her upright. The Abbess appears out of the smoke, kneeling in front of Wasp, arms outstretched. Wasp throws herself into that forgiving embrace.

Eloise lays a breakfast tray beside the bed. Cheerful sunbeams radiate from her face. 'You really are one of us now,' she declares. 'I hope it does not hurt too much.'

It hurts right enough, like a lump of flesh has been gouged from her arm. Wasp is forced to sleep, when she can sleep at all, on her right side facing the wall. During the day she suffers a dull ache. Night brings agony. Sometimes she's forced to get up and pace the room or sit on the edge of the bed, shrouded in her coverlet.

It's hard to think about Moth. For hours after the branding, Wasp lay in a bubble of misery. The girl who'd been the cause of this now seems the least important thing in the world. The thought of getting into more trouble, of even asking the wrong questions, leaves Wasp sick with fear. How brave she had thought herself, barging into the Cellar. How clever to escape a slow death in the Comfort Home. But the sight of those masked faces in the flickering gloom of the Scarlet Parlour was worse than any beating she'd previously endured.

The Fixer arrives at dusk to change her dressings. He checks the brand and declares it clean. 'A good job.'

'I'm glad you think so. It's been two days and it still throbs.'

'You'll need to endure discomfort for a while longer. But it will fade. You have leave to stay in your bedchamber for the rest of the week.'

'I don't regret what I did. The Cellar is a horrible place.'

'Better girls than Moth have been swallowed up by it. Think of it as a lid that lets the steam out of the pot. We're safe in the House. Safe because of what happens there. You forget how much you have to be thankful for.'

He doses Wasp with a sleeping draught. This time she slips away at once. No dreams.

Nightingale's Box

'Come with me.'

Wasp's half-awake eyes stare at Nightingale through tousled hair. Her face is puffy and disbelieving. She waves a hand in protest. 'Why are you here? I don't need to resume my duties yet.'

Nightingale indicates the wardrobe. 'Find a day gown and put on your slippers.'

Wasp thumps out of bed with the grace of a Shire horse. Nightingale notices the bandage on the girl's shoulder, the way she still favours it. That will pass soon. How quickly the hurt inside might heal is another matter.

Wasp dresses in silence then, at Nightingale's beckoning, follows her along the passage. Every step is full of defiance. 'Am I being punished again?' Wasp demands. 'Is this retribution for what happened at the Cellar? Isn't my brand enough?'

Nightingale presses a gloved fingertip to her lips, opens her bedroom door and waves Wasp inside. She enters reluctantly, as if some form of spidery trap awaits, but no peril lurks in the walls, carpets or curtains. Nightingale closes the door and retreats to a corner. She points to the shelf beside her bed – to the item that sits there.

'That box has been moved.'

'You brought me here to tell me that?'

Nightingale waves a finger. 'No one lays a hand on it but me. No one touches it, moves it or opens it. That rule is as fundamental to the House as any other. I know that casket's place on the shelf to within a hair's breadth. It has been tampered with.'

'Don't you keep it locked?'

'No, Wasp, I don't keep it locked. Not any more. That would defeat its purpose.'

'D'you expect me to admit to touching it?'

'I expect you to open the lid and tell me what you see inside.'

'Can't you look yourself, especially as you are so precious about who goes near it?'

'I could look myself, but to do so would likely kill me.'

'I don't understand. Is it a trap?'

'For me, yes. For you, not yet.'

'Suppose I don't do it?'

'You will.'

'Why?'

'Because you can see that I'm frightened of what's in that box.'

The girl thinks about that for a moment. She remains suspicious, and has a right to be, but the same determination that took her all the way to the Cellar will guide her hands now. 'You don't need to take it down,' Nightingale prompts. 'Just open the lid for a peek.'

She does as she is asked, her hands pink against the woodwork. Nightingale imagines a long sigh of air as the lid is prised open, though in truth it makes no sound at all.

'A muslin bag,' Wasp says, peering through the crack.

'Is it full?'

A shake of the head. 'No. Only half full. Tiny brown lumps of something are spilled across the bottom.'

Nightingale half sits, half collapses onto the bed. Her cheeks turn numb as the blood drains out of them. 'Then it's true.'

Wasp drops the lid and steps away from the shelf. 'What's true? What's the matter?'

'You're catching me at a difficult moment, Wasp. Before we discuss this further I want you to tell me something. What would you be prepared to do in order to attain something you wanted? Or believed you wanted?'

'I don't know if I can answer that. A part of me wants to run away, to start afresh somewhere else. Another part of me wants to go home, to face the people who wronged me, though I'm not yet sure how I would accomplish that.'

'You have no home outside the House.'

'My village. I want to undo what was done.'

'You are dead. You expect to resurrect yourself?'

'You can't kill me. Not that way. I never chose to come here. I was tricked into a carriage with locks and blinded windows. I'd sooner have been dragged behind a hurdle than suffer that.'

'You blame your people? It's their fault?'

'No, it's mine.'

'You can't go back. No one goes back. Think of the consequences. It's not simply a matter of turning up on your own doorstep.'

'I'm not sure I can live with the consequences of not doing so.'

'Run away or seek revenge – an interesting choice. Suppose you were forced into making it?'

'Why are you doing this to me? What kind of woman are you?'

Nightingale throws open her fingers. Calling cards, dozens of them, flutter to the rug. 'This is who I am. The sum of me. Other people's names scratched onto a piece of paper. That and a gold-trimmed day gown, and beautiful dresses that don't belong to me.'

'So? You had nothing when you arrived, like the rest of us.'

'I had a daughter.'

'A *child*? Was such a thing allowed?'

'I don't know. I could never discover if the Fixer took my baby away because she was in danger from the House or in danger from me. All I remember is a cry. When she was born. It was far away, beyond the cloud of the dream makers. The Fixer says he tried to place her in my arms, but I couldn't hold her, couldn't put her to my breast. We were on the road and on the run. He had to beg milk for her tiny belly. I don't recall her face. Did she look like me? Have my eyes, my cheeks, my hair? Even though I know none of these things I think about her every day.'

Nightingale leans over, tugs on the dresser drawer and pulls out a wad of toddler's garments.

'Are those your daughter's clothes?'

'No, Wasp, I stole them. The shopkeeper was so taken with my face I could've lifted the counter from under his nose and he'd not twitch an eye. I'm grateful I've not gone mad enough to steal a baby from its cot, though I've considered it more than once. I keep thinking I shall find her, and when I do she'll have nothing, and I'll have nothing to give her. So I take the clothes, from shops, washing lines and once out of a mother's hands. Though I daresay my child will have outgrown the lot by now I can't see her as anything other than an infant.'

She pinches her chin between thumb and forefinger. 'I don't know if I'd recognise her. I missed the first words, the first steps. Perhaps even now she's playing with friends, or picking flowers in the park with a woman she thinks of as her mama. Would my crashing into her life ruin things for both of us? I don't even know her name . . .'

Nightingale returns the garments to the drawer. 'You are surprised? Perhaps you thought me heartless? A witch with flint for a soul? It may be I was that once. Pain can gnaw at your nerve endings until it seems there's nothing left to feel.'

Wasp glances at the box. 'What was I looking at in there?'

'The dream makers. That's what I call them. An apothecary or herbalist would no doubt have another title. For me they drew a curtain over the sharp edges of the world. I became someone else. And because of that I thought I could be happy.'

'Are they poison?'

'No, a remedy. Of sorts. Do you want to try them? They will take you out of here. Lift you as far as you want to go. You will crave them like you would a lover, and while they are a part of you there's no need to come back. Ever.'

'No. You're afraid of that box. You said so yourself. Why do you even keep it there, on that shelf, in plain view?'

'It is part of my covenant with the Fixer. The contents of that box made a slave of me. He broke its chains by taking my baby away. I can make a captive of myself again any time I choose.'

'He makes you keep that box in your room?'

'He wants to see if the desire is still there.'

'And is it?'

'Yes. It still is. The box is both a torment and a means of escape. A terrible means. I can leave the House by throwing away my soul, or keep that lid closed and try to walk out of here with my head up. I have hopes, Wasp, hopes that I might see my daughter again. I need to stay in the real world, not flee to the dream one. And that, more than anything, is why I don't touch the box. One day I'm going to sit in the park with a large bonnet to keep off the sun. I want to watch the roses bloom and hear playing children laugh. I want to wear a soft, white woollen scarf around my shoulders and not care if clouds drizzle on me. I don't wish to be rich or blessed with a handsome husband. I had a slice of men before ever putting a foot over this doorstep. I'd like a room overlooking a lawn with a cedar tree spreading in one corner. The room will be filled with my things, trinkets and baubles, letters, cuts of coloured lace, items of no value except what they mean to me and the fact that they are *mine*.'

'Yet your box has been tinkered with.'

'Yes. Another symptom of an ever growing malaise.'

'Have you told the Abbess?'

'The Abbess is losing her wits. Not quite all together, no, and not all at once. You can see it here and there, in little ways, but soon I think these will roll into one big whole. She built this place and held it together through those self-same wits. Once they are gone all that will be left are the rats.'

'Rats?'

'Already they are gathering. They whisper, hold clandestine meetings, make plans. They scamper both inside and outside these walls. I won't lie. I know this has been building for a while. There are too many people with big ambitions. The House is a juicy pie and they all want their cut. Now you've come along and somehow put a spark to the tinder.'

'Me? How so?'

'Think, Wasp. The Abbess has no heir. If she falls, those rats I mentioned will scrabble over the pieces she leaves behind.'

'Did you ask me to look in the box just to tell me this?'

Still that defiance. 'The muslin pouch you saw was always full. Now it's half empty. The dream makers are a potent force. Their theft bodes trouble.'

Nightingale stands and paces around the bed, squeezing the material of her gloves together. Only a persistent thread of curiosity is keeping this girl here, she realises. If Wasp wishes to walk back out that door there is nothing to be done about it. As a Harlequin, Nightingale expects obedience from the other girls, but this one is not so easily leashed. She could be the saving of them all.

'Soon the House will be holding what is known as a Parade.

Those girls not on distant Assignments are dressed up and sent to the Scarlet Parlour. Clients enter and select the escort of their choice. Government ministers, peers, men of the highest rank all take their turn. It is quite the gathering point for our country's noble and illustrious. Someone of a certain disposition might think to use that influence to their advantage.'

'A Parade?'

'In truth it's no more than a dandied-up party. During such events the Masques are feted as the Toasts of the Town. Most of these cullies are on a trophy hunt. We watch them ride their aristocratic high horses then pauper themselves to beg a sweetmeat out of a Masque's hand. Everyone wallows in the attention. Some more than others.'

'So much for respecting clients.'

Nightingale gives a tight smile. 'The fleecing begins the moment clients step through the front door. They dine only on the finest French cuisine at extortionate prices. Bottles of claret are served at triple their worth. Girls are perfumed down to their toenails. Only the very air comes without charge, and rumour has it the Abbess would extract a price for that if she could. But this Parade, I suspect, will differ. I think the Queen is about to be deposed.'

'Then why not leave? I know you can. Moth saw you getting on a coach at the Meldrum inn. You could go looking for your daughter and not come back.'

'Only one person knows where my child is, and that is the man who gave her away. The Fixer. Both he and Kingfisher are the ropes that keep me bound to this room, no matter how far an Assignment or otherwise will take me.'

'Can't you do something about it?'

'God help me I have, and much as I want my daughter I fear for the consequences. But there is something else. The House exerts a thrall. Most of us have fallen under that spell, myself

284

included. We know no other home and the comforts provided here have made us idle and compliant. If turned out into the street I doubt we'd survive the week. You, however, have both a mind and a heart that won't sit still. Dragging me along to the Cellar proved that, and suffering a brand hasn't cowed you. I'd go so far as to say you might prove our only hope – my only hope. Because I suspect I shall never truly leave here until you lead me out by the hand.'

She let the girl go then, and marvelled at how easy opening her heart had proved. It must be dark times indeed. *You never cease to surprise yourself,* she thinks. Now she must become a Masque again. An Assignment at the theatre awaits and she needs to be at the dressing room early to have the pick of the gowns. Nightingale whispers out of her room, closes the door behind her and, before she can stop herself, lets out a short, sharp scream.

A bloodied apparition pads along the hall towards her, toes leaving scarlet pockmarks in the carpet. A loose pattern of hand-prints spreads across the front of its shift. Eyes scorch out of that red mask.

Nightingale feels a moan burble from the back of her throat. She searches for cuts, a wound, anything that can cause such a horror. She grabs the spectre's wrist. Her hand slides off, smearing some of the redness across her fingers. The scent of petals fills her nose.

'Rouge,' Nightingale whispers.

The Abbess's emblems are smothered by the thick paste. Her features have turned into a scarlet dough. Not a patch of her skin has been left uncovered. Nightingale can see it glimmering darkly through the translucent folds of the old woman's silk shift.

'Abbess, what have you done?'

'I wanted to look beautiful.'

'We must get this off you at once. All of it.' Nightingale steers the old woman into the bedchamber and kicks the door closed.

'Don't bring your box of sin near me, girl. I don't need your sorcery.'

'No sorcery, just a good clean.' Nightingale plucks the towel from the side of her washbowl, dampens it and starts wiping the Abbess's face and hands. Within moments the material is saturated with rouge. What will be said in the washhouse?

'You can't judge me,' the Abbess says. 'Look at your own eyes.'

'I won't touch the box. You know what it means.'

'There are some things even you would break your head and heart over. I doubt I'd do more than chip them at best. I'm not so witless I don't know what's happening. Nor am I alone in that. As long as I can speak I can think. Words are the threads which hold me together. Don't let me lose them. Don't let me lose everything. The House will unravel around me.'

'What can I do?'

'You? Nothing. Others will bring matters to a head. Watch carefully, then choose your path.'

'My path leads to my daughter. Where is she?'

'I don't know. She was gone shortly after the Fixer brought you to my doorstep.'

'He could have told you?'

'Why? That was a part of your gone-away life. Bringing it back might cause more trouble than either of you can cope with.'

'I must take that chance.'

'Then your time is coming, songbird, as surely as the tide.'

Full Circle

Wasp is handed an Assignment by Nightingale. Neither Kingfisher nor the Abbess is at breakfast. Rumours burble around the dining room. Nightingale quells the chatter by announcing the Abbess has a mild fever and has taken to her rooms. Wasp has never seen the Abbess's private place. Neither has anyone else she's spoken to. Apparently a number of chambers lead off from the Mirror Room, but no windows pierce that part of the building.

Dry-mouthed, Wasp takes her scroll upstairs and unfurls it. She reads too quickly, her eyes stumbling over the words. An important Ball requiring overnight attendance. Wasp's presence has been specifically requested, and Nightingale will accompany her.

Her eyes skim the rest of the scroll and catch something else, something scribbled along the bottom. In her anxiety she's almost overlooked it. Cramped lettering, different from the rest of the text, and hastily written:

Moth can't return to the Cellar. No client will touch her. She will be killed at the month's end.

And below that:

Don't blame the Abbess.

Wasp sucks down a gobbet of air and crumples the scroll against her chest. Moth would be taken care of, she'd been told. They hadn't ever lied to her, had he? Everything in the room seems to stand out in stark, brittle colours. In less than eight hours she'll be on Assignment. There doesn't seem enough time left in the world. The end of the month is only five days away. Five days. She has no reason to doubt the message. Moth had been sent to the Cellar. Wasp herself had been branded. People who could do that to young women were capable of anything. *We don't carry baggage in the House.* Again and again that warning. Indeed, what use would Moth be to them now? *I've heard things*, she'd said. *There is another place you don't want to go.*

Wasp drops the scroll onto the fire. She watches the parchment curl and burn. Even if she could pluck Moth out of this situation, where would she go? Mother Joan's? Far too close. Richard seems an unlikely saviour, but his money and connections might prove useful. How to get a message to him? No writing paper or quills are kept in the rooms. As far as friends and relatives are concerned the girls who live here are all hanged, transported or runaways. The Abbess might have a quill and inkpot tucked under her desk in the hall. A tenuous hope and too fraught with risk.

What if she waylays a boy in the square outside and sends him off with a spoken message and a promise that Richard will give him a shilling? Hazardous, as even walks around the square are usually taken with an escort.

Richard, whatever I've said to you in the past, however rejected you might feel, please book an Assignment and do it soon.

A busy evening in the dressing room. Half the House is due out on Assignment and the chamber is filled with chattering girls. Maids tease hair or help with awkward fastenings while Nightingale watches implacably from the corner. During the final days of her recovery, Wasp's mind has been working over the Harlequin's words. The temptation is there to talk it over with Hummingbird, but she'd likely laugh and wave it all out of the window.

Wasp discards three gowns before choosing one she can tolerate. She wants something eye-catching but not too frivolous. Her instructions are to wear ivory, and the confection she holds in her arms, while uncomfortably resembling a wedding dress, is loose enough about the hips to allow a night of dancing. Given the nature of the party she has also been instructed to bring her mask. Removing her day gown, she steps into the velvet cocoon and draws it up around her shoulders.

'You play your part with passion, Wasp.' Nightingale has ghosted up beside her. 'Have you dabbled in acting?'

'In a manner of speaking.'

'It will be a long journey for us tonight.'

'Us? Yes, the scroll mentioned you'd be coming.'

'This is a demanding Assignment. Your client is very exacting. He specifically requested your presence. But there are protocols involved with which I doubt you're familiar.'

'And you are familiar with them?'

'I know the tricks. We shall both need to work hard to make this a success.'

'Who is this client? Someone I've escorted before?'

'It's enough that he has requested you.'

'Where are we going? The Assignment never mentioned a destination.'

'Normally I'd say another country dance at yet another country house. They are all much the same. However, in this case I believe our host has something particular in mind.'

'A Masked Ball?'

'That and more. Now let me help you with those fastenings. They're more awkward than most.'

Her fingers are nimble on the clasps, and her touch surprisingly gentle. Finally she drapes a necklace around Wasp's neck. It sparkles when the light hits it. Reflected points bobble on the walls, following the rhythm of her breathing. Then comes the perfume. Nightingale wants to drench her in lavender. Wasp claims it brings on a sneezing fit, though in truth she'd cut her nose off and pickle it before willingly wearing what she has always regarded as an 'old woman's scent'. So her tormentor resorts to rose petal. Wasp now smells like her mother's flower patch. In her head she hears Hummingbird laughing.

A coach arrives within the half hour. Nightingale changed earlier and looks ready to conquer the night. Her mask is a porcelain masterpiece of shape and colour, her wig a tumble of flowered silver. Wasp's own hair, now grown to a manageable length, has been pinned back and concealed beneath a pink wig. Once aboard she tucks away a loose strand as the carriage rumbles out of the square. No name has been supplied for her client, either real or invented. Wasp tries to tease an answer out of Nightingale but finds herself cut off with a flick of one finger.

'Don't say anything. Either now or when we arrive. Stay close to me. Don't wander. Don't talk to anyone unless I say so.'

Fine, Wasp thinks. Her ivory gown crinkles as she settles back on the fat cushions. Leaving town, the carriage follows a road alongside a gushing river for about a mile and a half. A right fork plunges them into thick wood and everything outside turns black.

Wasp's hands feel slick inside her gloves. Nightingale sits in silence, back straight, staring through the window, though there's precious little to see. Wasp shifts, flutters her fan. Finally the Harlequin turns from the window.

'This is a seldom used route but quicker by a good half hour. You can stop fidgeting. We are almost there.'

No surprise this road is ill favoured. The potholes feel deep enough to sink a barn. The carriage lurches alarmingly. Wasp bites her tongue when they bump over a fallen tree branch. Her sense of disquiet grows, and the Harlequin's distracted attitude doesn't help.

After having her spine nearly shaken to pieces, Wasp is relieved when the coach rattles out of the trees. Beyond the window she glimpses an open space with a huge house lit up like a market fair. It looks familiar.

'Remember what I told you,' Nightingale says.

Wasp nods. Sight of the house is momentarily lost behind a tall hedge.

'Good. I hope you have a strong character, my young swan. Now put your mask on.'

A pair of iron gates open onto a crescent-shaped gravel drive. The carriage halts at the foot of a broad flight of steps. Other carriages draw up behind them. Some have two horses, some four.

Coachmen cling grimly to the back, hats bobbing with the rhythm of the leather springs. Wasp can hear laughter tinkling on the night air. Coloured lanterns jiggle on cord looped around the portico. As she takes it all in, a liveried footman scuttles down the steps and opens their door.

Wasp grasps the edge of her seat. 'I cannot go in there.'

'You can and shall. I shall brook no disagreement.'

'I am known here.'

Nightingale levers Wasp's arms from the seat and pilots her towards the steps. 'Don't go faint on me. Lord Russell and his guests await.'

A Night of Masks

Long poles impale the lawn, torches sparking from their tips. Lanterns loop in luminous moons along the drive to the foot of the front steps. Light bleeds from every window. This is Russell Hall as Bethany Harris has seldom seen it. During family parties she'd been obliged to stay in her room with curtains drawn. One night only she had been permitted to watch from a corner of the balcony overlooking the entrance hall. She had never witnessed anything so grand, though Lord Russell's face was tight.

'Don't ever become a part of that world,' he warned. 'Everything is plotted, like the steps of a dance.'

'But they look like gods.'

'Hardly. Tonight they will dance and talk. Cigars will be smoked. Port and canary drunk. The women will gossip and eye each other's dresses and find ever more complicated ways to show how much they hate one another. Tomorrow the men will go into the woods and hunt. It's the wrong time of year but they'll find something to kill. They are all so afraid of being considered ordinary they make grotesqueries of their lives.'

Wasp's gown rustles as Nightingale leads her up the steps. 'Why so reluctant, Wasp? Isn't this what you wanted?'

'I'm not ready.'

'You have matters here that need settling. You said so yourself. So settle them, and perhaps you will be a little less haunted.'

Footmen stand on either side of the door. Village lads most likely, their faces unrecognisable in the shadows cast by the lanterns. A babble of guests fills the hall, exchanging greetings and shedding cloaks into the arms of waiting servants. Everyone is dressed to the buttons and wearing a rainbow of assorted masks. For the first time, Wasp is able to move among guests without finding herself the centre of attention. It feels curiously liberating.

Nightingale draws Wasp into a side room. She recognises it as a parlour the late Lady Russell used for entertaining. Tall French windows open onto a paved terrace. Cool air gusts around the furnishings.

'Amuse yourself for a short while,' the Harlequin tells her. 'A matter needs attending to. House business.'

She disappears into the hubbub. Wasp is drawn to the windows and looks out over the gardens. Two paper lanterns on the edge of the lawn have blown out. A figure strides across the grass, taper in hand. Even at a distance, Wasp recognises the leather jerkin and hat pricked with a hawk feather. She'd wondered how she'd cope with such a moment, even rehearsing scenarios in her head. Faced with the reality of it her plans melt away, as she always suspected they would.

Gathering her skirts, Wasp crosses the terrace, slips between a pair of stone angels and sets off across the dark lawn. Walking the passages of the House has taught her silence, and her slippered feet are light on the grass. She catches him tinkering with the first of the lanterns. As he sets the taper to the wick his face illuminates in a moon of familiar shapes.

'Still keeping to your place, I see.'

The taper slides from his fingers. The flame sputters on the grass but remains stubbornly alight. They regard each other for a few moments, lanterns washing their faces with rainbows.

'Can I be of some service, Miss?'

Wasp slips off her mask. She hears his breath catch. 'Don't worry,' she tells him. 'I've not come back to bedevil you.'

'You're no spectre, Beth Harris. I know my own blood.' His gaze slides over her gown, her gloves, the expensive ribbons tied into her wig. 'Look at you. A painted whore.'

'Better than a lunatic.'

'Dead, that's what I heard you were. I never believed it. Not you. I'd know inside myself if such was true.'

'And you never tried to look for me?'

'Why would I, Beth? You'd only cause more heartbreak.'

'Did you know what kind of home Lord Russell placed me in? Did you even care? Look past the dress and the rouge – this is your daughter speaking.'

He shifts his feet. 'He is the squire. I was desperate. We all were. Took your mother a long time to get her wits back. Her heart broke, then fixed, then broke again. To see you here, like this, would kill her for sure. That's part of the reason I had to let you go. She's all I have left. I also had my duty to the squire and to God. You were beyond rod or sermon.'

'And George Russell?'

'He never believed the stories about you either, despite what his papa might have told him.'

He stoops to retrieve the taper. 'Why return now, Beth? You didn't come here dressed like that to hunt me out.'

'I was invited. I don't yet know by whom.'

'Has George Russell seen you?'

'I've not yet been presented to him. I doubt he will see past my face powder.'

'You've done many things I didn't expect, but becoming a whore was the last of them. That's what you are, isn't it? I don't reckon any of his lordship's gaggle would take you as a wife. The unmarried bucks always turn up with their harlots and pass them off as sweethearts.'

'A whore? My virtue was given, not sold.'

'Listen to that silver tongue. Is there any repentance left in your soul?'

Wasp presses a finger against her father's lips. 'Perhaps you'll learn the truth, but not from my mouth. You gave up that right when you sent me away. So far no one has recognised me, or knows we've met. It's our secret, and the dark will keep it safe.'

Wasp has shaken the grass from her slippers and is waiting in the parlour when Nightingale returns. 'We shall join the other guests now,' the Harlequin says. 'Stand beside me and keep your mouth closed, even if I point you out to someone or bring them over to see you. If drinks or sweetmeats are offered, don't touch them. It proved hard enough to stuff you into this dress. You've filled out so much.'

Charming, Wasp thinks. *So I'm to starve as well.*

The guests have been shepherded into a place off the main hall. The room is big and high and square. A fire is tucked into one wall but it's barely hot enough to cook a rabbit. Pale light floods from candle-spiked chandeliers, turning everything the colour of dumplings. People greet one another like old friends but no more warmth lurks in their eyes than in the darkening sky outside. Footmen drift in and out with trays of wine and sweetmeats. Wasp doesn't recognise anyone. Have they been conjured out of the walls?

'Remember what I told you,' Nightingale whispers into her ear.

Wasp is happy to oblige. She's no desire to go running around in this gilded den. Despite the society magazines, she doesn't understand anything these people are talking about. Their voices rise from a whisper to a boom then back again. Compared to the quiet elegance of the Masques they are grotesques, and a few smell like old kippers despite their lace-trimmed pomanders.

What do they think of me? Wasp wonders.

Nightingale moves among the guests, clasping hands in her impeccable fashion. A perfect ambassador for the House. No sign of Lord Russell or his son. Are they planning a dramatic entrance? Wasp heard of one party where the host, dressed like a canary, was lowered from the ceiling in a flower-bedecked cage.

A slender fellow with a scarlet mask and a neckcloth as big as a bed sheet snares Wasp's attention. He's talking to someone beside the punch bowl. Richard. It's *Richard*. The voice, mannerisms – there can be no doubting it. Conversation finished, he dips through the door into the hallway. Wasp fights the urge to run after him. She will talk to him later, preferably when Nightingale's distracted.

More talk, more drink. Outside, the purple sky has deepened to pitch. Wasp begins to feel more painted doxy than Masque, and the heavy wig is making her neck ache. Her skirts and petticoats weigh heavily and the lace gloves make her fingers itch. Guests glance at her from time to time then return to their gossip. Nightingale is talking to a stout fellow in an embroidered blue coat and a wig flecked with silver. Both hands are clasped in front of her. It hardly seems she's breathing.

A gaggle of roly-poly musicians arrive and station themselves near the windows. Guests trickle in and out. As the quintet tunes up, Wasp slips into the hall where the air isn't so thick. Spotting Richard is a fine piece of providence. Is he the mystery client who hired her? She must winkle an opportunity to catch him alone.

A painting mounted beside the staircase catches her eye. A study of the gardens. Wasp recognises the fountain and higgledy-piggledy flowerbeds. It's pretty. The prettiest picture she's seen. The sky is a bright summer blue, the grass a lush green. Each blade has been separately painted. She can almost smell it.

She lifts the picture from the wall and tilts it towards the light. Cotton puff clouds scud across the canvas. Ravens wheel in a spiral above the shadowed hedges. This is no cheap daubing from some market artist, but the work of Lord Russell. Wasp can't imagine the hours it must have taken.

'Do you like it?'

Standing beside her is a tall gentleman dressed in black with gold trim. His mouth beneath the black velvet mask is pinched but kind. Bright eyes peer at her through the disguise.

'I'm sorry, sir, I didn't hear you.'

'The floor swallows up your footsteps. People creep about this house like thieves.'

He eases the painting from her gloved hands and sets it back against the wall. 'I know most of the guests,' he continues. 'Some people you recognise even through the most elaborate disguise. With you I confess to being flummoxed, but that is the purpose of a Masked Ball, I daresay. It will make the final revelation all the sweeter.'

'Final revelation?'

'You don't know? The clock strikes midnight and the masks come off, to the delight of some and disappointment of others. Since you're one of the few visitors to express genuine appreciation of this painting perhaps you ought to see more.'

'My escort insists I stay in the parlour. If she finds me here she will be displeased.'

'Escort?'

'The lady in the bird mask.'

'If there is an issue I'm sure she can be persuaded you're in good hands.'

'Is there some doubt then?'

He laughs. 'I suspect I'm in more danger from you than you'll ever be from me. Come, I'll be delighted to show you around.'

Wasp worms her way around the stacks of canvases. Some are leaning against the walls, others seemingly sprout from the bare floor. Otherwise not a stick of furniture is present in this tucked-away room. 'So these are all Lord Russell's paintings?'

'Indeed. It's quite a pile, isn't it? Have you seen the gardens? How the flowers clash? In midsummer it's a nightmare. Everything is wrong. It makes you ill. That fool my father employs to tend his gardens has no sense of symmetry.'

'I always thought them rather beautiful.'

'Really? So you've seen them before?'

'Well, I—'

'These paintings were kept in a folly on the far side of the estate. Perhaps you've seen that also? A notorious dabbler, Lord Russell never used to be so interested in art. Each new pastime was a fleeting wonder. Every business venture, every speculation whether in land or shipping had him excited on Monday and bored by Tuesday. His stables were full of unridden horses. A new pianoforte, brought all the way from Austria, went out of tune for want of playing. I remember a stomach-heaving week when dinner guests were obliged to eat exotic dishes from the Orient. His restless whims cost a petty fortune. If he desired something he took it then lost interest.'

She keeps her voice level. 'Where is Lord Russell?'

'In Bath spa taking the waters. He has been troubled of late.

A family problem. I doubt any cure will be derived from the visit but it will serve him better than haunting his own rooms.'

Wasp pauses at one of the tall windows. The gardens are spread out below in a moon-kissed chequerboard of lawns and lantern-speckled hedges. As a girl she often ran behind her father as he performed his duties around the estate. She knows each turn of the path, every leaf-shaded corner. All of the things the House of Masques has forced into her seem to leak away. She's becoming Bethany Harris again. Beth is in the walls, the floor, in the footsteps along the passage. Like a mind gone too old and returning to childhood again.

So he does care.

Following this man up to the attic chambers, she'd been both surprised and relieved at her sense of calm. He was merely a genial guest pandering to a lady's whims before the dancing started. Whoever her mystery client turned out to be, she would use all her wiles to hide her identity when midnight's moment of revelation came.

The past is mine to conjure or lock away at will, she thinks.

Muted, as if in another world, the musicians launch into their first tune. 'Shouldn't you see to your other guests?' she says, turning.

George Russell's mask is in his hand. His eyes are half closed and full of pain. Reaching up, he tears off Wasp's disguise.

'I believe it's time to stop playing games now, Bethany. Don't you?'

A Covenant

'Did you hire me, Richard?'

'No.'

'Did you know I would be there?'

298

'Why the inquisition?'

'I have a history with that household. Were you aware of it?'

'People talk. I don't get involved in their petty scandals.'

'Do they have something to gossip about, then?'

His eyes follow the line of Wasp's skirts. 'Perhaps. In any case it was quite a pickle you found yourself in.'

Wasp lets out a long breath. Outside the window of Richard's carriage, Russell Hall's coloured lanterns are already dwindling. 'It was horrible. I thought I was in danger and I don't even know the reason.'

'In danger? From George? When you barged into my card game, which I was poised to win incidentally, and begged me to take you home I thought someone had threatened to shoot you. What became of your escort?'

'She's probably looking for me as we speak. How well do you know George?'

Richard shrugs. His mask lies on the seat beside him but his face is unreadable. 'A bright new spark in Parliament. That makes him a useful acquaintance. Up until now, though, he's been using his burgeoning career as an excuse to spend a great deal of time in town. Gossip has it he got into a scandal over some village girl and decided to quit the muddy hamlet his father owns. Servants can prove difficult when a bit of nonsense lodges inside their heads. I'm surprised he didn't take a stick to the girl.'

For the first time in weeks, Wasp feels herself blush to her roots. She hopes Richard won't notice in the dim light. 'You said, "Up until now". What's changed?'

'The change is in the shape of a young lady by the name of Annabel Talbot, a cousin of the Russells', whose engagement the Ball is in celebration of.'

'Engagement?'

'George is going to wed her, or at least her papa thinks he is.

'Twould be a good catch for the girl. Unfortunately there's nothing but dandelions drifting about in her head. Oh, she's a pretty, warmhearted soul, bred in the proper fashion. She'd make George a good wife, bear his heirs, turn a blind eye when he dips his wick elsewhere, that sort of thing. However, I've seen George debate in the Commons and I can't see him settling for such a soft prospect.'

'He recognised me, despite the clothes and mask.'

'Perhaps he knows you better than you think.'

'In any case I'm sorry you will miss your party.'

He flicks his hand. 'There are a hundred such frivolities in the course of a season.'

Wasp glances out of the window. 'We came by a shortcut. A track through the woods. It must be here somewhere. Can we take it now? I need to talk to you.'

'Hmm, I think I know it. The old drovers' road. An axle-breaker, as I recall. This is all very mysterious. Care to throw a little morsel my way?'

'You left me a card. A card that said I could count on you for help. I need that help now, more than I ever thought I would.'

Richard's face is a dim shadow against a greater blackness. She hears a rasp in his breath and his breeches rustling as he shifts his legs.

He's not going to do it, is her immediate thought. *The card was just a courtesy, like two people exchanging addresses with no intention of writing. He'll likely fumble for some excuse and drop me out of the coach the moment we're back in the city.*

He calls out instructions to the driver. A minute later the carriage makes an abrupt right turn. What little starlight glimmers outside the window is swallowed up. The springs jounce. Branches scratch the wooden panels. After half a mile of bone-breaking travel the driver pulls his team to a snorting halt in some tuckaway in the trees.

Richard settles back in his seat. 'We should be afforded enough privacy. This track is so little used not even the local footpads frequent it. I have to say this is quite an adventure.'

'It's too quiet. Your driver will overhear us.'

He leans his head out of the window. 'Ross, go and see to the horses. Don't come back until I call you.'

Wood creaks as the coachman climbs from his perch. Wasp waits until his soft footfalls recede.

How do I begin? she thinks. *How can I ask anything of this pampered boy?*

She opens her mouth and without any prompting the words spill out. Richard listens in silence. He offers her a kerchief, which she presses against her face. Outside, in the dark, something crashes through the trees sending twigs rattling to the forest floor. Richard leans forward. Wasp hears the whisper of thick material as a blanket is spread over her legs.

'You're shivering,' he explains.

'I have to save Moth. I need to get her out of that velvet-lined dungeon and away from the Abbess. It won't be easy. Kingfisher and Leonardo will be after her like hunting dogs. I was told the House of Masques holds everyone in its thrall, and it's true.'

'You've proved strong enough to come this far.'

'Have I? Throwing all my problems in your lap doesn't speak of courage. The Abbess branded me. Pressed a hot iron against my skin because I broke the rules. I'll have it for life. Not only on my arm but in my head and heart too.'

His mouth is inches from her ear. His breath comes in short, sharp bites. 'I have rooms in Portsmouth near the harbour. Father doesn't know about them. The landlord owns a shipping business and, thanks to my ministrations, enjoys favourable import duties on his cargoes. The place is hardly a palace but it's comfortable, at least for a while. I go there when Father is conducting private business in the city and use it as I please. You are welcome there. I doubt even the Abbess's bloodhounds could sniff you out.'

'Where is your father? Is he at the party?'

'Last I saw of him he was climbing the stairs with a bottle of canary tucked under one arm and the Duchess of Hambleton on the other. I shall be the last thing occupying his thoughts.'

Wasp sighs. 'I still don't know how I'm going to smuggle Moth out of the House. I've no idea where she's being kept and I can't keep asking.'

'Are your Sisters prone to bribery?'

'I suspect most would sell their mothers for a shilling.'

He fumbles in his jacket then drops something heavy into her lap. Coins jangle. 'That should be enough to open doors and seal mouths.'

Wasp slides the purse into her reticule. 'I don't know how to begin thanking you, Richard.'

'Indeed you do.'

He lays a hand on her arm. Wasp's mouth has gone dry. She tries to move. Her muscles won't obey. 'What are you doing?' she whispers.

A rogue lick of starlight peeks through the trees and illuminates his face. His teeth seem to leap out at her. 'You were so upset tonight I thought you might welcome a distraction.'

'Take your hand away. I am a Masque. No one touches me.'

His fingers caress her sleeve. 'Going against your Abbess carries a dreadful risk,' he murmurs into her ear. 'More so than even you know. Everything bears a price. You're getting by far the better bargain. You and that girl whose hide you're so keen on saving. This caper is going to cost.'

'Richard—'

'It's all I want. It's all I ever wanted. Not so much to ask, considering the life you must've led already.'

Friend's voice in her head. *You want a decent supper, lass, you'll have to pay for it.* And then her father. *You're nothing but a painted whore.*

A price. Always a price.

Wasp settles back against the seat. 'Just like your papa after all,' she says.

'No, you don't understand.' His fingers leave her arm and linger above her cheek. 'I only wish to touch your face.'

'My face?'

'Yes. A few moments, no more.'

'You are not permitted to—'

He waves her into silence. 'You rejected me in the park. You accuse me of setting up a clandestine Assignment then you interrogate me about George. Not satisfied with that, you go onto demand favours as if you and I were close kin. I am not here to be used. What I ask in return is little enough, don't you think?'

'I've done worse things,' Wasp murmurs, closing her eyes.

'I should accompany you into the House,' says Richard. 'I'll say you took ill at the party and I brought you home.'

'What about Nightingale?'

'She was busy with the other guests. I'm sure your Abbess will understand.'

'Keep your end of the bargain and I shall not burden you with anything more than we agreed to.'

Outside, city windows slide past in candlelit blocks. His face lights up, darkens, lights again. He's back on the opposite seat, slouching like some idle, pampered squire. The carriage turns into Crown Square and draws to a halt in front of the House.

Seated behind the reception table is Hummingbird. Candles flicker over the rolled-up scrolls of the following day's Assignments.

'Where is the Abbess?' Wasp asks. 'Still indisposed?'

Hummingbird puts down the quill she's been fingering. 'In a manner of speaking. You're back early.'

'Perhaps I can explain this unexpected return,' Richard says, stepping forward.

'Perhaps you can.'

Wasp casts around the otherwise empty hall. 'Why is Kingfisher not here?'

'Now that,' Hummingbird says, 'is a very good question.'

Wasp rouses Eloise and orders a hot posset to settle her stomach. The maid brings it to Wasp's bedchamber and places it on the bedside table.

'I had to heat the milk myself,' Eloise says. 'Cook is not about at this hour.'

'Fine. Please leave towels and a fresh shift outside my door.'

'Anything else, *enfant*, or am I permitted to enjoy a little sleep before daybreak?'

'Go to bed. I won't need anything more tonight.'

'Very well, but you will be sure to return that gown, *oui*?'

Too tired to care about the House's precious garments, Wasp dabs her aching body with a wet towel. If she has to humour Richard for the sake of herself and Moth then so be it. She wipes the smell of Nightingale's chosen perfume from her breasts and runs the towel over her face, clouding the water in the basin with face powder.

Feeling better, Wasp ties her hair behind her neck. She scoops up the ball gown and hooks it over the back of the chair. She pads naked to the window. Hummingbird has taken Richard into the Scarlet Parlour, something she lacks the authority to do. Wasp found herself dismissed. She heard neither Richard's explanation for their early return nor Hummingbird's response.

Outside, the moon drags itself from behind a patch of cloud and shivers Crown Square with pale light. Waiting as instructed, horses snorting and pawing the road, is Richard's carriage.

It's still there when, sleepless, she checks again two hours later.

Wasp turns over in her bed. Grey light trickles between the curtains. The air feels cold against her cheeks despite the orange bowl of embers hugging the bottom of the hearth. She swings her legs out from under the coverlet and stands, stretching. Richard's purse is tucked beneath her pillow. She'll have to think of a better hiding place. In the Comfort Home things were stuffed up sleeves or tucked into skirt linings. No such opportunity in a place where clothes and bed linen are changed daily.

She goes to the dresser, plucks a towel and rubs her face. The coarse material invigorates her skin. She pulls the curtains wide. Beneath a washed-out sky everything is the colour of ashes. Wasp half expects to see Richard's coach and team still waiting by the kerb, but apart from a scattering of hawkers pitching their wares no one else is abroad.

A knock on the door. Hummingbird slips uninvited into the room. Wasp isn't sure if she's pleased to see her old friend or not. The Masque's eyes are puffy and her hair unusually tangled. Her emblem resembles a livid welt on her pale cheek.

'Anything wrong?' Wasp ventures.

'That Kitten of mine is killing me.' Hummingbird perches on the edge of the bed. 'I'm going to put her in a room of her own before I commit murder.'

'Is she keeping you awake?'

'I don't think she knows the meaning of sleep. She spends night after night fidgeting and whispering. Again and again, hour after hour, and much worse than any other new girl. I've yelled at her, poked her, thrown a pillow at her head, but it doesn't make any difference. I've even threatened to tip a pitcher of water over her. Yet each morning she's up and about like a spring bunny while I've got my head under the pillow feeling like death.'

'I didn't think a Kitten could best you, Hummingbird.'

'Neither did I but, short of murder, what can I do?'

'She wasn't the sole reason for your late night.'

'Indeed not. Your escort hadn't even left before Nightingale turned up. She'd make a spitting cat look sweet-natured. Richard had to explain everything.'

'What did he say?'

'It doesn't matter. He's been recompensed for his trouble and Nightingale is a mite less put out. I'd tread softly around her for a day or two though. She thought you'd been kidnapped.'

'Where is the Abbess? Is she still unwell?'

'Yes.'

'What does the Fixer think?'

'The Fixer has troubles of his own. Are you coming to breakfast?'

'I'm not hungry. If I get an Assignment send it up.'

'Can I do this?'

Wasp holds both hands in front of her face. Her fingers shake so badly they're long, pink blurs. She flexes them, stretching the muscles, then balls them into fists. She must gamble everything on this one attempt. There's no other way. She can't go tiptoeing around the Masques, hoping one of them will tell her something.

They'll just as likely inform the Abbess, or the Abbess will find out anyway. Things might go wrong whatever Wasp chooses to do. She's already tried collaring Moth's former mentor, Red Orchid.

'I want to know where Moth is being kept.'

'Go and ask the Abbess.'

'I can't do that, as well you know.'

'So why do you think I can help?'

'You've been here longer than me. I'll wager there's not a rat in the rafters you can't account for. You're bound to know where Moth is. You'd make it your business to know.'

'Even if that were true why should I tell you anything? You're too stuck on that little duckling. Everyone says so.'

And that had been that.

Wasp sits on the edge of her bedroom chair, careful where she puts her legs. She's pinned up a fold in her gown to fashion a makeshift pocket for Richard's purse. The coins swing against her thigh whenever she moves. What if the fastening breaks and the purse tumbles out at the wrong moment?

She peers out of the window. It's going to work. It *has* to work. She'll find where Moth is being kept and a way to get her out. They'll go to Portsmouth with Richard and never have to come back here. He was right; she is using him, but perhaps he's the sort who likes that. A touch on the cheek is scant price to pay.

Mind made up, Wasp slips out of her room and hurries down the passage. On the stairs she bumps into a maid carrying a bundle of linen and sends the whole lot tumbling over the banisters. Shouting an apology, Wasp pushes through the hall curtain and down the long passage, skirts billowing in a cloud of taffeta. She shoves the mirror door open with both hands. It swings round on its hinges and bangs against the wall. Shattered glass spills across the floor.

The Fixer is standing beside a dome lantern. With him is Lapwing, one of the younger girls. A couple of weeks ago a carriage ran over her foot, breaking three of her toes. The Fixer is teaching her to walk properly again. He holds her arms while she faces him, her injured limb swathed in bandages.

The Fixer turns and regards the broken mirror. 'That will prove expensive to replace.'

Heat rushes into Wasp's cheeks. 'I wanted to talk to you.'

'Really?' His gaze flicks over her gown. 'Are you off somewhere, or just returned?'

Wasp's flush deepens. Her anger has fallen away. She feels like a child about to get slapped by her papa for smearing mud on her petticoat.

The Fixer steers Lapwing towards a stool and helps her sit. He rubs his hands, ambles over to his leather box and takes out a vial. 'You're certainly distressed about something,' he continues. 'This draught will calm you. It's my last one, so it's fortunate I'm seeing the apothecary later today. At any rate it should soothe your disposition.'

'I don't need remedies.'

'And I don't have time for conversation. I'm busy with someone as you can see. Go and calm yourself, as I said, then we can see what is so important that you feel obliged to blunder into my chambers.'

An amused look tickles Lapwing's pale face. Wasp seizes the only notion that enters her head. 'I can sweep up the mess.'

The Fixer holds out the vial. 'I think you've done enough.'

How could I have been so clumsy? Wasp bemoans as she skulks back along the passage, the Fixer's vial gripped in her fist. So much for playing the rescuer, the conquering heroine straight from the pages of a penny story sheet. Her demand to know Moth's whereabouts had turned to ashes on her tongue. How can she hope to help anyone this way?

Still, there remains a chance. The Fixer can't haunt the Mirror Room forever. Wasp could check each door, perhaps call Moth's name until she hears a response. Moth won't be gagged, will she? The door is likely locked but perhaps Richard's burly coachman can break it. He might even be able to handle the Fixer should there be an ugly scene. Once they have Moth inside Richard's carriage the battle will be won.

Wasp crosses the lobby. Two Masques pass her, put their heads together and whisper. She ignores them and hurries back upstairs. 'Can anything else go wrong today?' she mutters. Outside, in the grey folds of the city, someone is screaming. The voice ululates as if struggling to reach a too-high note. It penetrates her nerves before tailing off.

What if I forget about the whole thing? I could keep my own counsel and carry on with my life. After all, Moth's not my friend. She's a lost soul who needs someone to cling to. I'm not her mother or sister. I hardly know her. I've already been branded once. What good did helping people ever do me? Why should I care any more?

A scroll is lying on her bed. Last-minute Assignments aren't uncommon. As a Kitten, Wasp had watched more than one Masque dash, flustered, for the dressing room. Perhaps it's what she needs. A break, a chance to gather her thoughts. She picks up the scroll, tugs on the ribbon and reads the instructions. A simple enough job. A 'gentleman merchant' wants to promenade around the park then take supper. No special clothes or affectations. Perhaps they'll finish early and she can come home in time for this evening's Parade. She might have a better perspective on things by then.

But another note is scrawled along the bottom, same handwriting as before.

Ask Hummingbird about the baby.

Pain flares in Wasp's chest. She realises she's holding her breath and lets it out in a long whoosh. In the novels she had borrowed from the Russells' library, or the stories she read to the children, everything was clear. The good. The evil. In each there was a conflict, an adventure, a resolution with perhaps some love and betrayal thrown in for spice. Real life is confusing. Events seem to drift around in no particular order until something sticks. Heroic acts don't necessarily result in happy endings. By liberating Moth from the Cellar, has Wasp damned her further? *We don't carry baggage in the House.* Did Hummingbird tell her that? Or was it the Abbess?

Wasp folds the parchment. Who is the mystery confidant? Is it some sort of trick designed to trap her, to test her loyalty? Wasp has never taken note of her Sisters' handwriting so can't identify the script, but Hummingbird is the nearest thing she has to a friend.

She tosses the scroll on top of the dresser and collapses onto the bed. Outside, the screaming has started up again. It sounds like the end of the world.

A sharp wind churns around Crown Square. It flaps Wasp's skirts around her ankles and she grabs her bonnet to stop it being wrenched off. Apart from a few pedestrians blustering along, the square is empty. In the lee of the steps a pair of sedan bearers stand blowing into their hands beside a mud-splattered chair. Above, clouds boil across the rooftops.

Wasp squeezes her voluminous skirts into the sedan. It's an hour's trip across town and the bearers are in no mood to be gentle. Draughts whistle through chinks in the woodwork. Wasp hangs on, distracted by thoughts of Moth. One rescue had already ended in disaster; what would the result of another be? It would be easy to let it all go, to accept that everyone's lives belonged to the Abbess. No more brandings, no more guilt, no more trouble.

A yapping mongrel runs out in front of the lead bearer. He stumbles and the chair lurches forward. Wasp grabs the door handle for support. Moth can't survive the House. She can't survive life. Fate has plucked then crushed her. Abandoning her might be for the best.

Mightn't it?

And what about George Russell? What have you tried to convince yourself every night since the moment you accused him? That it was for the best? And what of his father? You could never be equals, so in the end who used whom?

She had known every crease and tuck of Lord Russell's body. Just to touch it made her shiver. Lord Russell understood the dark, passionate core that lurked inside her. He knew that in the Comfort Home she could make accusations until her throat was raw and they would be dismissed as the demented ravings of a lunatic.

What about the children, Bethany?

'I would have cared for them,' she whispers into clenched fists. 'Don't you see that? It was an act of compassion.'

Why? Because Lord Russell was your master? Because you were taught from birth to lower your eyes and curtsey to his kind, no matter what? You couldn't leave him alone, no matter how many times you both slaked your lust on one another. His appetites were as strong as yours, and you thought his bastard was the key to open the gate of his world. Only that didn't work, did it, Bethany? So you wanted to take Julia and Sebastian away. Forever. A mother will resort to desperate measures when faced with enough of a threat. And that's how you regarded yourself. A mother.

'No—'

You were bound for the turnpike. An hour's journey at most. But George caught you at the gate. He wore no cravat that day. His shirt was open, his throat soft and white. How perfect he looked.

'Where are you taking the children, Miss Harris?'

He stood in the lane, still in his riding boots. You had been caught on the fly, Julia and Sebastian wrapped tight in their travelling cloaks, small bundles tucked under their arms. The hired carriage was late. Its tardiness had damned you, so you muttered something about Pendleton market and fairings for the children, and even as you blurted out that lie his gaze fell on the bundles, then on your face. 'Oh,' he said, 'as I recollect Pendleton market is not held until Thursday. 'Tis remiss of you to be confused over such a trifling matter. You who are normally so precise in everything you do.'

He walked towards you. The children squeezed behind your skirts, bundles dropping to the ground.

'You are frightening the little ones.'

'Am I?' His voice was leaden. 'Who is really afraid of whom?'

He turned to the children. 'Go back to the house. Miss Harris and I have something to discuss.'

When he thought them far away he turned back to you and said, 'Must you steal someone else's children? Doing as you have done it's a miracle you didn't get one of your own.'

A summer of lies. Stays laced so tightly she could hardly breathe. Then pain. Too soon. Too soon by a season. A red-splattered blanket wrapped around a lifeless boy thing. Bundled out and taken into the night.

Julia and Sebastian. The children. My children.

'I did.'

'What?'

'I lost it. I miscarried and was torn up inside. I was told I could never have another. I'm not sure whether your father was sad or relieved.'

'You hoped to snare him? That he would set you and your bastard up in a nice house with a generous stipend? Or did you want more, Bethany Harris? Did you think he'd take you as a bride and you'd become mistress of Russell Hall, that everyone would fall under your thrall?'

'Oh George, no thought about how I felt, no lament for the lost child? I did want that child. I wanted it for myself.'

They stood there talking a while longer, voices even but their words carrying ever sharpening blades, until finally George said, 'You could go to the gallows for this,' and you realised you had to protect yourself, and what you had to do to protect yourself.

Rape? That's just what you told everyone. Anger and fear addled your thinking.

A bump as the bearers set the chair down. 'We've arrived, Miss.'

Twigs and early fallen leaves swirl into the chair. Wasp climbs out. She has to shout to be heard. 'What time will you return for me?'

The bearer cups his hands around his mouth. 'Weren't told aught about picking you up.'

Before she can say anything else the two men lift the sedan and set off at a fast trot. Wasp casts about. She's never been to this park before. Under the churning sky it's a brooding, foreign place of dark hedges and whiplashed trees. Petals, blown from their flower stems, flurry across the clipped grass.

A man is walking towards her, a bundle of yellow roses in his arms. He stops and describes a low bow.

'Allow me to present myself, Miss. I am Steven Cole, gentleman merchant and your company for the evening.' He thrusts the roses into her arms. Wasp, forgetting etiquette entirely, stares at him. His fine clothes are as fake as his plummy voice. The cravat is cotton, not silk, as is his shirt. Not a scrap of velvet has gone into the making of that embroidered jacket, and the rings he flourishes so extravagantly are nothing more than tin baubles.

His face is no better. All the powder in the world can't hide the old, puckered scars sweeping across both cheeks. His nose is bent at a horrible angle and half his teeth are black. Has a fairground bear attacked him?

Am I being punished? Wasp wonders.

Cole waits expectantly. Wasp dips a shallow curtsey that seems to satisfy him. 'We had best start walking,' he says, 'or I fear we shall soon have the park to ourselves. No point in hiring such a pretty object if no one's abroad to admire it.'

'Is this wise, sir? The weather looks evil.'

'A stiff breeze, no more. The hedges will shelter us.'

He starts off, stretching Wasp's pace, his awful, chewed-up visage grinning as he talks. He chats about London, the sea and the ships he claims to own. The bundle of roses is heavy in Wasp's arms. Enough flowers for three girls. She supposes she ought to feel flattered.

Around the park, hawkers are packing up their wares. Wasp's eyes water. Every rogue gust catching the underside of her bonnet drags on her wig. If it flies off there's nothing to be done about it. Cole leads her up a path between flowerbeds and around a fountain. Another gust catches the spray and gives them a soaking. People are abandoning the park in droves.

'Marvellous,' he declares, flinging his hands in the air. 'I spend a ransom on a Masque and there is no one to witness it. What use is that? Some of the best members of society are meant to walk and ride here. I don't see so much as a gig.'

While his back is turned, Wasp dumps half the roses behind a shrub and rearranges the others. When he faces her, all pretence at a smile is gone.

'Come, we shall try around the cooing seats and then think about supper.'

'How am I to get home?'

He scowls. 'What?'

'How am I meant to get home, sir? The sedan bearers say they have no arrangement to return for me.'

'Half an hour in my company and already you are talking of going back? One thing at a time, my doxy. I aim to have my money's worth out of you before the evening is done.'

He starts off again, Wasp tripping in his wake. Above, the clouds finally burst, spattering the gravel path with fat black raindrops. The wind drives water across the park in howling sheets. The roses wilt into sodden lumps in Wasp's arms.

'Very well,' Cole says, realising that, despite the cost, he isn't going to defeat nature. 'We shall not trifle with a chair. It is a short walk to my lodgings.'

'I am not permitted into private residences except by prior arrangement, sir.'

'So what do you propose to do? Stand here and drown? You admitted yourself you have no transport. I cannot leave you out in such vile conditions. We can take warmth and hot coffee in my rooms then arrange to go to supper. Don't make me insist.'

Wasp, who's shivering by now, doesn't have the heart to argue. She follows him out of the nearest gate. Her gown has turned into a wet mass that drags on her legs. Cole turns a corner, and then another. He encourages, distracts, and within five minutes has her completely lost.

The season is spiralling to an end and evening tumbles fast onto the city.

Cole's lodgings are on the ground floor of a narrow, gable-ended building that must have suffered the hard part of a hundred winters. He fumbles in the gloom for a key and waves her inside. A small room, blessedly warm and simply furnished. A fire chuckles behind a grate and candles have been left burning on the mantel. Cole removes his coat, throws it over the back of a chair and pours himself a drink from a bottle on the dresser. Then he locks the door.

'What are you doing?' Wasp demands.

'Cutpurses are at large in this part of town. They'd think nothing of coming into a man's room and stealing the gold from his teeth.'

'Aren't you going to fetch coffee?'

'The fire will warm you well enough.'

'A carriage, then? To take us to supper?'

He eyes her gown. 'You need to dry yourself first. Take the dress off and I'll hang it in front of the grate for you.'

Wasp's voice cranks up a notch. 'No, I can't—'

'Don't be coy. I brought up three daughters after their mama died. You mustn't risk catching a fever.'

'It's not appropriate. I'm a lady.'

Cole puts down his glass. 'Is that right? And what lady can be bought for a purse of coin, I ask you?'

Wasp's hands tighten on the flowers. 'What is it you want? Why have you really brought me here? If you want a harlot there are places where your money will be welcome.'

'Do you know a woman named Anna Torrance?'

'Who?'

'I don't know what name your House has given her. She's a tall girl, fair as sunshine, with a picture of a bird etched on one cheek and a pattern of red and white diamonds on the other.'

'What would you want with her?'

'I might as well be honest. She's got a child out there, and that could cause a great deal of trouble for some well-connected people. Trouble is, the whereabouts of that child is a mystery. The one man who knows has given us the slip. So I've a proposition for you of sorts.'

'I don't want to hear it.'

'Now that's a shame. Could put a fat purse in your hand. Your mistress don't need to know. It'll all be quiet and discreet.'

'You want me to lead her to you, is that it? Why don't you hire her yourself?'

'Easy to say, Miss, but hard to do. Can't just walk in there and pluck a body out. The Abbess likes the glint of sovereigns as much as the rest of us, but she's got a nose for a rat and no amount of money will stop her sniffing us out. You lot don't matter so much, but her Harlequins are a different tale, and while young Torrance is in that gilded cage I can't touch her. She got away from me and my kin once already. Her quack friend was cleverer than we gave him credence for. But you don't know who she is or where she came from, do you?'

'What makes you think I could persuade her to go anywhere?'

'Because you've done it before, at that bawdy house, the one called the Cellar. Word gets around, especially in our circles. Help us out, and afterwards you can go wherever you want, especially with a purse to smooth things along.'

'How do you know so much about me?'

Cole grins and taps his broken nose with a forefinger. 'Wasn't supposed to come to this, but that doctor of yours – oh, he's a slippery fish. Maybe if we have his prize girl he'll prove more willing to settle our business with him.'

'So you're after the Fixer too?'

'The Fixer? If you're talking about Dr John Cannon then he's the man with the answers, though fixing ain't something he's always good at from what I've heard. It's no use looking outraged. 'Twas Anna Torrance herself who put us onto his tail. She paid my master to do a little persuading, but her own father, a man not to let things lie, got word of the matter and paid more. So if we catch two little rabbits in the same snare we earn a fee twice over. That's good business to my mind.'

He puts down his glass. 'I'd hoped we could settle this in the park. But it seems the weather had other notions.'

She slaps him across the face. He stumbles backwards with a mulish bellow of surprise. A red palm print burns on his left cheek. Both eyes go as wide as sovereigns and his breath pumps out in long, heavy gasps.

'I shall not be your Judas,' she says.

'Well, I'm truly sorry to hear that. Hiring you cost good money. I daresay I'd like it back.'

'Masques don't carry money.'

He shrugs. 'I reckon I'll have to make you change your mind then.'

He moves towards her. She waits, fingers now hooked into claws. *Come on. I took it in the Comfort Home and I can take it from you.*

But Steven Cole, gentleman merchant, does something unexpected.

He dies.

A Dangerous Errand

The bag is gone.

The Fixer doesn't know exactly when he lost it, only that it's no longer slung over his shoulder. It has likely burst on the cobbles, the contents strewn across the road. Vital medicines, yet worthless to any thief. He has no time to curse their loss.

The men were waiting for him outside the apothecary. Three of the buggers. 'Where is the child?' he was asked, and with that one question knew immediately that his days at the House were over. From their faces he also knew these men would not be put off by appeals of ignorance. Two carried staves and made no effort to hide them.

He'd fought like an animal. A broken nose for one, a few missing teeth for another. In the end he'd put all three down long enough to buy a few seconds to run. Losing his pursuers will depend on how well they know the curving back alleys and lanes of this city quarter. Pounding feet warn the Fixer they're close.

He clutches his side. A stave had caught him on the ribs, possibly cracking one.

It can't be a coincidence. They knew he frequented that apothecary, and when to expect him. Was the storekeeper behind it, for a fat bribe perhaps? If so, what had led them to that particular shop in the first place?

He cuts a corner, stumbles and barrels into a wall. Pain rips up his side. The lane runs between two warehouses and he hauls himself behind a stack of empty crates. A fierce gale is kicking up with rain not far behind. He sits in the gloom and tries to quieten his breathing. *Where is the child?* The question knocks about inside his head.

Voices at the mouth of the lane. 'Should we split up?' someone asks.

'Naw, look at the beating he gave us. You think you'll fare better on your own? Frankly it's no loss to me if we don't find him. Let someone else get their teeth knocked out.'

They move off down the main thoroughfare. The Fixer counts off five minutes before leaving the sanctuary of the crates. He knows a good back route to the House from here. It's unlikely those brutes will find him now.

You knew this day would come, John. You've been ready for it ever since you arrived. Yet here he is, beaten and bleeding again. Who could have betrayed him? *Who?*

'Babies,' the Fixer whispers. 'It's always about babies.'

Whatever people think of him now, it was true he'd been a doctor once. Clara Hawley finished that, but was it her fault or his? Dr John Cannon, as he was called then, was in no doubt she would die. Most of her blood had spilled over the front of his silk shirt. Two guineas and countless fittings had been the cost of that extravagance, and now it wasn't even fit to burn. The baby was in the wrong position; any quack could've surmised that. It was likely dead too. Cannon suspected the umbilical cord was wound around its neck. Not having to worry about the child sometimes made saving the mother easier, but Clara was already halfway to God and wouldn't be turning back from that journey. Her skin had taken on a terrible pallor. Both hands were claws on her prayerbook. He'd tried slipping it from her grasp but suspected nothing would persuade her to let go. She had scant other comfort.

Music seeped through the walls. The party was at its peak. Five minutes after arriving, Clara's waters had broken, much to the irritation of their host. 'You're a doctor, Cannon,' he'd said. 'Be a fellow and see to this, will you? And, for pity's sake, be discreet.'

Clara's young husband, already drunk, was puking his gizzards into the privy. Oh, the lad had tried, Cannon conceded that much. He'd stood beside her, full of endearments and noble, hand-holding intentions. Maybe the child was his, maybe it wasn't. In any case at the first spattering of blood he had to be carried from the room.

Now it's just me and you, like it was before.

'My baby—' A heat-drenched whisper.

'Don't you do this to me, Clara Hawley,' Cannon muttered. 'Have you any notion how long it took me to rise in society? My place is balanced on a sword edge and because of you I could lose the lot. I need you to live.'

He should've opened the windows. The room stank. He kept blinking to clear the sweat from his eyes. How much had he drunk? The punch had been concocted to deceive. Two glasses of that and perhaps a brandy on top. Then there had been the generous swig from Crabbe's hip flask on the way here. 'A warmer for the journey' he'd called it.

Pain speared Cannon's jaw. He was grinding his teeth again. A habit from childhood. 'A wonder you don't wear them to the bone,' his mother had declared.

He tried to get another hold on the child. A shudder coursed through Clara's body.

'Damn it.'

He stood listening as the last breath rattled from her lungs. The Bible slid from her fingers and thumped onto the floor. The baby wasn't coming, not ever. Her eyes were closed, her muscles already relaxing.

Cannon searched the cramped dressing room he'd been obliged to use. The wardrobe offered nothing. Likewise the drawers. He tore a curtain from its rings and draped it over the body.

A noise from the door. Crabbe stepped into the room, glass in hand. He glanced at the covered figure. 'So you lost her? The child too?'

'She was damned from the moment she conceived. I couldn't get the baby out. The mother hadn't a whimper of strength left.'

'You mean it's inside her yet?'

'Even in death she clung onto it. And it's sapped the soul right out of her.'

'Was it your child, John? I know you were tupping her. That could prove a damned expensive distraction.'

'I don't know. Maybe.'

'They'll want someone's hide for this. You're not of their blood, no matter how many parties you attend or fine clothes you buy. You can smoke their cigars, sup their port and play as many hands of hazard as you like. I've no doubt they find you entertaining but they've drawn borders around themselves. It's a matter of breeding. At the very least you'll be ruined. At worst, dead.'

'Clara should never have been let out of confinement. I had no help. Not so much as a scullery maid.'

'I've no hand for this sort of thing.'

'You're not to blame. At sea I was nicknamed "the fixer". I led people to believe I could fix anything. This is the price of my vanity. I was fonder of parties than practising my craft. I've turned rusty as an old door hinge.' He held up blood-drenched fingers. 'I couldn't get my rings off. They cut her inside. God forgive me. I should never have come off the ships.'

'Flog yourself later, John. You'll have time enough, I suspect.'

'What shall we do?'

'I'm off downstairs for another serving of canary. You are going to run. I'll make sure you get away, but you'll owe me.'

'What is it you want?'

Crabbe emptied his glass. 'Everything.'

And he had taken just that. Even the job tarring slaves at the docks had been secured through Crabbe's contacts. The Fixer thought himself safe until the night spat out another pregnant girl. A decision had been made there too.

You're not fit to be a mother, he'd told her.

The skies open. Wind-driven rain cuts his cheeks and plasters his shirt against his broken chest.

'Anna,' he mutters through bloodied lips, 'what have you done?'

'Where is Kingfisher?'

Leonardo puts down his clay pipe and regards the Fixer over the top of the flickering lantern.

'He hath taken his little African bird and flown. I suspect thou knowest that already.'

'But all those trinkets he's garnered over the years are still in his quarters. They were precious to him.'

Leonardo shrugs. 'He hath found a trinket that breathes.'

'Why would he leave without telling me? Damn it, I freed him from a *cage*.'

'In here,' Leonardo taps his chest, 'he doth not believe thou canst save him. Through this girl he will find his soul again.'

The Fixer imagines Kingfisher standing in front of him. That look on his face. That *voice*. 'You pulled me out of slavery. Would you not expect me to do the same? Do you really see me as a man, John Cannon, or something you saved to salve your conscience? Or suit your purposes? That is what my countrymen and women do, is it not? Suit the white man's purpose?'

The girl was the only thing he was ever secretive about. I should have foreseen this.

He'd tried to be sympathetic. Was Kingfisher not simply doing what the Fixer himself had done with Anna? So, a blind eye had been turned, again and again, as she was tucked away in Kingfisher's quarters. He fed her with food from his own plate, took out her pot, bribed the washerwoman for some fresh clothes. He'd never have managed it if the Abbess hadn't fallen sick, and the nature of that illness was a mystery in itself. The Fixer had gently probed but been waved away at every turn. It was Hummingbird's doing. She seemed to have set herself up as the old woman's keeper and now everything was falling apart. Stumbling into Kingfisher's quarters had left the Fixer in no doubt. The bed, the dresser, the fireside table with a cup of the fruit juice Kingfisher preferred. Orange. Another expensive whim the Abbess indulged. All were untouched. But there, sitting amidst everything, the bracelet made of hair. His wife's hair. In that instant the Fixer realised things had irrevocably changed.

Leonardo picks up his pipe. 'He is a clever man, that darkie. Can squeeze coin out of a kerbstone if need be. He'll not go hungry or be in want of a roof.'

'So that's it? He left no message?'

'Only that you must give her back the child.'

'I see. It seems he was a better friend than I imagined.'

The coachman gestures at the Fixer's injuries. 'From the look of thee, doctor man, thou hast more troublesome things to consider.'

He nods. 'My past is catching up right enough.'

'Not just *thy* past, I think.'

'No, not just mine. At least this time they didn't have swords.'

Leonardo shakes his head. 'No refuge is to be found here, doctor man. Trouble is brewing inside the House as well as out. I drive these girls in their coaches. I work the yard while they take the air. I serve and pamper them, and overhear every word they utter. Thou art best gone before the wolves descend on us all.'

'If I leave a note will you pass it to Nightingale?'

'I shall.'

Unexpected Choices

'Sir? Mister Cole?'

The merchant isn't going to answer, now or ever. He's fetched up against the bottom leg of the bed, his dead eyes staring at the ceiling. His left arm is curled tight, the fingers clenched; his right has fallen across his chest. The rug is half wrapped around him, concealing most of his lower body. Two seconds ago he'd been thrashing around on the floor like a landed trout.

'I was told to—' Those were his last words. Nothing profound. Not even a proper sentence. She thought someone might come running to investigate the racket but five minutes have passed without so much as a footstep in the lane. The room has no other door.

She slides the key out of Cole's coat pocket and checks outside. The sky is a massive bruise. The wind has fallen to irregular gusts but the sheeting rain is far from spent. Wasp peers up the lane. If lucky she might catch a chair. Some diehards work the roads whatever the weather.

Nothing moves in the visible oblong of street. No, there, tucked into a doorway near the corner, a shivering linkboy, torch sputtering in his hand. Early for him to be out, but the weather has brought a premature dusk. Wasp runs up the alley, raindrops stinging her face. She grabs the boy by the shoulder. He gawps like a frightened rabbit, the torch nearly slipping from his fingers.

'Do you know Crown Square?' Rain streams down Wasp's hair and into her eyes. Everything is a watery blur.

''Course I do,' he says, pulling free of her grasp.

'Go to the house with the polished black door. Knock and ask for Hummingbird. Bring her here. Tell her Wasp sent you.'

He shook his head. 'That's the whores' palace. I'll get a beating if I go there.'

'You'll fetch worse from me if you don't.'

The boy squirms. 'My da won't like it.'

'He won't have to know, will he? Go now and you'll get a shilling when you return.'

'I'll have the shilling now.'

'No, you won't, you little tinker. I'm not having you disappearing into the murk. A shilling in your hand when you get back – that's a promise.'

The boy leaves at a fast trot, torch fading into the murk. Wasp returns to the room. She fetches a chair from the corner, sets it beside the hearth and sits down to wait in the mottled firelight.

'So you killed him?' Hummingbird nudges the rug off Cole's corpse with her foot.

'He kept asking me things. I'm hired out to entertain, not to be interrogated. All I did was slap him. He had some sort of seizure and there wasn't anything I could do.'

'We'll have to dump his carcass.'

'Dump him?'

'We can't afford to get caught up in this. Now, help me. Empty his purse to make it look like a robbery.'

'What?'

'Come on. This is no time to turn sweet.'

'How are we going to move him? Didn't you bring Leonardo?'

'That little Bible spouter? I'm not getting him involved. I have a chaise outside and before you ask I drove it here myself. You were lucky I got your message, though why promise that brat a shilling? It cost a good pair of earrings to entice him to talk, and those were a gift from one of my best clients.'

'Where is the boy?'

'Scampered back into the same gutter he came from, I expect. Now, grab the cully's legs.'

'Hummingbird, what if someone sees us?'

'Then we say he passed out over too much wine and we're helping him back to his coach. Stop fussing.'

Hummingbird slides back into her voluminous cloak and draws up the hood. She hooks both hands under Cole's armpits while Wasp takes his ankles.

'He's too heavy.'

'Then we'll drag him.' She nudges the door open and together the girls bundle the corpse outside. The carriage is backed into the lane. Hummingbird climbs inside and they manoeuvre Cole up the steps. It seems to take forever. Wasp's muscles ache and she can see her companion struggling. By the time they have him inside both are gasping.

'Right,' Hummingbird says, catching her breath. 'Empty his pockets like I told you. I'll drive us to a place where we can safely ditch him.'

'He'll be missed, won't he?'

'Cullies disappear in this city every day.'

'I can't believe this has happened. If we're caught everyone will think I murdered him.'

'Well, you did, more or less.'

'That's not fair.'

'No time to argue. We'll have time to talk when we return to the House.'

'It's just—' Wasp shakes her head.

'Another problem, Sister? Bigger than the one you already have on your hands?'

'Perhaps.'

'All right, but let's ditch the cully first.'

'Where did you get the chaise?'

'A favour from a client. Every so often we clop around in it. He taught me to drive as a novelty, I suspect. Unlike your friend here, he's not one for asking questions.' Hummingbird draws up her hood, climbs back onto the driver's perch and clicks the horse forward.

Wasp rifles Steven Cole's corpse. His eyes are cracked open, his cooling face frosted with raindrops. There's nothing much to take. A purse with sixpence in it and a fob watch with the hands missing. She drops them into her reticule and straightens. Her hair is sticking to her cheeks and her gown smells of stale rainwater but there's more to worry about than the House's precious chattels.

Ten minutes later Hummingbird stops the carriage. 'Let's get this business done.'

The chaise is sitting at the mouth of an alley crammed between two rows of terraced houses. The rain has eased but the streets remain blessedly quiet. Between them they drag Cole's body down the carriage steps and into the gutter. One of his shoes flips off.

'Are you going to leave him like that?' Wasp asks.

'What do you expect me to do? Say a prayer? Dig a grave and erect a headstone? I'll wager in half an hour his jacket is gone. A half hour after that, his shirt and breeches too. Nobody will know or care who he is. You ought to be thankful.'

'Suppose someone enquires at the House? Finds out who he was with?'

'People don't make those sorts of enquiries, not if they have a shred of sense. Now get back inside.'

As they drive off, Wasp leans out and peers back into the murk. Cole resembles a pile of rags. She draws her head back and rubs the rain out of her eyes. There it was again. Death. Everywhere. Even skulking through the sunniest summer lanes of her village, when Tommy Button, the washerwoman's toddler, chased a butterfly down a well and drowned for it. It had been Wasp's own father who pulled him, dripping and soulless, from the dark water, while everyone except his hysterical mother shook their heads and declared 'The Lord gives and the Lord takes'. And in the Comfort Home the Lord cut his harvest there too: Jenny Brewster, barely more than sixteen years old and disowned because she threw fits, screamed and uttered the foulest language for no good reason so that her parents believed her possessed. She'd taken to her mattress with a fever and was found the next day staring dead-eyed at the floor with blood around her nose. No eulogy-spouting cleric for her, but corn sacks for her shroud and two hefty labourers bearing shovels and a barrel of quicklime. Wasp had watched her carted out of the front door like so many potatoes.

Death. Can it ever be cheated?

Wasp reaches over and tugs Hummingbird's arm. 'I need to talk to you. Now. Before we get back to the House.'

'Can't it wait?'

'No.'

'Oh, very well, but it's hardly the best time.' Hummingbird pulls into the lee of a bridge spanning a sluggish, muddy river. 'Horse is getting skittish. He wants feeding. I hope this won't take long.'

The chaise is wretchedly small and their legs press together. The stink of the river invades the confined space. Hummingbird's cloak is slick with water. Drops run down her nose and chin.

'What was I doing with that man?' Wasp begins.

Hummingbird raises her eyebrows.

'Yes, I was on Assignment, at least that's what I was supposed to think. But then he started asking questions about Nightingale.'

'Nightingale?'

'Yes, and someone called John Cannon. I think he meant the Fixer. Some business ties them both together and this fellow, Cole, talked about getting a fee. Where do you suppose he came from?'

'There are all kinds of men whose services may be hired. In a sense they are harlots too. They breed in the same gutters as the cheapest whores.'

'No way home.'

'What?'

'I had no way home. The sedan bearers who delivered me to Cole had no instructions to pick me up again. Nothing was said about a carriage either. Someone must be fixing the Assignments.'

'This is all very fanciful.'

'Don't tell me it's not possible. The Abbess has seemingly vanished with this supposed illness. You must know what's going on?'

'Don't be so harsh. I'm no Harlequin. The Abbess doesn't confide in me. I wouldn't set someone like Cole on you. I'm your friend. Besides, Nightingale is the one giving out Assignments these days. Perhaps you should take your questions to her.'

'You must help me.'

'Wasp, I'm sure I'd love to, but if this goes too far we'll both fetch a lot more than a hot arm. Your obsession with Moth isn't helping.'

'You're my friend. You just said so.'

'Who are you, Moth's mother? Are you seeking atonement for your sins? You won't save your soul by saving her neck. If a path to redemption is what you want then you should pursue a more useful cause and a better means of achieving it than this.'

'You don't know what I've done or need to do. Perhaps I am Moth's "mother". Perhaps I feel I do owe her something, yet for a time I was ready to turn my back. I thought myself such a failure that any attempt on my part to interfere would only lead to more trouble.'

Hummingbird sighs – a long, low sound like wind gusting through an alley. 'But you've interfered too much already.'

'That's a horrid thing to say.'

'Bawdy houses lie in every port and back street. You can't wish them away.'

'How could I leave her in the Cellar after what I witnessed? Yet since that night I've dithered along in the hope that everything will resolve itself. Now, accident or not, someone else is dead. I have to try and help Moth . . . or lose my wits. Call that selfish if you like, but I intend to get her out of the House.'

'Really? And afterwards?'

'There won't be an afterwards. I'm leaving with her. I'm done with this nest of horrors.'

Hummingbird shifts on the narrow seat. 'Not a good idea, Sister. Our Emblems mark us out wherever we go. People only need to glance at us to know what we are. Even if you run far enough you'll still draw attention to yourself. These coloured pictures are our manacles. One day soon they could be our weapons. Think about that.'

'The Emblems can be removed.'

'True, if you are determined enough.' Hummingbird dips into the folds of her cloak and draws out a long-handled hairbrush. She flicks a catch on the base and the handle slips off. Underneath is a steel blade tapering to a vicious point. It glints in the light from the coach lantern. 'Most girls keep a little something to get them out of trouble.'

'No. Don't cut me.'

'I could heat the blade in the lantern flame. Two seconds pressed against your cheek would be enough to set you free.'

'I'll be scarred.'

'Vanity or liberty, Wasp. I can't pander to both.'

'I'll help Moth, then fret about the picture on my face.'

Hummingbird slides the knife back into its handle. 'As you wish.'

A Final Choice

Nightingale is screaming inside. Her hands are fat with gloves. Three pairs. Lace, then kid, then winter leather, yet she can still imagine feeling the wooden grain of the box through the material. She listens, eyes screwed closed, as the muslin bag slops open onto the roof, spilling the dream makers into the gutter with a tiny tick-tick rattling. Can she smell them, or is it her imagination? It's rained all evening. The air beyond the open window is thick and damp. City scents assault her. Smoke, dung, cooking meat.

But still . . .

She lets go of the box. It clatters down the slates and disappears over the lip of the roof. A moment later there's a splintered crash as it hits the yard below. Nightingale's legs fold and she slides onto the rug. She has no one left. 'The darkie hath taken his pot of black gold and fled' was how Leonardo put it, but no fanciful slant could change the bare fact that Kingfisher has abandoned them. The Fixer, too, has jumped from the same ship, even though he's seemingly gone to swim in different waters. Leonardo might use rich language but he lacks the imagination to make up stories. Nightingale accepted the truth of his words even before he'd finished uttering them. He had entered the House to find her, an act almost unheard of, and broken the news in his uniquely Biblical manner. She had tried to protest but he shook his misshapen head.

'Young bird, he had to go. Thou hast set the dogs on him.'

'The Fixer would understand why, or he knows nothing of me.'

'He is prepared to forgive. Thou canst go to him, but thy box of witchery cannot. Thou must settle the storm within these walls first.'

'Where is he?'

'The city harbour. He will take a ship bound for the colonies and sign on as surgeon. A new life for him. In time he may send for you. Both of you.'

'Both of us?'

Astonishingly, Leonardo smiled. His teeth were perfectly white in that ugly face. She had never noticed before. He dropped a jangling purse and sealed letter onto the table. 'Best make thy mind up,' he said.

So 'the witchery' is gone. Already, if only in her imaginings, she can feel the cravings starting to bite. Week by week the Fixer had given her just enough to keep them at bay. She could almost pretend each dose was medicine. The box was never an easy solution, not even a temporary one. Once the lid was opened it was over, one way or the other. She couldn't hope to face her daughter with such a Damoclean sword dangling above her head.

You had no right to be a mother. Look at what you did to yourself.

The addiction is not as strong as it once was but weeks of pain lie ahead. Leonardo has delivered the Fixer's terms. He still has her on a leash, but the pull of the House is equally strong. Something has to break.

Nightingale peels off the top two layers of gloves. Outside, the passageway is empty. She hurtles down the stairs in her slippers, dodging the scraps of party litter that have escaped the Scarlet Parlour. For hours she'd stood in her mask while the revellers had fawned and preened. Most were packed off to the Cellar where special treats were apparently to be had, others slinked back to wives and mistresses.

But not everyone had gone.

She ducks behind the hall table and scrabbles through the litter in the drawers. What a rat's nest. Rolls of parchment and piles of old calling cards tumble onto the floor. How did the Abbess ever make sense of this mess?

'Ah, here it is.' Her hand closes around a polished wooden stock.

So the stories are true.

A Confrontation

Wasp scurries up the front steps of the House. 'Go straight upstairs and don't talk to anyone,' Hummingbird had instructed. 'Wait in your bedchamber until I join you.'

She claimed she could get a message to Richard but wouldn't be pressed as to how. 'I have my methods. Give me half an hour to return the carriage.'

'Can't we use it to get away? Richard could meet us in Portsmouth.'

'Pox it, Wasp, you are such a dreamer. I doubt whisking Moth out of the House is illegal but stealing a coach will put us on a prison barge. Just wait in your bedchamber and don't do anything impulsive.'

'Hummingbird, thank you.'

'Just go.'

A quiet and empty hall. No lingering girls. Only half the candles in the overhead chandelier are lit. Jaundiced light throws pale shadows over the walls.

Unnerved by the silence, Wasp checks the dining room. Crumpled napkins, greasy plates lying in cracked piles, a tipped-up bottle of port bleeding red onto the carpet. At the top table, a chair lies on its side.

Where are the maids? Why has no one cleared this up?

On impulse she crosses the hall to the Scarlet Parlour. Inside, the room resembles a deserted battleground. Playing cards are scattered across the rugs and a fug of pipe smoke clings to the tapestries. Wasp's foot catches an empty brandy decanter. It skitters across the carpet and fetches up against the wainscoting. 'Where are you all?' she whispers, plucking a silk neckcloth from the back of the sofa.

Abandoning the parlour, Wasp removes her shoes and pads up the thick stair carpet. Not a sound anywhere. She slips into her own room. Dark, the curtains drawn, the hearth dead and full of ashes. She sparks her tinderbox and puts a sputtering flame to the bedside candle. A soft glow fills the room, though the cold air has a musty smell to it. Her bed is still rumpled from this morning, the coverlet lying half on the floor.

Wasp pulls off one of the pillowcases and twists it between her hands. It was a trick she learned in the Comfort Home. Someone with an eye on her footwear once hit her across the side of the head with a knotted shawl. The blow sent her reeling. Fortunately a wild kick caught her assailant in the face. She lost two rotten teeth and Wasp kept her shoes.

The knotted pillowcase dangles from her fingers. In the tick-tock quiet the crude weapon makes her feel better. A half hour passes. She judges the time from the doleful chiming of the clock down the hall.

The door breezes open. Wasp's fingers tighten on the linen club, but it's only Hummingbird.

334

'Do you mean to brain me with that thing?' she remarks, sitting on the edge of the bed.

Wasp drops the pillowcase onto the mattress. 'Of course not. I'm just anxious.'

Hummingbird takes her hand. 'Well, I've sent a message to Richard. I've no guarantee he'll act on it though.'

'What shall we do in the meantime?'

'You were the one with the big plan, Wasp. I suppose we'd better go and find Moth.'

'You do know where she is, then?'

'In the Mirror Room?'

'How shall I slip her out? Do you have an idea about that too?'

'Some distraction or other. We'll think of something. Now, let's go and hunt out your friend.'

'Hummingbird, there's something else.'

'What now? Hasn't enough happened already?'

'Someone has been writing notes at the bottom of my Assignments. Warnings about Moth. At first I wondered if it might be you, but the last one killed that notion.'

'I'm certainly not the type to leave clandestine messages. Why don't you show me these notes. I might recognise the handwriting.'

'They were etched onto the scrolls.'

'And you burned them after reading?'

'As I was taught.'

'What convinced you I wasn't the mystery author?'

'The final one said I should ask you about the baby.'

'The baby?' A mongrel expression flits across Hummingbird's face, half surprise, half anger. 'Now there's a question, Wasp. Of all the things you could've asked me it had to be about that. Tell me, do you know what brought me to the House?'

'No, of course not.'

'I once saw a "gentleman" beat a harlot to death because he hadn't the coin in his purse to pay her. Nobody took him to task for it. That's the power men can wield over us if you let them.'

'So? My village had its share of wife beaters and tricksters.'

'But have you ever been violated? Ever had a man take you when you didn't want to be taken? Must be so if you spent time in a madhouse. How did you feel when their tongues were squirming inside your mouth? When they were poking you with their disease-ridden pintles? Ever seen someone die of the pox?'

Wasp grimaces. 'Stop it, please.'

'Do you want to know what my crime was? A simple coach journey. I was travelling with my uncle in his chaise. We pulled into an inn for the night, but it was busy. One room left, so Uncle told the landlady I was his wife, see? "'Tis separate beds, child," Uncle explained. "You trust me, do you not?"

'So there I was, all tucked up and my head full of dreams. But some time in the night a black urge got a hold of Uncle. I woke to find him pulling my shift up over my head. I tried to scream, but his hand was firm over my mouth and all my thrashing and squirming counted for naught. I lay rigid, staring at the ceiling. I couldn't stop him taking his pleasure, but I could dampen his wick. Afterwards he beat me for going cold. I held my fat, bloody lip, even when I got home. When my mother remarked on my bruises, Uncle laughed and put it down to an attack of the vapours. "She went for a stroll through the woods behind the inn without telling me," he said over his roast beef dinner. "Foolish girl managed to lose her way and plummeted headlong into some thick undergrowth. That's where I found her. A bit the worse for wear but no real harm done."

'That was me, you see? Always prone to hysteria. Always fanciful and liable to burst into tears. I once saw a cat kill a mouse and bawled the whole day. I was put to bed, with some laudanum mixed with brandy, while Uncle stayed downstairs laughing and sipping port.

'That could have been the end of it. But when my blood stopped and I felt the first stirrings inside me I knew I'd be accused of other things. So I poisoned Uncle's breakfast. It was simple. Our local apothecary was so blind and befuddled he'd give you anything. Uncle sat, as smart as a dandy, eating the death I'd mixed into his soup. Some time later the maid, who'd gone to town with my parents, found him dead on the dining-room floor. Poor girl fainted clean away, so I heard. I was already halfway to London courtesy of Uncle's gold pocket watch and a side of ham from the larder.'

'And your unborn child?'

'I gave birth screaming on the floor of a flophouse with a gypsy hag for a midwife. She wanted to buy the child. I said no. The house was owned by a man who liked to fight dogs in a pit cut out of the floor of an old coach house. I'd been thieving for him to meet the rent. Very nimble-fingered, I was, but I couldn't do it any more because I refused to leave the baby. I wouldn't whore for him either. I said if he threw me out I'd snitch to the first constable I found. They wouldn't hang me if I turned informant. Transported to Parts Beyond the Seas, maybe, but I could live with that.

'I forgot about the dogs. I'd grown so used to the sound of snarling, the smell of blood and shit wafting out of the door of that coach house. The animals were kept starving to make them fight better. When I was asleep he let them out of their pens and threw my newborn into the pit. That's what he told me, though I know now he was likely lying and the hag took the baby after all. But I went to tell the magistrates. I was in such a state I could hardly talk. The owner, when called in for questioning, said I must have done it. He was tupping the gypsy and she backed up his

337

story. They said I'd tried to get a Wise Woman to kill the baby because I couldn't live with the shame of its being a bastard, and ended up murdering it myself out of spite.'

Wasp stares aghast. 'You had a child. A *child*.'

'Yes, Wasp, and I'm hardly alone in that. Many a busy womb has found refuge under this roof. Not all so-called crimes women commit involve theft or murder . . . So there you have it. Any more questions?'

'No.'

'Then let's go.'

They hurry downstairs in a flurry of skirts. The candles flickering in the sconces appear subdued, as if the air in the passage is sucking the life from them. Tapestries seem limp and washed out. Everything has lost its gloss.

'I can't hear anything,' Wasp whispers.

'These walls swallow up sound. They're at least four feet thick.'

'The Mirror Room door – it's open.'

A crack, nothing more. Wasp hesitates, straining to sense any movement, beyond. 'I still can't hear—'

Hummingbird pushes the door wide and steps through. Taken aback, Wasp follows her into the Mirror Room. She regards the polished floor, the light globe with its flame turned low, the circle of mirrors reflecting eternity.

'Empty.'

'Really?' says Hummingbird.

'I don't understand. I thought you said . . . What are you doing?'

Hummingbird nudges off her slippers. They fall onto the floorboards with a muted thump. White-stockinged feet whisper on the varnished oak, pirouetting like a pair of collared doves in some bizarre love dance. She pulls the pins from her hair and lets it tumble in a soft curtain over her shoulders. Both arms rise, hands poised. Skirts rustle as she dances from mirror to mirror. 'Your plot seems to have turned sour, Wasp. Where are you going to run to now?'

A sick feeling spreads from Wasp's belly into her throat. 'You knew this room would be empty.'

'Empty?' Hummingbird chuckles like a mischievous child. 'It's far from empty. Take a look around you. Rooms, passages, nooks and crannies. Chambers within other chambers. A labyrinth.' She pauses in front of one of the tall mirrors and raps it with her knuckles. 'They reflect the world back at you while hiding another world of their own.'

'You're talking in riddles. I don't like it.'

'I'm simply answering your question.' She raps the glass again. 'People can disappear, become lost, be forgotten.' She moves to another mirror and runs her hand, almost lovingly, over the smooth glass.

'Where's the Abbess?'

'Abbess?' Hummingbird's hair swings about her cheeks in a dark spray. 'The Abbess's crown is as wooden as the desk she sits behind.'

She moves to another mirror, flicks some unseen catch and swings it open. Lamps hanging from the ceiling light the passage beyond. A short, whispered walk and they come to another, smaller, round chamber. The walls and floor are covered in frippery. Sagging bookcases, dusty trunks, yellowed books and papers piled high. Hats, hundreds of them, are heaped in a disordered mess amongst odd shoes and the other remnants of long-ago fashions. In the middle of it all is a dressing table with a looking-glass so old it reflects the world with an unsettling greenish hue. A figure sits ghostlike in a cotton nightshift, stroking her face and peering at her reflection.

Wasp's voice catches in her throat. 'Abbess?'

The figure doesn't stir. 'Am I still beautiful?' she whispers. Her skin is pink and bare. All her paper tattoos are piled on the dresser before her like autumn leaves.

Hummingbird runs her hand along the back of the chair. 'I don't know what the concoction is, exactly. It keeps her quiet in the evenings and lets her live out her fantasy during the day.'

Wasp takes in the Abbess's wide, glassy eyes. 'The dream makers. You stole them from Nightingale.'

'Age has bent this woman's body into the ground and is taking her mind with it. At first the changes were so slight no one noticed. Then there was an incident. Then another, and another. The Abbess knew what was happening. She asked me to help her. Instead I've sent her somewhere else. Somewhere better than her rotting mind could go on its own.'

'And you let her sit here, alone in this sty?'

'All these things,' Hummingbird gestures around the room, 'are from her past. She brought them here herself. Every kerchief, every curled scrap of paper holds meaning. Yes, she eats with us from porcelain with a silver fork, and holds audience in a room as fine as any palace. But in the end she comes here to remember where she came from and the things she had to fight for. That's what she told me once, that the sum of a person's life is their memories.'

Hummingbird caresses the Abbess's shoulder with her fore-finger. 'I clean her teeth, brush the snaggles out of her hair and empty her pot, just like a loving daughter. She was always a strong woman. The Abbess never suffered a day's illness in all the time I've known her. She was a little too fond of gin, yes, and perhaps smoked richer things than a pipe from time to time, but her constitution was as solid as the stones of this house. Without me she wouldn't have a life at all.'

'But Nightingale? The Harlequins?'

'Give a vain woman a title and a better dress than anyone else and it keeps her in her place. The Harlequins are a bunch of pampered Kittens, even more obedient to the Abbess than the best behaved of Masques. Cellar whores have twice their wits.'

Wasp squints in the muddied light. 'Who are you, Hummingbird? Who are you really?'

'A lost soul, like you. We've not been put here by chance, Wasp, but by a catalogue of lies, broken promises and male indifference. What can be stolen from a woman in a moment is seldom regained in a lifetime. Nothing has changed over the centuries. We are closeted, robbed of power, reduced to menials and brood mares. Except for the true courtesans. In ancient Greece they were the *hetaerae*, publicly displaying their wealth while turning the heads, hearts and minds of the men who supposedly governed. They had no official social status, and it was that which freed them. We are the dispossessed. The cast-offs. Because we're not a part of society we can't sin against it. No Masque has ever entered the Royal Court. We're always kept on the margins – admired, esteemed, but never admitted. This is one apple that needs to be cut to the core. Our nets are cast wide and carefully baited. The big fish will gleefully bite. We shall catch them all. We'll slip in through the back door and lodge for life in their gilded halls.'

Hummingbird glances at the figure in front of the mirror. 'Despite everything, in the end she's just another bawdy-house keeper. But enough of that. I don't wish to spoil the coming charade.'

Back in the Mirror Room the lamp has been turned high, burning shadows behind the dozen or so figures now encircling it. Most are strangers but one or two Wasp recognises. The man who held the party on the river barge, and there at the back . . .

Oh dear heaven.

'I want our Emblems to be seen in high places,' Hummingbird says. 'Every lord, duke or Member of Parliament must crave a Masque on his arm. Is that not so, Richard?'

He swaggers up. Who would have thought that boyish body was capable of such a thing, yet his feet are surprisingly gentle on the floorboards. He leans towards Wasp. She tries to back off, but Richard shakes his head and whispers 'No, no' like a father cooing at a swaddled babe. He takes Wasp's head in his hands and she shivers because they feel like cold fish against her cheeks. Before she can utter a squeak his lips press against her own. Dry, hard lips, that she reckons haven't known a tender kiss in all their years. A sour taste fills her mouth. She tries to push him off but he goes on making those stupid cooing noises. Now his hand strokes Wasp's forehead. She supposes her own face must have turned a shade of blue, she's that close to choking.

Finally a release. 'Now, Wasp,' he says, 'be a clever girl.'

She backs towards the passage to the Abbess's room, but Hummingbird's blocking the door. A knife slides from her cuff and hovers at the other girl's throat. Wasp recognises it as the blade from Hummingbird's hairbrush. 'I'm sorry about this, Wasp, I really am.'

'You said you were my friend.'

'I *am* your friend. Don't you understand? You can hold the world in your hands, consort with princes and kings. The House is a tool to crack open the juiciest treasures. It can't be allowed to go blunt. Just one more step and everything is yours.'

She brushes Wasp's cheek with the backs of her fingers. Wasp flinches.

Hummingbird's grin is like broken glass. 'Don't be hard on Richard. He hasn't been the same since meeting you, my little mad girl. Oh, he dreams about you, Wasp. Dreams of doing things that even your battered mind could never conjure up. I understand how you could turn his head. Tonight will prove a test of loyalty in many ways.'

A mirror door on the far side of the chamber swings open and Moth is pushed into the room. She's clad in a white shift, not a linen day gown but something much finer – silk perhaps. Her hair has been bundled up into a knot behind her skull. She is barefoot.

Now the trick is complete. Wasp could weep over her own stupidity.

Richard hauls Moth to the middle of the room and forces her to her knees. The lantern throws her shadow in a hundred different directions. 'Get me a parson,' she whimpers. 'Please fetch a parson.'

Anticipation shivers through Hummingbird's cohorts. They're like hungry dogs about to be thrown a shank of bloodied meat.

'You know what to do,' Hummingbird says in Wasp's ear. 'Take that step.'

'I can't do it.'

'You're one of us.'

'One of whom? These brave souls slobbering over the life of a girl? You've been tormenting her all this time, haven't you? Making hissing noises outside her bedchamber door, filling her ears full of terrors about the Cellar and the bad things that happen to disobedient girls. Did you remain silent when she stole that piece of ribbon because you knew I'd tell, that I'd be punished by the Sisters and likely foul any chance of friendship I'd had with Moth? What a cursed toad you are, and I hate myself for not seeing it. I'll never be like you.'

'You've been groomed for this moment, Sister, ever since I dropped that nest of wasps on your bed. Now you must choose between lives. Hers or yours.' Hummingbird offers the blade. Wasp stares at it.

'You can't really mean this.'

'Why not? Moth is dead anyway. She would've been executed for her persistent thieving, or starved in some ditch. We are all dead. That's the first thing the Abbess tells us. Besides, why should you care? Richard told me about your adventures at Russell Hall. You were quite the talk of the district. How many hearts and souls have you already broken? Your mother's? Your employer? His son? And the children you were supposed to care for? Kingfisher betrayed his own people. The Fixer let a woman die birthing his bastard. Now they've fled into the dark. Are you going to run? And keep running? We are the broken and the damned. Admit it. You're not capable of friendship. Or love. You are the perfect Masque.'

Wasp takes the knife and steps forward. Moth's face is like a cake someone has tipped onto the floor. One sweep of the knife and the task would be done.

'Do it,' Hummingbird urges. 'Do it and join the circle. This is your real initiation. You dealt with that worthless cully, Cole. I saw this strength in you from the beginning, Sister.'

'If I refuse will she go free?'

'Refuse? You consider that a choice?'

Moth's bruised lips ripple open. 'You can't save me this time, Bethany. Honestly, I'd rather die than go back to the Cellar.'

'Forgive me,' Wasp whispers, but something has already broken inside the other girl's eyes.

'*Damn you, witch. Leave them alone!*'

A new voice. Nightingale has burst into the chamber. Her eyes are insanely bright, her face flushed. An undersized pistol is clutched in one hand. Where has that come from? Did she conjure it out of the air?

A sigh ripples around the lamplit faces. The circle wafts forward then ebbs again. Thoughts gallop through Wasp's mind. Is this part of the game? Is the evening about to take another perverse twist?

'We seem to have another guest.' Amusement flickers on Hummingbird's lips. 'Never mind, I like surprises. Would you care to tell me where you got that weapon? I doubt it would kill a rabbit.'

'Don't be dim. You heard the rumours about Kingfisher keeping a pistol in case of serious trouble at the door. You've gossiped about it often enough.'

Hummingbird plucks something out of her sleeve. Nestled in her palm is a cluster of the brown crystals. 'Is this what you want? I've no further use for it. Take it, return to your room and put your head back in the clouds.'

'No.'

'Are you sure? Look at yourself, Nightingale. Have you seen your face, listened to your breathing? That look in your eyes could turn a wolf to stone. You *need* this.'

'Don't bring that poison anywhere near me.'

'Then would you mind telling me what you do want?'

'Let Moth go. Wasp too.'

'Why?'

'I have my reasons.' She cocks the hammer on the pistol. 'You're in no position to argue.'

Hummingbird laughs. 'Are you planning to shoot us all?'

'A splendid notion.'

'Do you have a dozen other guns tucked inside your gown? Both your guardians have flown the coop. Why not go after them? Perhaps you'll find your child, since you think yourself such a willing mother. Your time at the House is finished. Put that plaything away and leave. Now.'

'Who are you to speak of motherhood? You killed your own child.'

'Nightingale?' Wasp's voice is hoarse with fright.

'That's right, Wasp. Did you ask her about the baby?'

'You left me those notes?'

'Yes, I did, and I have no doubt she spun you some fantasy about gypsy hags and violations by evil men with eyes full of lust for her sweet young body. She's a liar. She has been from the very beginning. The baby was real enough, but she murdered it. She blamed her lover and he was hanged, but his family knew what was in her heart. That's why she fled here. She's had her eye on the House from the start and, by God, she's a patient little whore. Such a creature is capable of anything.'

'How do you know these things?'

'The Abbess's mind is slipping right enough, and this slipped out of her mouth.'

The circle begins to fold in on itself. 'Quite the tittle-tattle, aren't you?' Hummingbird says. 'And what about your own saintly past? Will you make a declaration about that? Be truthful, Nightingale. I'm sure Wasp would be delighted to hear the circumstances that brought you to the House.'

'I already told her, you bitch.'

A flash of powder, a sharp report. The lamp's glass globe shatters. Burning oil sprays out in a bright yellow fountain, turning bodies into screaming torches. Fire is reflected a dozen times, a thousand times, from mirror to mirror. Infinity. The tide of flame engulfs Hummingbird, transforming her gown into a bright inferno. She spreads both arms wide. Her face is a yellow mask, her lips pulled back in a snarl. Glass cracks and shatters.

Nightingale catches hold of a whimpering Moth. 'That door,' she tells Wasp. 'That one there.'

They plunge into the passage. Wasp pulls the door shut behind them. On the other side fingers scrabble on the glass, trying to find purchase.

'Curse it, the Abbess is still in there,' Nightingale says.

'Will the fire spread?'

'Not if it's contained. Those rooms were originally built to hold wines and spirits. Have you seen the way brandy burns? Once the door is locked any fire would eventually choke on its own smoke. That's why there are no windows.'

'Is there any way to lock the door?'

Nightingale stares at her. 'Wasp, do you know what you are saying?'

'Is there?'

'Yes.'

'Then lock it.'

Nightingale regards her for a moment longer, then reaches over and fiddles with a concealed catch. A *thunk* as a bolt slides home.

A few girls are milling about the hall. Some are still in their party dresses. Other faces peer through the banisters or stare from the upstairs landing.

No one leaves. Nobody runs away.

'Go back to your rooms,' Wasp says.

In a whisper they are gone.

Nightingale opens the front door. Cool air wafts into the lobby bringing a scratching of dead leaves. 'Come on,' she urges. 'We have to reach the stables. I didn't expect to leave by the front door.'

She runs, pulling Moth with her. Wasp follows. Crown Square is mercifully empty. They stumble along the side lane to the courtyard and stable block. Leonardo is waiting with one of the House coaches and a fresh team. Wasp baulks. Nightingale shoves her in the back. 'Don't worry. Leonardo has been converted to the path of the righteous.'

'Very holy of him.'

'He's not stupid, and he can take me to the Fixer. Now hurry.'

Before they can climb aboard, the splintered dark disgorges a figure, as tall and black as the night surrounding him. He walks up to the coach, eyes luminous and full of sparks. Nightingale brandishes the empty pistol. He smiles. 'I am not afraid of you or your gun, Anna.'

'It makes little difference to me whether I pull the trigger or not,' Nightingale retorts. 'You won't stop me. I won't be a prisoner any longer.'

Kingfisher shrugs. 'Perhaps you will kill me. Then again you might miss, or the pistol could misfire. Much has taken place these past few weeks.'

'Fetch your little foundling from wherever you've hidden her and leave.'

'A storm has finally broken in the House, yes?'

'More like the end of the world. Don't worry, your stolen girls are safe with me. Go back to your homeland.'

'When my countrymen are still here? No, Anna, this city has not seen the back of me. I have more hunting to do. Remember that whenever it gets dark.'

'You have no money, Kingfisher. The Abbess owned everything.'

'No, not everything. I have my mementoes, which are all I shall claim back from this place. Go follow your own path, Anna, and leave me to mine.'

In a breath he's gone.

Once his charges are aboard, Leonardo sends the team out of the Square at a fast trot. Wasp settles back on the seat, breathing hard. Nightingale hands her a blanket and wraps another around Moth's shoulders. The girl is crying softly, her face in her hands.

'What now?' Wasp says. 'Have we left one disaster only to fall into something worse? Who were those other people with Hummingbird?'

348

'Politicians and minor gentry, selling themselves to the House in the hope of grasping a bigger slice of an already too rich cake.'

'Did you have a part in any of this?'

She shakes her head. 'If that's what Hummingbird suggested then it isn't true.'

'You look ill.'

'Worse is to come. But I shall live through it. I have to live through it because I've been given a chance to start afresh.'

'Where?'

'A new world. There's a place for me, I think. And my daughter.'

'Nightingale, you'll—'

'Anna. My name is Anna Torrance.'

'Anna, you'll see your child?'

She holds up a letter. The wax seal is broken. 'The Fixer's legacy. There's no telling if the people caring for her will wish to give her up, or if she'll want to leave the only parents she's known. But it's only right she learns about her mother even if she never sees me again. She'll be so young, and I don't even know her name. I never had the time or wits to choose one. I need to prove I deserve her.'

'Why the notes? About the goings-on in the House? Things would've been so much clearer if you'd spoken to me.'

'I couldn't tell you anything to your face without your thinking it was another cruel game. I'm sorry for everything.'

'What if it had gone wrong? We could all have died tonight.'

'I know.'

'One of the men there, Richard, offered help if I ever wanted to leave the House. I'd planned to go with Moth. Like the Mirror Room, that notion has gone up in flames.'

'I know of him. He has his bank in a thumbscrew thanks to the House's influence. He thought to carve quite a career for himself. Others were bribing Hummingbird with cartloads of money to obtain favours. The whole city was choking on her poison. She thought me too witless to know what was going on around me, or too helpless to intervene if I did.'

'Where do we go now?'

'Leonardo knows a guesthouse about a mile outside the city boundary. The landlord keeps his counsel and you won't be troubled. You can catch your breath.'

'Moth isn't going with you?'

'I fear the Fixer has overstretched himself already.'

Moth sits up. 'I won't be parted from Bethany.'

Wasp squeezes her arm. 'You don't need me. You've suffered hardships that would drive me from my wits. You are stronger than I am.'

Anna gives a tight smile. Perspiration is standing out on her forehead in fat, translucent drops. 'Moth is a brave girl. I confess, she had more faith in you than I. Like Hummingbird, I was curious as to where your true loyalties lay.'

Wasp slumps on the seat. 'I'm glad you thought I was worth it.'

'I took you to Russell Hall to help you make a decision. Has that decision been made?'

'I suspect I made it the moment I told you to lock the Mirror Room door.'

Constance throws a fit when she sees who's standing on the front step. She doesn't utter a word, merely flaps her hands before running back inside. The door swings on its hinges, squeezing the warm air spilling out of the hallway. *At least she didn't slam it in my face*, Wasp thinks. She had a morbid image of standing in a darkening street while the world fell asleep around her.

Finally another figure appears on the threshold.

'Hello, Mother Joan,' Wasp says, nudging Moth forward. 'My friend needs help. I told her I'd find her a home.'

Mother Joan frowns. 'I don't understand. That girl is troublesome. Why bring her to my door again?'

'You gave me another chance.'

Mother Joan glances at the sobbing young woman then ushers them both inside. Standing in the parlour, with no sign of the chequerboard and the dressing-up clothes locked away, Wasp keeps her explanation brief. Mother Joan listens without judgement. 'You would have her become my charge?' she says finally.

'It doesn't have to be forever, but it might prove a blessing for both of you. Moth can't be Polly, or one of Polly's friends. She's no good at putting on an act and you said you're tired of pretence. Take her as she is. I'm not saying it won't be difficult.'

'I daresay it will take perseverance, but in the words of my husband I can be a stubborn old crow. A young voice in the house again would be a sweet and welcome thing. Mr Slocombe would agree. If the girl is willing then so am I.'

'I can still come and see you,' Wasp tells Moth. 'This is a dear, dear lady. You'll be happy, I promise.'

'Very well,' Moth sniffs. 'If you think I ought to stay here then I shall.'

'And what of you, Bethany?' Mother Joan asks. 'Have you found a home anywhere?'

Wasp glances back into the street. 'I hope so.'

The legal and political wrangle following the events at the House is matched in scandal only by its dearth of reliable witnesses. Two clients, desperate to escape the flames, managed to force open the back door with the sheer weight of their overstuffed bodies. To those abroad in the streets, the sight of screaming men – one with his hair on fire – was enough to send them scurrying back into their homes. Others, including Hummingbird and the Abbess, were presumed burned to their bones. The blaze, as Nightingale predicted, did not spread.

There is an inquiry of sorts, held in a discreet courtroom with no public access. The examiner is determined proceedings will not degenerate into a rowdy farce. Helping with the questioning is an old hand on the city benches, one Mr Slocombe. Down to the cuffs of his jacket he cuts an impressive figure.

Wasp, whose stay at the inn has been paid for by the Slocombes, is present during Moth's questioning. The examiner, at Mr Slocombe's prompting, is gentle. Moth weeps a lot, and elicits a few gasps, but in the end can tell the hearing very little.

Wasp's interrogation follows a similar pattern, and she answers everything as honestly as she dares. At one point she's obliged to reveal her branded arm. Every neck in the place stretches to catch a peek.

Mr Slocombe is called upon to make a brief statement. He says he became involved with the House only to help his spouse, and expressed horror at the growing corruption within. Mother Joan herself sits in the gallery, nothing on her face betraying what she might be thinking. 'I was aware my wife was becoming dependent on these visits,' Mr Slocombe explains, 'but had no notion of the level of influence the House hoped to wield over me.'

At the end of the day, Wasp is intercepted by Mother Joan, who cuts an elegant figure in ivory gown and bonnet. 'My husband tells me no further action is to be taken,' she says. 'Everything of import has been dealt with discreetly. They'll claim you're just another bawdy house in a city full of such dens.'

She presses a note into Wasp's hand. 'Would you like me to take you?' she asks, once Wasp has read the message.

The carriage clatters to a halt. Wasp peers into the street. Another coach is drawn up outside the House. The blinds are drawn, the horses placid between the shafts.

'I don't know if I'm ready for this,' Wasp says.

'One last task,' Mother Joan replies. 'One more ghost to lay to rest.'

Wasp steps down into the road. A harsh breeze whips her hair around her cheeks. She imagines it smells of smoke and cinders. A slap of the reins and Mother Joan's coach is gone, rattling off into the evening.

Wasp takes a deep breath and crosses the square. *After what I have witnessed, how can anything frighten me again?* Yet her hand is moist on the carriage handle. Lanterns illuminate the face of the man inside. Wasp sits opposite. He offers her a flask but she waves it away.

'Are you going to ask me to come back?' she says.

'The warden told me you were dead. He showed me a grave. For a moment I almost believed it.'

'Perhaps it would have been better if you had.'

'My father never told me where you had been taken. I had to work through that village, tongue by tongue, filling pockets with my own gold. I was like a gleaner, picking up grains of wheat from a vast field. Letting you go should have been easy. Men in my position cast lives aside the way they throw out a worn pair of riding boots. Father was too ill to suspect what I was about. I don't know if his indisposition was due to guilt or a broken heart.'

'And the party? Was it you who hired me?'

353

'I heard about this remarkable girl from Richard. The more he was in his cups, the more he revealed. He was quite smitten and gave an excellent description. Your voice, mannerisms, the cut of your cheeks. Everything. I told him I would engage you as a favour. But it was I who wanted to see you.'

'To right wrongs? To punish me? Or to say you could have loved me after all?'

A smile softens the edges of George Russell's mouth. 'No, and I shall not pretend otherwise. I admit to my own character. I would have possessed you, suffocated you and left you broken. Yet you painted me blacker than could ever be proven. We are both to blame, Bethany Harris. Both of a like mind and heart. We would devour one another. You wished to use Julia and Sebastian and would have stolen those innocents at a pinch rather than lose them. Yes, my sweet, I now understand what was in your head that afternoon. You would not be put aside so easily. You saw yourself as having power over all our lives. And what would you have done after the deed? Lived in triumph whilst my family fell to pieces? I saw the look on your face.'

'George, I didn't intend to hurt the children. When you caught us that afternoon I believed that you would either never let me go or I would lose everything. I thought Julia and Sebastian might be poisoned against me. I wanted to take them away from that, to talk to them properly, even if in the end it meant saying farewell. I'm no child stealer.'

'Did you really think so poorly of me? Was every touch an assault? Each sideways glance an act of brutality?'

Wasp shakes her head. 'A squire, his son and a girl from the local village? No romantic story, however fanciful, would dare invent such a plot. I'd have proved the ruin of *you*, George, and scandal would have blighted the children's lives.'

He reaches over and clasps her hands, squeezing the knuckles of each finger as his father did in the happy days. 'Don't blame your own papa. He truly thought you'd lost your wits, that obsession had conquered you and poisoned your thoughts. He was told doctors would take care of you until you were able to return to your family. He never doubted that. Neither did I. Unfortunately my father had other plans. I only learned of these after you had been taken away. No one informed me directly. Rumours gusted up from the servants' quarters. I heard you'd gone mad, that you'd intended to hurt the children to spite my family. Father put duty before his heart and it almost killed him.'

'Did you believe the rumours?'

'I've spent a lot of time and money searching for you. I wanted to hear the truth from your own mouth, or the truth as you perceived it.'

'I don't know if I loved your father, George. I certainly felt passion, but love and passion aren't the same, are they?'

'Not always, though you told me you were with child. That was a hard thing to accept.'

'Would things have proved different had it been yours?'

'I don't know. Did you really lose the child, or did Father hire a Wise Woman to get rid of it? A deed carried out with your consent?'

'You think I could do such a thing?'

'No, Bethany, not really. And despite our differences I could not think such a thing of my father either. Afterwards you discovered you were barren, is that not so? You'd never have another. But you weren't about to let such a trifle stop you. Not when you could be mother to Julian and Sebastian.'

'Do they ever mention me?'

'No one talks about you. It's more than they dare. I can't take you back even if I wanted to. Society lays down strict rules for families such as ours. We have little of the freedoms the common man enjoys. The belief that Lord Russell, the squire, would consider favouring you over his son and heir was the most grievous blunder you made. I shall no doubt marry that society girl he chose. She will bring a comfortable dowry and an opportunity to slip a finger into her family's affairs. I shall help you, Bethany, in the best way I can. In the *only* way I can. I shall leave your life forever.'

Wasp takes a final look at this man who has taken nothing yet still cost her so much. If their paths cross again he will be a stranger to her, and she to him. He bows as she leaves the carriage. 'Farewell, Miss Harris.'

'Farewell, George.'

Those are the last words they ever exchange.

Finalities

The brassy 'clang' of the door knocker sounds unnaturally loud in the near empty square. The black-painted door swings inward, revealing a girl in a gold-trimmed day gown. She blinks in the daylight, fingers stroking a slender, unadorned neck. One cheek sports a diamond pattern, the other a picture of a wild flower. Primrose, one of the Harlequins. Obviously tired yet still beautiful. Wasp hadn't much noticed her before. A testament to how Nightingale's brightness cast everyone into shadow.

'It's you,' she says. 'I wondered if you'd come back.'

She steps aside. Wasp brushes past her into the hall. Cold. Gloomy. No candles burning. 'How are you faring?'

'We go through a semblance of life. Rooms are cleaned, bed linen changed. Meals arrive from the kitchen and empty plates sent back. We pace the corridors like ghosts.'

'Shall we talk in the Scarlet Parlour?'

Primrose shakes her head. 'It has remained untouched since the night of the fire. No one goes in there. Some like to pretend the Abbess is still in her place on the divan, keeping the beating heart of the House healthy. They don't wish to believe otherwise. The maids are too frightened to clear up. Perhaps they think they will see her phantom.'

'Not very likely.'

'I suppose not. It took days to purge the smell of ashes from the Mirror Room. Labourers stripped away the burned wood, rebuilt the floor then whitewashed the walls and ceiling. So far they have not been paid. They are patient but cannot remain so indefinitely. I know nothing of the House accounts. We brought in a man of law to try to unravel the complicated knot the Abbess had tied. He called us a "viable business". Can you believe that? Our hearts and souls are mere commerce to him. Money is plentiful, the House deeds are in order and any one of us can claim to be the Abbess's heir. Nobody outside these walls can ever touch our "business". I wonder how much the Abbess paid to obtain such a tight entail. Hummingbird did well to hook that secret out of the old woman's head.'

'So you could continue?'

'We could, I daresay, if we had the wit for it. But we are too used to being told what to do. Even Harlequins like myself are little better than servants with a bit of extra gilding. The Abbess *was* the House. At first I wondered whether she planned for it to die with her. Certainly without her, or someone like her, everything will unravel. Soon we shall find ourselves at the riverside taverns fighting with the harlots for custom.'

'Did anyone other than Hummingbird know the Abbess was losing her wits?'

'We all knew. It was like watching rot creep up the walls and knowing some day it would bring the roof down upon your head.

We also know both Kingfisher and the Fixer are gone. Leonardo came back and told us. He is out there, in his stables, waiting to take someone to an Assignment. We've had no shortage of requests. Look at these cards.' Primrose sweeps her hand over the hall table. 'You can't put a gag on scandal. We are more in demand than ever, but with no Abbess, no doctor and no one to procure Kittens the House will wither.'

'Leave, all of you. Sell everything and go.'

'We are all dead, remember. We have nowhere to go.' She looks up. 'What about you, Wasp? Do *you* have somewhere to go?'

Assuming the Mantle

She stands in front of the mirror, face scrubbed, hair tied back. A smock, trimmed with silver, flows from her shoulders and whispers around her feet. Laid out before her is an array of coloured patches cut in the shape of flowers, birds, insects. A paper testament to the beauty of creation. One by one she fixes them to her face, neck and arms, covering the tattoo on her cheek. Her eyes, peering out from this mosaic, are satisfied.

She leaves the room she once shared with a girl called Hummingbird. That ghost has been expunged. The carpet is soft beneath her slippered feet, the polished banister cool against her fingertips. She imagines for a moment a whiff of smoke on the air, but those chambers have been cleaned and purified with sulphur. The outside door to the Mirror Room has been barred with iron, the one leading from the lobby nailed shut. Perhaps they will remain that way for good. Many decisions will need to be made over the next few months.

The Cellar has closed, the building sold. Those that could be saved have been, the other harlots must work their trade elsewhere.

A Harlequin passes her on the landing, as sweet as a peach and dressed for an Assignment. A smile is on her mouth and in her eyes. *We have survived*, the smile says. *We can do this. We can go on.*

Each Masque has been given the same instruction: 'They live in every city, town and village. The lost. The fallen. The disinherited. We have learned not to see; now we must sharpen our eyes. While on Assignment look for them everywhere, from town house parlours to the most wretched gutters. Pass the word. Have it whispered in their ears. The work of a moment. *There is somewhere you can go.*'

Mother Joan made it easy. 'Now that the Abbess is dead there is the matter of ownership of the House. It is a question my husband is able to resolve, if required,' her letter said. 'A single name will suffice.'

Ownership of the House had not proved an issue. No one contested it. The authorities wanted to tuck the matter away, forget about it and move on. The big fish of the American War was still in want of frying. The King's wits were as loose and unreliable as a beggar's teeth and his son looked set to bankrupt Parliament. Who ultimately cared about the wishes of a gaggle of gilded courtesans?

Descending the stairs, the patchwork woman runs her hand along the banister. Spotless. Eloise has proved a firm taskmaster.

The new arrival stands in the middle of the lobby, her face made gaunt by the bright chandelier overhead. She shivers, despite the shawl Red Orchid has thrown across her shoulders. A week on the streets has already robbed much of the muscle from her bones. Her hair is lank and stringy, her face smeared where she has tried to wash it in rainwater. But underneath the ravages of the city she is built well, with good cheekbones and an elegance her torn dress can't disguise. Leonardo found her sleeping in his carriage. At some point she had scaled the yard wall, as the scabs on her knees testify, and made her bed in the coach house. 'That one is a fighter,' Leonardo testified. 'She didst kick my shins black when I laid hands upon her.'

Her eyes widen when she sees the patched apparition approaching from the stairs, but defiance is there too – a strength which will likely save her.

The woman once known as Bethany Harris smiles and holds out both hands.

'Welcome,' she says. 'I am the Abbess, and we are going to be friends.'

IAN GARBUTT has worked in journalism and publishing. He was awarded a Scottish Arts Council New Writer's Bursary and attended Napier University in Edinburgh where he obtained a Master of Arts with Distinction in Creative Writing. Historical fiction is his speciality, and he has published two novels for Piatkus under the pseudonym of Melanie Gifford.